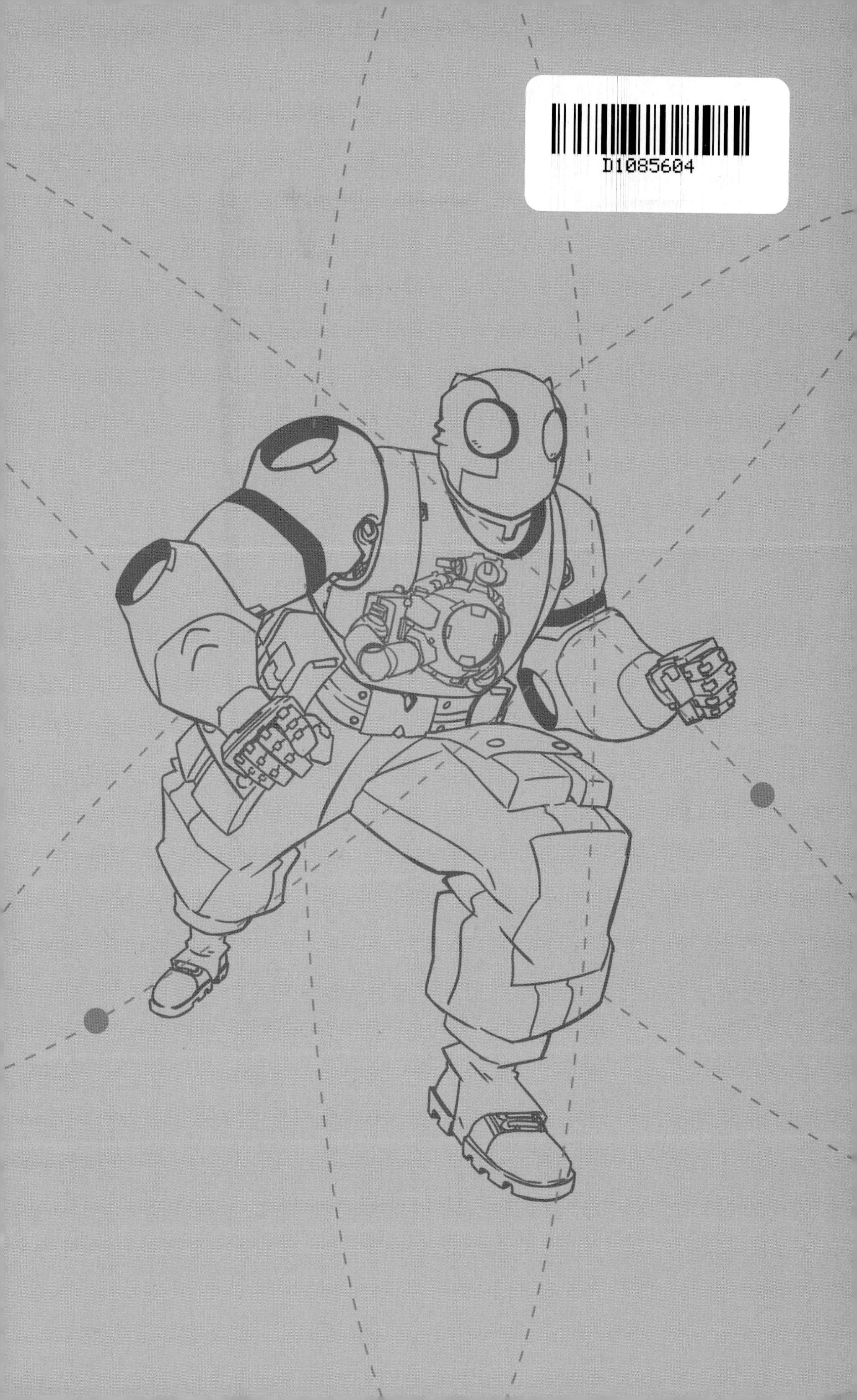

IDW

Facebook: **facebook.com/idwpublishing**
Twitter: **@idwpublishing**
YouTube: **youtube.com/idwpublishing**
Tumblr: **tumblr.idwpublishing.com**
Instagram: **instagram.com/idwpublishing**

COVER ART BY
MEREDITH McCLAREN

COLLECTION EDITS BY
DAVID MARIOTTE

ORIGINAL DESIGN BY
JEFF POWELL

COLLECTION DESIGN
ERIC TRAUTMANN /
FEDORA MONKEY STUDIO

PUBLISHER
GREG GOLDSTEIN

978-1-68405-451-0   22 21 20 19   1 2 3 4

REAL SCIENCE ADVENTURES: THE NICODEMUS JOB.
MARCH 2019. FIRST PRINTING. Atomic Robo, the Atomic Robo
logo, all characters and their distinctive likenesses featured
herein are trademarks and/or registered trademarks of Brian
Clevinger and Scott Wegener. All Rights Reserved. The IDW logo
is registered in the U.S. Patent and Trademark Office. IDW
Publishing, a division of Idea and Design Works, LLC. Editorial
offices: 2765 Truxtun Road, San Diego, CA 92106. Any similari-
ties to persons living or dead are purely coincidental. With the
exception of artwork used for review purposes, none of the
contents of this publication may be reprinted without the
permission of Idea and Design Works, LLC. Printed in Korea.
IDW Publishing does not read or accept unsolicited submissions
of ideas, stories, or artwork.

Greg Goldstein, President and Publisher
John Barber, Editor-in-Chief
Robbie Robbins, EVP/Sr. Graphic Artist
Cara Morrison, Chief Financial Officer
Matt Ruzicka, Chief Accounting Officer
Anita Frazier, Senior Vice President of Sales & Marketing
David Hedgecock, Associate Publisher
Jerry Bennington, VP of New Product Development
Lorelei Bunjes, VP of Digital Services
Justin Eisinger, Editorial Director, Graphic Novels & Collections
Eric Moss, Senior Director, Licensing and Business Development

TESLADYNE LLC

Ted Adams, IDW Founder

ATOMIC ROBO
PRESENTS
REAL SCIENCE ADVENTURES

The Nicodemus Job

WORDS
BRIAN CLEVINGER

ART
MEREDITH McCLAREN

COLORS
J.N. WIEDLE (MAIN STORY)
SHAN MURPHY (BACK-UP)

LETTERS
TESS STONE

— **EDITS** —
LEE BLACK

INTRODUCTION

ONE OF THE GREAT THINGS ABOUT working in pulp entertainment is that it's my *job* to be a fan of other creators. From a drunken lunch with the *Burn Notice* showrunner where we mocked each other's show, to fanboying with Seanan McGuire while developing her books for television, to finding writers to adapt my favorite Aussie military thriller series, I'm very blessed to have an excuse to talk to people whose work I love because their work is my work.

This is *not* the case with *Atomic Robo*.

I have no legitimate business excuse to be as wildly cheerleader-y as I am for this series. No, I love *Atomic Robo* because I just *love* *Atomic Robo*. The collected volumes sit on my office bookshelf for the express purpose of being loaned to every writer who works with me. The wee stickers I get from the Kickstarters are distributed to those writers' children, who run around screaming Dr. Dinosaur quotes. Because Doctor Dinosaur is, of course, the true protagonist of the series.

Brian and Scott and their various collaborators give us great pulp entertainment somehow lovingly mixed in with high-quality banter and sight gags. It's as if *Doc Savage* got into a three-way with the *Thin Man* and an entire bookshelf of gonzo '70s sci-fi. They can land a joke, they can write pathos—Bernard, oh Bernard—and spin a proper long-form conspiracy arc. The entire series fits into the big, ragged "genre entertainment" bag, but find me another series that so effortlessly glides between monster-fighting mechas, secret cyber-history, steampunk Westerns, cthulhoid horror, and World War II meat-and-potatoes Nazi punching with a side dish of Evil-Brain-in-a-Jar. When I started a new self-published comic series, Brian's the guy I emailed for advice on plotting. There's an amazing mastery of the form on display here.

Not to mention bloody work ethic. I can barely keep a side project webcomic going for more than a few months. They've been hammering these books out like (ancient cursed) clockwork for years now, without any drop in quality. To paraphrase my first Line Producer in television: "There is nothing more important than the timely delivery of quality scripted material. Everything else can and will go horribly wrong." When the business models shifted, they adapted to the Kickstarter and webcomic structure seamlessly. The *Atomic Robo* folk are, in short, the comic creators I want to be when I grow up.

It's a particular pleasure to write the introduction of *The Nicodemus Job*. Chris Downey and I had created *Leverage* as an homage to the great con and heist shows of the '70s. Basically, we were just trying to find a way to get someone to pay us to remake the *Rockford Files* episode of "Never Send a Boy King to do a Man's Job" over and over again.

Along the way we found ourselves codifying old forms of crime writing, figuring out ways to replicate what had very much been a tradition of one-off stories, and evolve them to fit long term narrative. From this emerged the idea of cons and heists as a unified genre in the way film noir is a genre; it's not about the tech or the camera angles, it's all about how and why characters solve the story problems, with not just crime but certain types of crime. I like to think our clarification of these ideas contributed to the bump in con and heist genre forms in other geek media. We didn't discover the rules for Running the House, Breaking the Box, Cracking the Bolts and Eyes, then Dodging the Heat, but we did enjoy holding them up and rotating them around for other curious fellow travelers.

Then along comes an email: "Hey, so we took a run at adapting the *Leverage* crime style to a heist during the height of the Byzantine Empire," and I was *delighted*. An experiment is only successful once it's been replicated. This book validates some of the thinking Chris and I had about crime-writing. The *Robo* team distilled the elements of the con and heist genre just as elegantly as they sampled all the above-mentioned traditions, putting their own special spin on it. *The Nicodemus Job* is the kind of story I love most: the kind I wish I'd written, but know I couldn't.

All I'm doing at this point is stalling you from starting a great story for the sole purpose of telling you how great the creators of the story are, so I'm going to let you go. But come back when you're done. We need to have a serious talk about how we both want to see a whole series of these adventures. I want some sort of Robin Hood crime cult established in the *Atomic Robo* universe. I want crossovers, Easter eggs, deep mythology. Put simply: I want more. And I guess that's the best compliment you can ever give a story.

John Rogers
Leverage/Blue Beetle

I had a blast discovering these characters, their histories, and their Constantinople. About halfway through writing this thing it became clear there was a whole franchise of ideas with these folks at the center of them. I hope we get to see at least one more.

And I'm stealing that Robin Hood crime cult, John.

Brian Clevinger
RVA, 2018

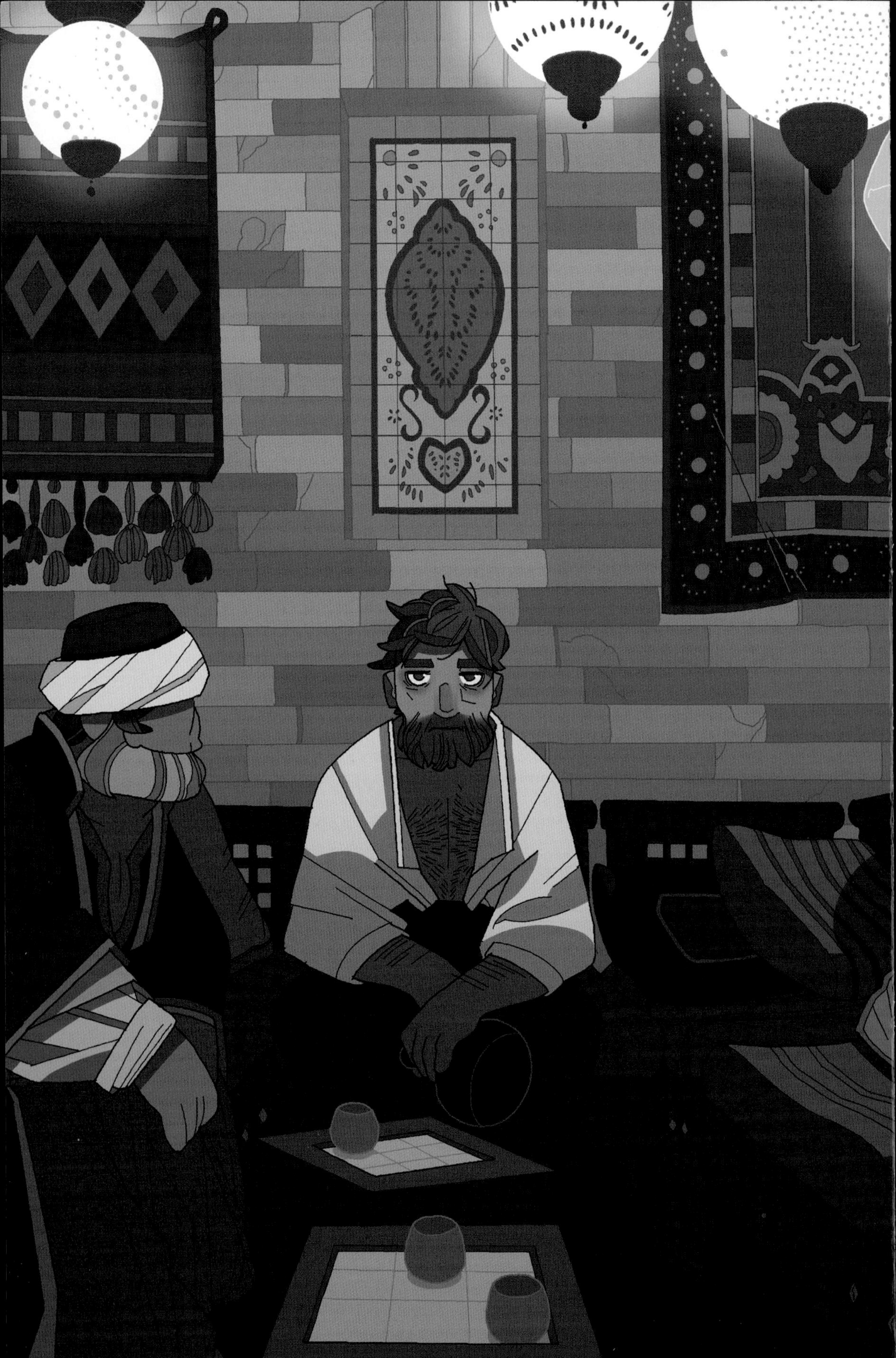

ART BY MEREDITH McCLAREN

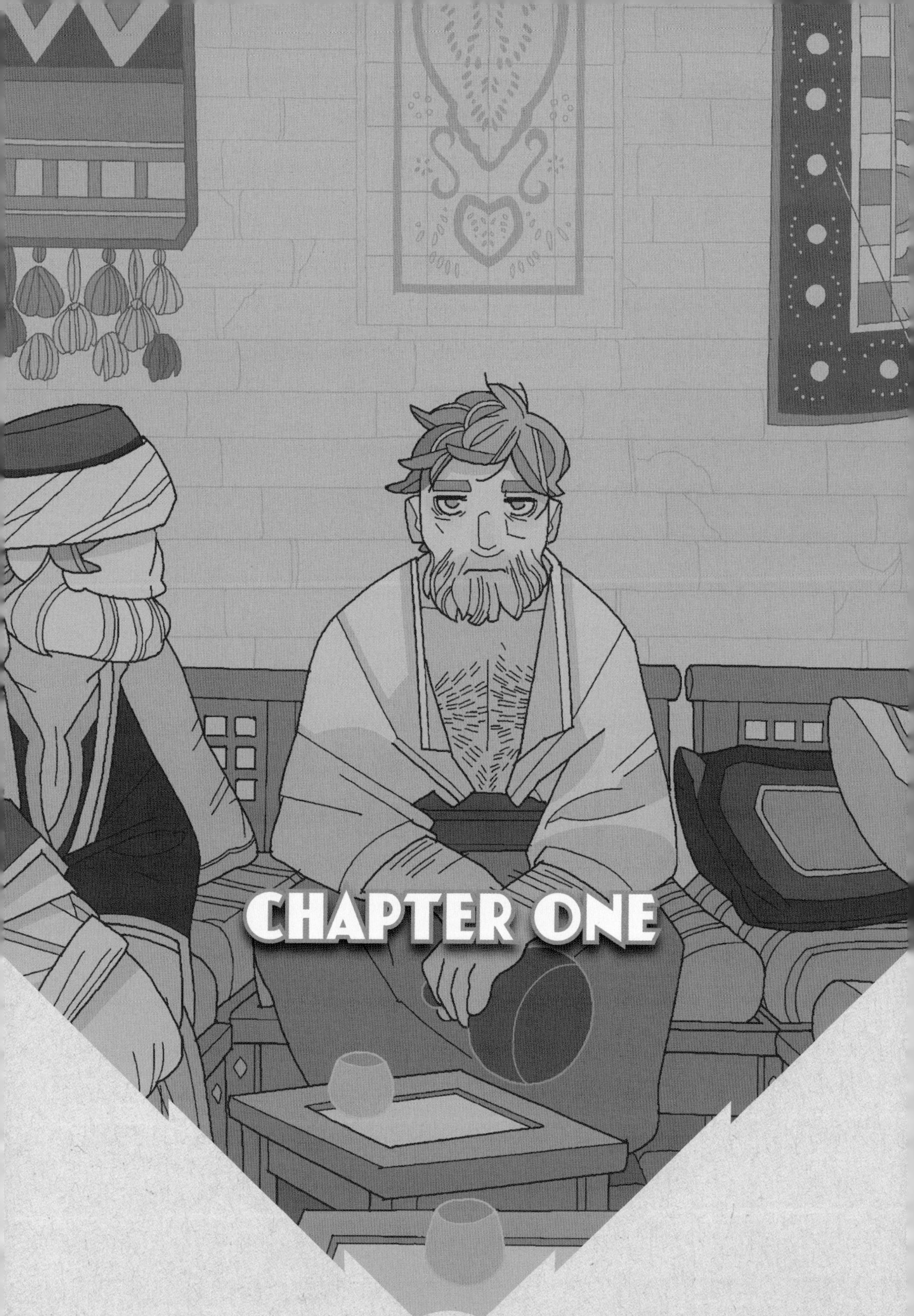

CHAPTER ONE

1

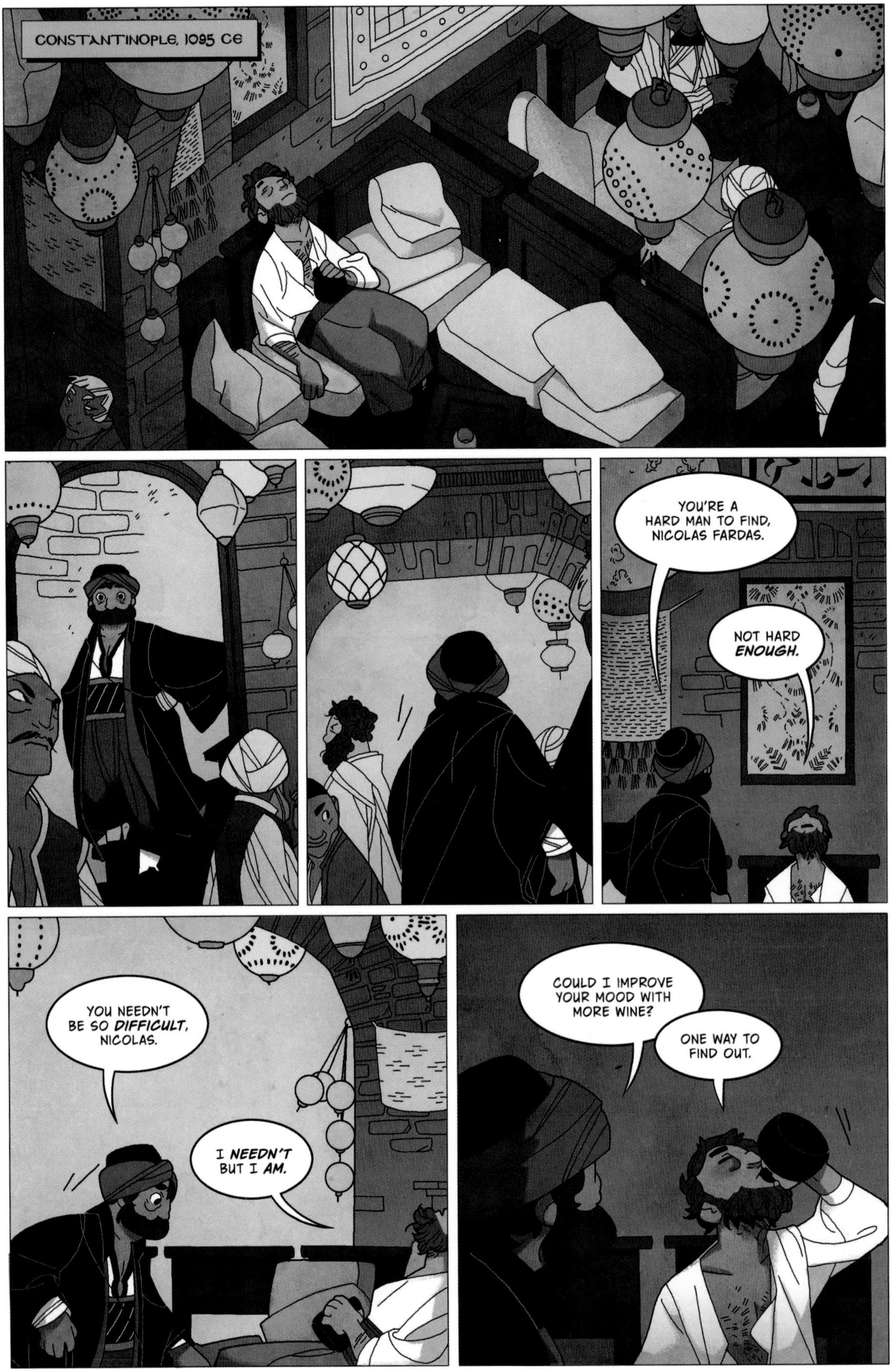
CONSTANTINOPLE, 1095 CE
YOU'RE A HARD MAN TO FIND, NICOLAS FARDAS.
NOT HARD ENOUGH.
YOU NEEDN'T BE SO DIFFICULT, NICOLAS.
I NEEDN'T BUT I AM.
COULD I IMPROVE YOUR MOOD WITH MORE WINE?
ONE WAY TO FIND OUT.

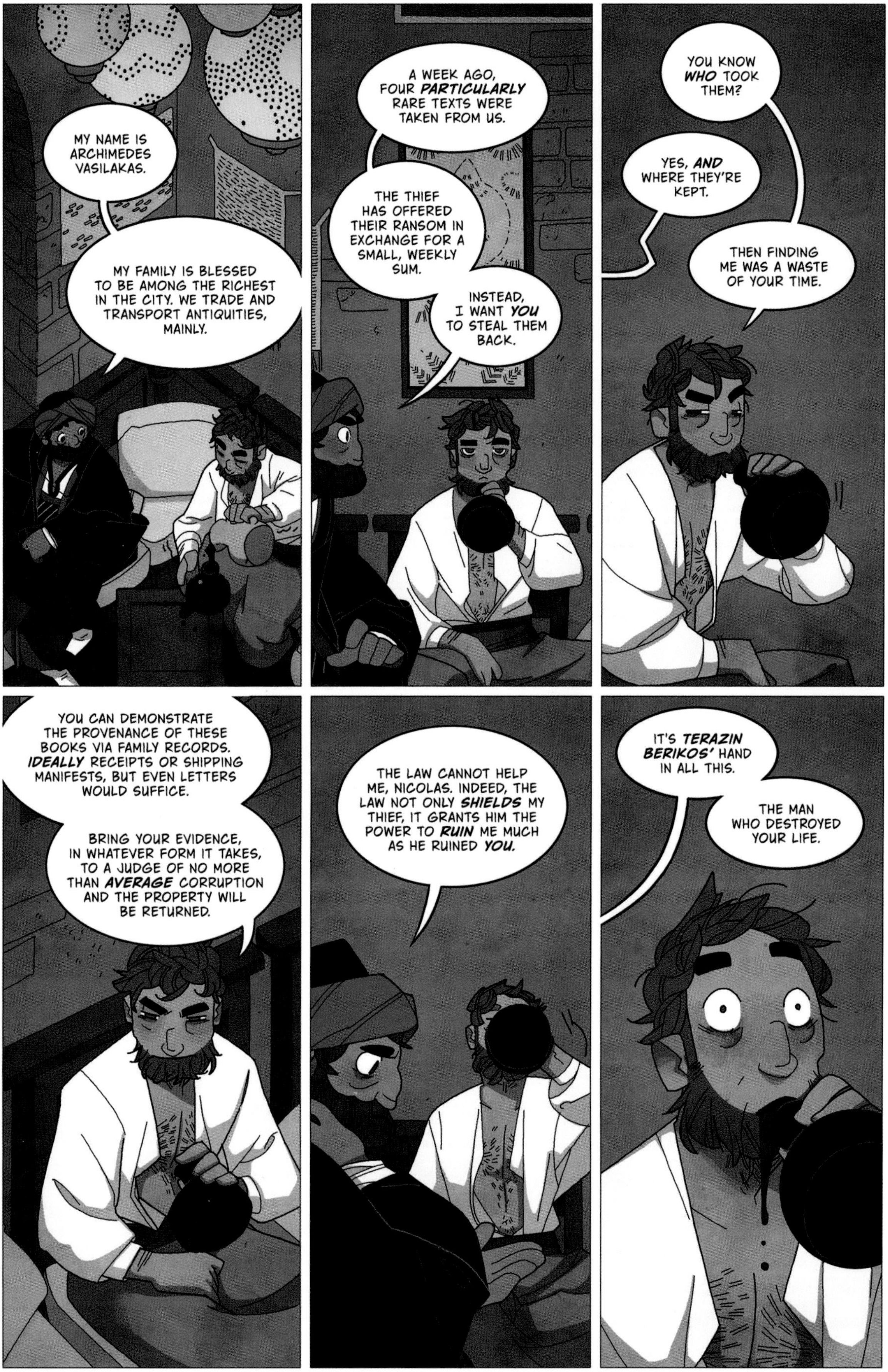
MY NAME IS ARCHIMEDES VASILAKAS.
MY FAMILY IS BLESSED TO BE AMONG THE RICHEST IN THE CITY. WE TRADE AND TRANSPORT ANTIQUITIES, MAINLY.
A WEEK AGO, FOUR **PARTICULARLY** RARE TEXTS WERE TAKEN FROM US.
THE THIEF HAS OFFERED THEIR RANSOM IN EXCHANGE FOR A SMALL, WEEKLY SUM.
INSTEAD, I WANT **YOU** TO STEAL THEM BACK.
YOU KNOW **WHO** TOOK THEM?
YES, **AND** WHERE THEY'RE KEPT.
THEN FINDING ME WAS A WASTE OF YOUR TIME.
YOU CAN DEMONSTRATE THE PROVENANCE OF THESE BOOKS VIA FAMILY RECORDS. **IDEALLY** RECEIPTS OR SHIPPING MANIFESTS, BUT EVEN LETTERS WOULD SUFFICE.
BRING YOUR EVIDENCE, IN WHATEVER FORM IT TAKES, TO A JUDGE OF NO MORE THAN **AVERAGE** CORRUPTION AND THE PROPERTY WILL BE RETURNED.
THE LAW CANNOT HELP ME, NICOLAS. INDEED, THE LAW NOT ONLY **SHIELDS** MY THIEF, IT GRANTS HIM THE POWER TO **RUIN** ME MUCH AS HE RUINED **YOU.**
IT'S **TERAZIN BERIKOS'** HAND IN ALL THIS.
THE MAN WHO DESTROYED YOUR LIFE.

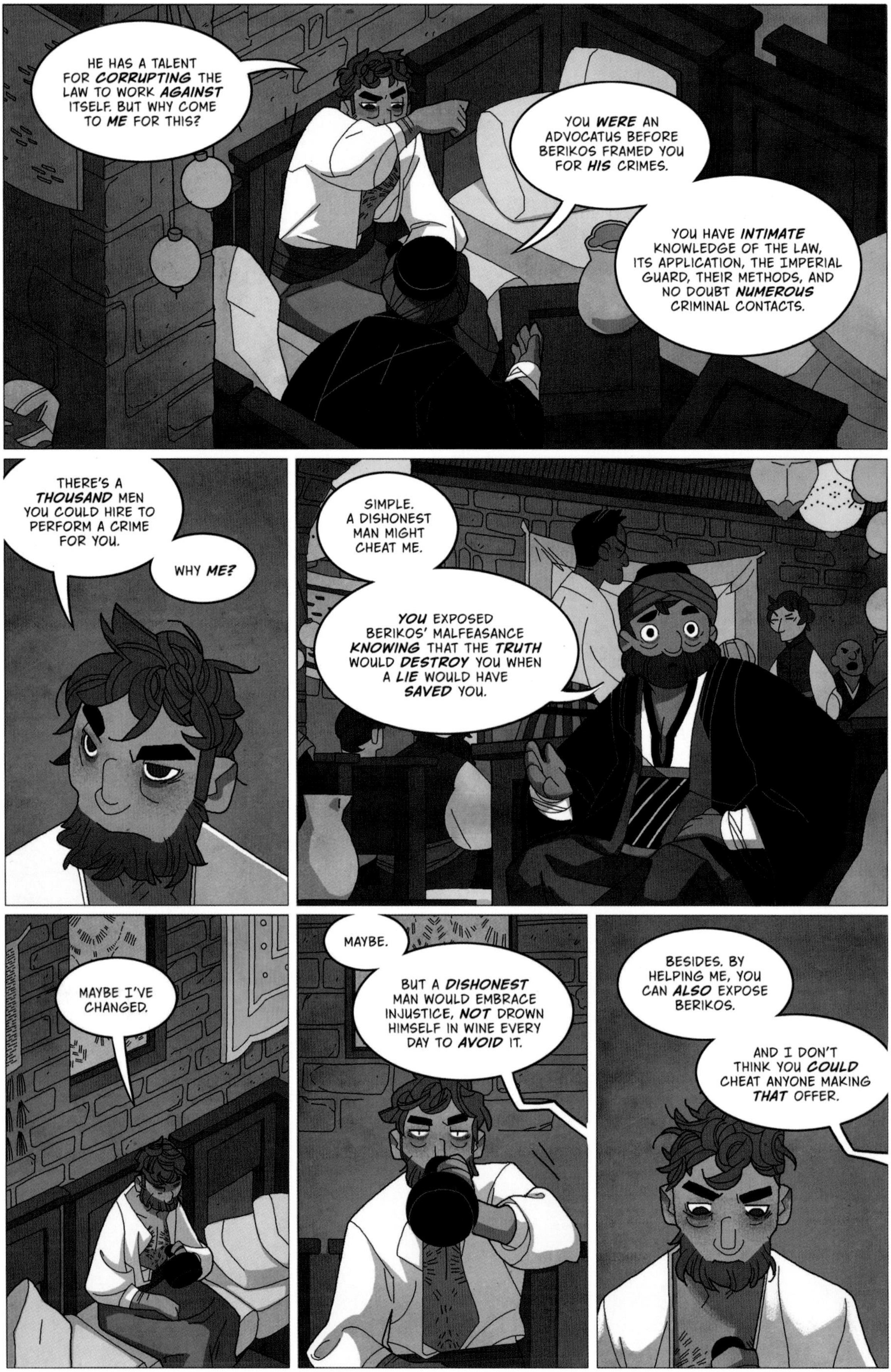
HE HAS A TALENT FOR CORRUPTING THE LAW TO WORK AGAINST ITSELF. BUT WHY COME TO ME FOR THIS?
YOU WERE AN ADVOCATUS BEFORE BERIKOS FRAMED YOU FOR HIS CRIMES.
YOU HAVE INTIMATE KNOWLEDGE OF THE LAW, ITS APPLICATION, THE IMPERIAL GUARD, THEIR METHODS, AND NO DOUBT NUMEROUS CRIMINAL CONTACTS.
THERE'S A THOUSAND MEN YOU COULD HIRE TO PERFORM A CRIME FOR YOU.
WHY ME?
SIMPLE. A DISHONEST MAN MIGHT CHEAT ME.
YOU EXPOSED BERIKOS' MALFEASANCE KNOWING THAT THE TRUTH WOULD DESTROY YOU WHEN A LIE WOULD HAVE SAVED YOU.
MAYBE I'VE CHANGED.
MAYBE.
BUT A DISHONEST MAN WOULD EMBRACE INJUSTICE, NOT DROWN HIMSELF IN WINE EVERY DAY TO AVOID IT.
BESIDES. BY HELPING ME, YOU CAN ALSO EXPOSE BERIKOS.
AND I DON'T THINK YOU COULD CHEAT ANYONE MAKING THAT OFFER.

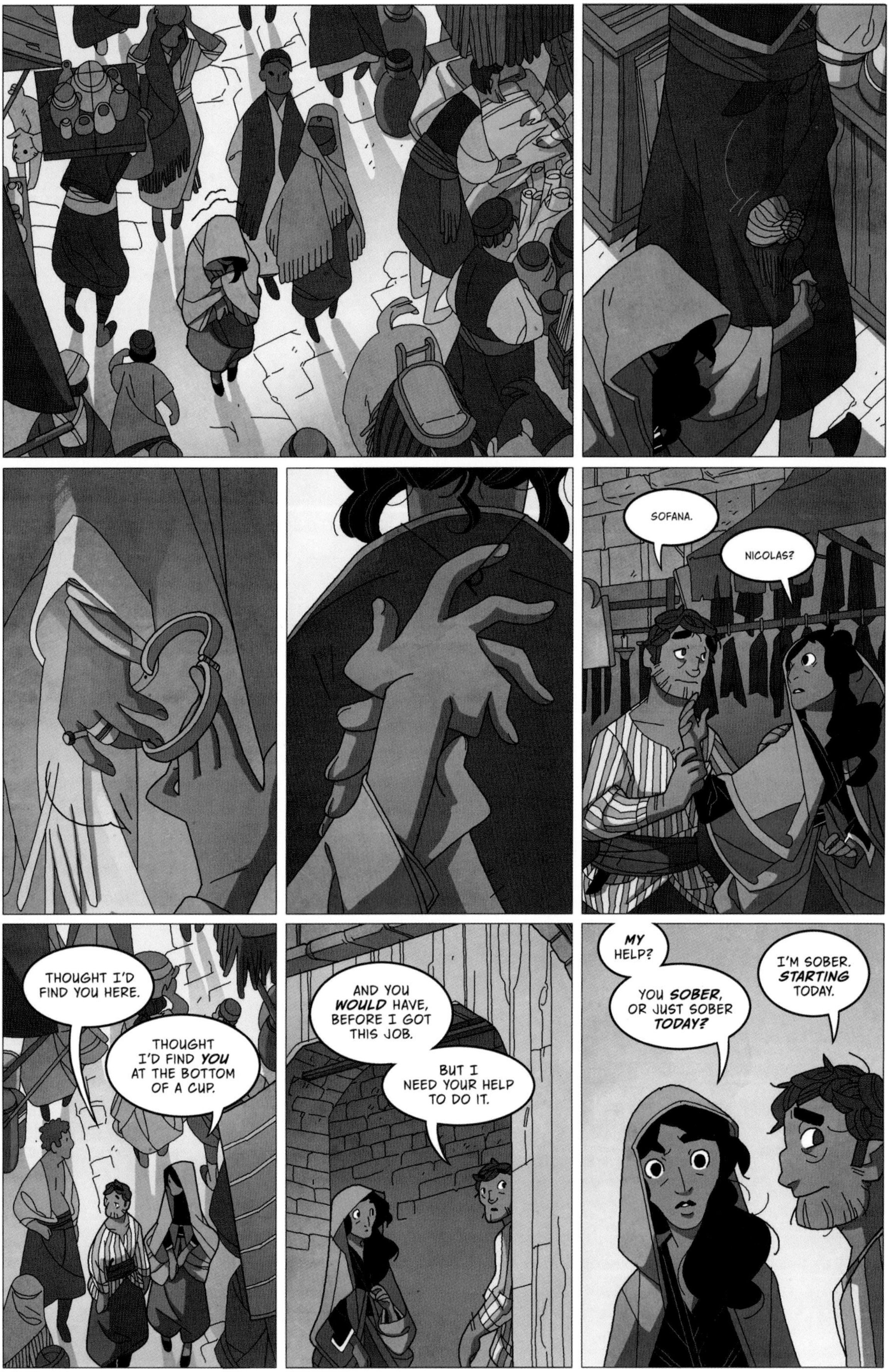
SOFANA.
NICOLAS?
THOUGHT I'D FIND YOU HERE.
THOUGHT I'D FIND *YOU* AT THE BOTTOM OF A CUP.
AND YOU *WOULD* HAVE, BEFORE I GOT THIS JOB.
BUT I NEED YOUR HELP TO DO IT.
MY HELP?
YOU *SOBER*, OR JUST SOBER *TODAY?*
I'M SOBER. *STARTING* TODAY.

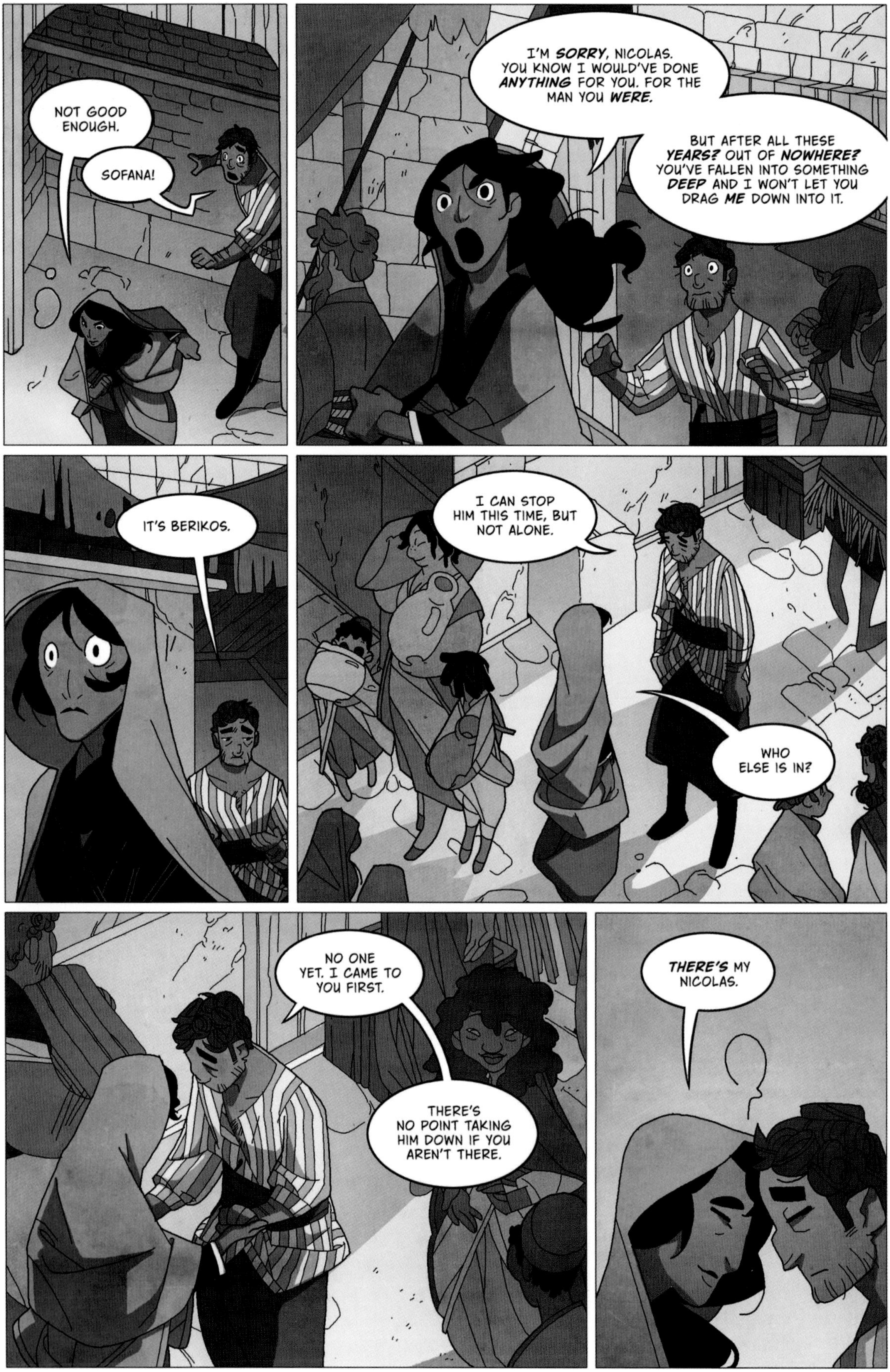
NOT GOOD ENOUGH.
SOFANA!
I'M SORRY, NICOLAS. YOU KNOW I WOULD'VE DONE ANYTHING FOR YOU. FOR THE MAN YOU WERE.
BUT AFTER ALL THESE YEARS? OUT OF NOWHERE? YOU'VE FALLEN INTO SOMETHING DEEP AND I WON'T LET YOU DRAG ME DOWN INTO IT.
IT'S BERIKOS.
I CAN STOP HIM THIS TIME, BUT NOT ALONE.
WHO ELSE IS IN?
NO ONE YET. I CAME TO YOU FIRST.
THERE'S NO POINT TAKING HIM DOWN IF YOU AREN'T THERE.
THERE'S MY NICOLAS.

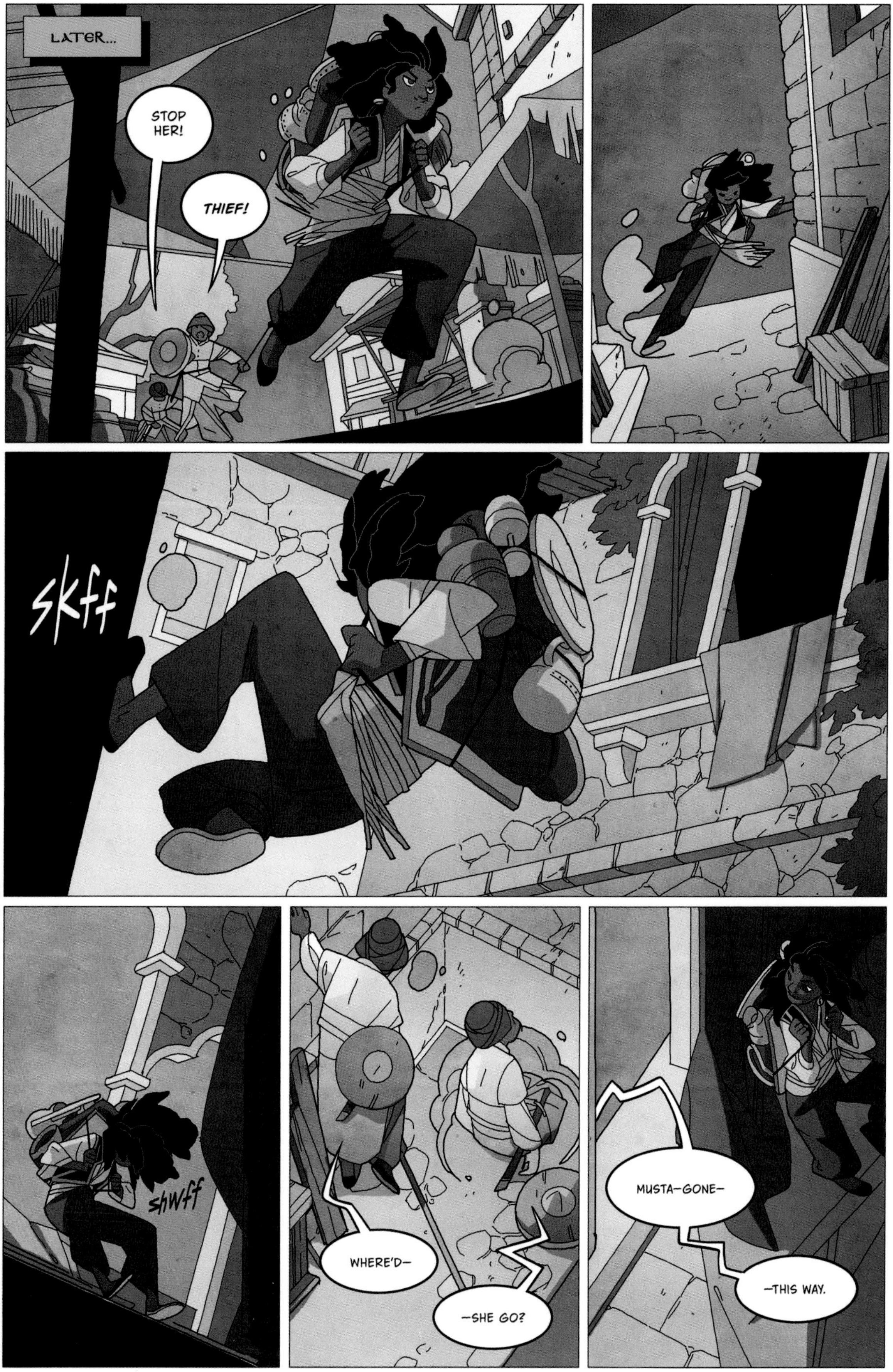
LATER...
STOP HER!
THIEF!
SKFF
SHWFF
WHERE'D–
–SHE GO?
MUSTA–GONE–
–THIS WAY.

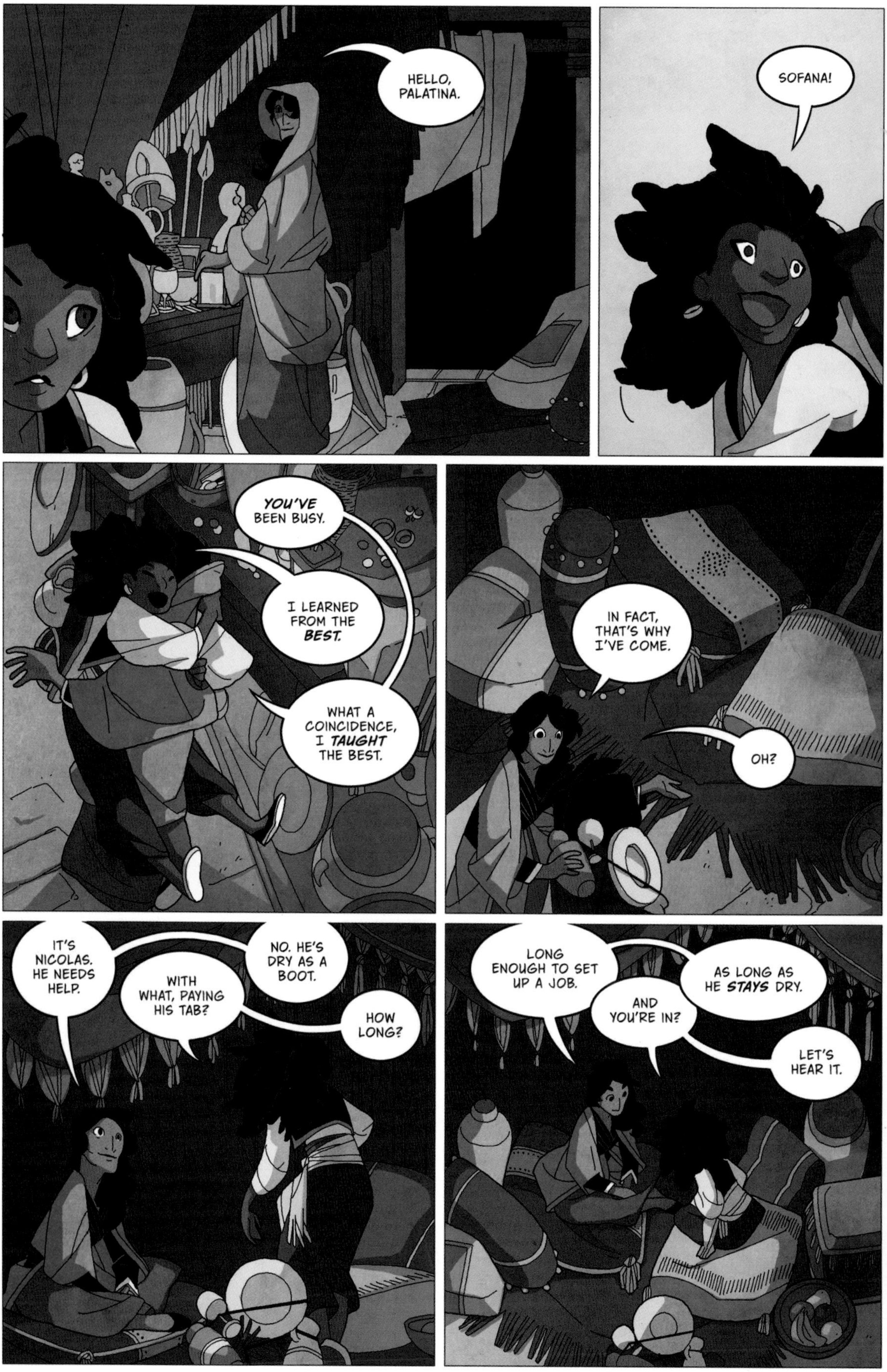
HELLO, PALATINA.
SOFANA!
YOU'VE BEEN BUSY.
I LEARNED FROM THE BEST.
WHAT A COINCIDENCE, I TAUGHT THE BEST.
IN FACT, THAT'S WHY I'VE COME.
OH?
IT'S NICOLAS. HE NEEDS HELP.
WITH WHAT, PAYING HIS TAB?
NO. HE'S DRY AS A BOOT.
HOW LONG?
LONG ENOUGH TO SET UP A JOB.
AS LONG AS HE STAYS DRY.
AND YOU'RE IN?
LET'S HEAR IT.

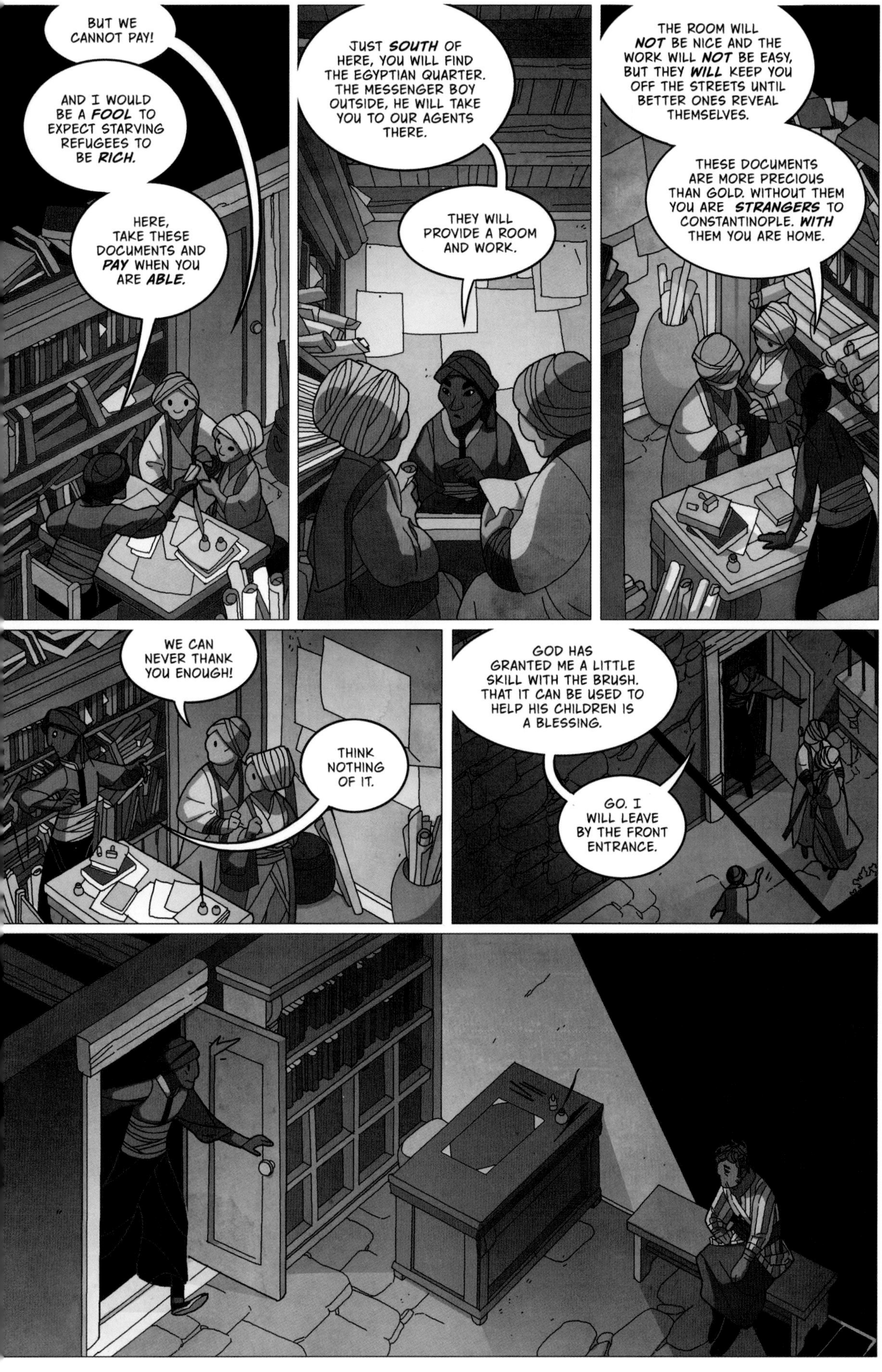
BUT WE CANNOT PAY!
AND I WOULD BE A FOOL TO EXPECT STARVING REFUGEES TO BE RICH.
HERE, TAKE THESE DOCUMENTS AND PAY WHEN YOU ARE ABLE.
JUST SOUTH OF HERE, YOU WILL FIND THE EGYPTIAN QUARTER. THE MESSENGER BOY OUTSIDE, HE WILL TAKE YOU TO OUR AGENTS THERE.
THEY WILL PROVIDE A ROOM AND WORK.
THE ROOM WILL NOT BE NICE AND THE WORK WILL NOT BE EASY, BUT THEY WILL KEEP YOU OFF THE STREETS UNTIL BETTER ONES REVEAL THEMSELVES.
THESE DOCUMENTS ARE MORE PRECIOUS THAN GOLD. WITHOUT THEM YOU ARE STRANGERS TO CONSTANTINOPLE. WITH THEM YOU ARE HOME.
WE CAN NEVER THANK YOU ENOUGH!
THINK NOTHING OF IT.
GOD HAS GRANTED ME A LITTLE SKILL WITH THE BRUSH. THAT IT CAN BE USED TO HELP HIS CHILDREN IS A BLESSING.
GO. I WILL LEAVE BY THE FRONT ENTRANCE.

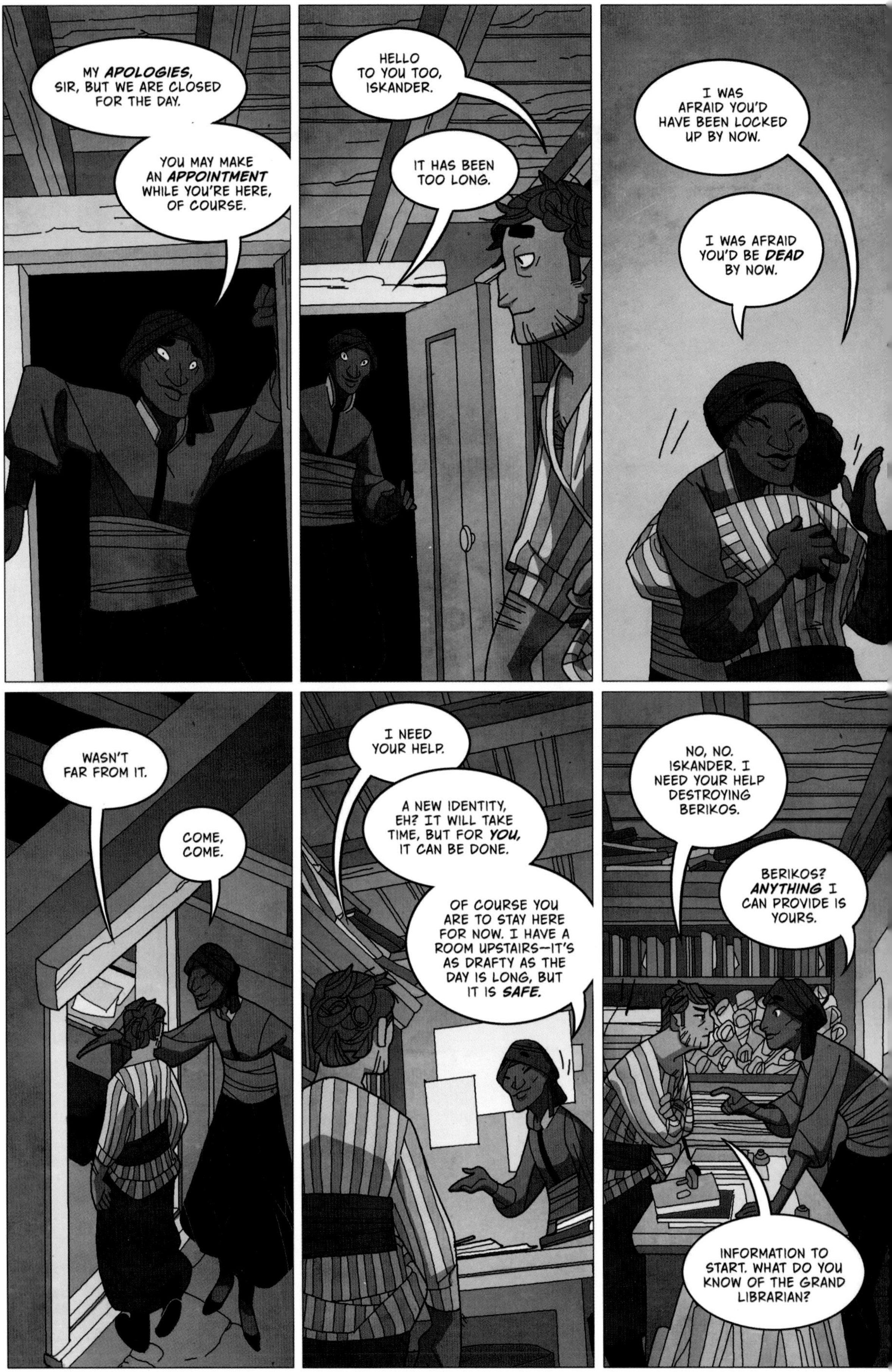
MY APOLOGIES, SIR, BUT WE ARE CLOSED FOR THE DAY.
YOU MAY MAKE AN APPOINTMENT WHILE YOU'RE HERE, OF COURSE.
HELLO TO YOU TOO, ISKANDER.
IT HAS BEEN TOO LONG.
I WAS AFRAID YOU'D HAVE BEEN LOCKED UP BY NOW.
I WAS AFRAID YOU'D BE DEAD BY NOW.
WASN'T FAR FROM IT.
COME, COME.
I NEED YOUR HELP.
A NEW IDENTITY, EH? IT WILL TAKE TIME, BUT FOR YOU, IT CAN BE DONE.
OF COURSE YOU ARE TO STAY HERE FOR NOW. I HAVE A ROOM UPSTAIRS—IT'S AS DRAFTY AS THE DAY IS LONG, BUT IT IS SAFE.
NO, NO. ISKANDER. I NEED YOUR HELP DESTROYING BERIKOS.
BERIKOS? ANYTHING I CAN PROVIDE IS YOURS.
INFORMATION TO START. WHAT DO YOU KNOW OF THE GRAND LIBRARIAN?

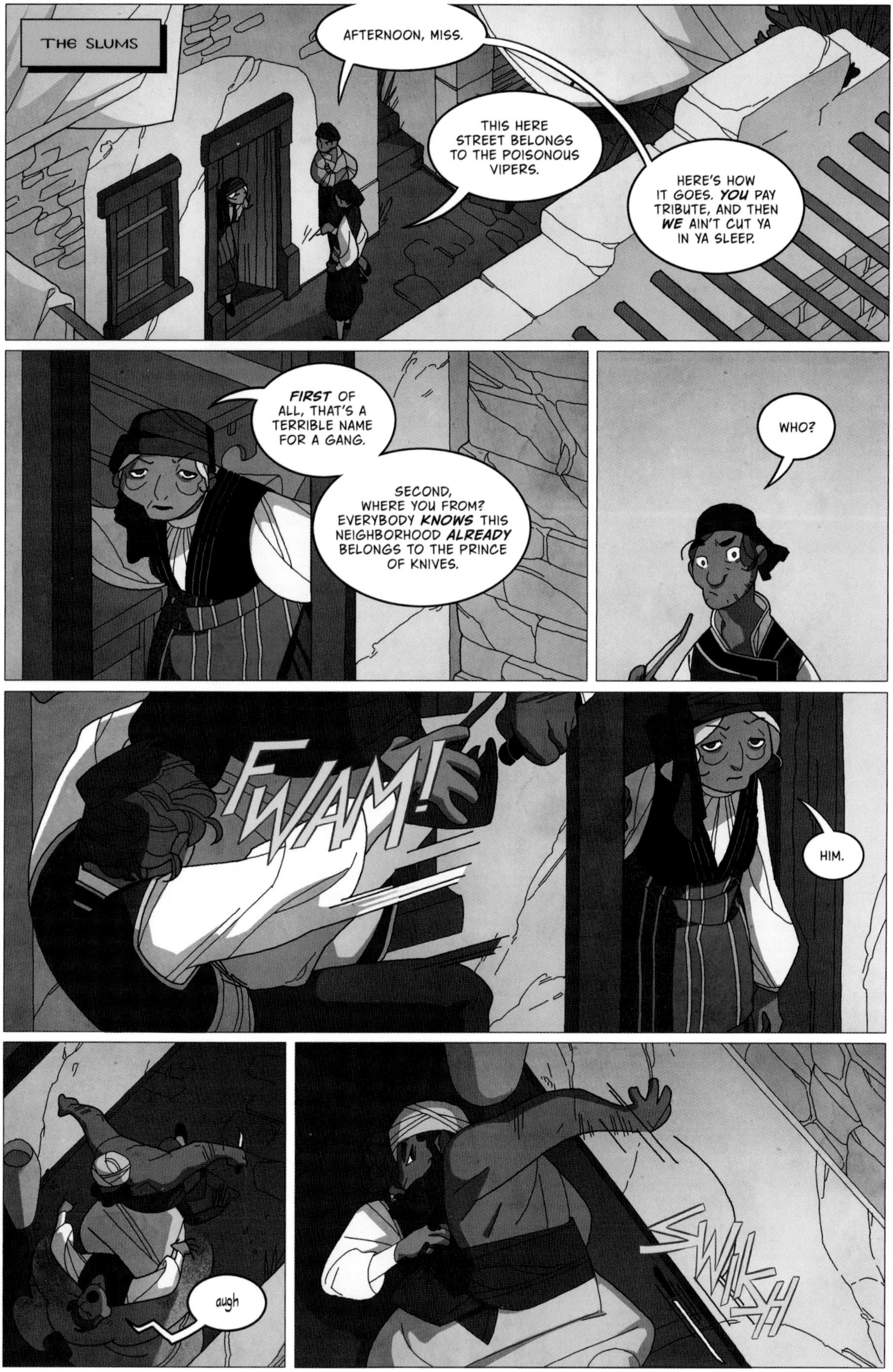
THE SLUMS
AFTERNOON, MISS.
THIS HERE STREET BELONGS TO THE POISONOUS VIPERS.
HERE'S HOW IT GOES. YOU PAY TRIBUTE, AND THEN WE AIN'T CUT YA IN YA SLEEP.
FIRST OF ALL, THAT'S A TERRIBLE NAME FOR A GANG.
SECOND, WHERE YOU FROM? EVERYBODY KNOWS THIS NEIGHBORHOOD ALREADY BELONGS TO THE PRINCE OF KNIVES.
WHO?
FWAM!
HIM.
augh
SWAKH

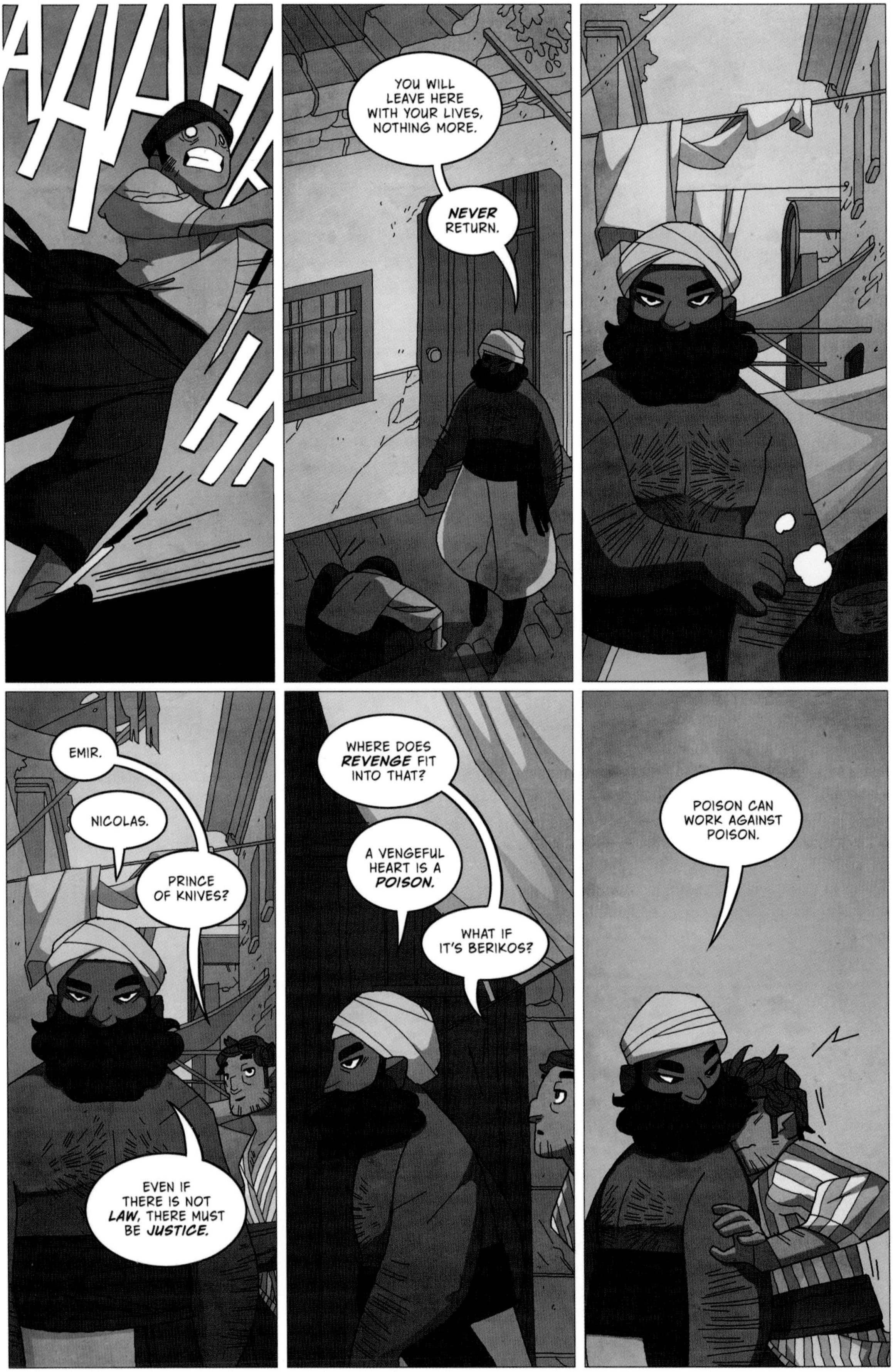

AAAH
HH
YOU WILL LEAVE HERE WITH YOUR LIVES, NOTHING MORE.
NEVER RETURN.
EMIR.
NICOLAS.
PRINCE OF KNIVES?
EVEN IF THERE IS NOT LAW, THERE MUST BE JUSTICE.
WHERE DOES REVENGE FIT INTO THAT?
A VENGEFUL HEART IS A POISON.
WHAT IF IT'S BERIKOS?
POISON CAN WORK AGAINST POISON.

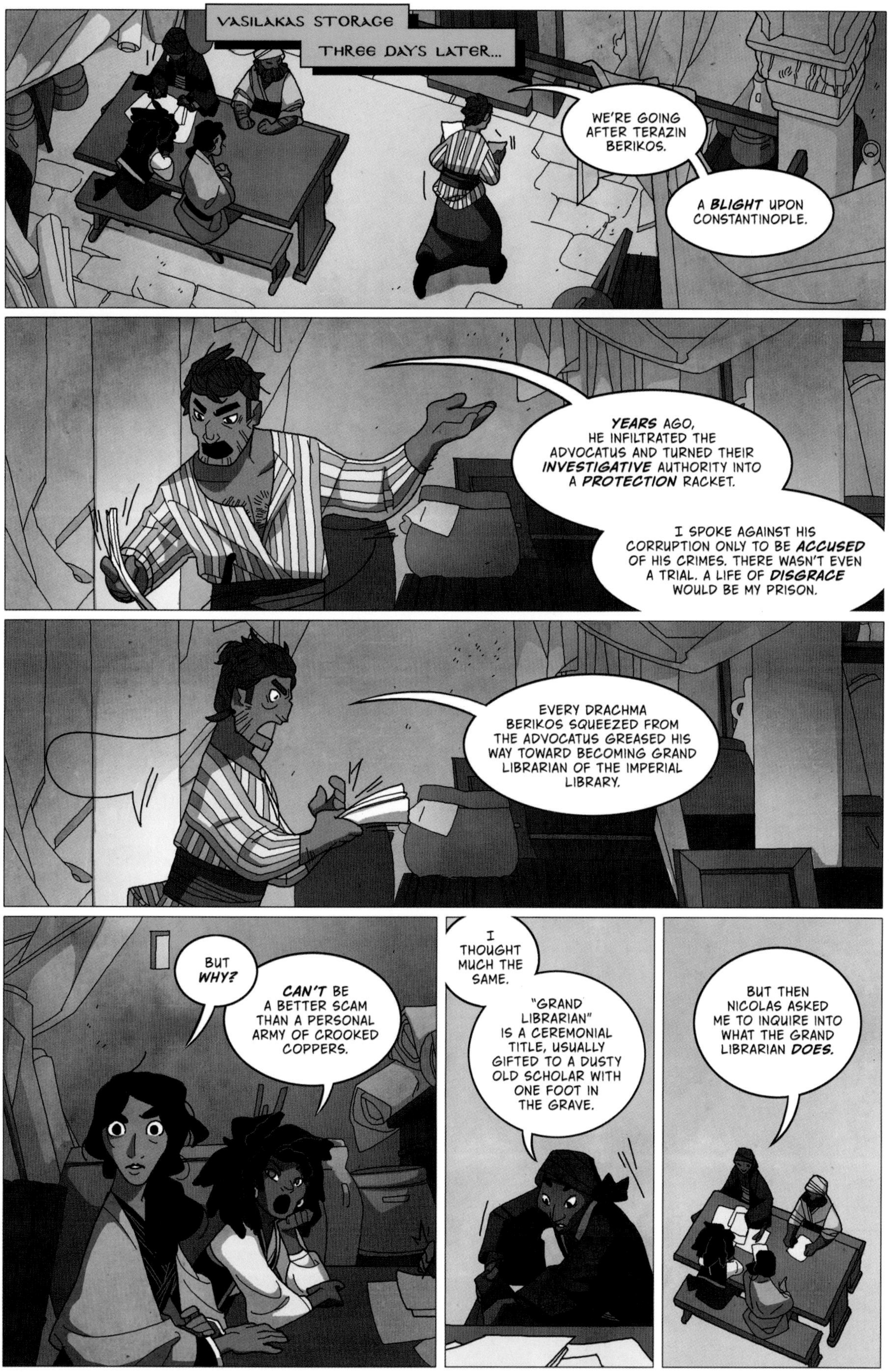
VASILAKAS STORAGE
THREE DAYS LATER...
WE'RE GOING AFTER TERAZIN BERIKOS.
A BLIGHT UPON CONSTANTINOPLE.
YEARS AGO, HE INFILTRATED THE ADVOCATUS AND TURNED THEIR INVESTIGATIVE AUTHORITY INTO A PROTECTION RACKET.
I SPOKE AGAINST HIS CORRUPTION ONLY TO BE ACCUSED OF HIS CRIMES. THERE WASN'T EVEN A TRIAL. A LIFE OF DISGRACE WOULD BE MY PRISON.
EVERY DRACHMA BERIKOS SQUEEZED FROM THE ADVOCATUS GREASED HIS WAY TOWARD BECOMING GRAND LIBRARIAN OF THE IMPERIAL LIBRARY.
BUT WHY?
CAN'T BE A BETTER SCAM THAN A PERSONAL ARMY OF CROOKED COPPERS.
I THOUGHT MUCH THE SAME.
"GRAND LIBRARIAN" IS A CEREMONIAL TITLE, USUALLY GIFTED TO A DUSTY OLD SCHOLAR WITH ONE FOOT IN THE GRAVE.
BUT THEN NICOLAS ASKED ME TO INQUIRE INTO WHAT THE GRAND LIBRARIAN DOES.

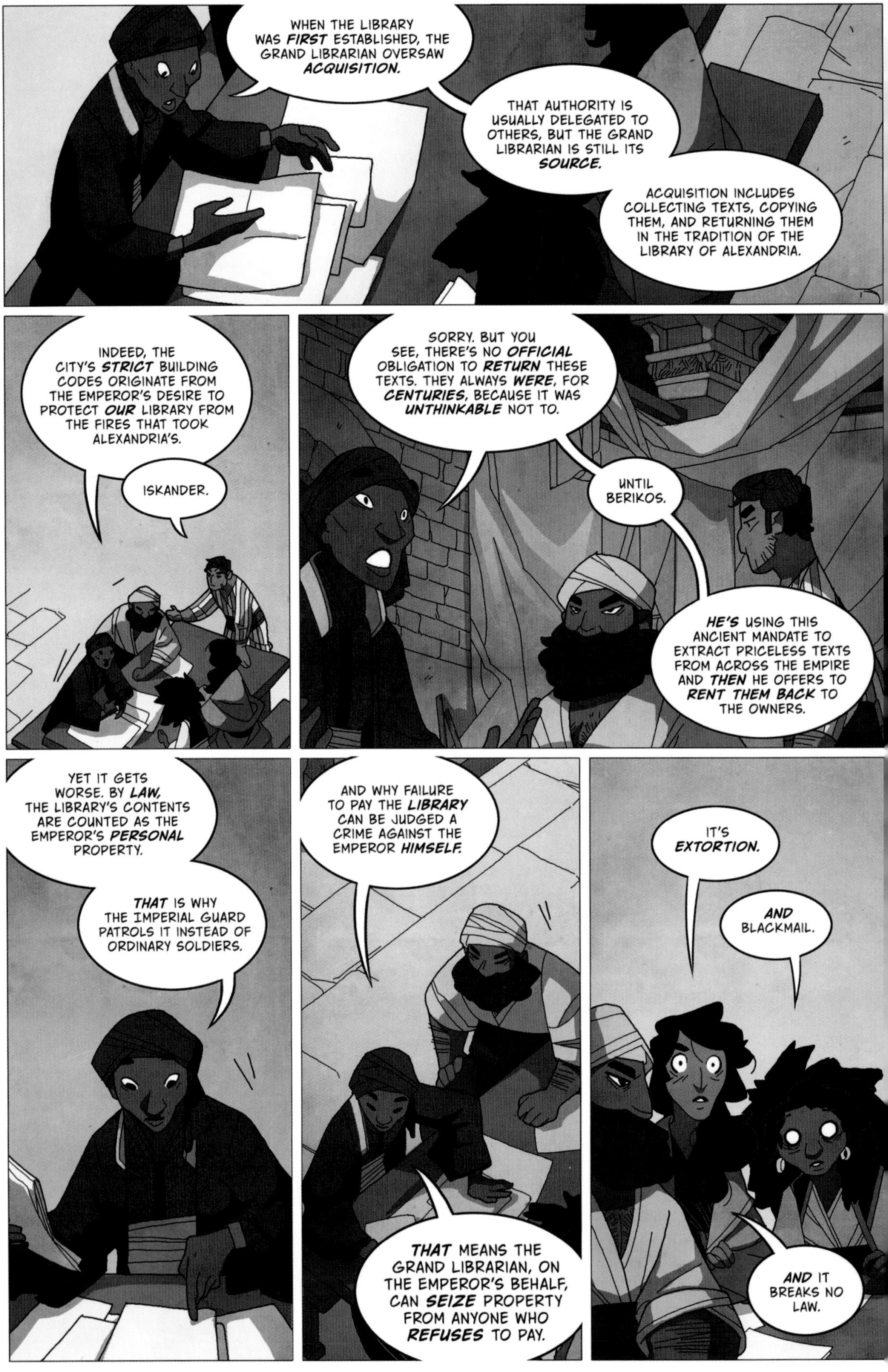

WHEN THE LIBRARY WAS FIRST ESTABLISHED, THE GRAND LIBRARIAN OVERSAW ACQUISITION.
THAT AUTHORITY IS USUALLY DELEGATED TO OTHERS, BUT THE GRAND LIBRARIAN IS STILL ITS SOURCE.
ACQUISITION INCLUDES COLLECTING TEXTS, COPYING THEM, AND RETURNING THEM IN THE TRADITION OF THE LIBRARY OF ALEXANDRIA.
INDEED, THE CITY'S STRICT BUILDING CODES ORIGINATE FROM THE EMPEROR'S DESIRE TO PROTECT OUR LIBRARY FROM THE FIRES THAT TOOK ALEXANDRIA'S.
ISKANDER.
SORRY. BUT YOU SEE, THERE'S NO OFFICIAL OBLIGATION TO RETURN THESE TEXTS. THEY ALWAYS WERE, FOR CENTURIES, BECAUSE IT WAS UNTHINKABLE NOT TO.
UNTIL BERIKOS.
HE'S USING THIS ANCIENT MANDATE TO EXTRACT PRICELESS TEXTS FROM ACROSS THE EMPIRE AND THEN HE OFFERS TO RENT THEM BACK TO THE OWNERS.
YET IT GETS WORSE. BY LAW, THE LIBRARY'S CONTENTS ARE COUNTED AS THE EMPEROR'S PERSONAL PROPERTY.
THAT IS WHY THE IMPERIAL GUARD PATROLS IT INSTEAD OF ORDINARY SOLDIERS.
AND WHY FAILURE TO PAY THE LIBRARY CAN BE JUDGED A CRIME AGAINST THE EMPEROR HIMSELF.
THAT MEANS THE GRAND LIBRARIAN, ON THE EMPEROR'S BEHALF, CAN SEIZE PROPERTY FROM ANYONE WHO REFUSES TO PAY.
IT'S EXTORTION.
AND BLACKMAIL.
AND IT BREAKS NO LAW.

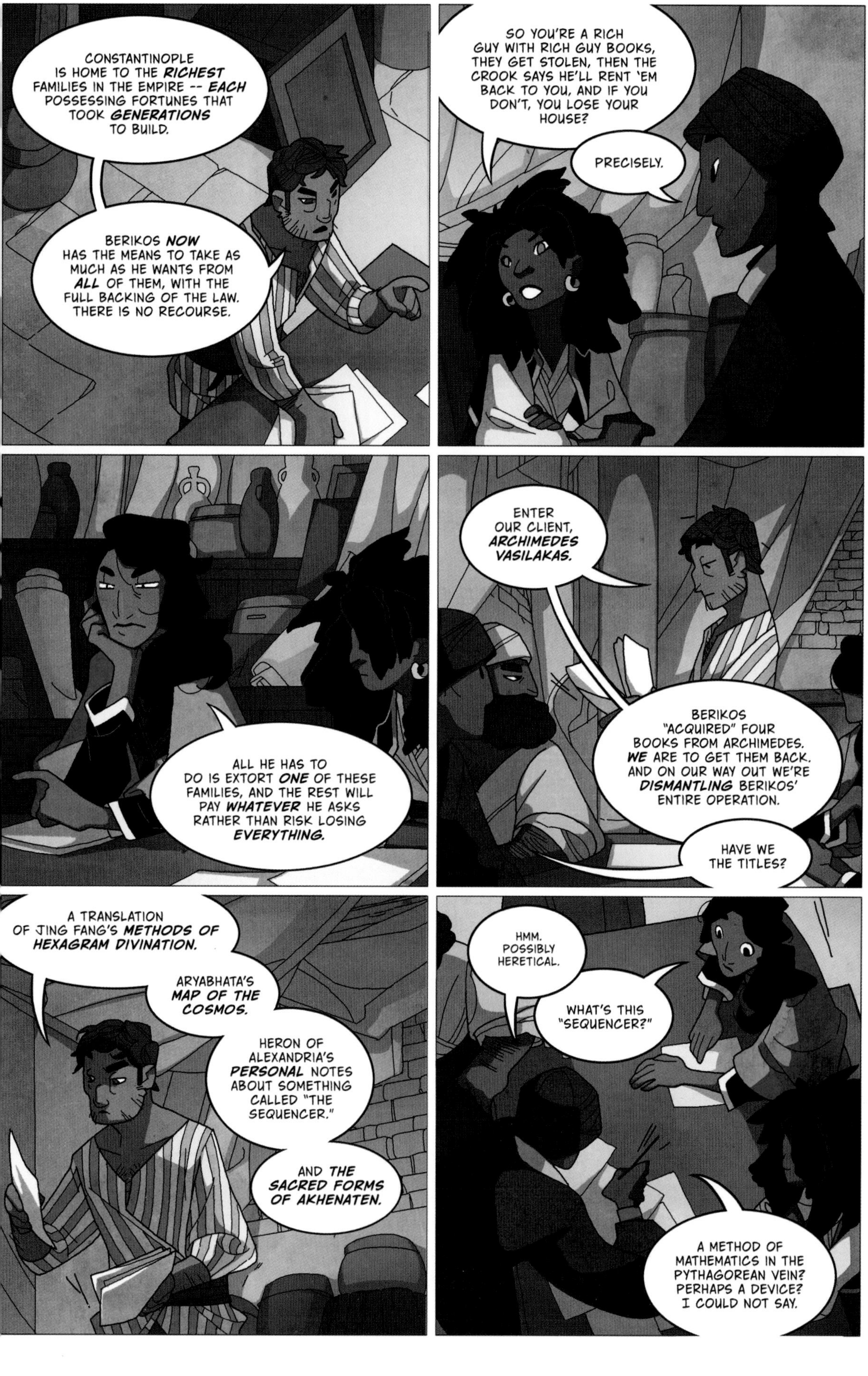
CONSTANTINOPLE IS HOME TO THE *RICHEST* FAMILIES IN THE EMPIRE -- *EACH* POSSESSING FORTUNES THAT TOOK *GENERATIONS* TO BUILD.
BERIKOS *NOW* HAS THE MEANS TO TAKE AS MUCH AS HE WANTS FROM *ALL* OF THEM, WITH THE FULL BACKING OF THE LAW. THERE IS NO RECOURSE.
SO YOU'RE A RICH GUY WITH RICH GUY BOOKS, THEY GET STOLEN, THEN THE CROOK SAYS HE'LL RENT 'EM BACK TO YOU, AND IF YOU DON'T, YOU LOSE YOUR HOUSE?
PRECISELY.
ALL HE HAS TO DO IS EXTORT *ONE* OF THESE FAMILIES, AND THE REST WILL PAY *WHATEVER* HE ASKS RATHER THAN RISK LOSING *EVERYTHING.*
ENTER OUR CLIENT, *ARCHIMEDES VASILAKAS.*
BERIKOS "ACQUIRED" FOUR BOOKS FROM ARCHIMEDES. *WE* ARE TO GET THEM BACK. AND ON OUR WAY OUT WE'RE *DISMANTLING* BERIKOS' ENTIRE OPERATION.
HAVE WE THE TITLES?
A TRANSLATION OF JING FANG'S *METHODS OF HEXAGRAM DIVINATION.*
ARYABHATA'S *MAP OF THE COSMOS.*
HERON OF ALEXANDRIA'S *PERSONAL* NOTES ABOUT SOMETHING CALLED "THE SEQUENCER."
AND *THE SACRED FORMS OF AKHENATEN.*
HMM. POSSIBLY HERETICAL.
WHAT'S THIS "SEQUENCER?"
A METHOD OF MATHEMATICS IN THE PYTHAGOREAN VEIN? PERHAPS A DEVICE? I COULD NOT SAY.

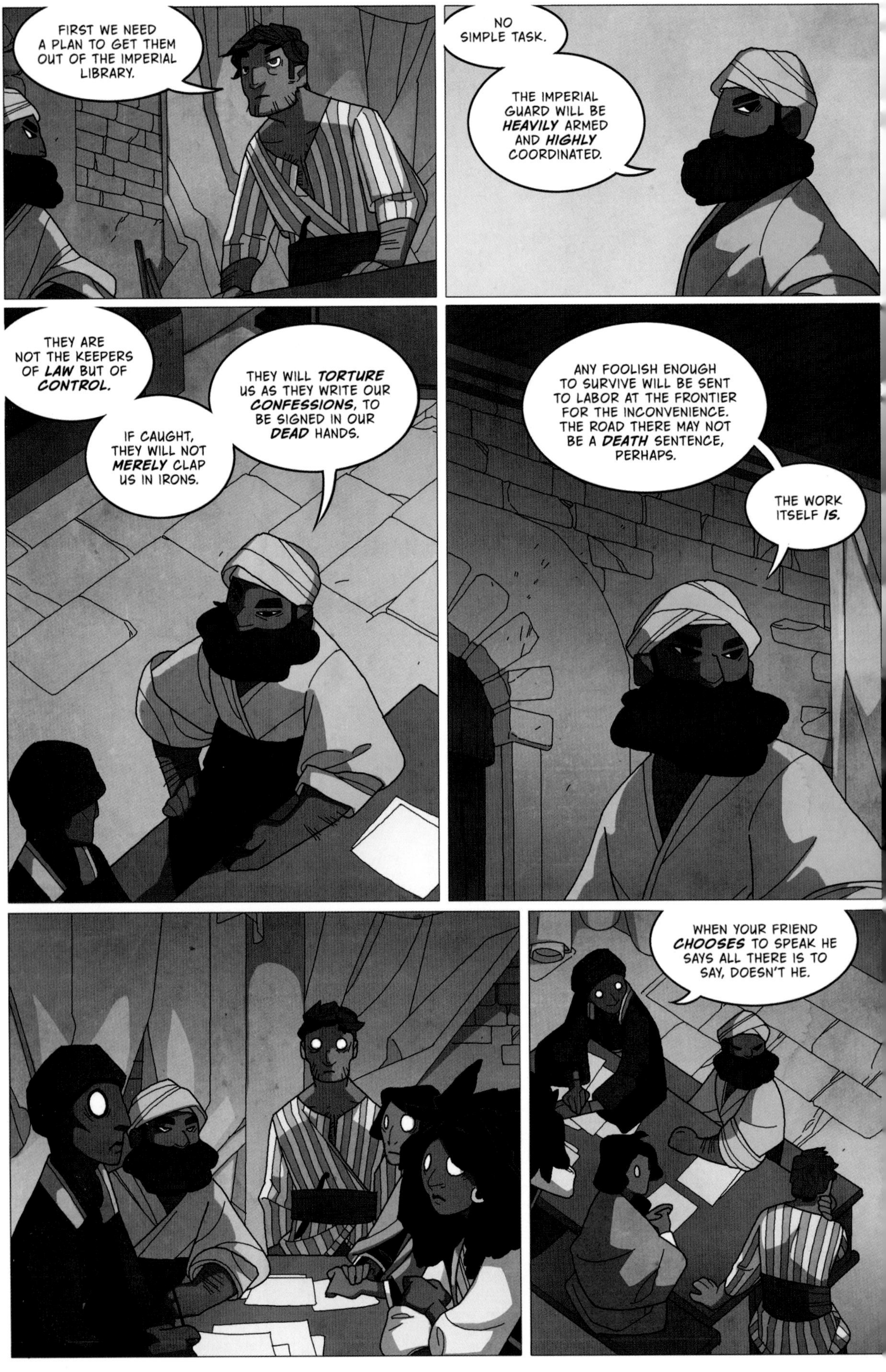
FIRST WE NEED A PLAN TO GET THEM OUT OF THE IMPERIAL LIBRARY.
NO SIMPLE TASK.
THE IMPERIAL GUARD WILL BE HEAVILY ARMED AND HIGHLY COORDINATED.
THEY ARE NOT THE KEEPERS OF LAW BUT OF CONTROL.
IF CAUGHT, THEY WILL NOT MERELY CLAP US IN IRONS.
THEY WILL TORTURE US AS THEY WRITE OUR CONFESSIONS, TO BE SIGNED IN OUR DEAD HANDS.
ANY FOOLISH ENOUGH TO SURVIVE WILL BE SENT TO LABOR AT THE FRONTIER FOR THE INCONVENIENCE. THE ROAD THERE MAY NOT BE A DEATH SENTENCE, PERHAPS.
THE WORK ITSELF IS.
WHEN YOUR FRIEND CHOOSES TO SPEAK HE SAYS ALL THERE IS TO SAY, DOESN'T HE.

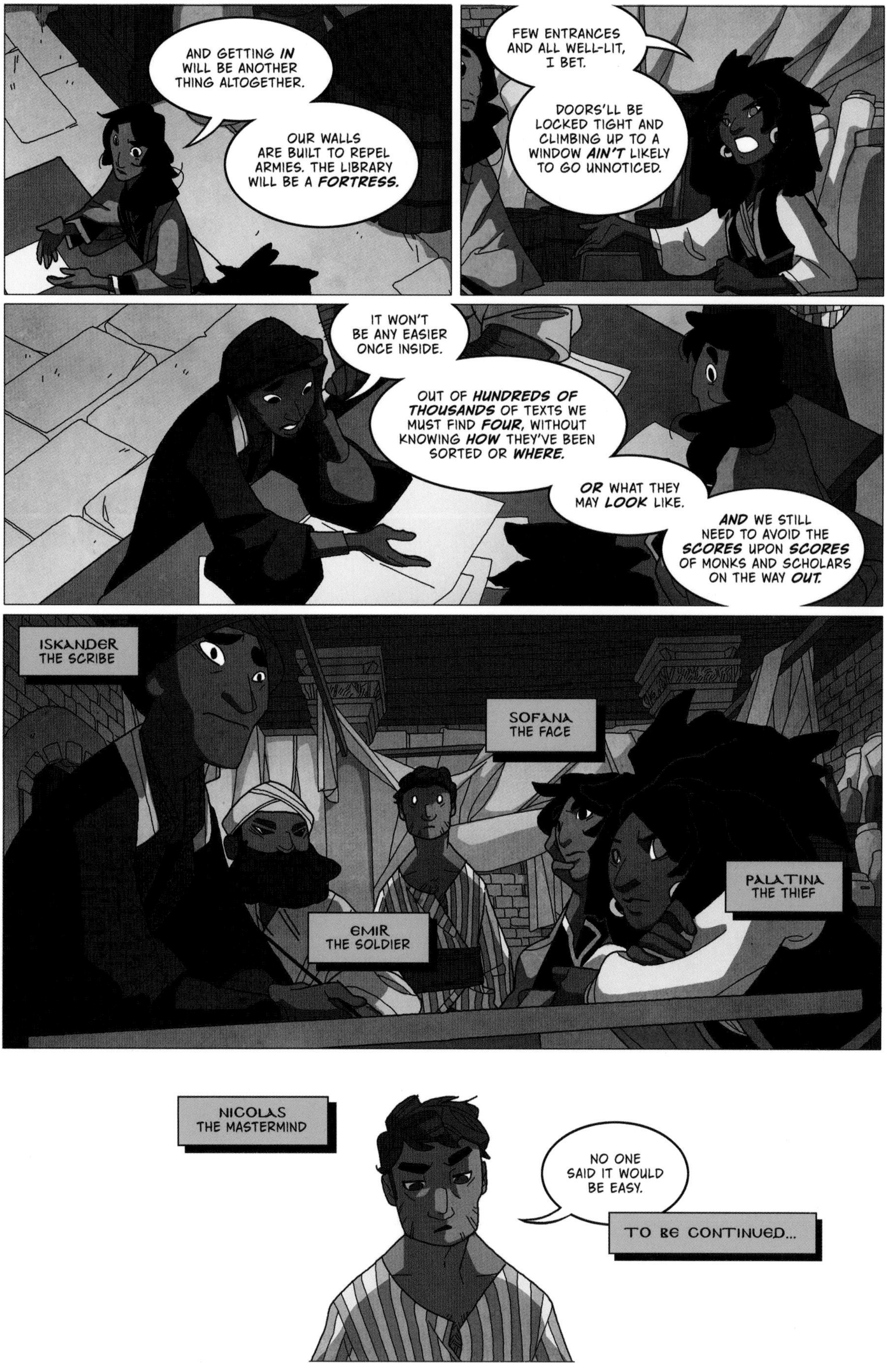
AND GETTING IN WILL BE ANOTHER THING ALTOGETHER.
OUR WALLS ARE BUILT TO REPEL ARMIES. THE LIBRARY WILL BE A FORTRESS.
FEW ENTRANCES AND ALL WELL-LIT, I BET.
DOORS'LL BE LOCKED TIGHT AND CLIMBING UP TO A WINDOW AIN'T LIKELY TO GO UNNOTICED.
IT WON'T BE ANY EASIER ONCE INSIDE.
OUT OF HUNDREDS OF THOUSANDS OF TEXTS WE MUST FIND FOUR, WITHOUT KNOWING HOW THEY'VE BEEN SORTED OR WHERE.
OR WHAT THEY MAY LOOK LIKE.
AND WE STILL NEED TO AVOID THE SCORES UPON SCORES OF MONKS AND SCHOLARS ON THE WAY OUT.
ISKANDER THE SCRIBE
SOFANA THE FACE
PALATINA THE THIEF
EMIR THE SOLDIER
NICOLAS THE MASTERMIND
NO ONE SAID IT WOULD BE EASY.
TO BE CONTINUED...

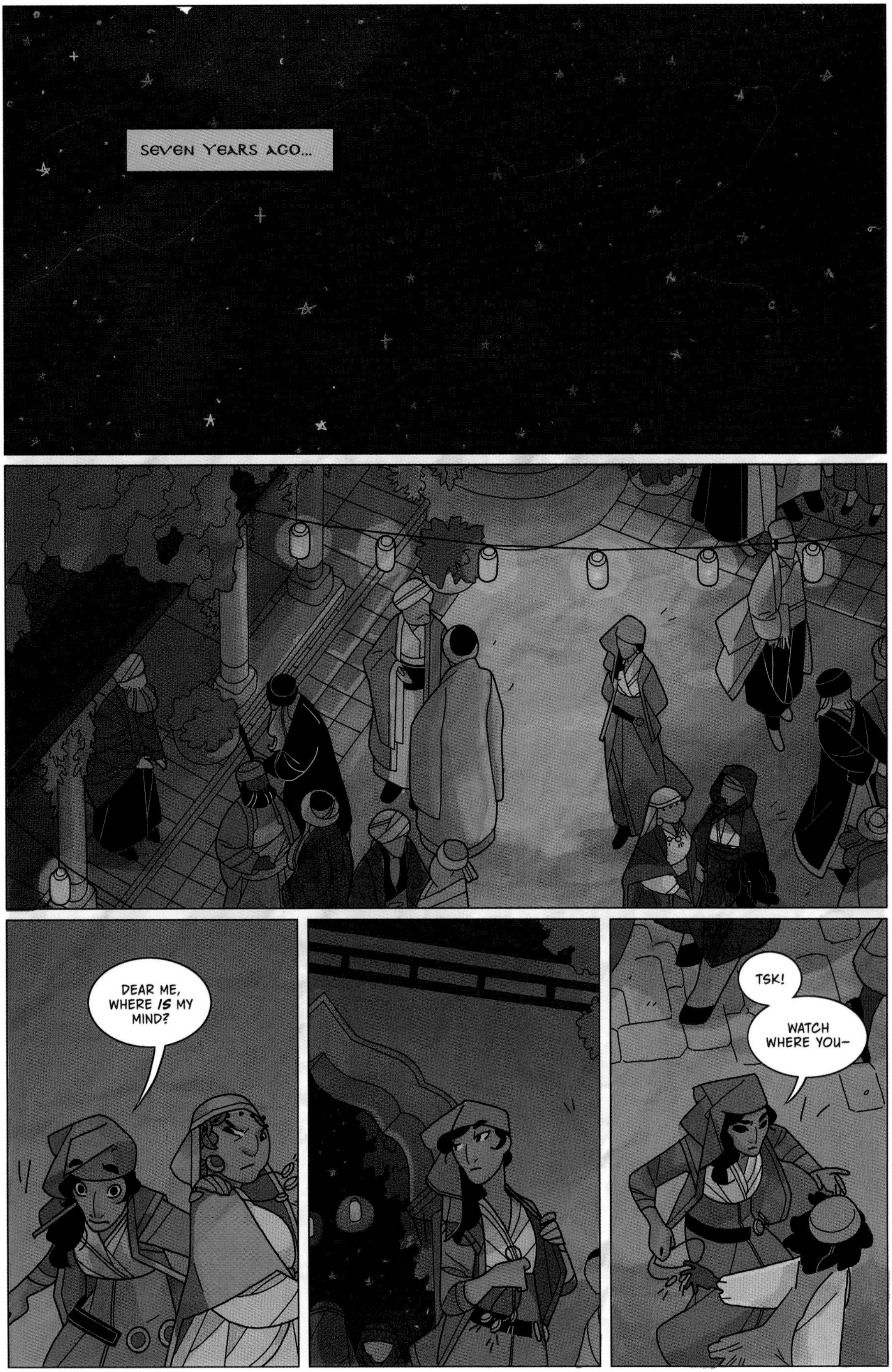
SEVEN YEARS AGO...
DEAR ME, WHERE IS MY MIND?
TSK!
WATCH WHERE YOU–

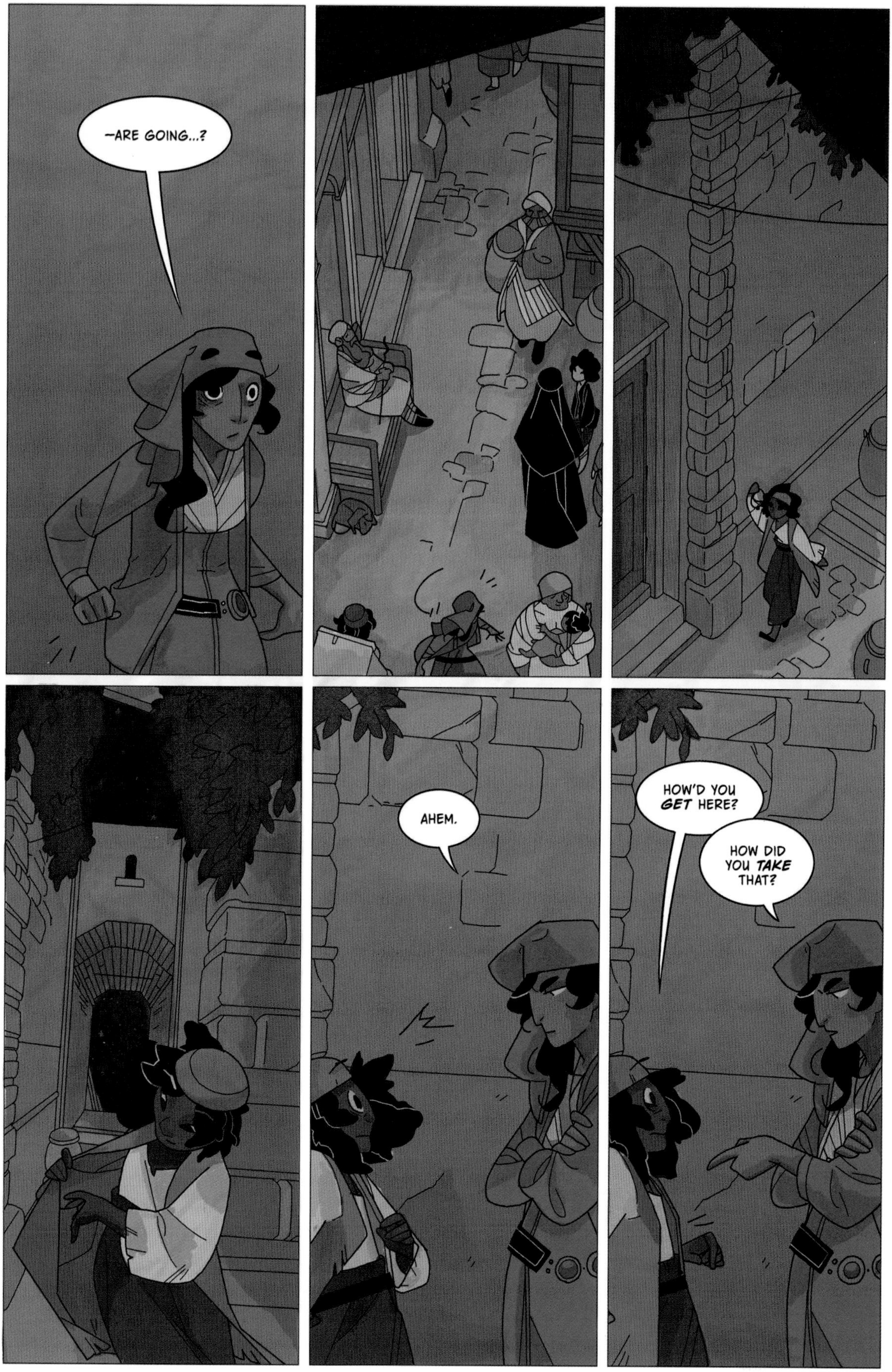
—ARE GOING...?
AHEM.
HOW'D YOU GET HERE?
HOW DID YOU TAKE THAT?

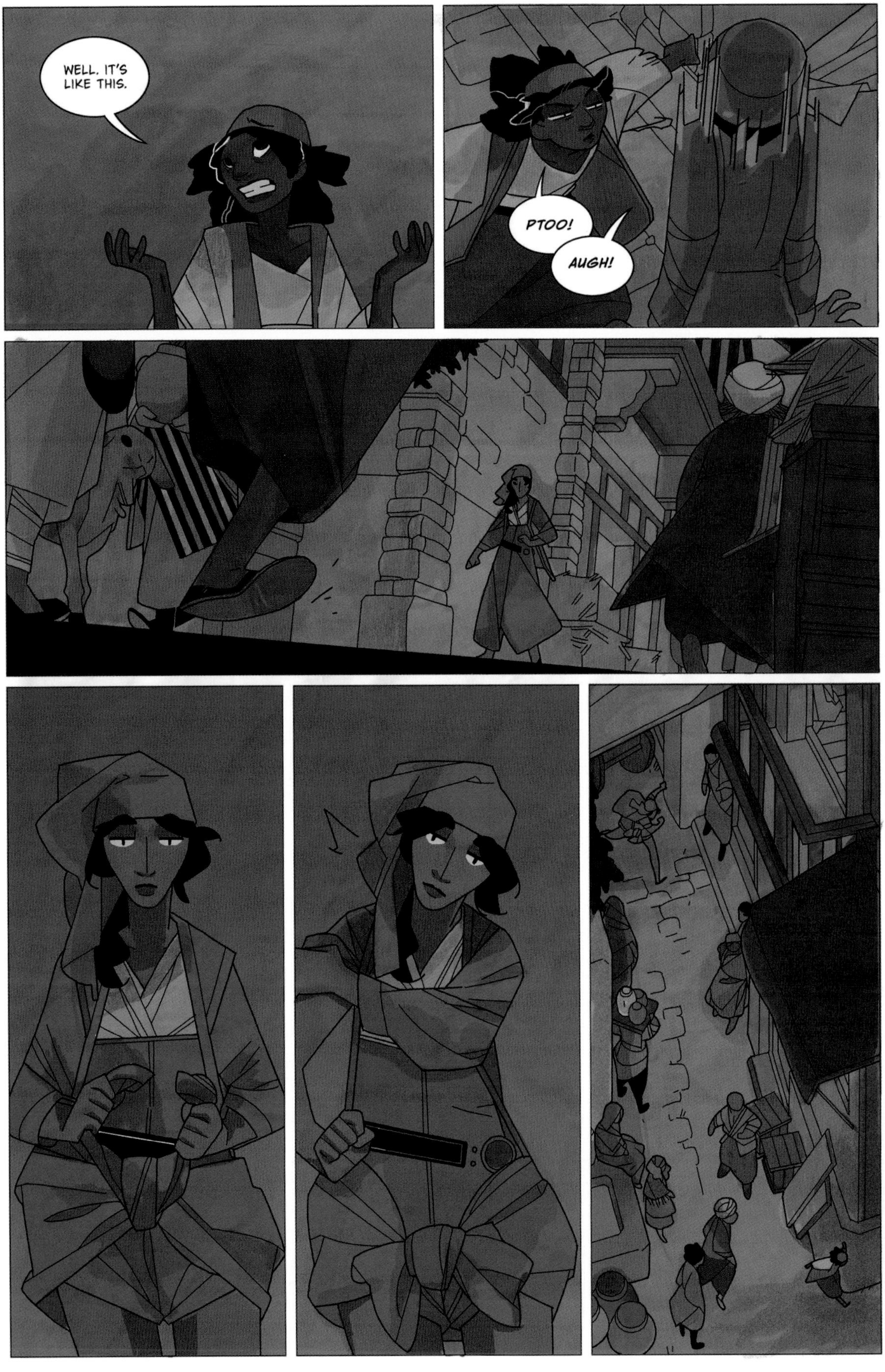
WELL. IT'S LIKE THIS.
PTOO!
AUGH!

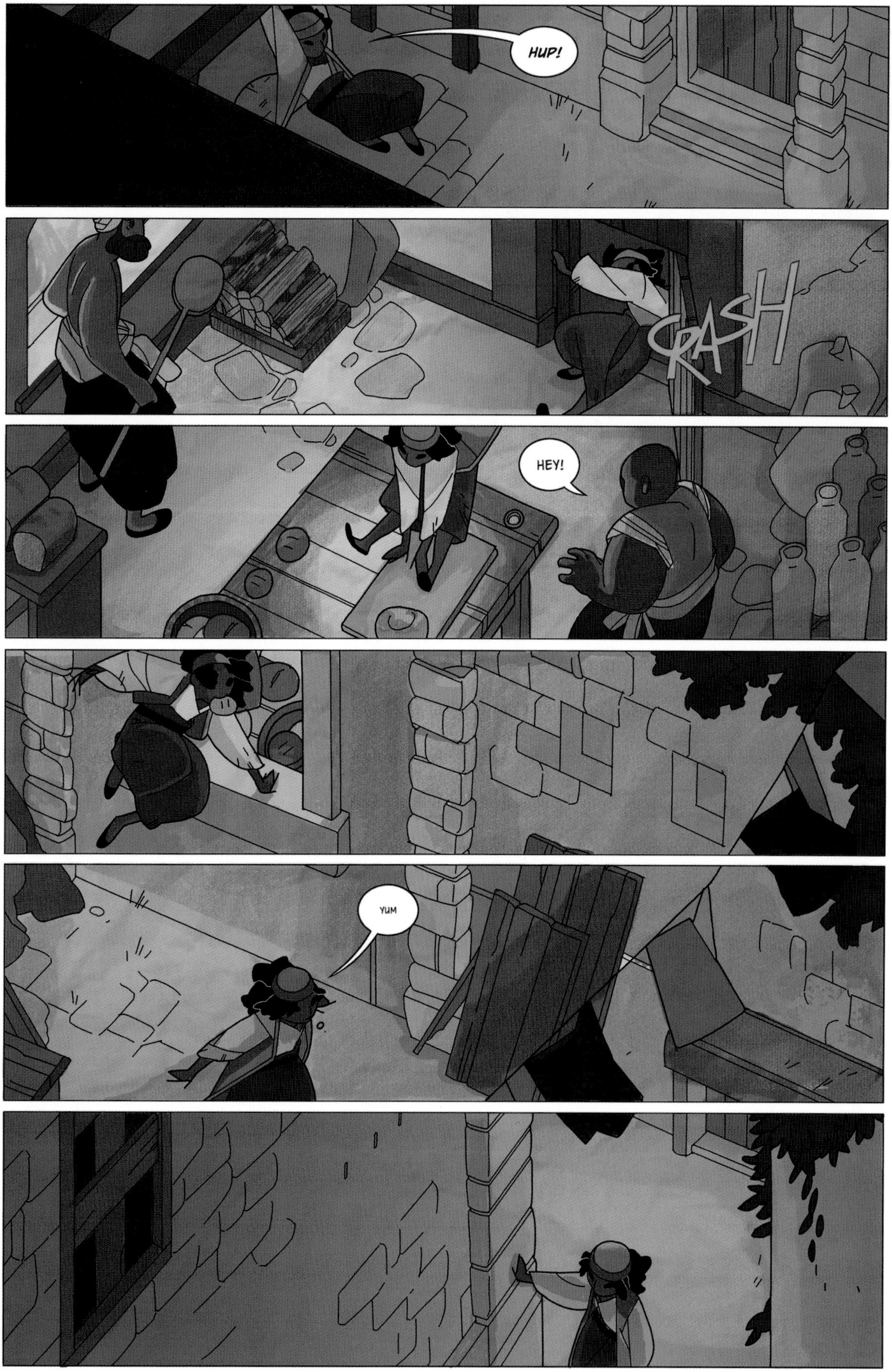
HUP!
CRASH
HEY!
YUM

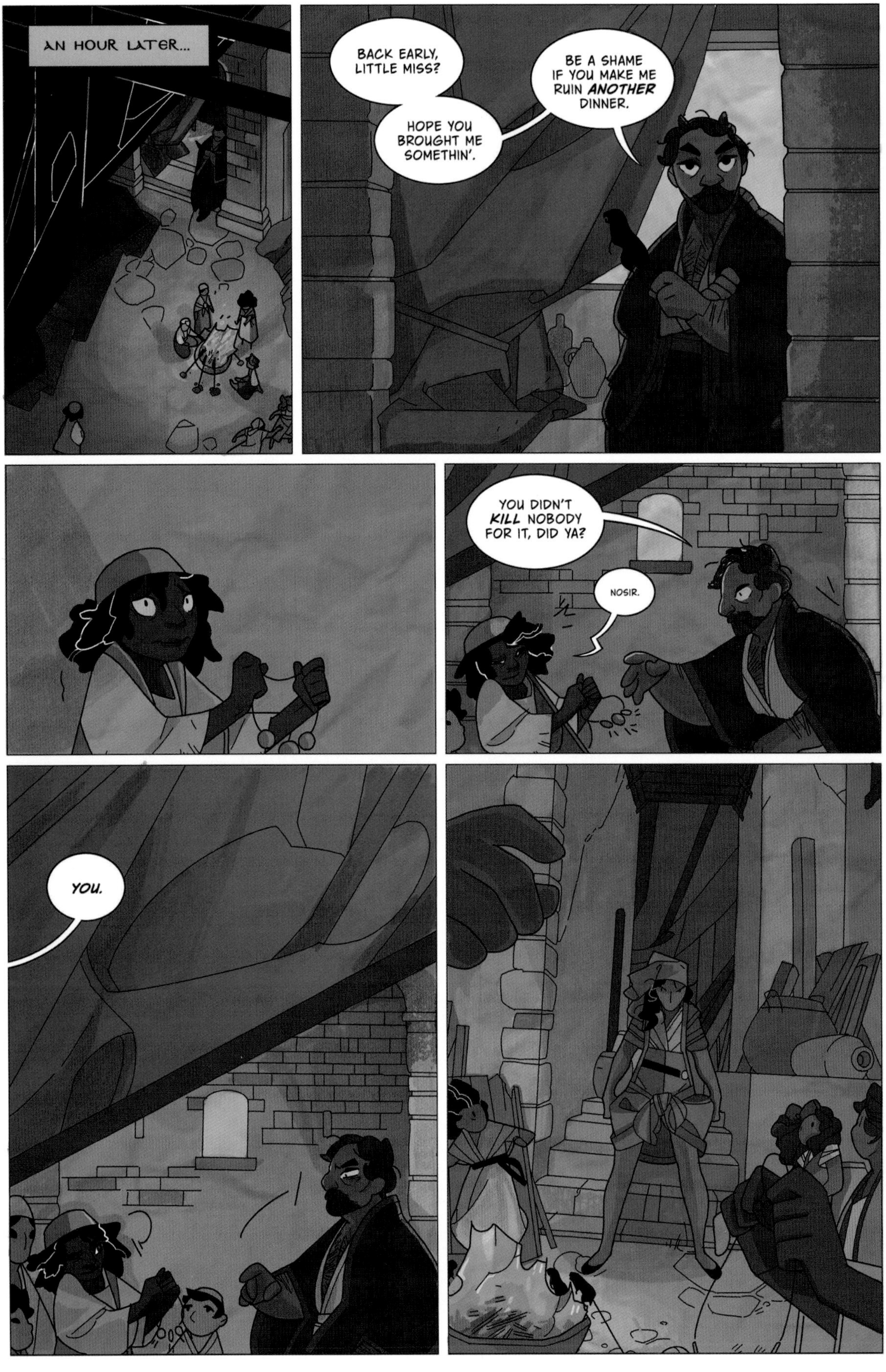
AN HOUR LATER...
BACK EARLY, LITTLE MISS?
HOPE YOU BROUGHT ME SOMETHIN'.
BE A SHAME IF YOU MAKE ME RUIN *ANOTHER* DINNER.
YOU DIDN'T *KILL* NOBODY FOR IT, DID YA?
NOSIR.
YOU.

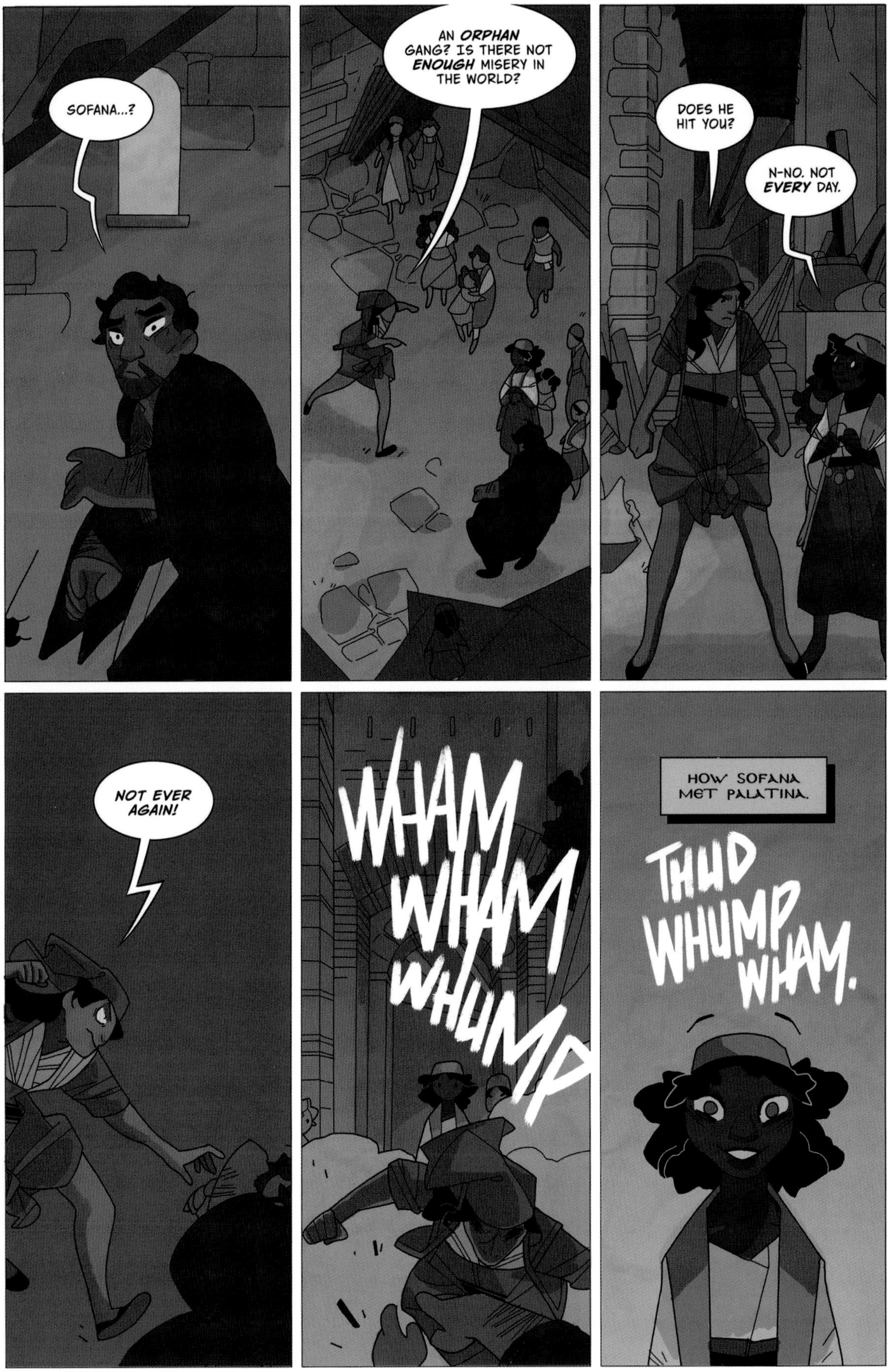
SOFANA...?
AN ORPHAN GANG? IS THERE NOT ENOUGH MISERY IN THE WORLD?
DOES HE HIT YOU?
N-NO. NOT EVERY DAY.
NOT EVER AGAIN!
WHAM
WHAM
WHUMP
HOW SOFANA MET PALATINA.
THUD
WHUMP
WHAM.

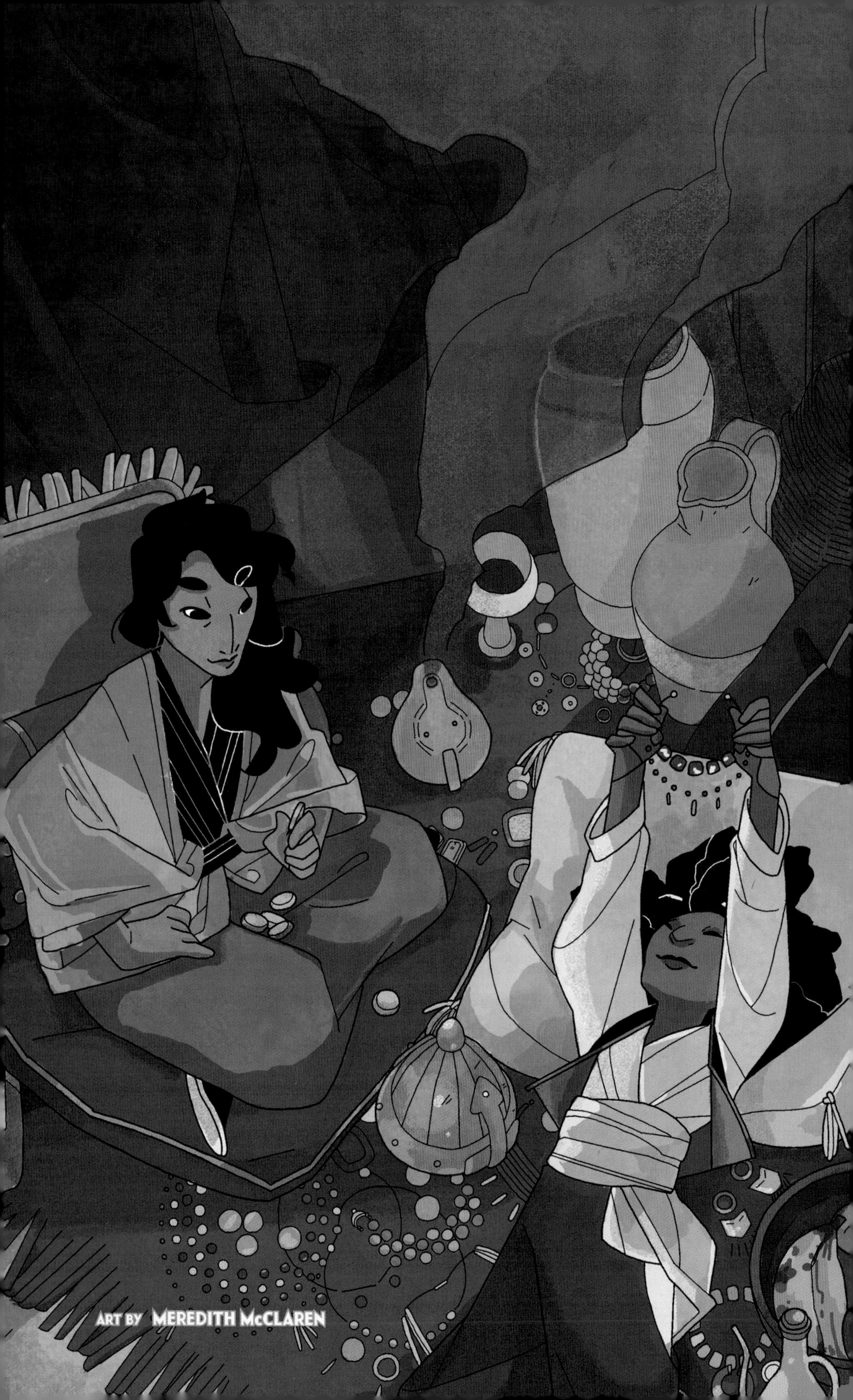
ART BY MEREDITH McCLAREN

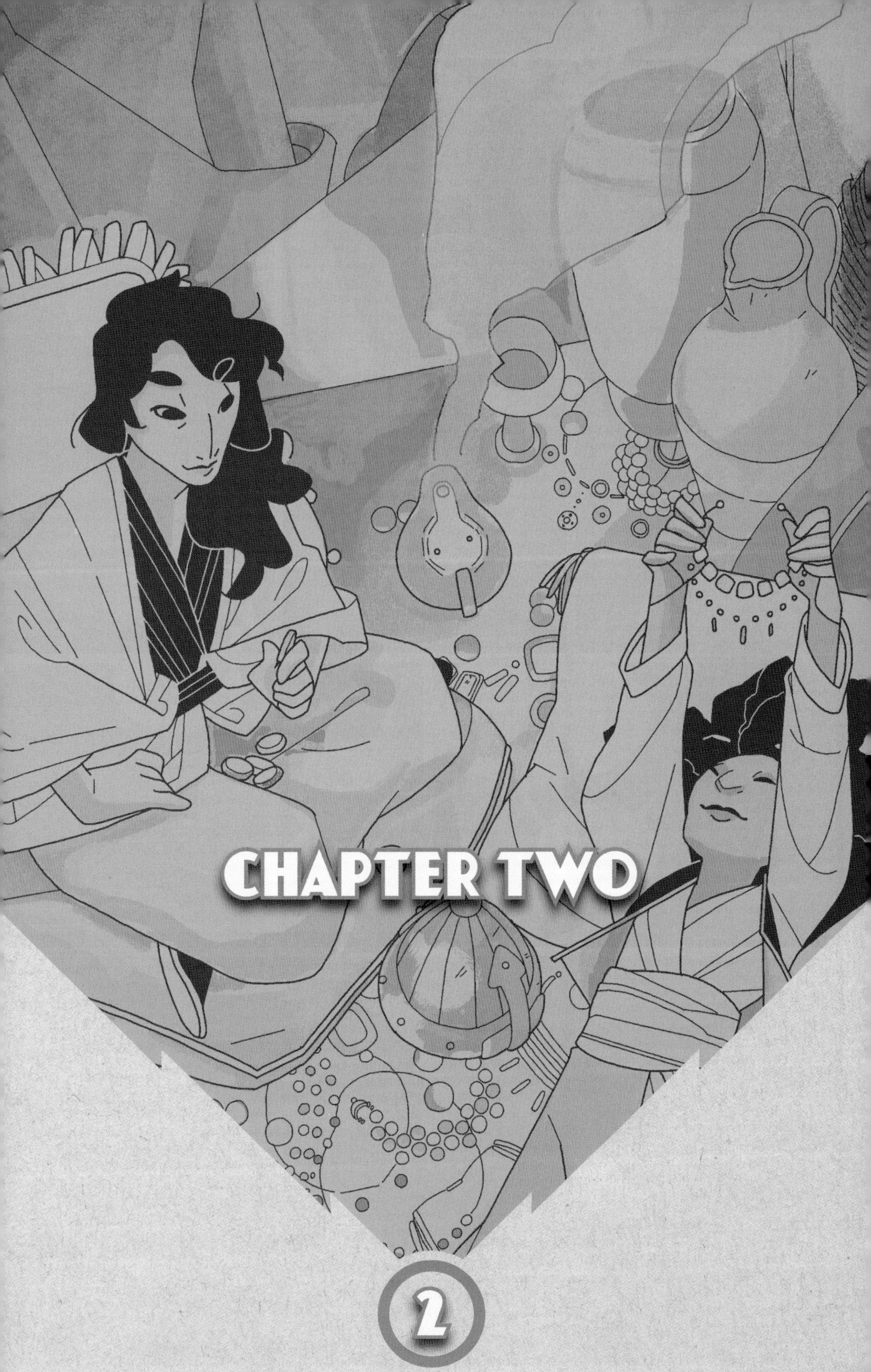

CHAPTER TWO

2

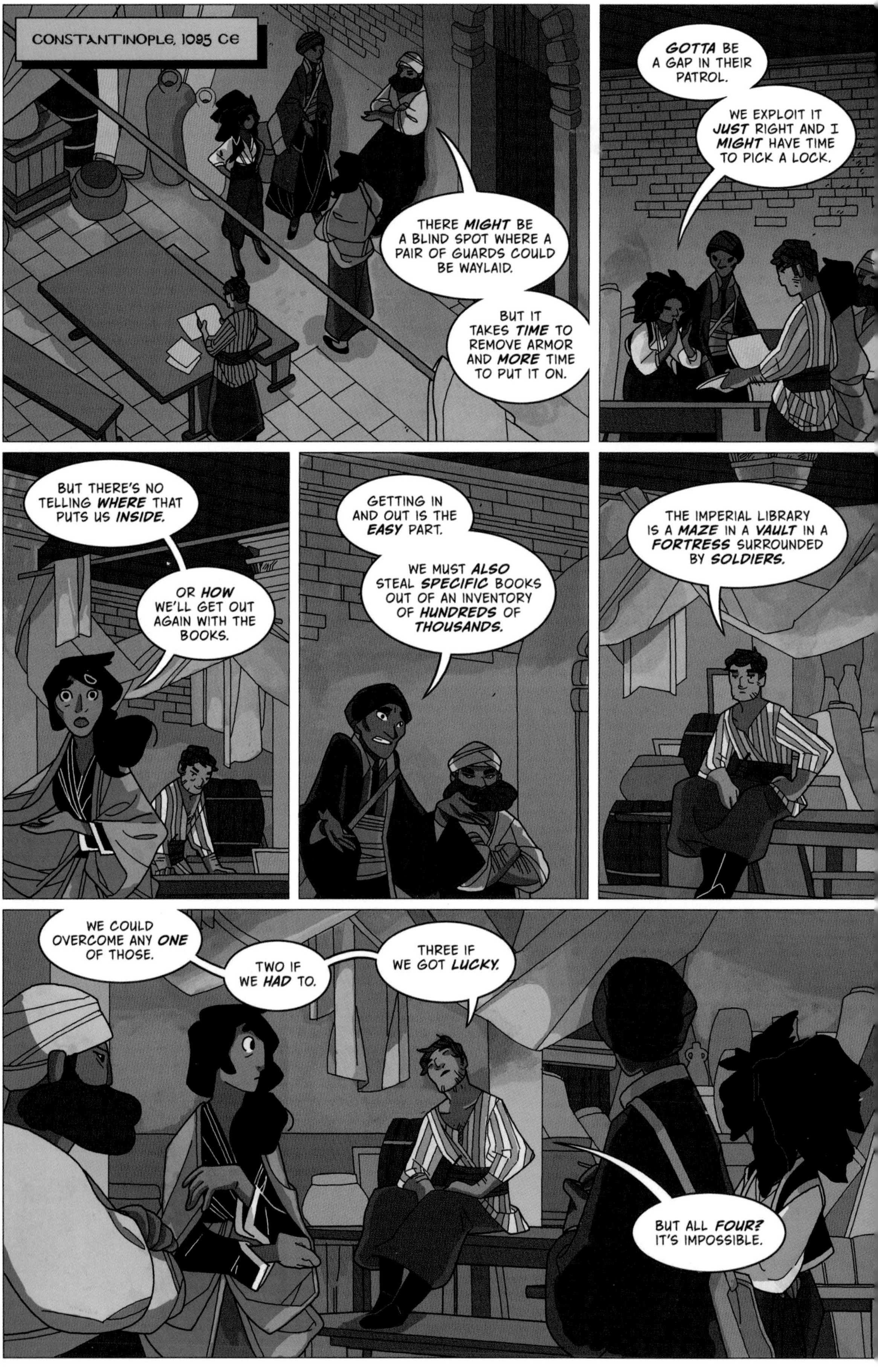
CONSTANTINOPLE, 1095 CE
THERE MIGHT BE A BLIND SPOT WHERE A PAIR OF GUARDS COULD BE WAYLAID.
BUT IT TAKES TIME TO REMOVE ARMOR AND MORE TIME TO PUT IT ON.
GOTTA BE A GAP IN THEIR PATROL.
WE EXPLOIT IT JUST RIGHT AND I MIGHT HAVE TIME TO PICK A LOCK.
BUT THERE'S NO TELLING WHERE THAT PUTS US INSIDE.
OR HOW WE'LL GET OUT AGAIN WITH THE BOOKS.
GETTING IN AND OUT IS THE EASY PART.
WE MUST ALSO STEAL SPECIFIC BOOKS OUT OF AN INVENTORY OF HUNDREDS OF THOUSANDS.
THE IMPERIAL LIBRARY IS A MAZE IN A VAULT IN A FORTRESS SURROUNDED BY SOLDIERS.
WE COULD OVERCOME ANY ONE OF THOSE.
TWO IF WE HAD TO.
THREE IF WE GOT LUCKY.
BUT ALL FOUR? IT'S IMPOSSIBLE.

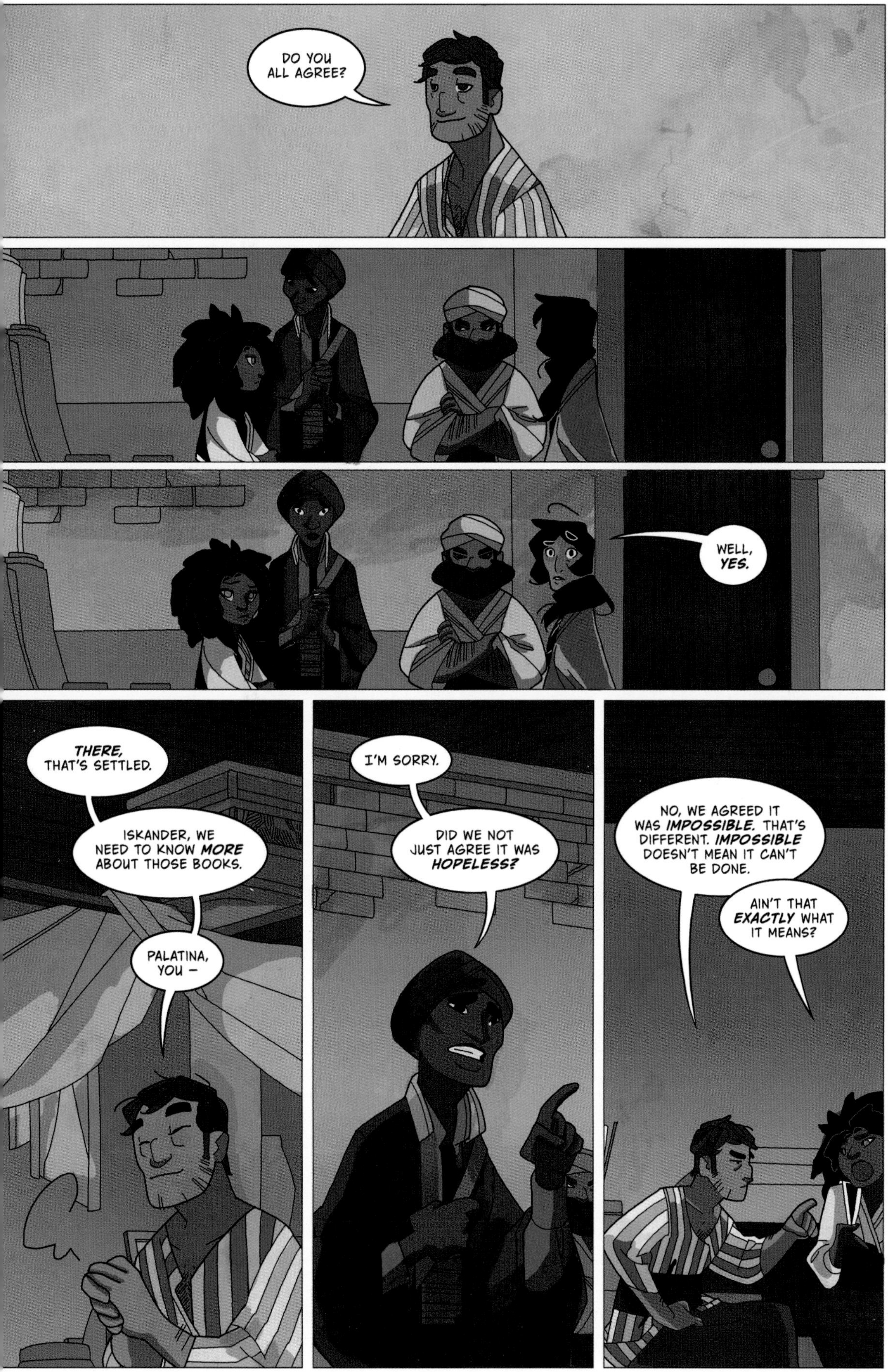
DO YOU ALL AGREE?
WELL, YES.
THERE, THAT'S SETTLED.
ISKANDER, WE NEED TO KNOW MORE ABOUT THOSE BOOKS.
PALATINA, YOU –
I'M SORRY.
DID WE NOT JUST AGREE IT WAS HOPELESS?
NO, WE AGREED IT WAS IMPOSSIBLE. THAT'S DIFFERENT. IMPOSSIBLE DOESN'T MEAN IT CAN'T BE DONE.
AIN'T THAT EXACTLY WHAT IT MEANS?

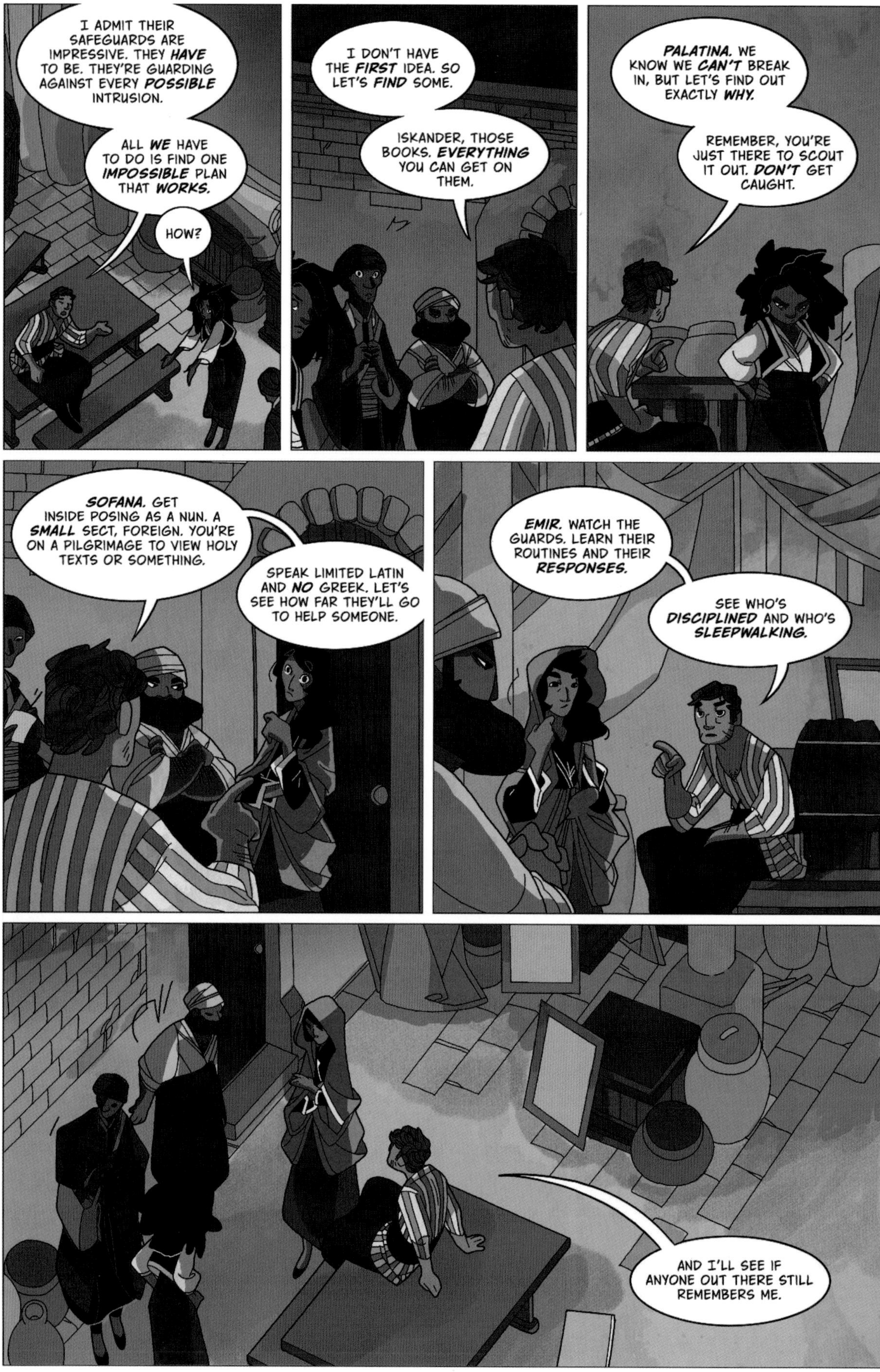
I ADMIT THEIR SAFEGUARDS ARE IMPRESSIVE. THEY HAVE TO BE. THEY'RE GUARDING AGAINST EVERY POSSIBLE INTRUSION.
ALL WE HAVE TO DO IS FIND ONE IMPOSSIBLE PLAN THAT WORKS.
HOW?
I DON'T HAVE THE FIRST IDEA. SO LET'S FIND SOME.
ISKANDER, THOSE BOOKS. EVERYTHING YOU CAN GET ON THEM.
PALATINA. WE KNOW WE CAN'T BREAK IN, BUT LET'S FIND OUT EXACTLY WHY.
REMEMBER, YOU'RE JUST THERE TO SCOUT IT OUT. DON'T GET CAUGHT.
SOFANA. GET INSIDE POSING AS A NUN. A SMALL SECT, FOREIGN. YOU'RE ON A PILGRIMAGE TO VIEW HOLY TEXTS OR SOMETHING.
SPEAK LIMITED LATIN AND NO GREEK. LET'S SEE HOW FAR THEY'LL GO TO HELP SOMEONE.
EMIR. WATCH THE GUARDS. LEARN THEIR ROUTINES AND THEIR RESPONSES.
SEE WHO'S DISCIPLINED AND WHO'S SLEEPWALKING.
AND I'LL SEE IF ANYONE OUT THERE STILL REMEMBERS ME.

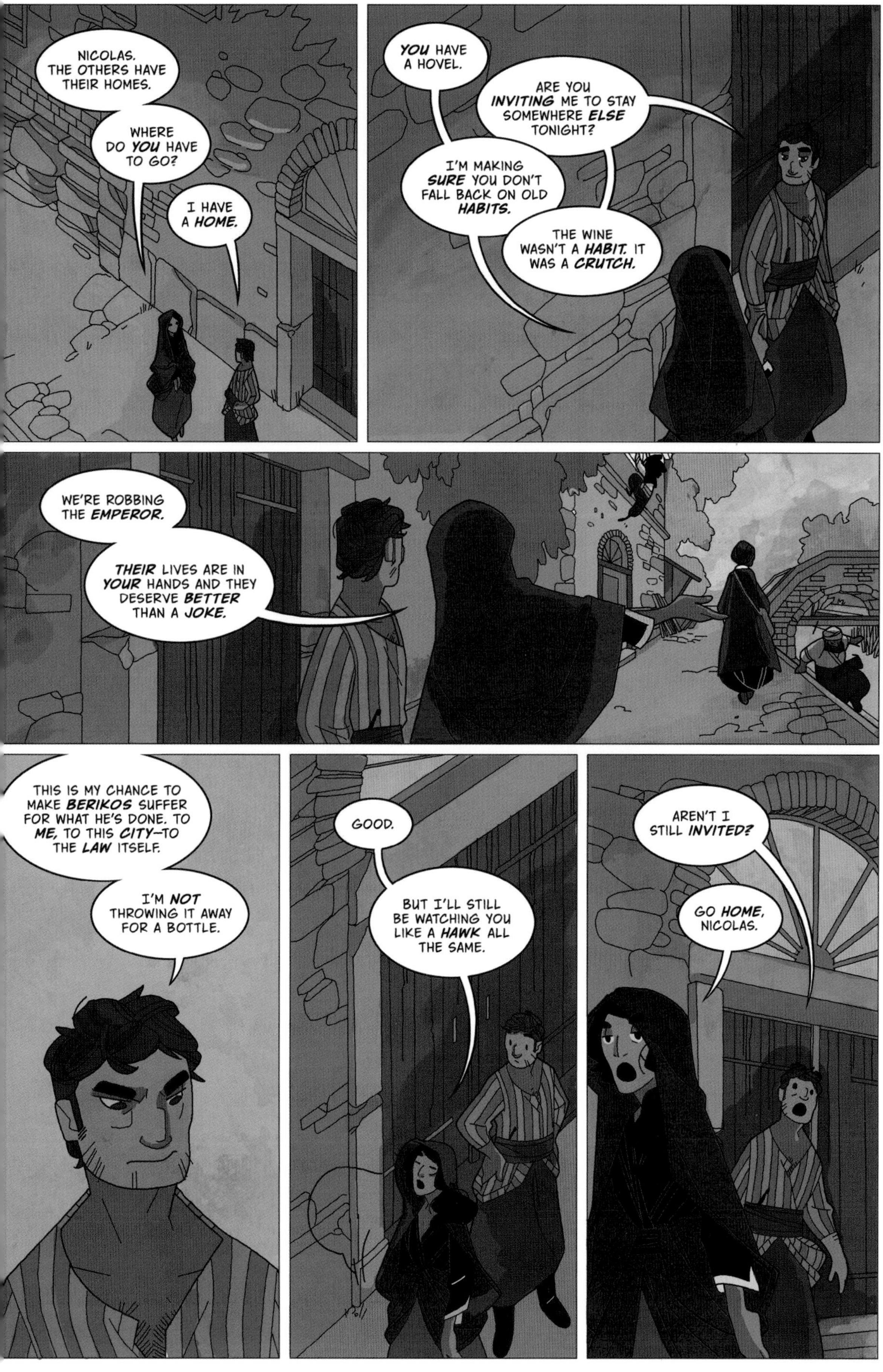
NICOLAS. THE OTHERS HAVE THEIR HOMES.
WHERE DO YOU HAVE TO GO?
I HAVE A HOME.
YOU HAVE A HOVEL.
ARE YOU INVITING ME TO STAY SOMEWHERE ELSE TONIGHT?
I'M MAKING SURE YOU DON'T FALL BACK ON OLD HABITS.
THE WINE WASN'T A HABIT. IT WAS A CRUTCH.
WE'RE ROBBING THE EMPEROR.
THEIR LIVES ARE IN YOUR HANDS AND THEY DESERVE BETTER THAN A JOKE.
THIS IS MY CHANCE TO MAKE BERIKOS SUFFER FOR WHAT HE'S DONE. TO ME, TO THIS CITY—TO THE LAW ITSELF.
I'M NOT THROWING IT AWAY FOR A BOTTLE.
GOOD.
BUT I'LL STILL BE WATCHING YOU LIKE A HAWK ALL THE SAME.
AREN'T I STILL INVITED?
GO HOME, NICOLAS.

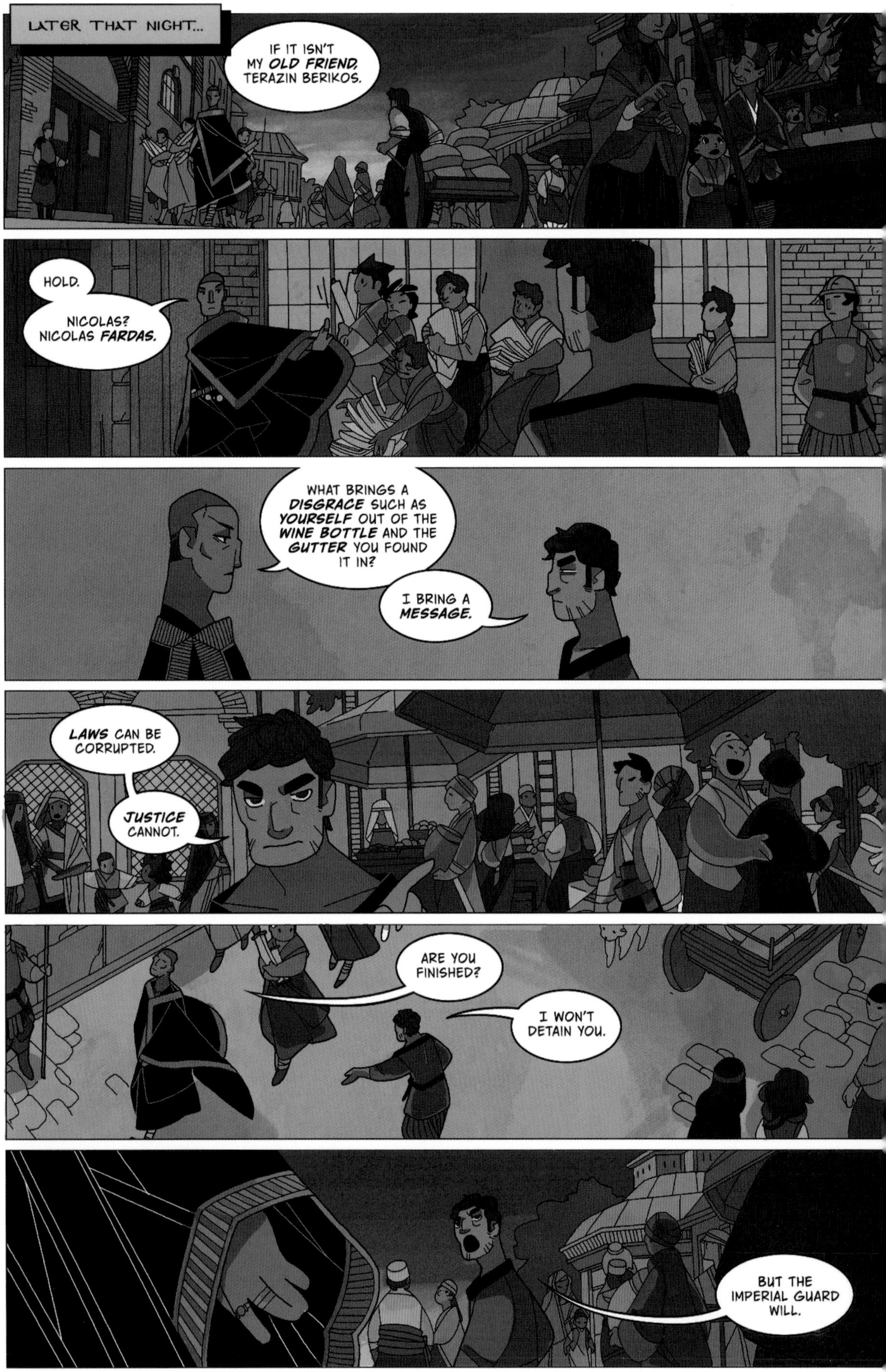
LATER THAT NIGHT...
IF IT ISN'T MY OLD FRIEND, TERAZIN BERIKOS.
HOLD.
NICOLAS? NICOLAS FARDAS.
WHAT BRINGS A DISGRACE SUCH AS YOURSELF OUT OF THE WINE BOTTLE AND THE GUTTER YOU FOUND IT IN?
I BRING A MESSAGE.
LAWS CAN BE CORRUPTED.
JUSTICE CANNOT.
ARE YOU FINISHED?
I WON'T DETAIN YOU.
BUT THE IMPERIAL GUARD WILL.

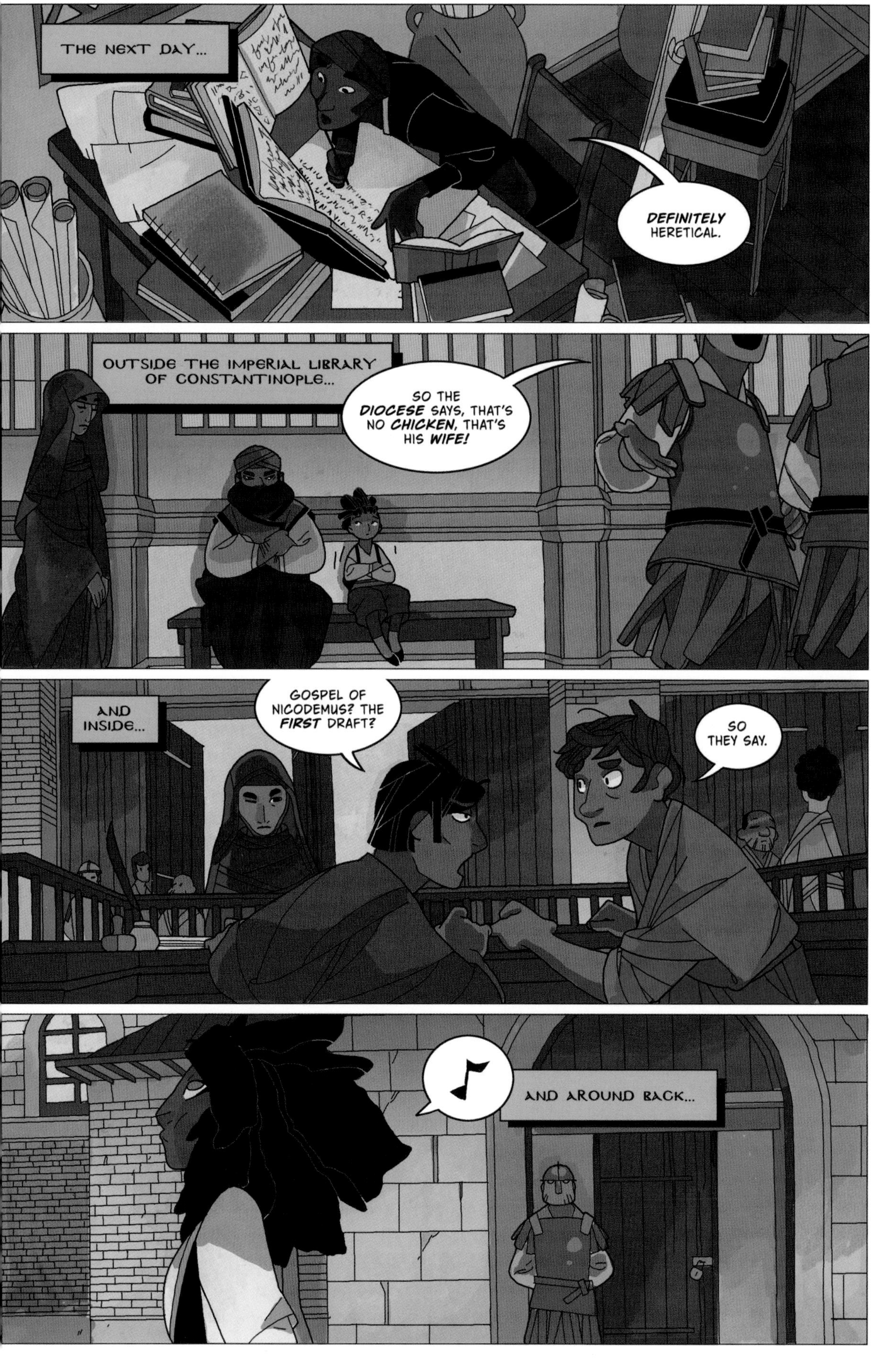
THE NEXT DAY...
DEFINITELY HERETICAL.
OUTSIDE THE IMPERIAL LIBRARY OF CONSTANTINOPLE...
SO THE DIOCESE SAYS, THAT'S NO CHICKEN, THAT'S HIS WIFE!
AND INSIDE...
GOSPEL OF NICODEMUS? THE FIRST DRAFT?
SO THEY SAY.
AND AROUND BACK...

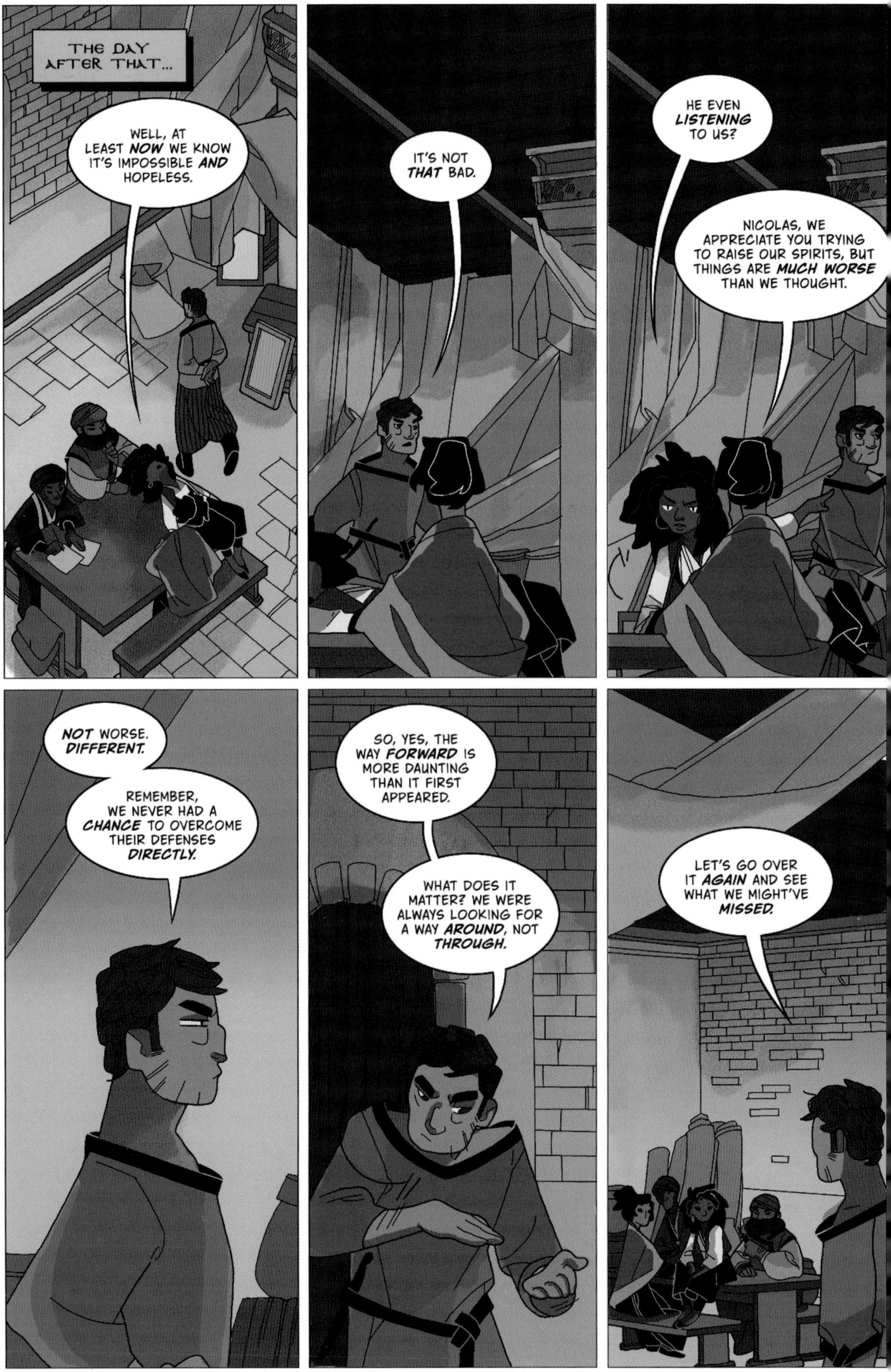
THE DAY AFTER THAT...
WELL, AT LEAST NOW WE KNOW IT'S IMPOSSIBLE AND HOPELESS.
IT'S NOT THAT BAD.
HE EVEN LISTENING TO US?
NICOLAS, WE APPRECIATE YOU TRYING TO RAISE OUR SPIRITS, BUT THINGS ARE MUCH WORSE THAN WE THOUGHT.
NOT WORSE. DIFFERENT.
REMEMBER, WE NEVER HAD A CHANCE TO OVERCOME THEIR DEFENSES DIRECTLY.
SO, YES, THE WAY FORWARD IS MORE DAUNTING THAN IT FIRST APPEARED.
WHAT DOES IT MATTER? WE WERE ALWAYS LOOKING FOR A WAY AROUND, NOT THROUGH.
LET'S GO OVER IT AGAIN AND SEE WHAT WE MIGHT'VE MISSED.

THE IMPERIAL GUARD HAVE THE BEST *ARMAMENTS, TRAINING,* AND *DISCIPLINE* IN ALL THE EMPIRE.

PATROLS WERE *FREQUENT.* AND EVERYWHERE. THERE IS *NEVER* A DOOR UNGUARDED *OR* CORNER UNWATCHED.

PERHAPS A DOZEN GUARDS COULD REACH THE MAIN ENTRANCE WITHIN A HEARTBEAT—WITH FIFTY *MORE* NOT FAR BEHIND.

HAHA, THAT OLD DIOCESE!

YOU EVER HEAR THE ONE ABOUT THE SIX-INCH ORGANIST?

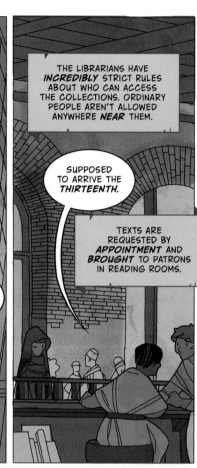

THE LIBRARIANS HAVE *INCREDIBLY* STRICT RULES ABOUT WHO CAN ACCESS THE COLLECTIONS. ORDINARY PEOPLE AREN'T ALLOWED ANYWHERE *NEAR* THEM.

SUPPOSED TO ARRIVE THE *THIRTEENTH.*

TEXTS ARE REQUESTED BY *APPOINTMENT* AND *BROUGHT* TO PATRONS IN READING ROOMS.

THEY LET ME IN AS A SPECIAL FAVOR DUE TO MY "PILGRIMAGE," BUT EVEN SO, IT TOOK THEM AN *HOUR* TO COME AROUND TO THE IDEA.

AND I WAS UNDER *CONSTANT* SCRUTINY BY *BOTH* A LIBRARIAN *AND* A GUARD.

DOORS ARE *GUARDED* AND *LOCKED* FROM *BOTH* SIDES.

OH GOSH, MISS, NO. YOU'RE *CLEAR* ON THE WRONG SIDE OF TOWN.

WHAT YOU WANT TO DO IS...

WINDOWS ARE NO GOOD NEITHER.

TOO HIGH UP, *TOO* LOUD TO GET IN, *AND* YOU GUYS COULDN'T MAKE THE CLIMB ANYWAY.

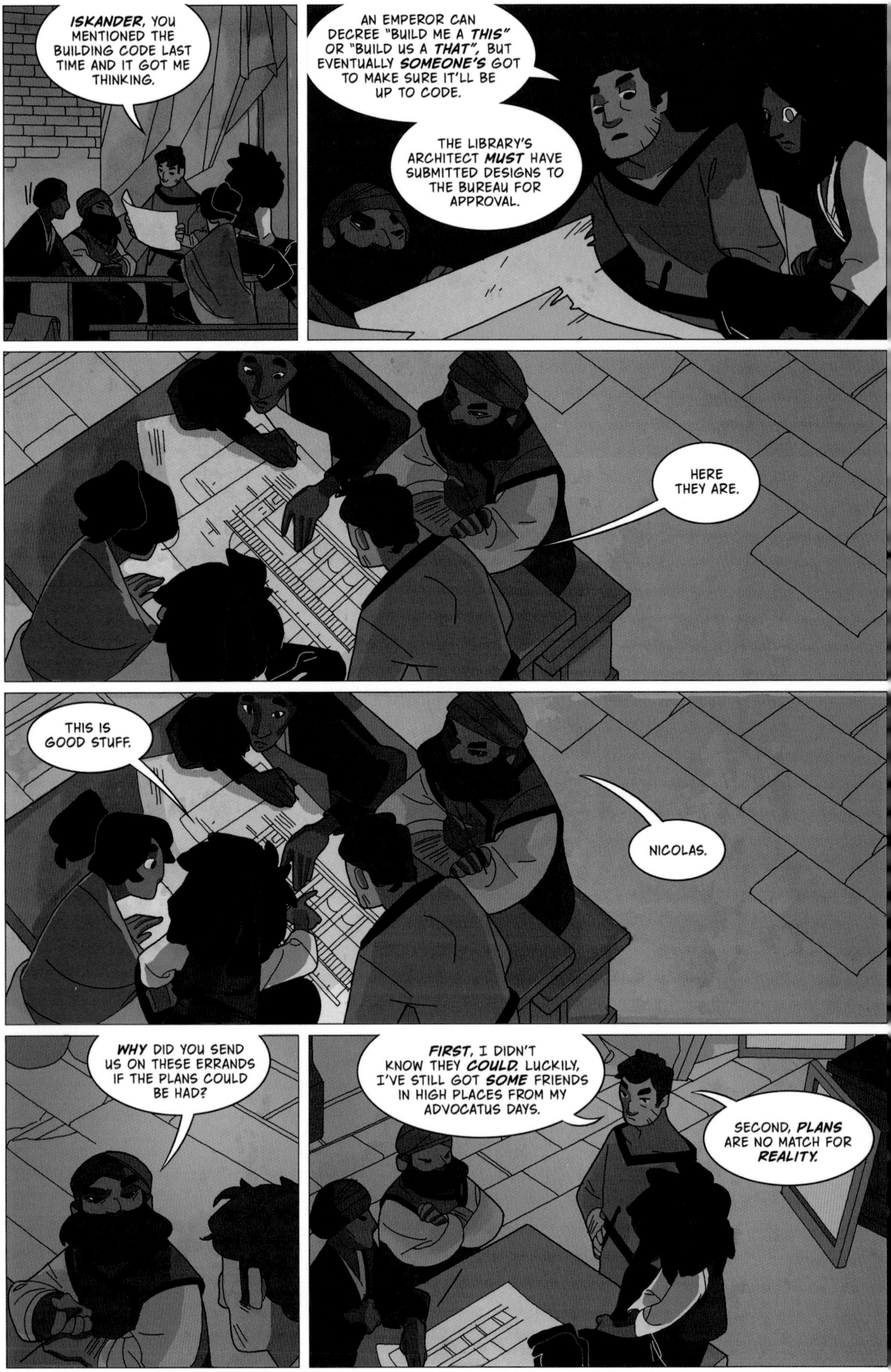
ISKANDER, YOU MENTIONED THE BUILDING CODE LAST TIME AND IT GOT ME THINKING.
AN EMPEROR CAN DECREE "BUILD ME A THIS" OR "BUILD US A THAT", BUT EVENTUALLY SOMEONE'S GOT TO MAKE SURE IT'LL BE UP TO CODE.
THE LIBRARY'S ARCHITECT MUST HAVE SUBMITTED DESIGNS TO THE BUREAU FOR APPROVAL.
HERE THEY ARE.
THIS IS GOOD STUFF.
NICOLAS.
WHY DID YOU SEND US ON THESE ERRANDS IF THE PLANS COULD BE HAD?
FIRST, I DIDN'T KNOW THEY COULD. LUCKILY, I'VE STILL GOT SOME FRIENDS IN HIGH PLACES FROM MY ADVOCATUS DAYS.
SECOND, PLANS ARE NO MATCH FOR REALITY.

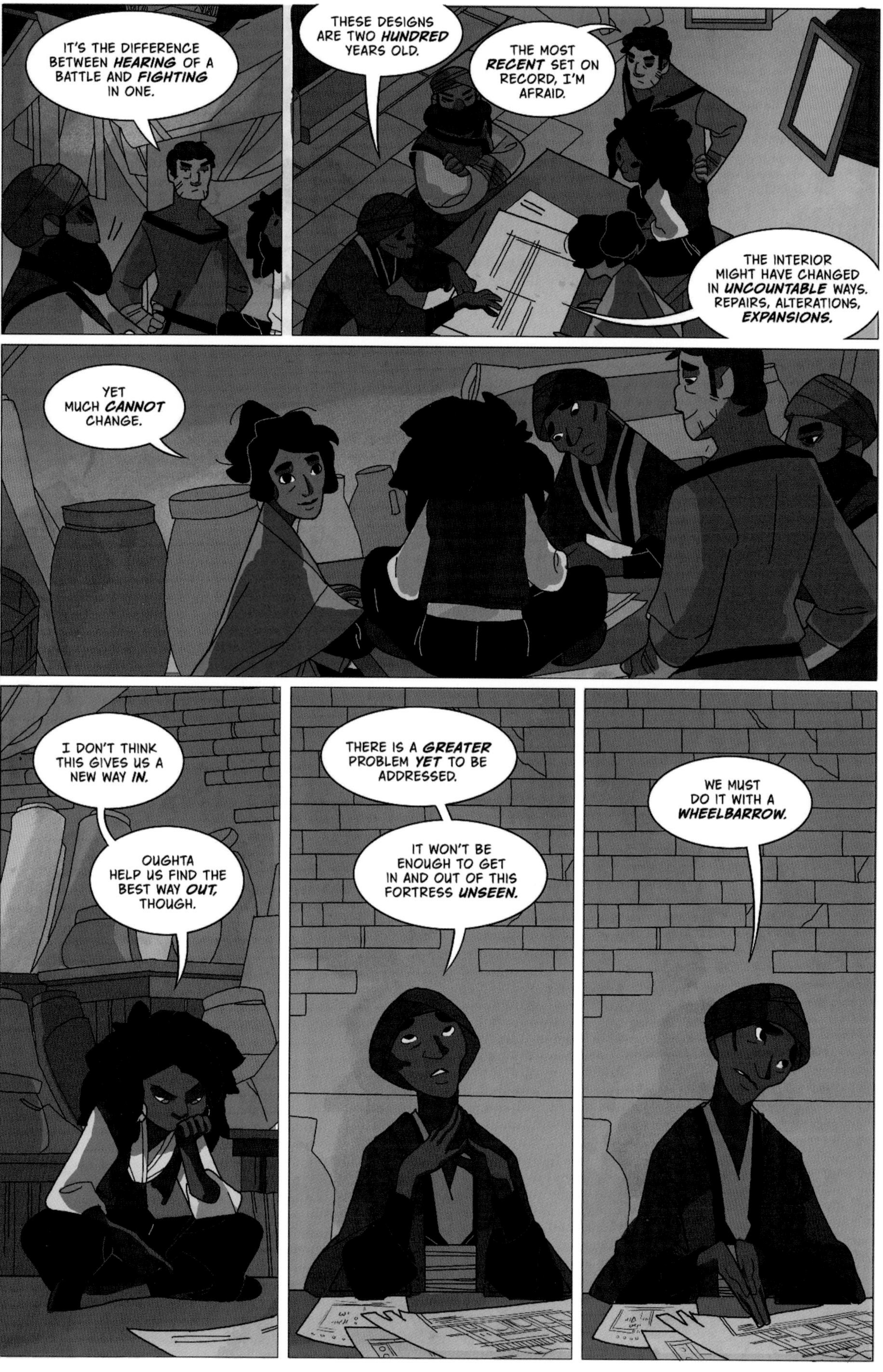
IT'S THE DIFFERENCE BETWEEN HEARING OF A BATTLE AND FIGHTING IN ONE.
THESE DESIGNS ARE TWO HUNDRED YEARS OLD.
THE MOST RECENT SET ON RECORD, I'M AFRAID.
THE INTERIOR MIGHT HAVE CHANGED IN UNCOUNTABLE WAYS. REPAIRS, ALTERATIONS, EXPANSIONS.
YET MUCH CANNOT CHANGE.
I DON'T THINK THIS GIVES US A NEW WAY IN.
OUGHTA HELP US FIND THE BEST WAY OUT, THOUGH.
THERE IS A GREATER PROBLEM YET TO BE ADDRESSED.
IT WON'T BE ENOUGH TO GET IN AND OUT OF THIS FORTRESS UNSEEN.
WE MUST DO IT WITH A WHEELBARROW.

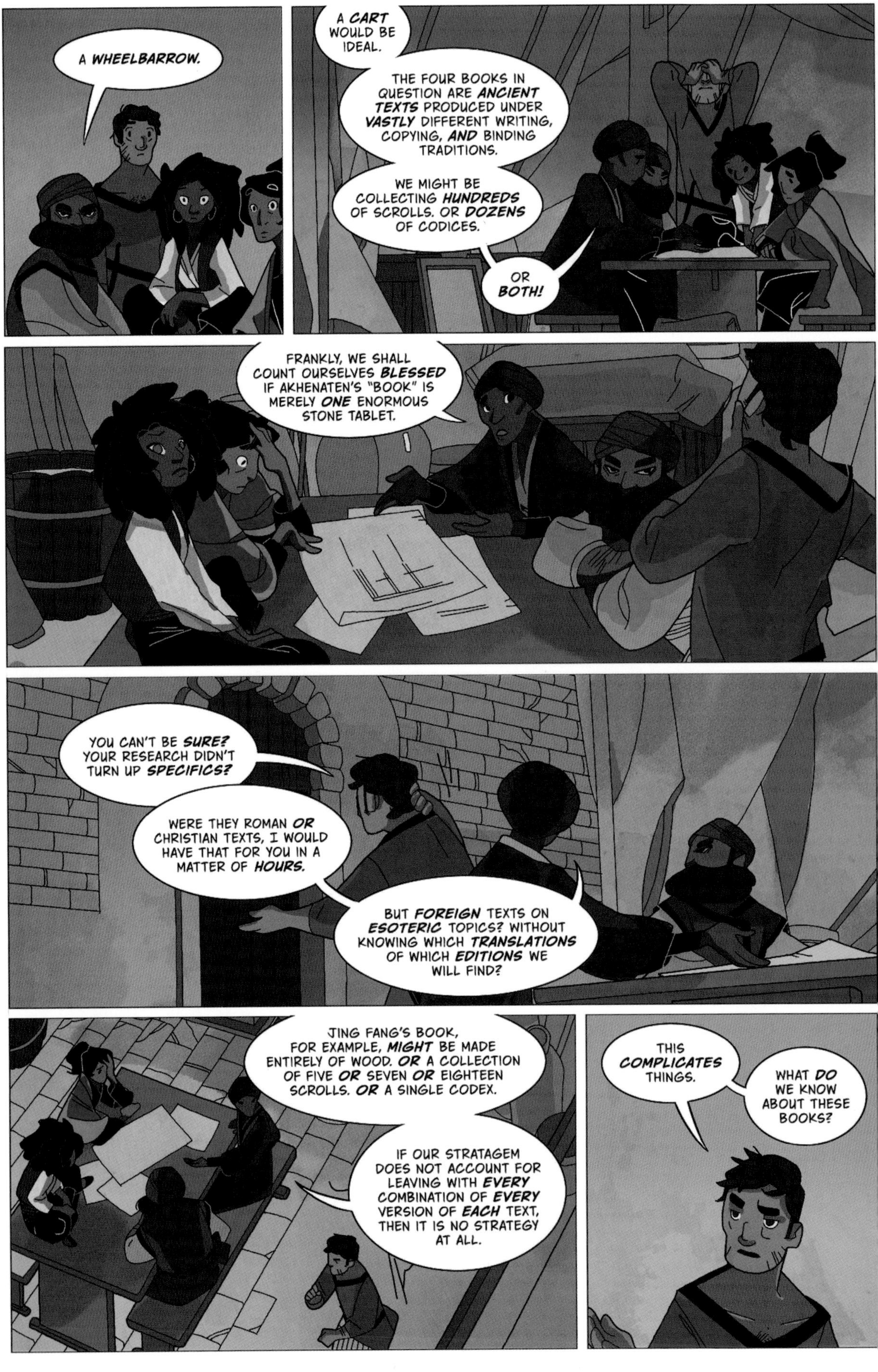
A WHEELBARROW.
A CART WOULD BE IDEAL.
THE FOUR BOOKS IN QUESTION ARE ANCIENT TEXTS PRODUCED UNDER VASTLY DIFFERENT WRITING, COPYING, AND BINDING TRADITIONS.
WE MIGHT BE COLLECTING HUNDREDS OF SCROLLS. OR DOZENS OF CODICES.
OR BOTH!
FRANKLY, WE SHALL COUNT OURSELVES BLESSED IF AKHENATEN'S "BOOK" IS MERELY ONE ENORMOUS STONE TABLET.
YOU CAN'T BE SURE? YOUR RESEARCH DIDN'T TURN UP SPECIFICS?
WERE THEY ROMAN OR CHRISTIAN TEXTS, I WOULD HAVE THAT FOR YOU IN A MATTER OF HOURS.
BUT FOREIGN TEXTS ON ESOTERIC TOPICS? WITHOUT KNOWING WHICH TRANSLATIONS OF WHICH EDITIONS WE WILL FIND?
JING FANG'S BOOK, FOR EXAMPLE, MIGHT BE MADE ENTIRELY OF WOOD. OR A COLLECTION OF FIVE OR SEVEN OR EIGHTEEN SCROLLS. OR A SINGLE CODEX.
IF OUR STRATAGEM DOES NOT ACCOUNT FOR LEAVING WITH EVERY COMBINATION OF EVERY VERSION OF EACH TEXT, THEN IT IS NO STRATEGY AT ALL.
THIS COMPLICATES THINGS.
WHAT DO WE KNOW ABOUT THESE BOOKS?

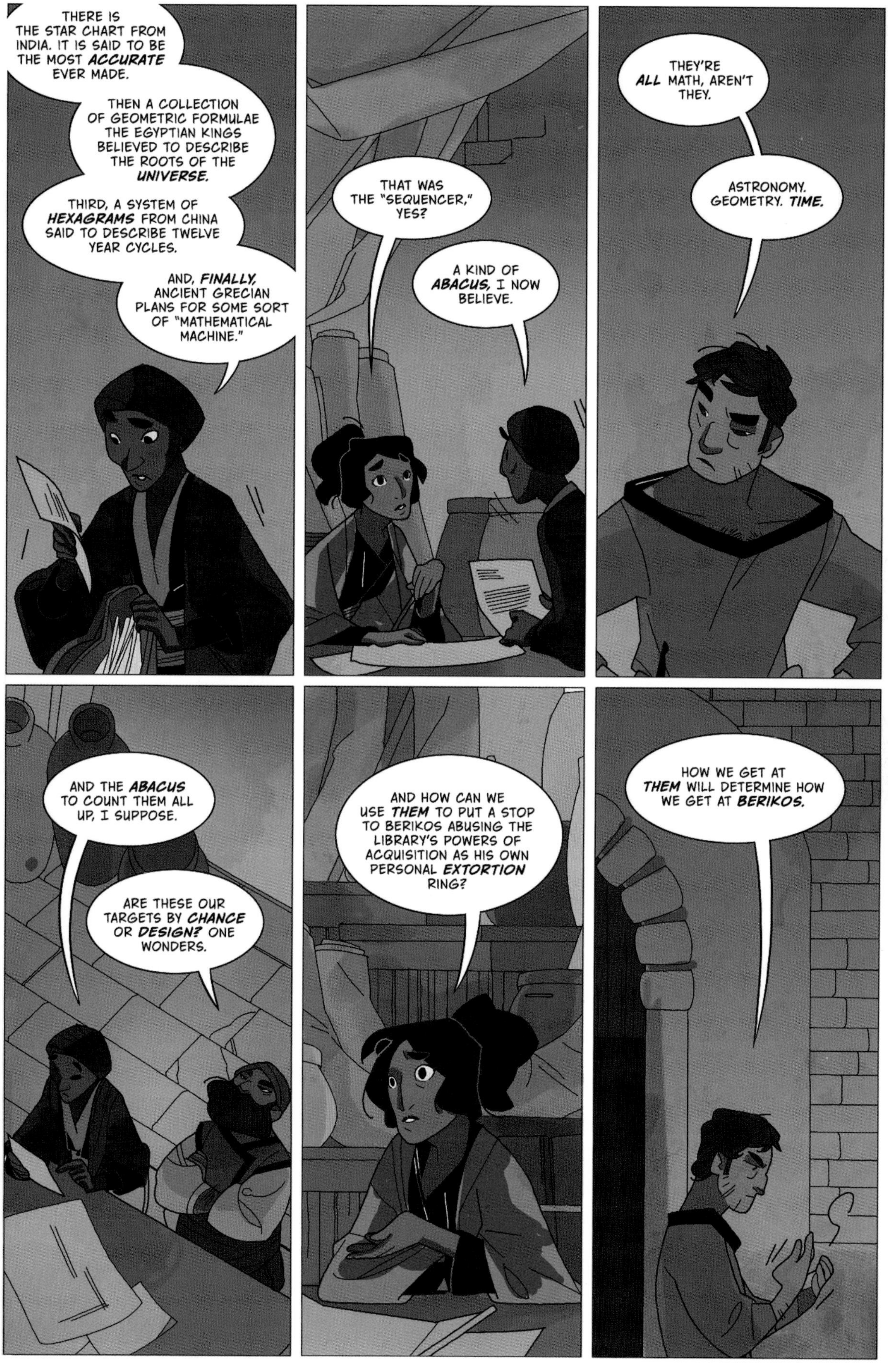
THERE IS THE STAR CHART FROM INDIA. IT IS SAID TO BE THE MOST ACCURATE EVER MADE.
THEN A COLLECTION OF GEOMETRIC FORMULAE THE EGYPTIAN KINGS BELIEVED TO DESCRIBE THE ROOTS OF THE UNIVERSE.
THIRD, A SYSTEM OF HEXAGRAMS FROM CHINA SAID TO DESCRIBE TWELVE YEAR CYCLES.
AND, FINALLY, ANCIENT GRECIAN PLANS FOR SOME SORT OF "MATHEMATICAL MACHINE."
THAT WAS THE "SEQUENCER," YES?
A KIND OF ABACUS, I NOW BELIEVE.
THEY'RE ALL MATH, AREN'T THEY.
ASTRONOMY. GEOMETRY. TIME.
AND THE ABACUS TO COUNT THEM ALL UP, I SUPPOSE.
ARE THESE OUR TARGETS BY CHANCE OR DESIGN? ONE WONDERS.
AND HOW CAN WE USE THEM TO PUT A STOP TO BERIKOS ABUSING THE LIBRARY'S POWERS OF ACQUISITION AS HIS OWN PERSONAL EXTORTION RING?
HOW WE GET AT THEM WILL DETERMINE HOW WE GET AT BERIKOS.

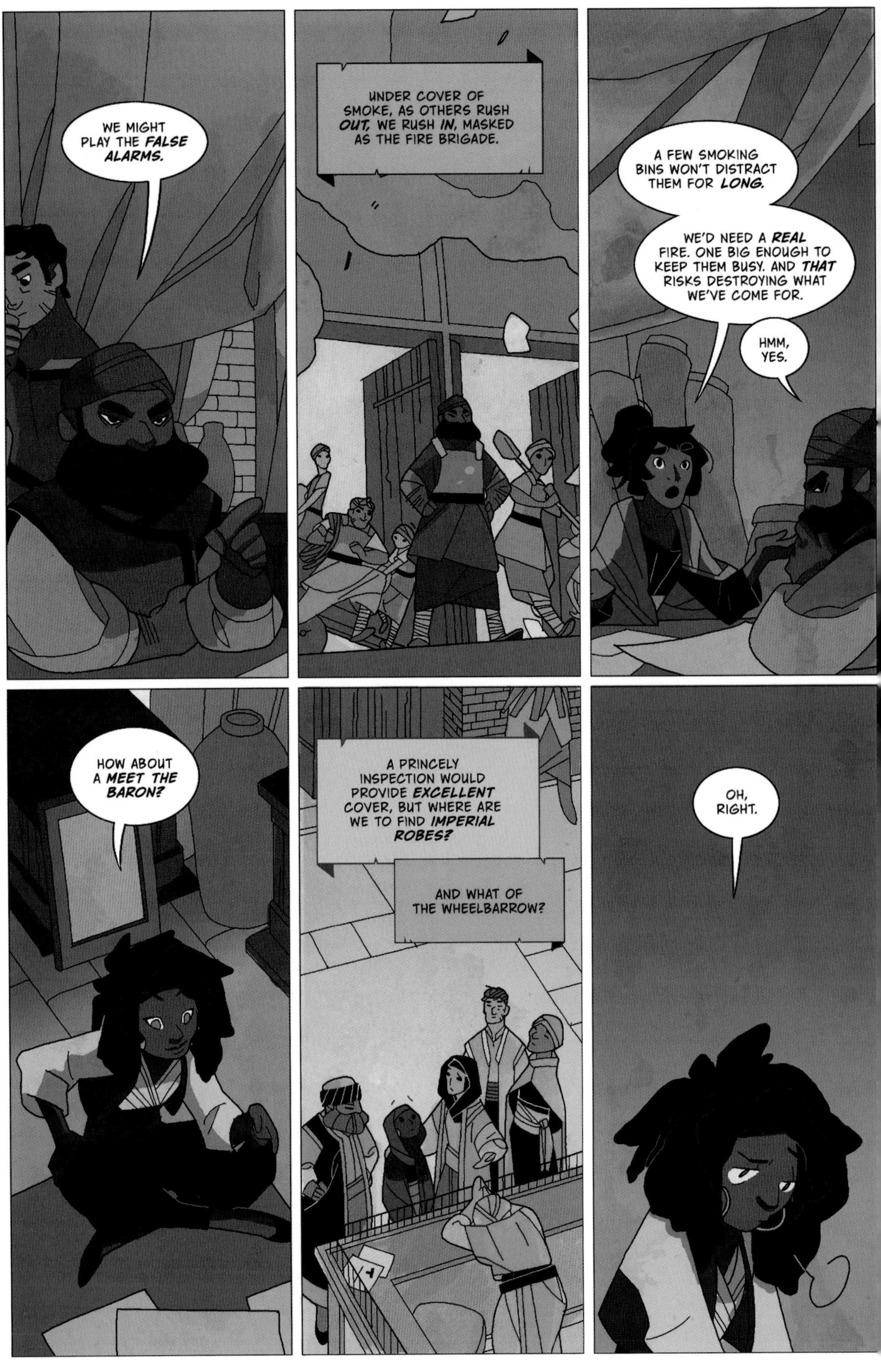
WE MIGHT PLAY THE FALSE ALARMS.
UNDER COVER OF SMOKE, AS OTHERS RUSH OUT, WE RUSH IN, MASKED AS THE FIRE BRIGADE.
A FEW SMOKING BINS WON'T DISTRACT THEM FOR LONG.
WE'D NEED A REAL FIRE. ONE BIG ENOUGH TO KEEP THEM BUSY. AND THAT RISKS DESTROYING WHAT WE'VE COME FOR.
HMM, YES.
HOW ABOUT A MEET THE BARON?
A PRINCELY INSPECTION WOULD PROVIDE EXCELLENT COVER, BUT WHERE ARE WE TO FIND IMPERIAL ROBES?
AND WHAT OF THE WHEELBARROW?
OH, RIGHT.

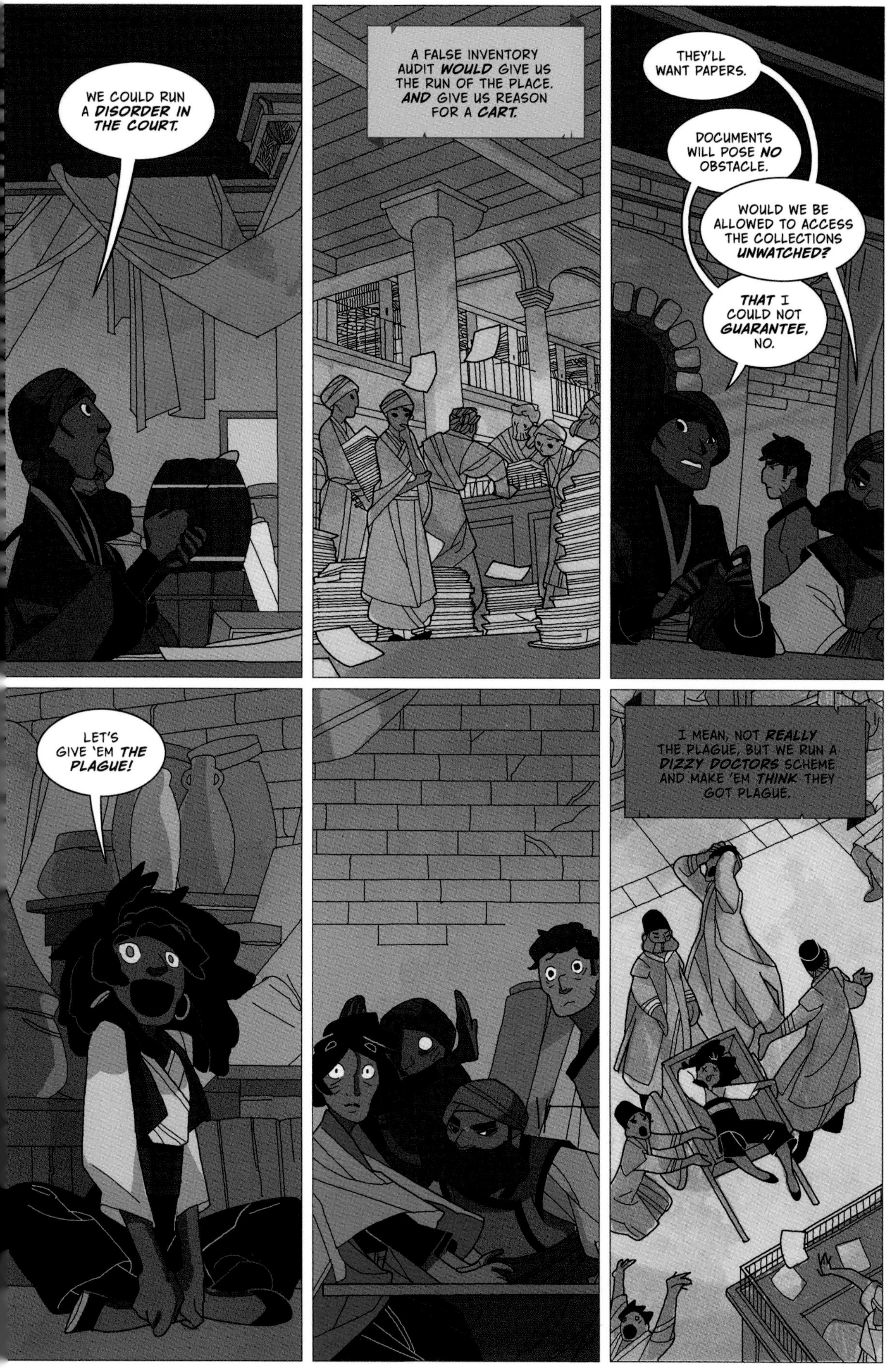
WE COULD RUN A DISORDER IN THE COURT.
A FALSE INVENTORY AUDIT WOULD GIVE US THE RUN OF THE PLACE. AND GIVE US REASON FOR A CART.
THEY'LL WANT PAPERS.
DOCUMENTS WILL POSE NO OBSTACLE.
WOULD WE BE ALLOWED TO ACCESS THE COLLECTIONS UNWATCHED?
THAT I COULD NOT GUARANTEE, NO.
LET'S GIVE 'EM THE PLAGUE!
I MEAN, NOT REALLY THE PLAGUE, BUT WE RUN A DIZZY DOCTORS SCHEME AND MAKE 'EM THINK THEY GOT PLAGUE.

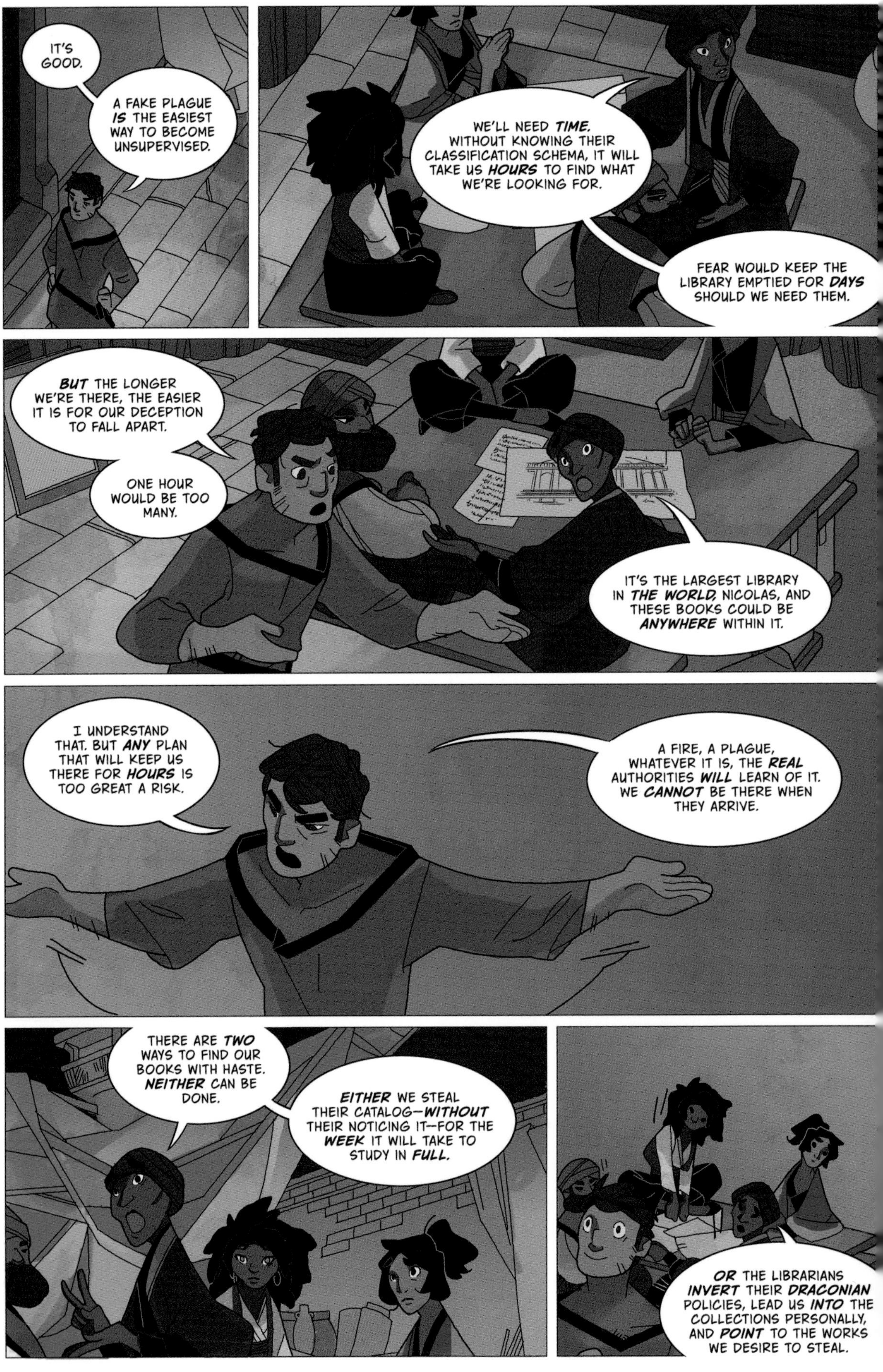
IT'S GOOD.
A FAKE PLAGUE IS THE EASIEST WAY TO BECOME UNSUPERVISED.
WE'LL NEED TIME. WITHOUT KNOWING THEIR CLASSIFICATION SCHEMA, IT WILL TAKE US HOURS TO FIND WHAT WE'RE LOOKING FOR.
FEAR WOULD KEEP THE LIBRARY EMPTIED FOR DAYS SHOULD WE NEED THEM.
BUT THE LONGER WE'RE THERE, THE EASIER IT IS FOR OUR DECEPTION TO FALL APART.
ONE HOUR WOULD BE TOO MANY.
IT'S THE LARGEST LIBRARY IN THE WORLD, NICOLAS, AND THESE BOOKS COULD BE ANYWHERE WITHIN IT.
I UNDERSTAND THAT. BUT ANY PLAN THAT WILL KEEP US THERE FOR HOURS IS TOO GREAT A RISK.
A FIRE, A PLAGUE, WHATEVER IT IS, THE REAL AUTHORITIES WILL LEARN OF IT. WE CANNOT BE THERE WHEN THEY ARRIVE.
THERE ARE TWO WAYS TO FIND OUR BOOKS WITH HASTE. NEITHER CAN BE DONE.
EITHER WE STEAL THEIR CATALOG—WITHOUT THEIR NOTICING IT—FOR THE WEEK IT WILL TAKE TO STUDY IN FULL.
OR THE LIBRARIANS INVERT THEIR DRACONIAN POLICIES, LEAD US INTO THE COLLECTIONS PERSONALLY, AND POINT TO THE WORKS WE DESIRE TO STEAL.

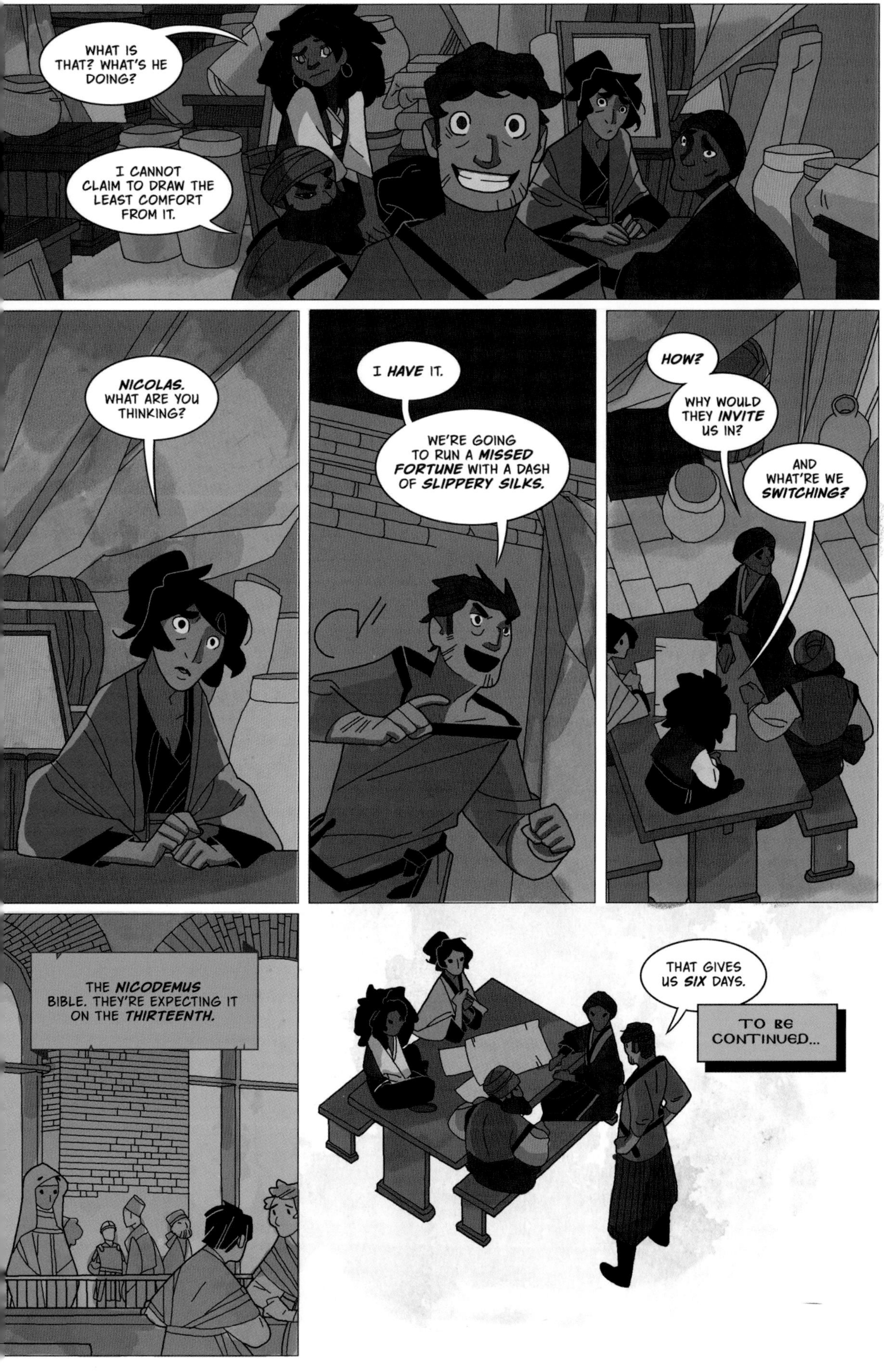
WHAT IS THAT? WHAT'S HE DOING?
I CANNOT CLAIM TO DRAW THE LEAST COMFORT FROM IT.
NICOLAS. WHAT ARE YOU THINKING?
I HAVE IT.
WE'RE GOING TO RUN A MISSED FORTUNE WITH A DASH OF SLIPPERY SILKS.
HOW?
WHY WOULD THEY INVITE US IN?
AND WHAT'RE WE SWITCHING?
THE NICODEMUS BIBLE. THEY'RE EXPECTING IT ON THE THIRTEENTH.
THAT GIVES US SIX DAYS.
TO BE CONTINUED...

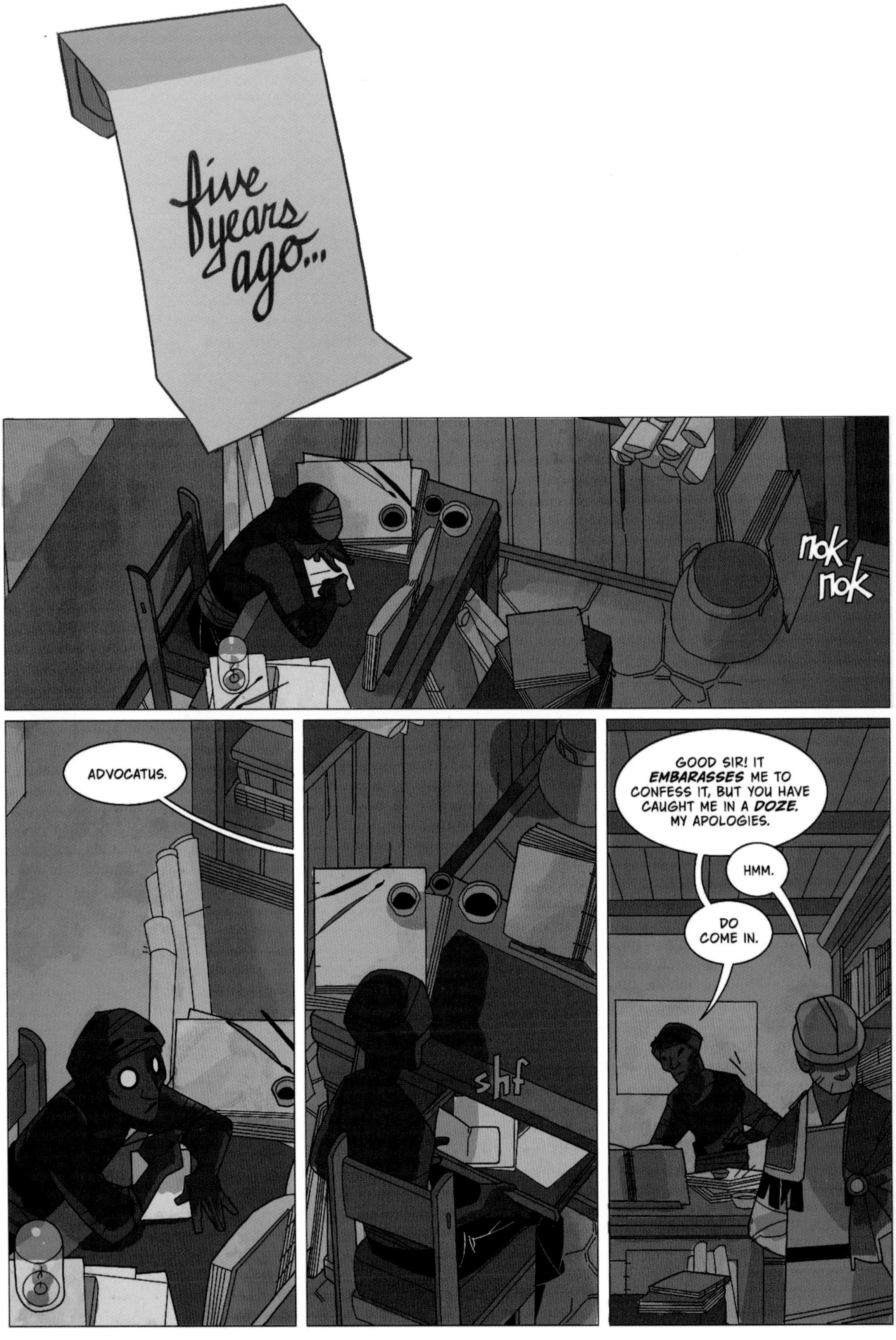
five years ago...
nok nok
ADVOCATUS.
shf
GOOD SIR! IT EMBARASSES ME TO CONFESS IT, BUT YOU HAVE CAUGHT ME IN A DOZE. MY APOLOGIES.
HMM.
DO COME IN.

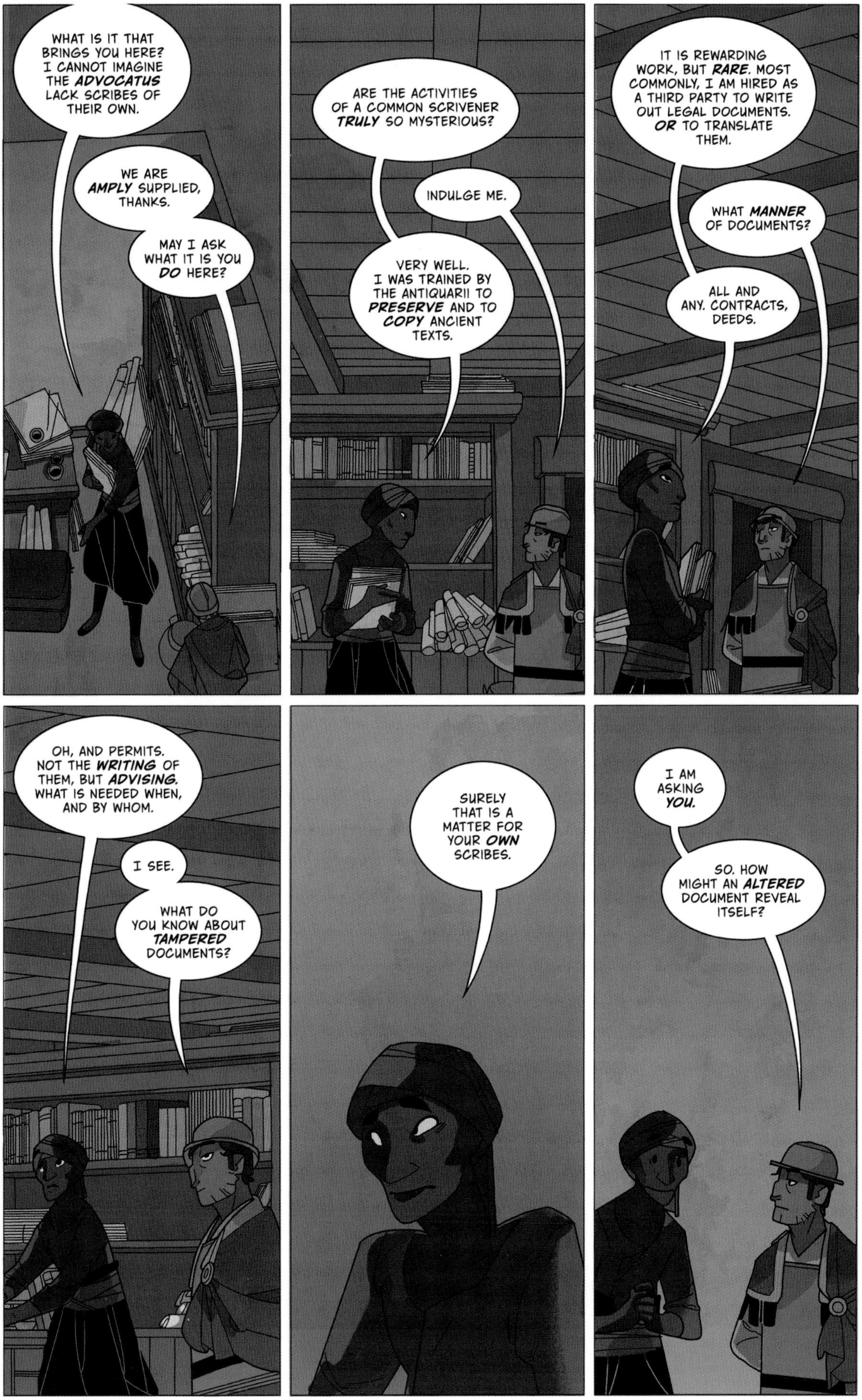
WHAT IS IT THAT BRINGS YOU HERE? I CANNOT IMAGINE THE ADVOCATUS LACK SCRIBES OF THEIR OWN.
WE ARE AMPLY SUPPLIED, THANKS.
MAY I ASK WHAT IT IS YOU DO HERE?
ARE THE ACTIVITIES OF A COMMON SCRIVENER TRULY SO MYSTERIOUS?
INDULGE ME.
VERY WELL. I WAS TRAINED BY THE ANTIQUARII TO PRESERVE AND TO COPY ANCIENT TEXTS.
IT IS REWARDING WORK, BUT RARE. MOST COMMONLY, I AM HIRED AS A THIRD PARTY TO WRITE OUT LEGAL DOCUMENTS. OR TO TRANSLATE THEM.
WHAT MANNER OF DOCUMENTS?
ALL AND ANY. CONTRACTS, DEEDS.
OH, AND PERMITS. NOT THE WRITING OF THEM, BUT ADVISING. WHAT IS NEEDED WHEN, AND BY WHOM.
I SEE.
WHAT DO YOU KNOW ABOUT TAMPERED DOCUMENTS?
SURELY THAT IS A MATTER FOR YOUR OWN SCRIBES.
I AM ASKING YOU.
SO. HOW MIGHT AN ALTERED DOCUMENT REVEAL ITSELF?

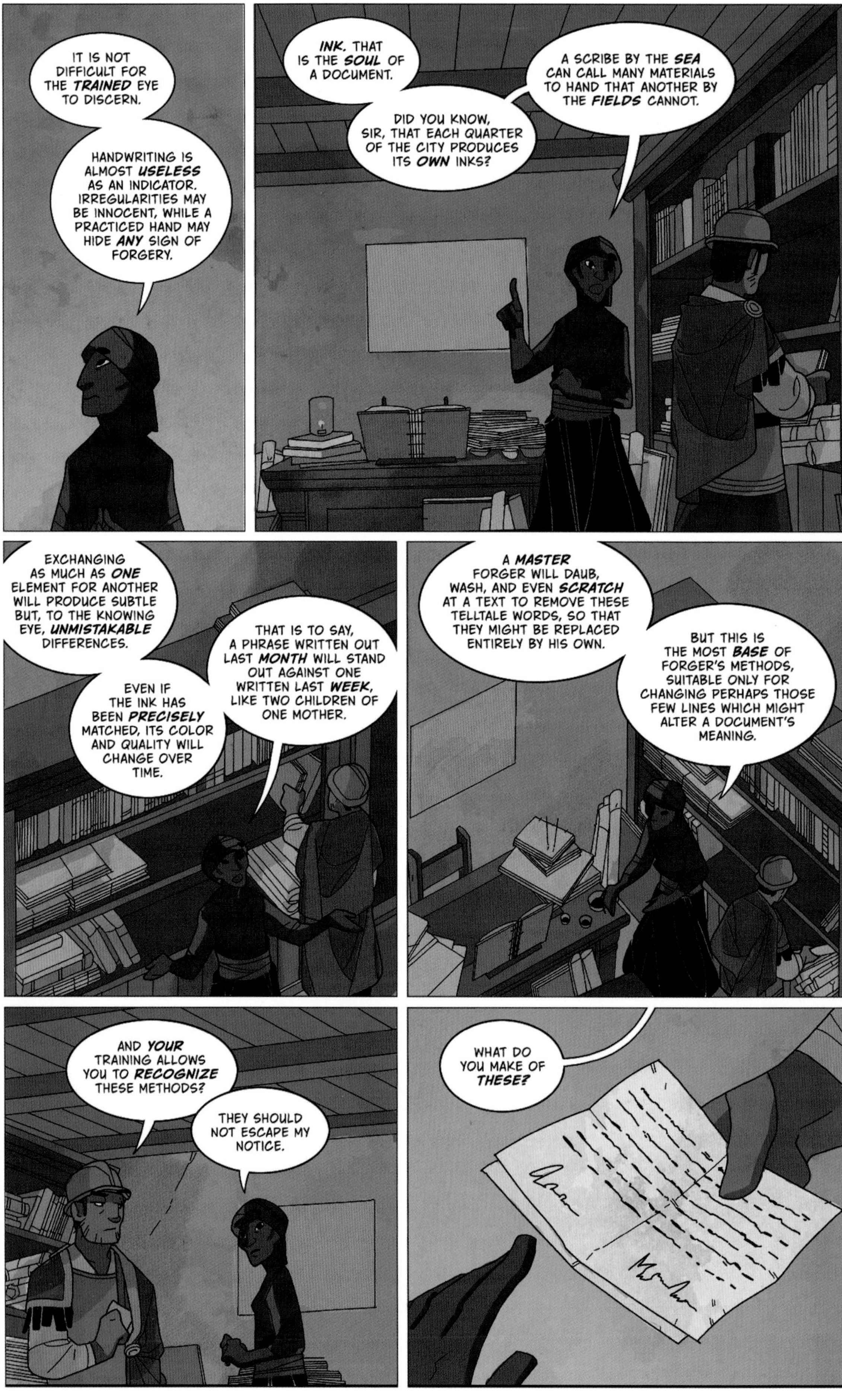
IT IS NOT DIFFICULT FOR THE TRAINED EYE TO DISCERN.
HANDWRITING IS ALMOST USELESS AS AN INDICATOR. IRREGULARITIES MAY BE INNOCENT, WHILE A PRACTICED HAND MAY HIDE ANY SIGN OF FORGERY.
INK. THAT IS THE SOUL OF A DOCUMENT.
DID YOU KNOW, SIR, THAT EACH QUARTER OF THE CITY PRODUCES ITS OWN INKS?
A SCRIBE BY THE SEA CAN CALL MANY MATERIALS TO HAND THAT ANOTHER BY THE FIELDS CANNOT.
EXCHANGING AS MUCH AS ONE ELEMENT FOR ANOTHER WILL PRODUCE SUBTLE BUT, TO THE KNOWING EYE, UNMISTAKABLE DIFFERENCES.
EVEN IF THE INK HAS BEEN PRECISELY MATCHED, ITS COLOR AND QUALITY WILL CHANGE OVER TIME.
THAT IS TO SAY, A PHRASE WRITTEN OUT LAST MONTH WILL STAND OUT AGAINST ONE WRITTEN LAST WEEK, LIKE TWO CHILDREN OF ONE MOTHER.
A MASTER FORGER WILL DAUB, WASH, AND EVEN SCRATCH AT A TEXT TO REMOVE THESE TELLTALE WORDS, SO THAT THEY MIGHT BE REPLACED ENTIRELY BY HIS OWN.
BUT THIS IS THE MOST BASE OF FORGER'S METHODS, SUITABLE ONLY FOR CHANGING PERHAPS THOSE FEW LINES WHICH MIGHT ALTER A DOCUMENT'S MEANING.
AND YOUR TRAINING ALLOWS YOU TO RECOGNIZE THESE METHODS?
THEY SHOULD NOT ESCAPE MY NOTICE.
WHAT DO YOU MAKE OF THESE?

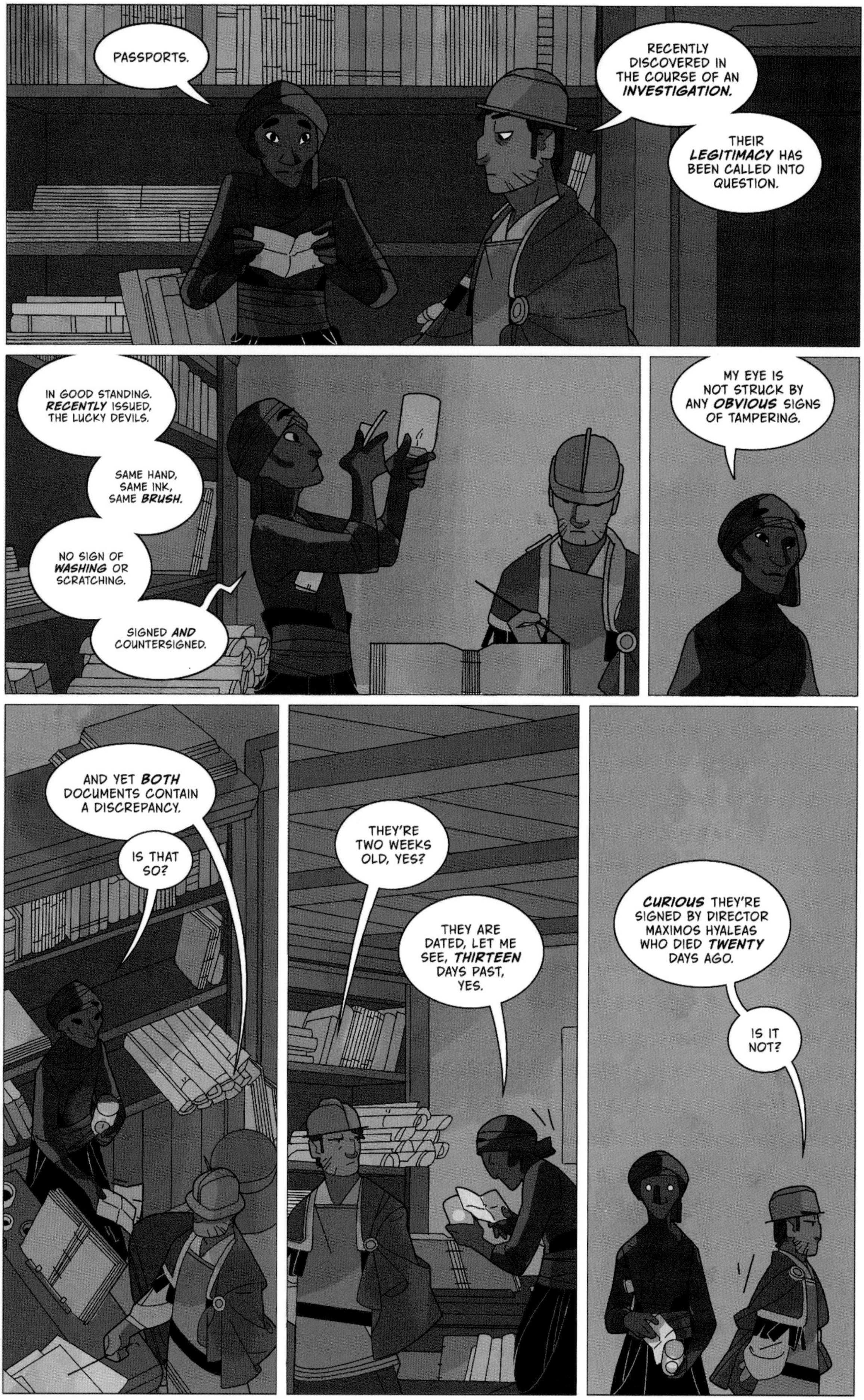
PASSPORTS.
RECENTLY DISCOVERED IN THE COURSE OF AN *INVESTIGATION.*
THEIR *LEGITIMACY* HAS BEEN CALLED INTO QUESTION.
IN GOOD STANDING. *RECENTLY* ISSUED, THE LUCKY DEVILS.
SAME HAND, SAME INK, SAME *BRUSH.*
NO SIGN OF *WASHING* OR SCRATCHING.
SIGNED *AND* COUNTERSIGNED.
MY EYE IS NOT STRUCK BY ANY *OBVIOUS* SIGNS OF TAMPERING.
AND YET *BOTH* DOCUMENTS CONTAIN A DISCREPANCY.
IS THAT SO?
THEY'RE TWO WEEKS OLD, YES?
THEY ARE DATED, LET ME SEE, *THIRTEEN* DAYS PAST, YES.
CURIOUS THEY'RE SIGNED BY DIRECTOR MAXIMOS HYALEAS WHO DIED *TWENTY* DAYS AGO.
IS IT NOT?

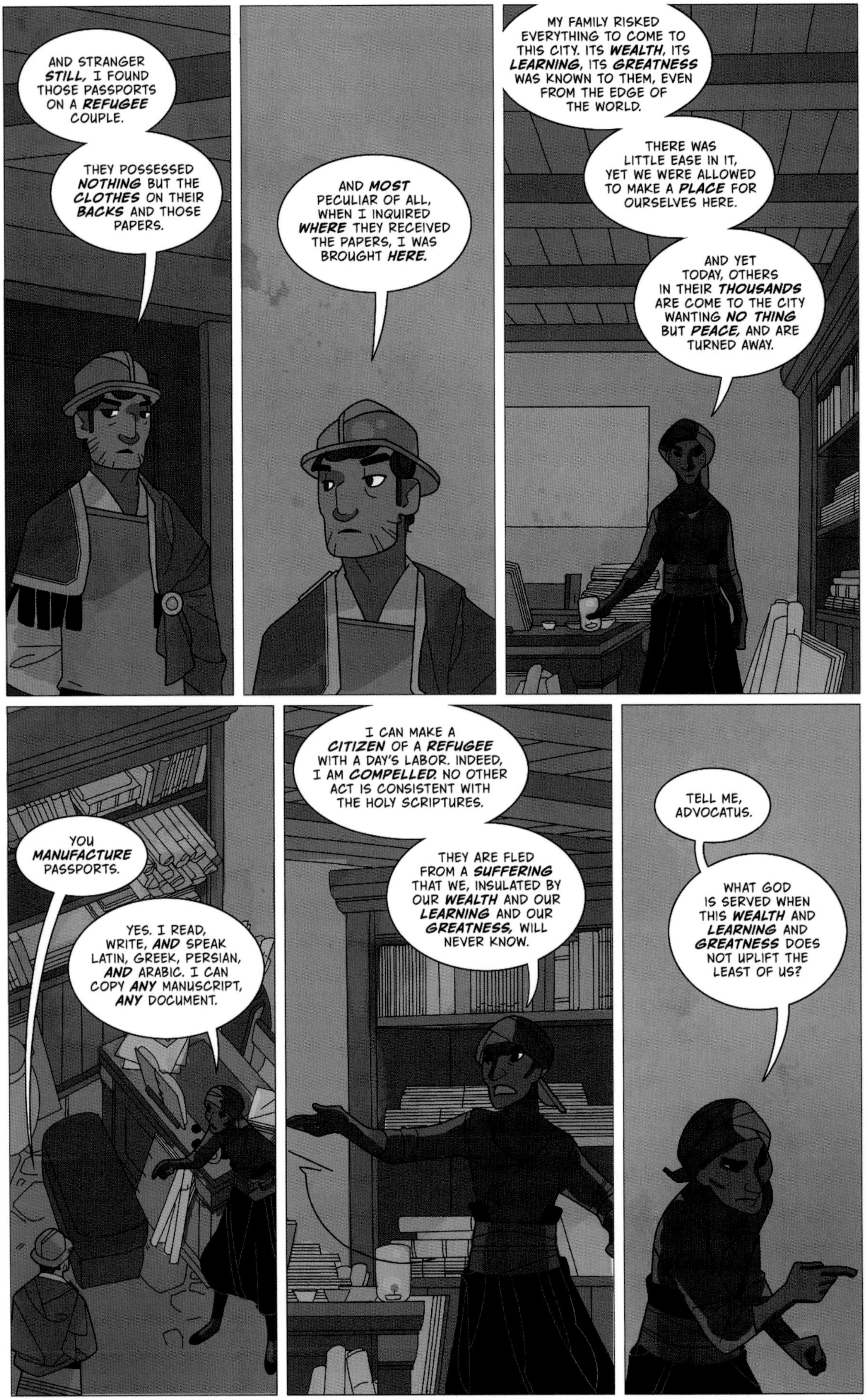
AND STRANGER STILL, I FOUND THOSE PASSPORTS ON A REFUGEE COUPLE.
THEY POSSESSED NOTHING BUT THE CLOTHES ON THEIR BACKS AND THOSE PAPERS.
AND MOST PECULIAR OF ALL, WHEN I INQUIRED WHERE THEY RECEIVED THE PAPERS, I WAS BROUGHT HERE.
MY FAMILY RISKED EVERYTHING TO COME TO THIS CITY. ITS WEALTH, ITS LEARNING, ITS GREATNESS WAS KNOWN TO THEM, EVEN FROM THE EDGE OF THE WORLD.
THERE WAS LITTLE EASE IN IT, YET WE WERE ALLOWED TO MAKE A PLACE FOR OURSELVES HERE.
AND YET TODAY, OTHERS IN THEIR THOUSANDS ARE COME TO THE CITY WANTING NO THING BUT PEACE, AND ARE TURNED AWAY.
YOU MANUFACTURE PASSPORTS.
YES. I READ, WRITE, AND SPEAK LATIN, GREEK, PERSIAN, AND ARABIC. I CAN COPY ANY MANUSCRIPT, ANY DOCUMENT.
I CAN MAKE A CITIZEN OF A REFUGEE WITH A DAY'S LABOR. INDEED, I AM COMPELLED. NO OTHER ACT IS CONSISTENT WITH THE HOLY SCRIPTURES.
THEY ARE FLED FROM A SUFFERING THAT WE, INSULATED BY OUR WEALTH AND OUR LEARNING AND OUR GREATNESS, WILL NEVER KNOW.
TELL ME, ADVOCATUS.
WHAT GOD IS SERVED WHEN THIS WEALTH AND LEARNING AND GREATNESS DOES NOT UPLIFT THE LEAST OF US?

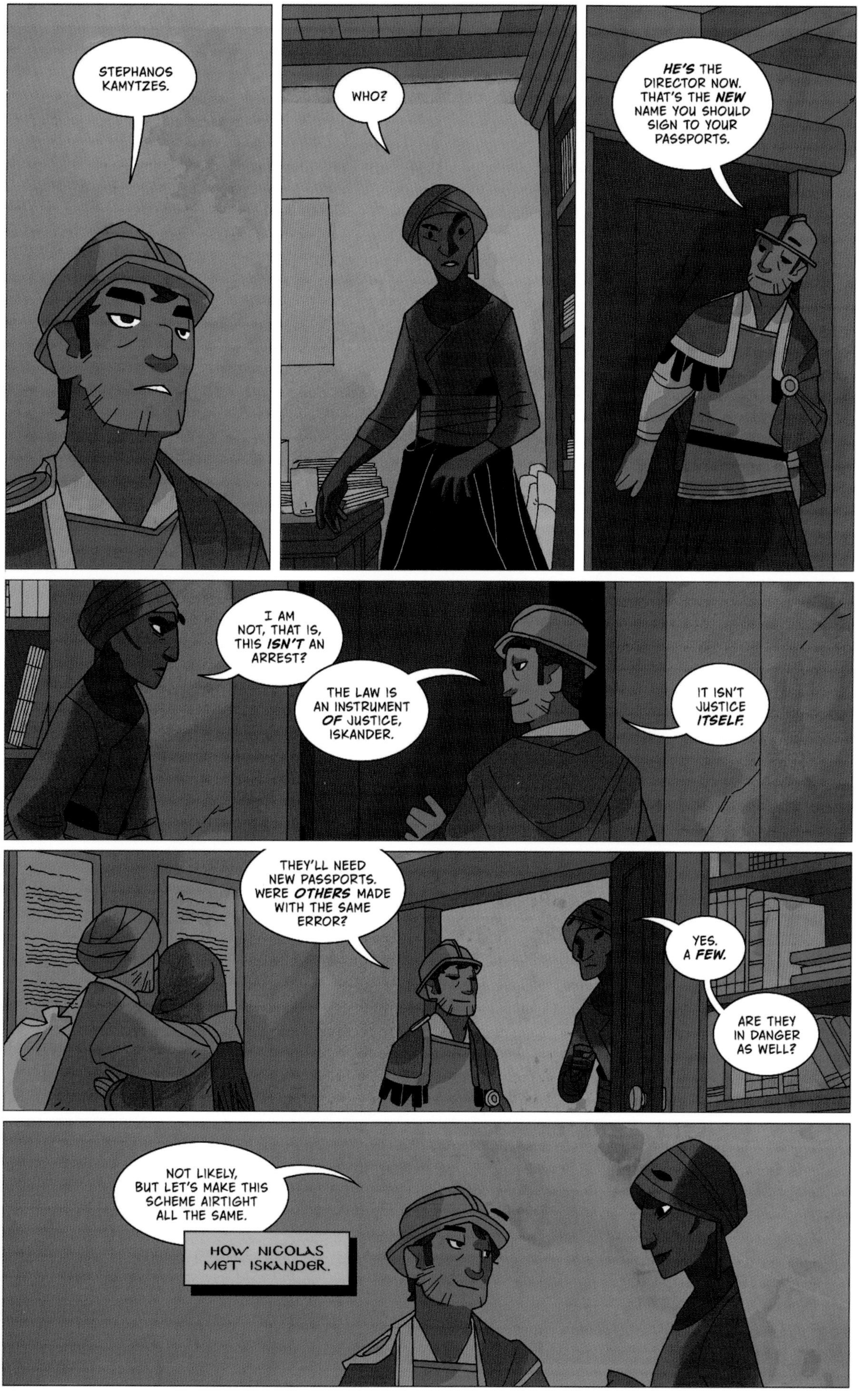
STEPHANOS KAMYTZES.
WHO?
HE'S THE DIRECTOR NOW. THAT'S THE NEW NAME YOU SHOULD SIGN TO YOUR PASSPORTS.
I AM NOT, THAT IS, THIS ISN'T AN ARREST?
THE LAW IS AN INSTRUMENT OF JUSTICE, ISKANDER.
IT ISN'T JUSTICE ITSELF.
THEY'LL NEED NEW PASSPORTS. WERE OTHERS MADE WITH THE SAME ERROR?
YES. A FEW.
ARE THEY IN DANGER AS WELL?
NOT LIKELY, BUT LET'S MAKE THIS SCHEME AIRTIGHT ALL THE SAME.
HOW NICOLAS MET ISKANDER.

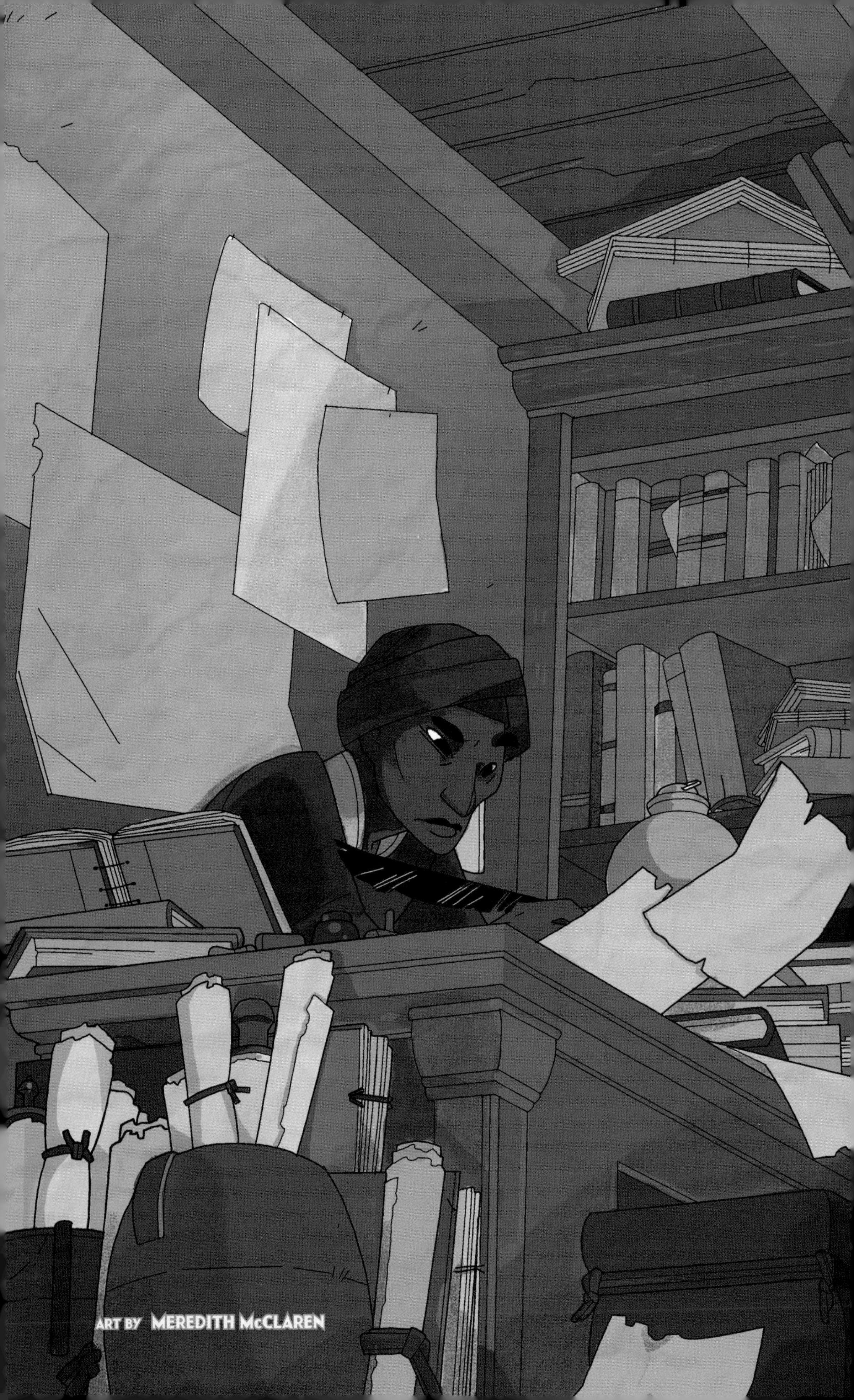
ART BY MEREDITH McCLAREN

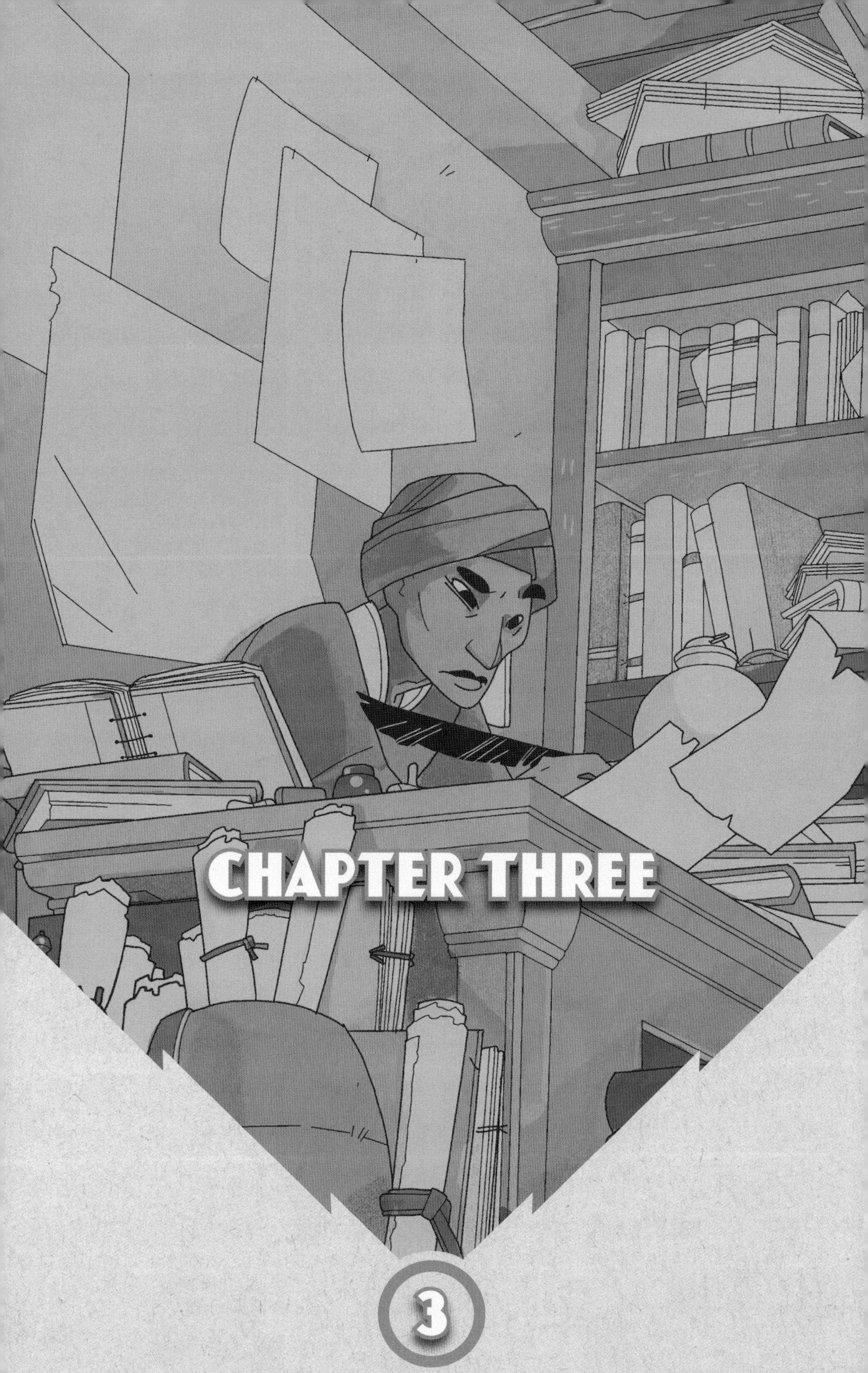

CHAPTER THREE

3

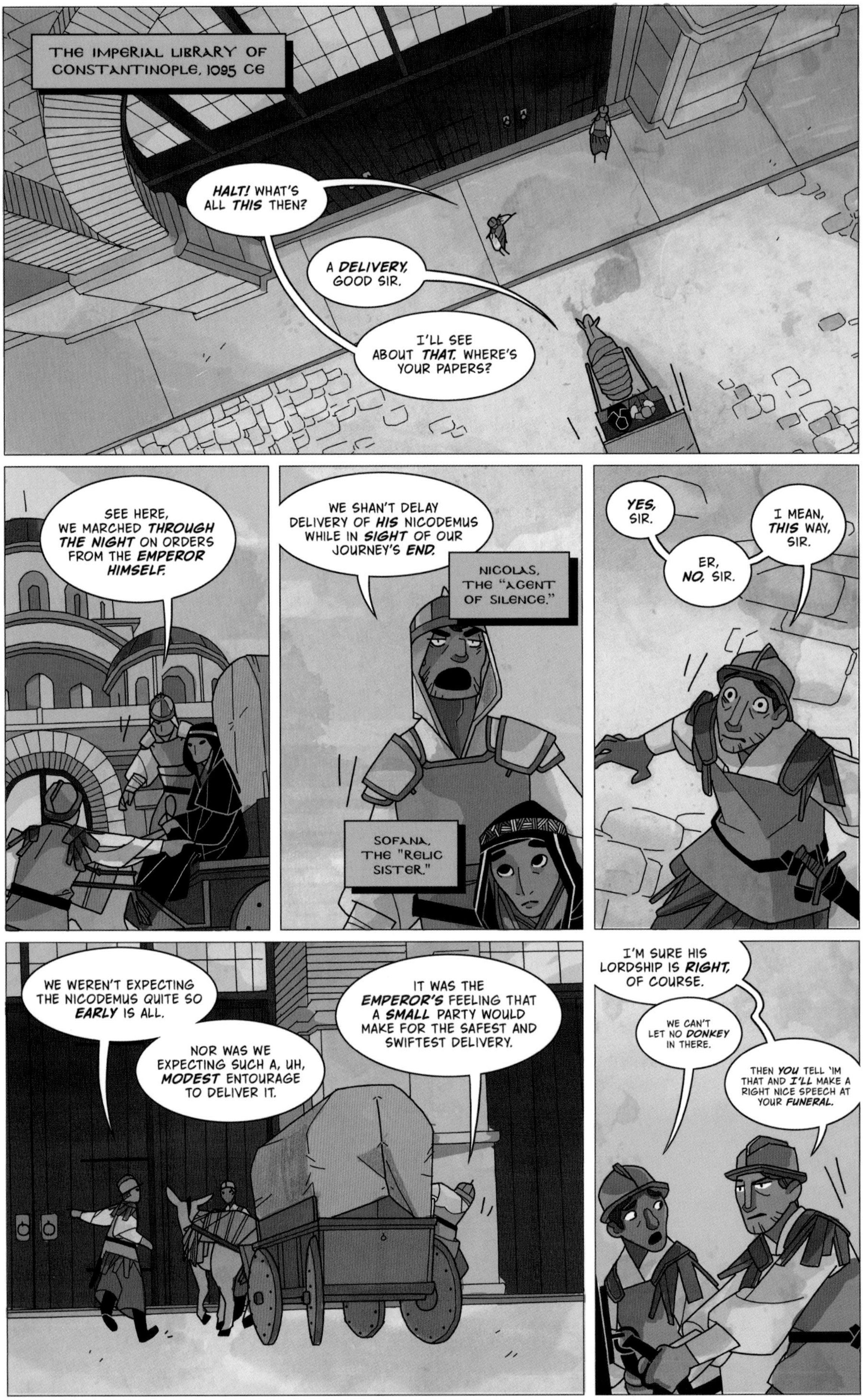
THE IMPERIAL LIBRARY OF CONSTANTINOPLE, 1095 CE
HALT! WHAT'S ALL THIS THEN?
A DELIVERY, GOOD SIR.
I'LL SEE ABOUT THAT. WHERE'S YOUR PAPERS?
SEE HERE, WE MARCHED THROUGH THE NIGHT ON ORDERS FROM THE EMPEROR HIMSELF.
WE SHAN'T DELAY DELIVERY OF HIS NICODEMUS WHILE IN SIGHT OF OUR JOURNEY'S END.
NICOLAS, THE "AGENT OF SILENCE."
SOFANA, THE "RELIC SISTER."
YES, SIR.
ER, NO, SIR.
I MEAN, THIS WAY, SIR.
WE WEREN'T EXPECTING THE NICODEMUS QUITE SO EARLY IS ALL.
NOR WAS WE EXPECTING SUCH A, UH, MODEST ENTOURAGE TO DELIVER IT.
IT WAS THE EMPEROR'S FEELING THAT A SMALL PARTY WOULD MAKE FOR THE SAFEST AND SWIFTEST DELIVERY.
I'M SURE HIS LORDSHIP IS RIGHT, OF COURSE.
WE CAN'T LET NO DONKEY IN THERE.
THEN YOU TELL 'IM THAT AND I'LL MAKE A RIGHT NICE SPEECH AT YOUR FUNERAL.

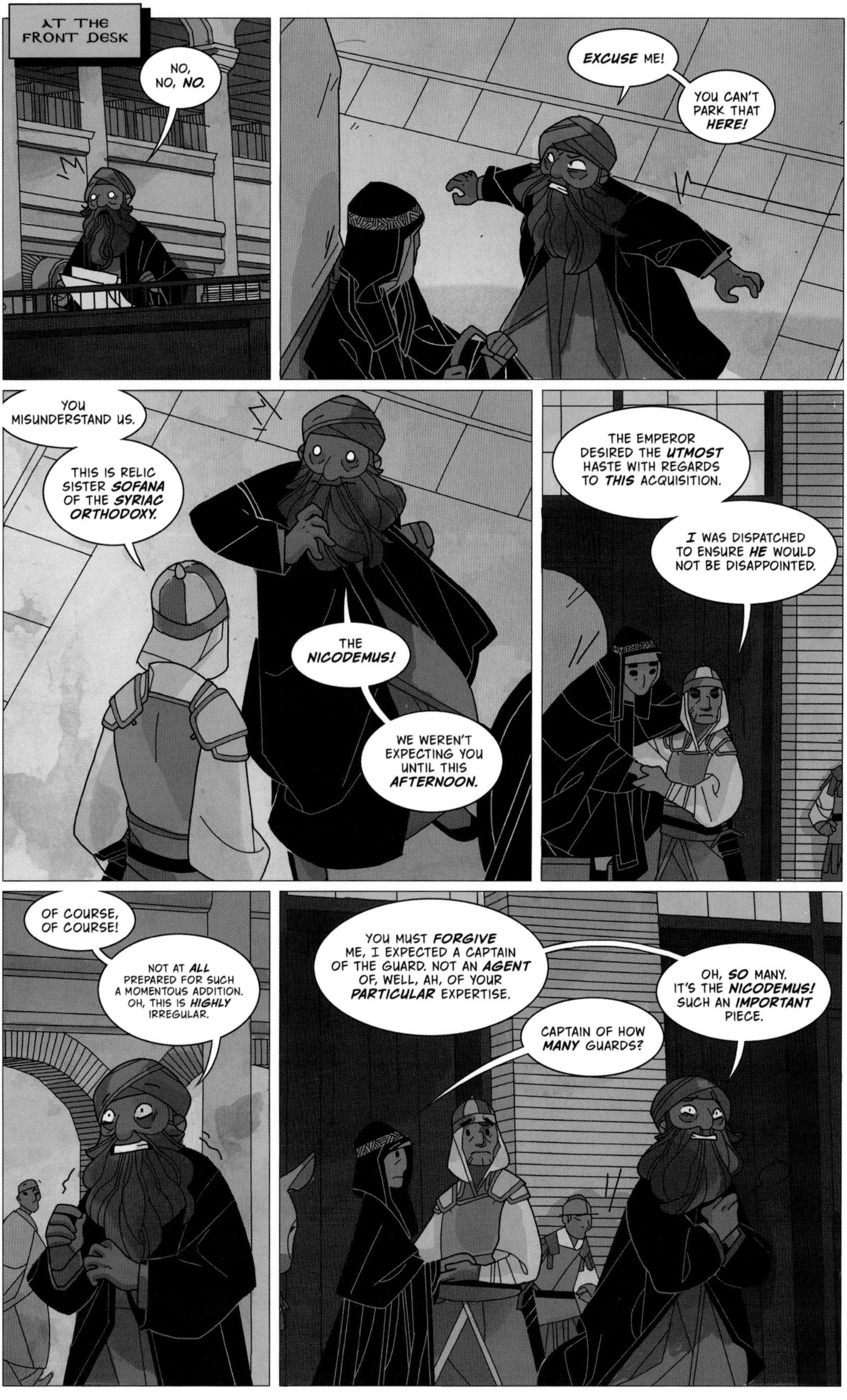
AT THE FRONT DESK
NO, NO, NO.
EXCUSE ME!
YOU CAN'T PARK THAT HERE!
YOU MISUNDERSTAND US.
THIS IS RELIC SISTER SOFANA OF THE SYRIAC ORTHODOXY.
THE NICODEMUS!
WE WEREN'T EXPECTING YOU UNTIL THIS AFTERNOON.
THE EMPEROR DESIRED THE UTMOST HASTE WITH REGARDS TO THIS ACQUISITION.
I WAS DISPATCHED TO ENSURE HE WOULD NOT BE DISAPPOINTED.
OF COURSE, OF COURSE!
NOT AT ALL PREPARED FOR SUCH A MOMENTOUS ADDITION. OH, THIS IS HIGHLY IRREGULAR.
YOU MUST FORGIVE ME, I EXPECTED A CAPTAIN OF THE GUARD. NOT AN AGENT OF, WELL, AH, OF YOUR PARTICULAR EXPERTISE.
CAPTAIN OF HOW MANY GUARDS?
OH, SO MANY. IT'S THE NICODEMUS! SUCH AN IMPORTANT PIECE.

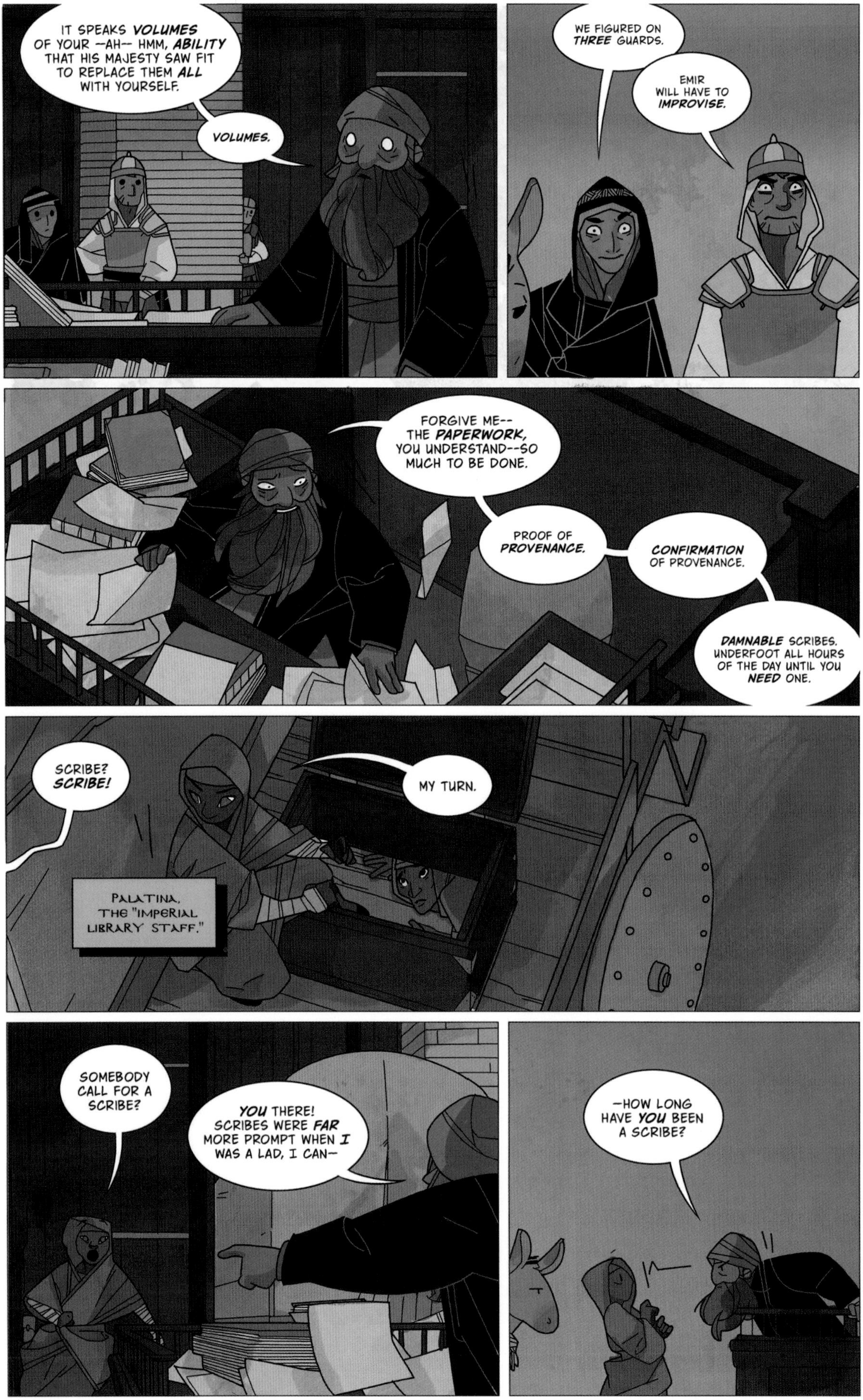
IT SPEAKS VOLUMES OF YOUR --AH-- HMM, ABILITY THAT HIS MAJESTY SAW FIT TO REPLACE THEM ALL WITH YOURSELF.
VOLUMES.
WE FIGURED ON THREE GUARDS.
EMIR WILL HAVE TO IMPROVISE.
FORGIVE ME-- THE PAPERWORK, YOU UNDERSTAND--SO MUCH TO BE DONE.
PROOF OF PROVENANCE.
CONFIRMATION OF PROVENANCE.
DAMNABLE SCRIBES. UNDERFOOT ALL HOURS OF THE DAY UNTIL YOU NEED ONE.
SCRIBE? SCRIBE!
MY TURN.
PALATINA, THE "IMPERIAL LIBRARY STAFF."
SOMEBODY CALL FOR A SCRIBE?
YOU THERE! SCRIBES WERE FAR MORE PROMPT WHEN I WAS A LAD, I CAN--
--HOW LONG HAVE YOU BEEN A SCRIBE?

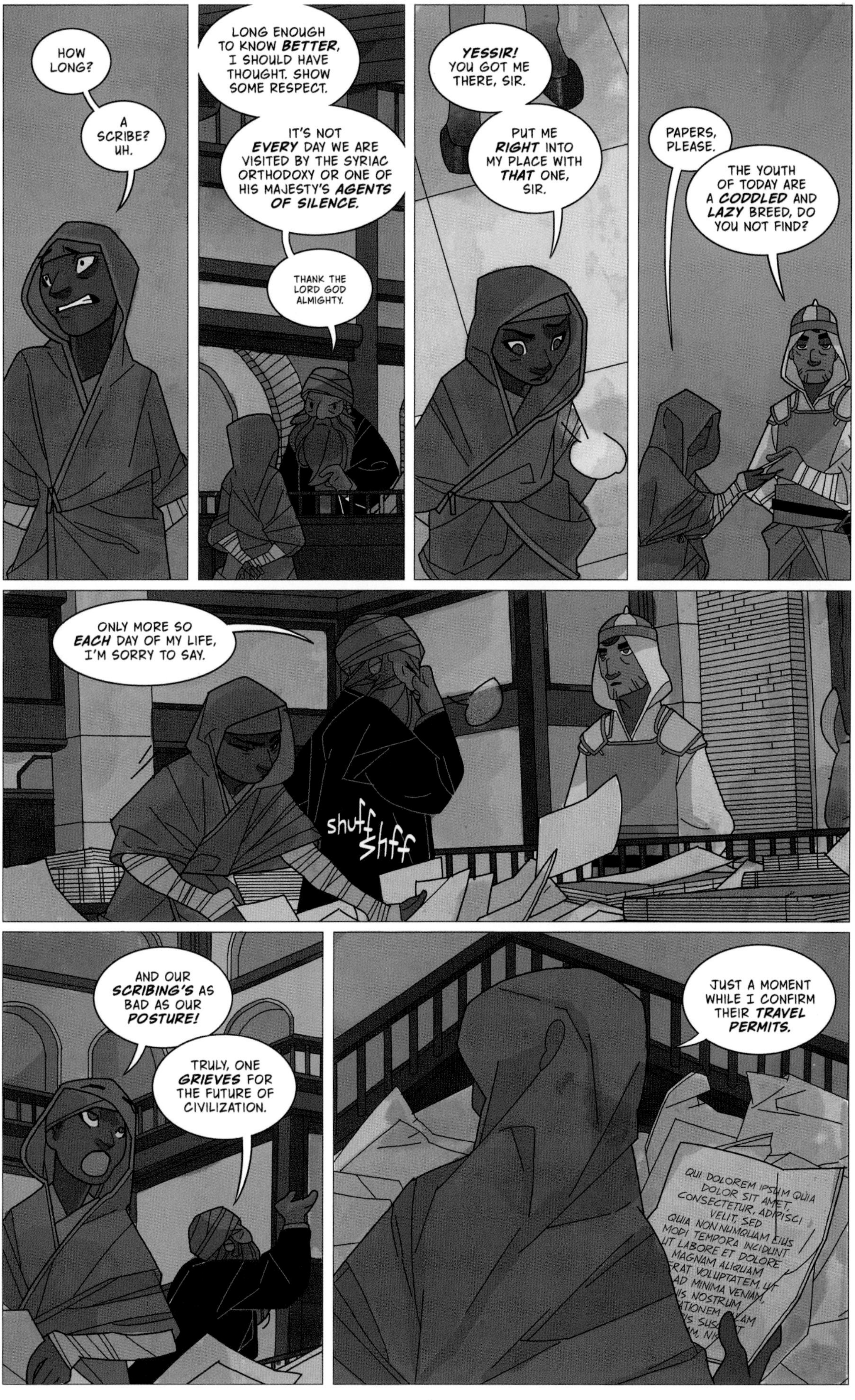
HOW LONG?
A SCRIBE? UH.
LONG ENOUGH TO KNOW BETTER, I SHOULD HAVE THOUGHT. SHOW SOME RESPECT.
IT'S NOT EVERY DAY WE ARE VISITED BY THE SYRIAC ORTHODOXY OR ONE OF HIS MAJESTY'S AGENTS OF SILENCE.
THANK THE LORD GOD ALMIGHTY.
YESSIR! YOU GOT ME THERE, SIR.
PUT ME RIGHT INTO MY PLACE WITH THAT ONE, SIR.
PAPERS, PLEASE.
THE YOUTH OF TODAY ARE A CODDLED AND LAZY BREED, DO YOU NOT FIND?
ONLY MORE SO EACH DAY OF MY LIFE, I'M SORRY TO SAY.
shuff shff
AND OUR SCRIBING'S AS BAD AS OUR POSTURE!
TRULY, ONE GRIEVES FOR THE FUTURE OF CIVILIZATION.
JUST A MOMENT WHILE I CONFIRM THEIR TRAVEL PERMITS.
QUI DOLOREM IPSUM QUIA
DOLOR SIT AMET,
CONSECTETUR, ADIPISCI
VELIT, SED
QUIA NON NUMQUAM EIUS
MODI TEMPORA INCIDUNT
UT LABORE ET DOLORE
MAGNAM ALIQUAM
RAT VOLUPTATEM. UT
AD MINIMA VENIAM,
IS NOSTRUM
ATIONEM ULLAM

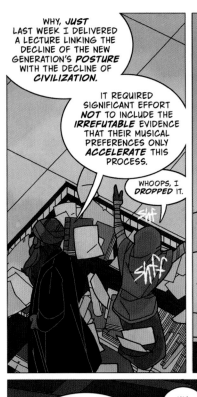

WHY, *JUST* LAST WEEK I DELIVERED A LECTURE LINKING THE DECLINE OF THE NEW GENERATION'S *POSTURE* WITH THE DECLINE OF *CIVILIZATION.*

IT REQUIRED SIGNIFICANT EFFORT *NOT* TO INCLUDE THE *IRREFUTABLE* EVIDENCE THAT THEIR MUSICAL PREFERENCES ONLY *ACCELERATE* THIS PROCESS.

WHOOPS, I *DROPPED* IT.

shf

shff

JUDGING BY THE RESPONSE, I SUSPECT MY *NEXT* LECTURE SERIES SHALL CENTER UPON PUBLIC *YAWNING* AS THE PRIMARY INDICATOR OF *MORAL DECAY.*

THERE IT IS.

shff

shwff

PERMITS *CONFIRMED.* THEIR SEAL IS *GENUINE.*

THE IMPERIAL LIBRARY OF CONSTANTINOPLE *WELCOMES* THE SYRIAC DELEGATION!

flitter

flutter

SISTER, AS THE HONORED SERVANT OF THE NICODEMUS, HOW DO YOU PROPOSE WE TRANSPORT IT TO THE *COLLECTIONS?*

UM, WELL.

THIS *CART* SERVED AS AN ABLE VESSEL THESE MANY DAYS AND NIGHTS. WE WOULD NOT DENY IT THE *COMPLETION* OF ITS TASK.

shf

OF COURSE, OF COURSE.

BUT TO PERMIT AN *ANIMAL* WITHIN THE *HALLOWED* HALLS OF THE IMPERIAL LIBRARY'S VAULT IS SIMPLY, AH—WITH *RESPECT,* SISTER, IT IS *UNTHINKABLE.*

THIS WILL NOT DO.

THE CART *MUST* BE TAKEN. IT CONTAINS, UH...

...THE *ALTAR,* YES, FROM WHICH I *MUST* INTONE THE RITES TO *COMPLETE* MY MISSION!

MY HANDS ARE *TIED,* SISTER.

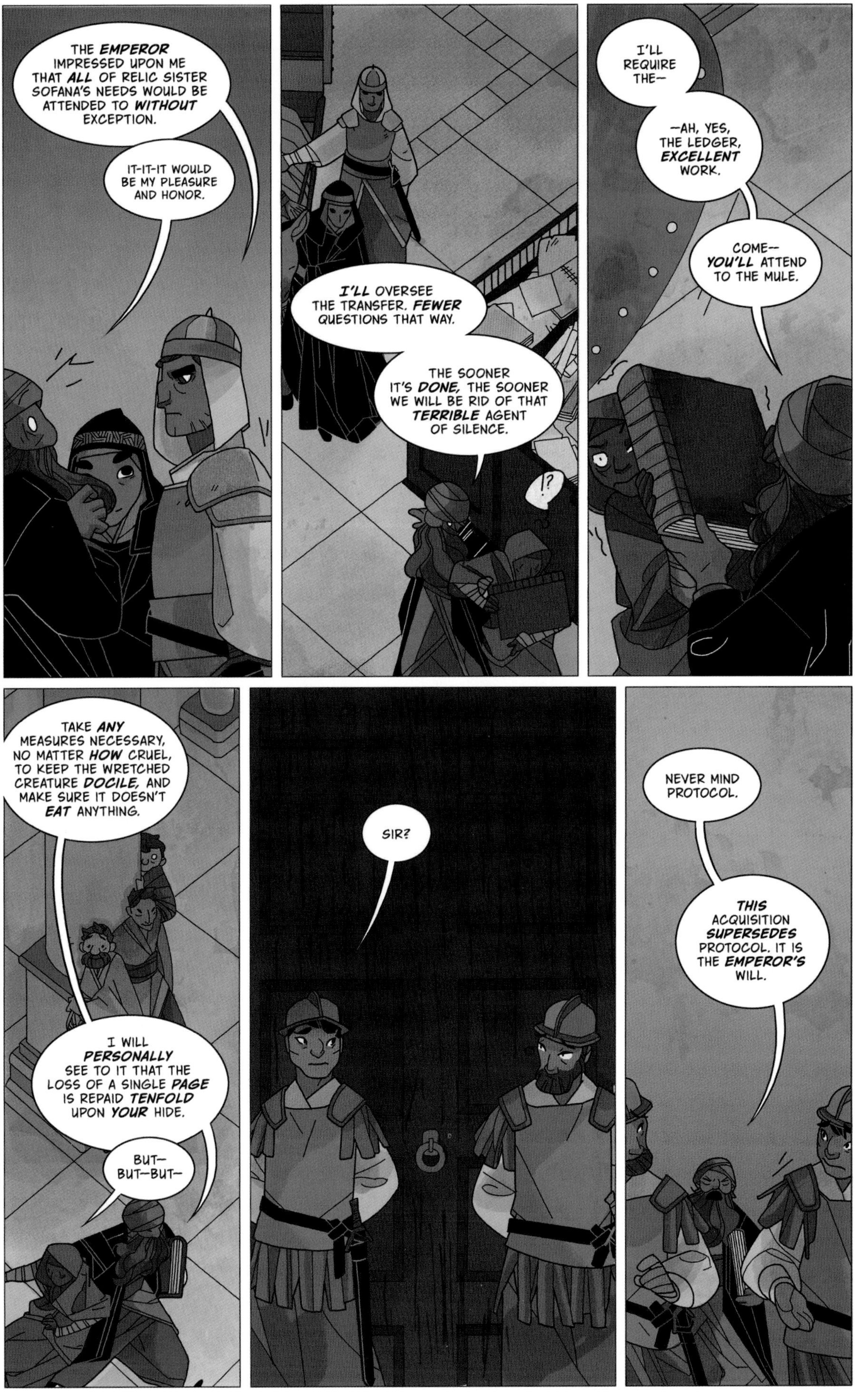
THE EMPEROR IMPRESSED UPON ME THAT ALL OF RELIC SISTER SOFANA'S NEEDS WOULD BE ATTENDED TO WITHOUT EXCEPTION.
IT-IT-IT WOULD BE MY PLEASURE AND HONOR.
I'LL OVERSEE THE TRANSFER. FEWER QUESTIONS THAT WAY.
THE SOONER IT'S DONE, THE SOONER WE WILL BE RID OF THAT TERRIBLE AGENT OF SILENCE.
!?
I'LL REQUIRE THE—
—AH, YES, THE LEDGER, EXCELLENT WORK.
COME— YOU'LL ATTEND TO THE MULE.
TAKE ANY MEASURES NECESSARY, NO MATTER HOW CRUEL, TO KEEP THE WRETCHED CREATURE DOCILE, AND MAKE SURE IT DOESN'T EAT ANYTHING.
I WILL PERSONALLY SEE TO IT THAT THE LOSS OF A SINGLE PAGE IS REPAID TENFOLD UPON YOUR HIDE.
BUT— BUT—BUT—
SIR?
NEVER MIND PROTOCOL.
THIS ACQUISITION SUPERSEDES PROTOCOL. IT IS THE EMPEROR'S WILL.

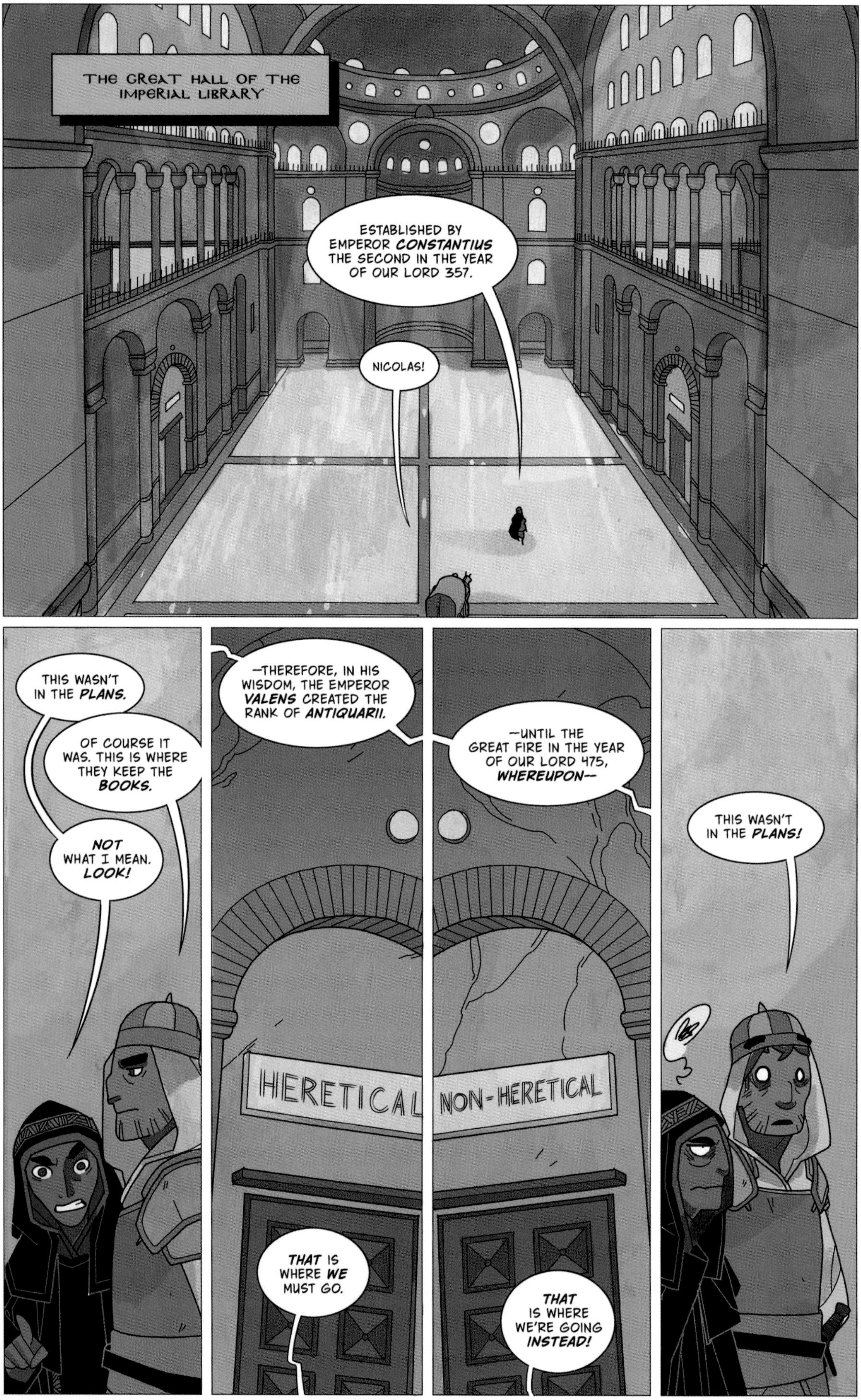
THE GREAT HALL OF THE IMPERIAL LIBRARY
ESTABLISHED BY EMPEROR CONSTANTIUS THE SECOND IN THE YEAR OF OUR LORD 357.
NICOLAS!
THIS WASN'T IN THE PLANS.
OF COURSE IT WAS. THIS IS WHERE THEY KEEP THE BOOKS.
NOT WHAT I MEAN. LOOK!
—THEREFORE, IN HIS WISDOM, THE EMPEROR VALENS CREATED THE RANK OF ANTIQUARII.
—UNTIL THE GREAT FIRE IN THE YEAR OF OUR LORD 475, WHEREUPON—
HERETICAL
NON-HERETICAL
THAT IS WHERE WE MUST GO.
THAT IS WHERE WE'RE GOING INSTEAD!
THIS WASN'T IN THE PLANS!

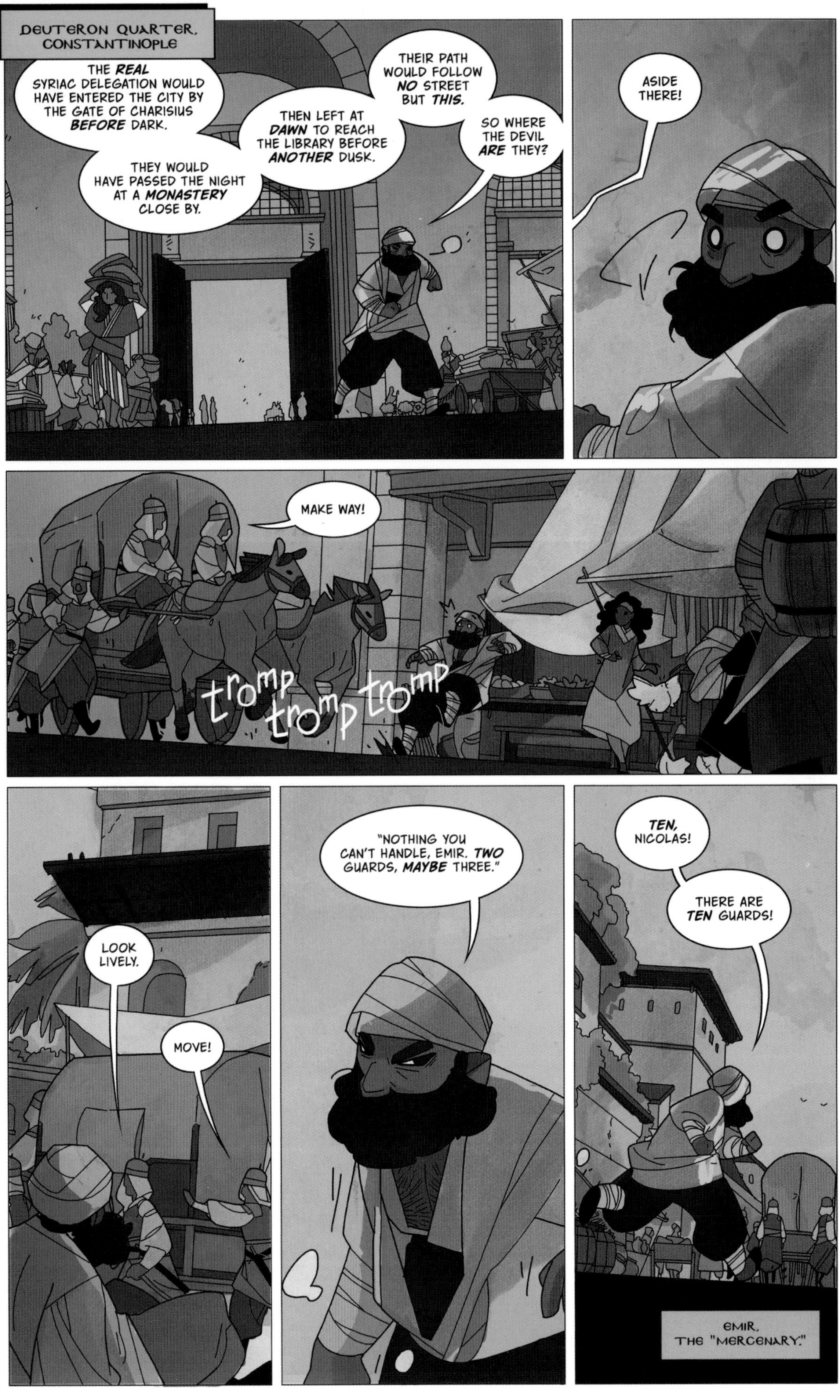
DEUTERON QUARTER, CONSTANTINOPLE
THE REAL SYRIAC DELEGATION WOULD HAVE ENTERED THE CITY BY THE GATE OF CHARISIUS BEFORE DARK.
THEY WOULD HAVE PASSED THE NIGHT AT A MONASTERY CLOSE BY.
THEN LEFT AT DAWN TO REACH THE LIBRARY BEFORE ANOTHER DUSK.
THEIR PATH WOULD FOLLOW NO STREET BUT THIS.
SO WHERE THE DEVIL ARE THEY?
ASIDE THERE!
MAKE WAY!
tromp tromp tromp
LOOK LIVELY.
MOVE!
"NOTHING YOU CAN'T HANDLE, EMIR. TWO GUARDS, MAYBE THREE."
TEN, NICOLAS!
THERE ARE TEN GUARDS!
EMIR, THE "MERCENARY."

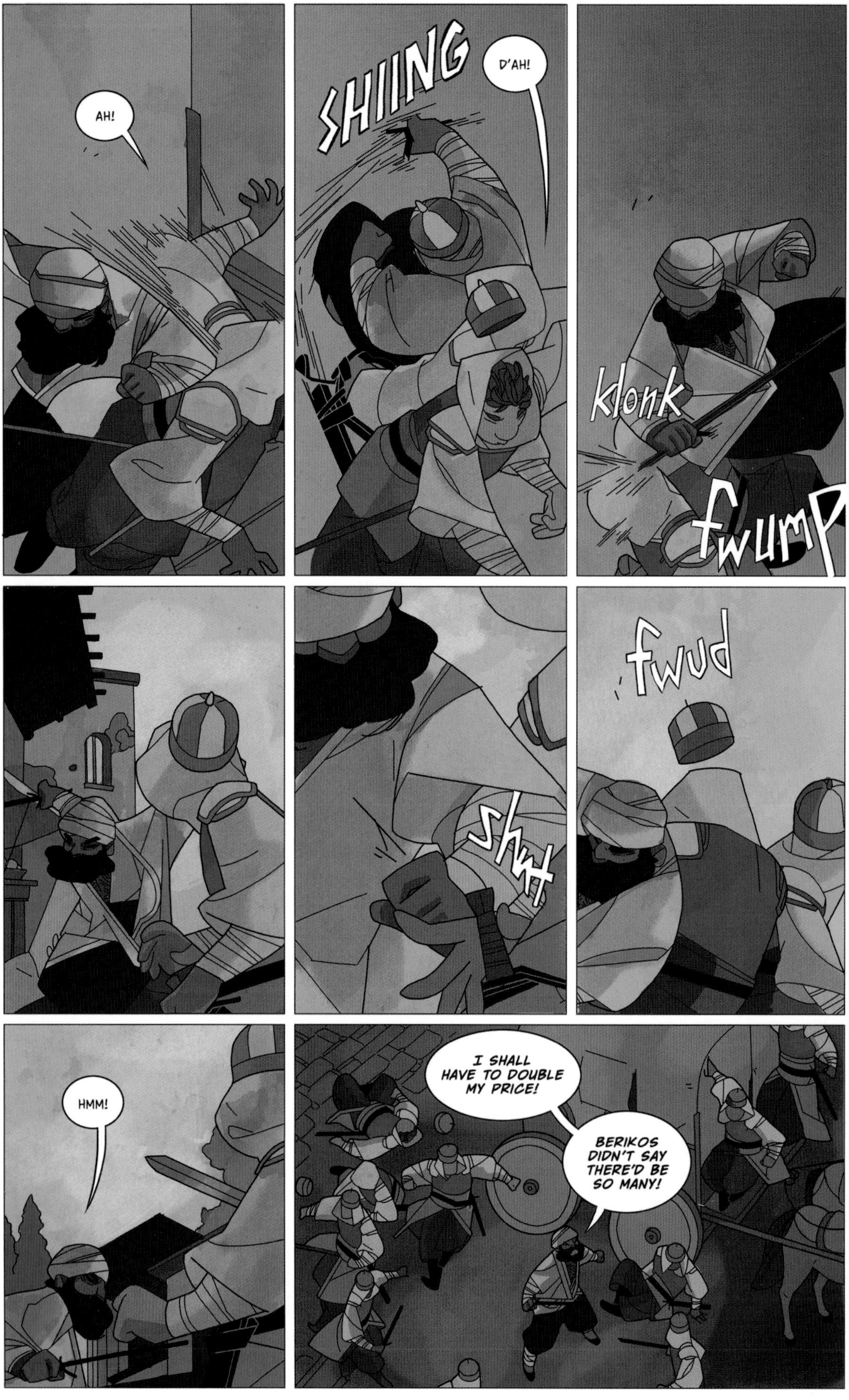
AH!
SHIING
D'AH!
klonk
fwump
fwud
shwt
HMM!
I SHALL HAVE TO DOUBLE MY PRICE!
BERIKOS DIDN'T SAY THERE'D BE SO MANY!

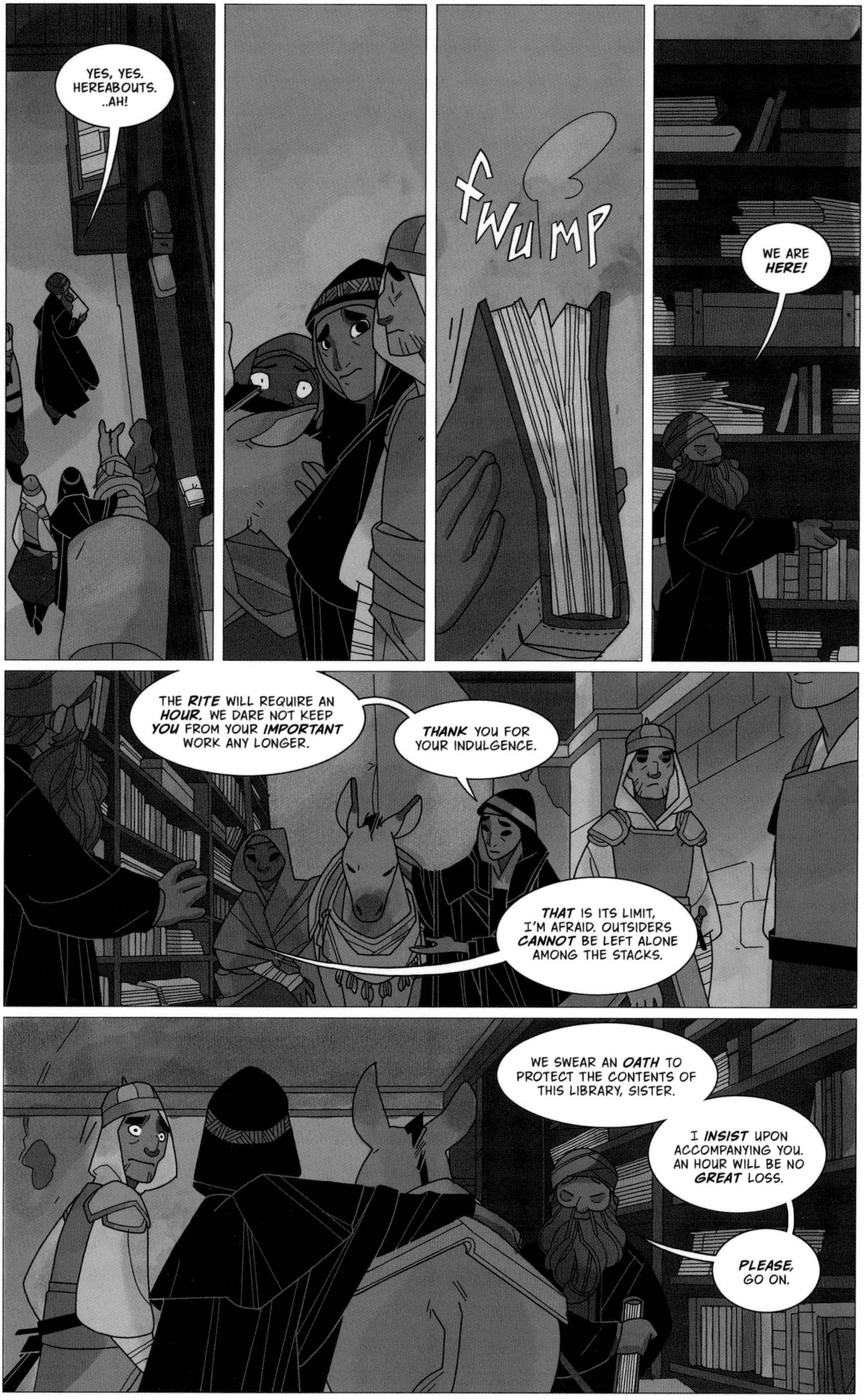
YES, YES. HEREABOUTS. ..AH!
FWUMP
WE ARE HERE!
THE RITE WILL REQUIRE AN HOUR. WE DARE NOT KEEP YOU FROM YOUR IMPORTANT WORK ANY LONGER.
THANK YOU FOR YOUR INDULGENCE.
THAT IS ITS LIMIT, I'M AFRAID. OUTSIDERS CANNOT BE LEFT ALONE AMONG THE STACKS.
WE SWEAR AN OATH TO PROTECT THE CONTENTS OF THIS LIBRARY, SISTER.
I INSIST UPON ACCOMPANYING YOU. AN HOUR WILL BE NO GREAT LOSS.
PLEASE, GO ON.

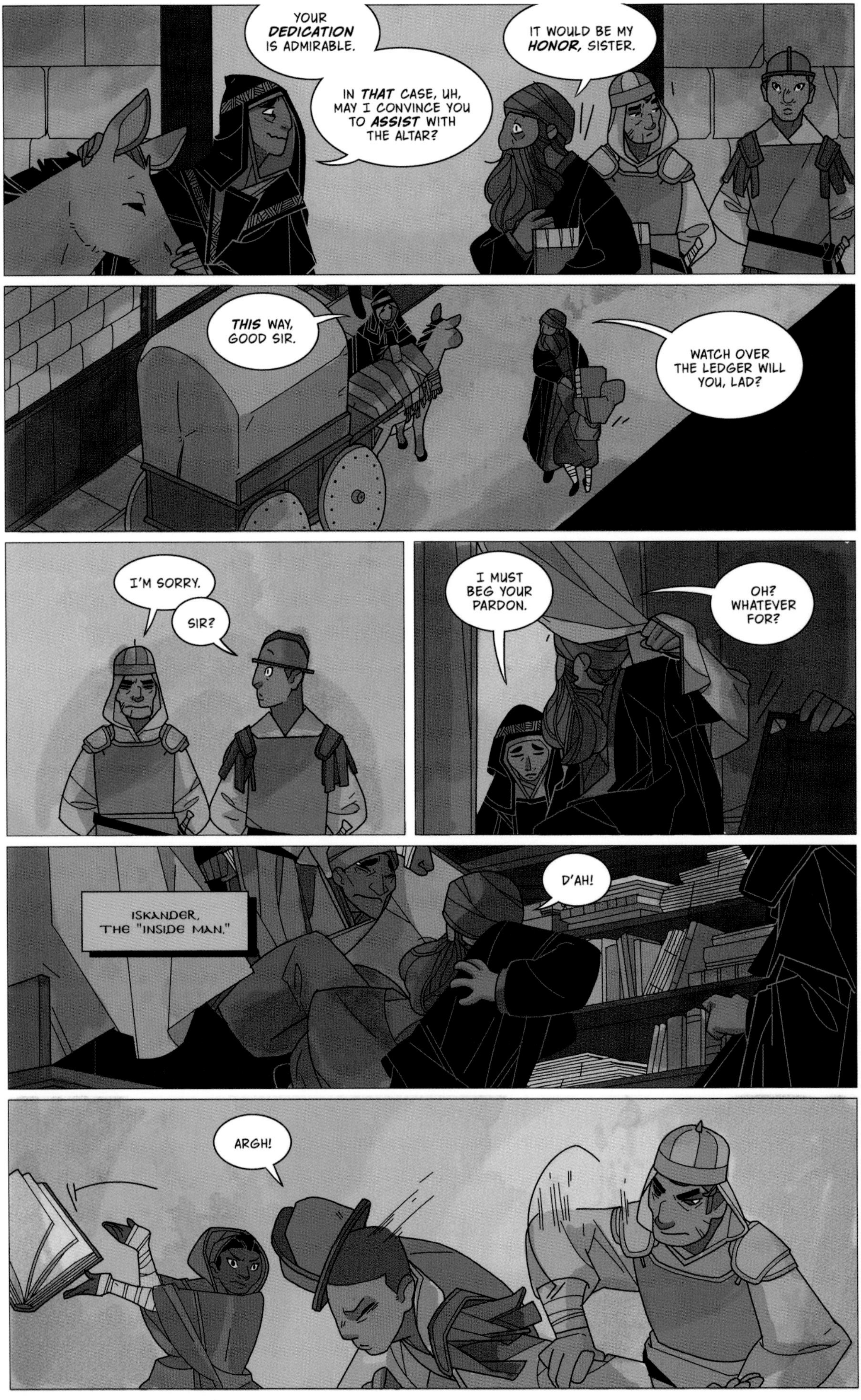
YOUR DEDICATION IS ADMIRABLE.
IT WOULD BE MY HONOR, SISTER.
IN THAT CASE, UH, MAY I CONVINCE YOU TO ASSIST WITH THE ALTAR?
THIS WAY, GOOD SIR.
WATCH OVER THE LEDGER WILL YOU, LAD?
I'M SORRY.
SIR?
I MUST BEG YOUR PARDON.
OH? WHATEVER FOR?
ISKANDER, THE "INSIDE MAN."
D'AH!
ARGH!

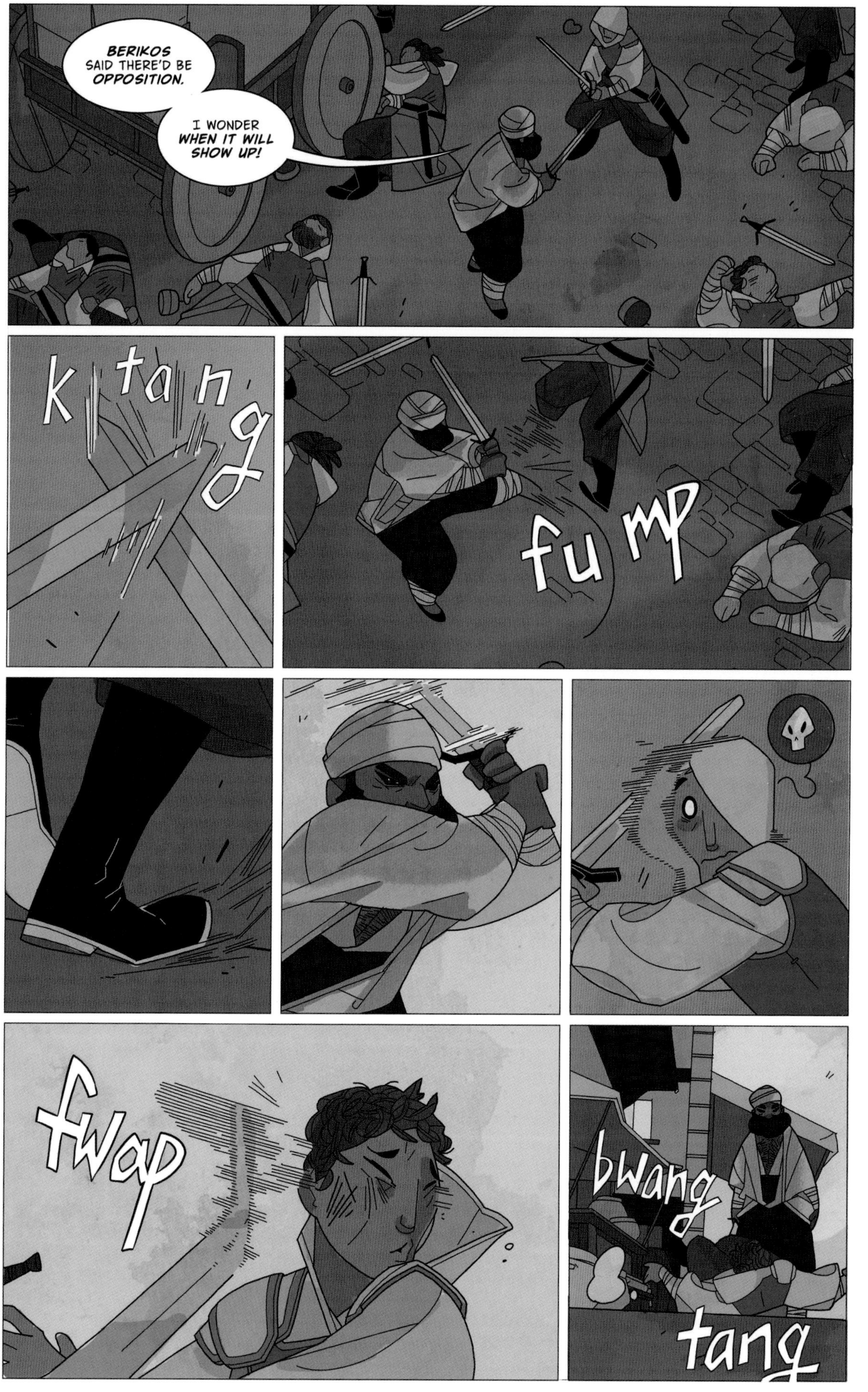
BERIKOS SAID THERE'D BE OPPOSITION.
I WONDER WHEN IT WILL SHOW UP!
ktang
fump
fwap
bwang
tang

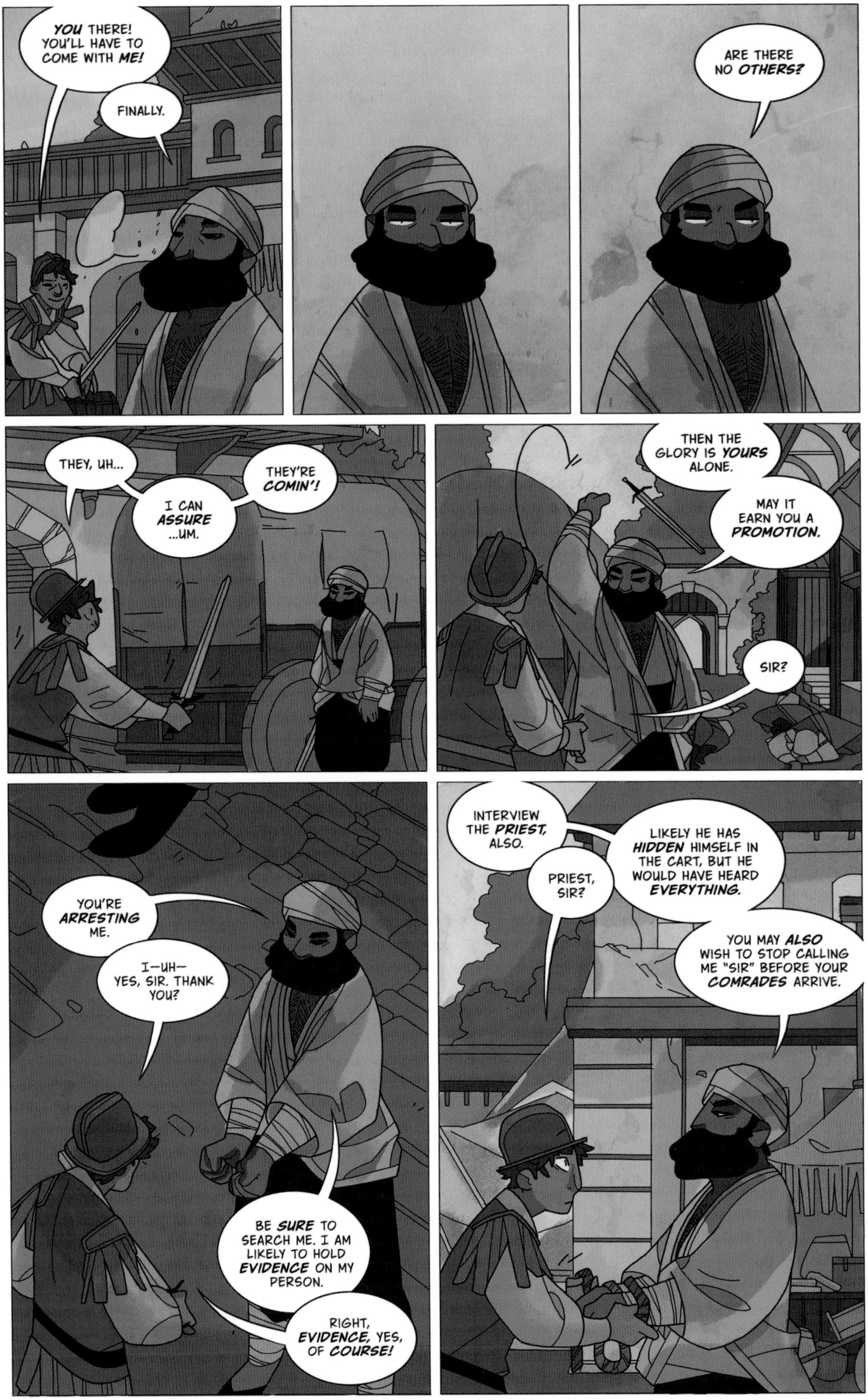

YOU THERE! YOU'LL HAVE TO COME WITH ME!
FINALLY.
ARE THERE NO OTHERS?
THEY, UH...
I CAN ASSURE ...UM.
THEY'RE COMIN'!
THEN THE GLORY IS YOURS ALONE.
MAY IT EARN YOU A PROMOTION.
SIR?
YOU'RE ARRESTING ME.
I—UH— YES, SIR. THANK YOU?
BE SURE TO SEARCH ME. I AM LIKELY TO HOLD EVIDENCE ON MY PERSON.
RIGHT, EVIDENCE, YES, OF COURSE!
INTERVIEW THE PRIEST, ALSO.
PRIEST, SIR?
LIKELY HE HAS HIDDEN HIMSELF IN THE CART, BUT HE WOULD HAVE HEARD EVERYTHING.
YOU MAY ALSO WISH TO STOP CALLING ME "SIR" BEFORE YOUR COMRADES ARRIVE.

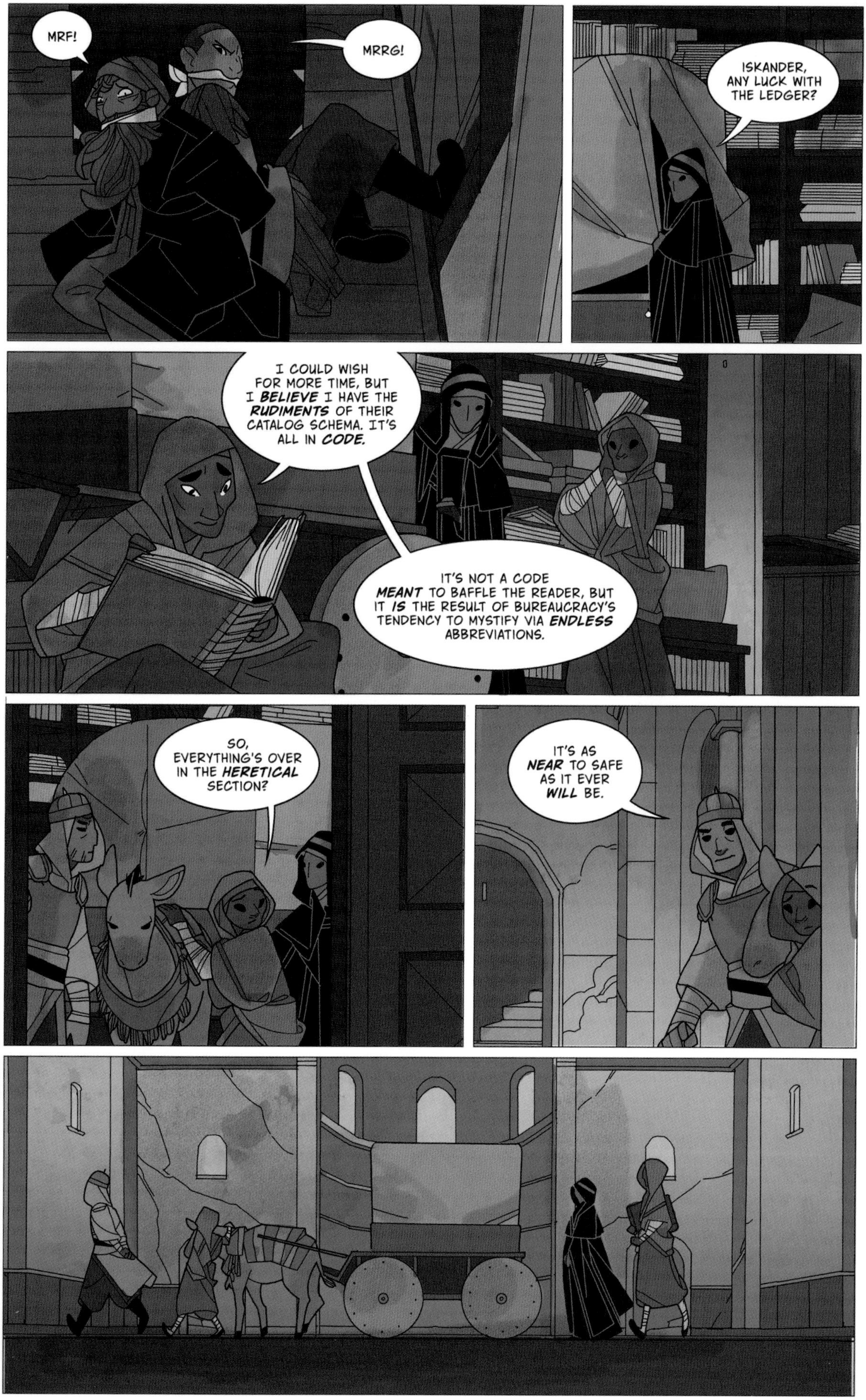
MRF!
MRRG!
ISKANDER, ANY LUCK WITH THE LEDGER?
I COULD WISH FOR MORE TIME, BUT I BELIEVE I HAVE THE RUDIMENTS OF THEIR CATALOG SCHEMA. IT'S ALL IN CODE.
IT'S NOT A CODE MEANT TO BAFFLE THE READER, BUT IT IS THE RESULT OF BUREAUCRACY'S TENDENCY TO MYSTIFY VIA ENDLESS ABBREVIATIONS.
SO, EVERYTHING'S OVER IN THE HERETICAL SECTION?
IT'S AS NEAR TO SAFE AS IT EVER WILL BE.

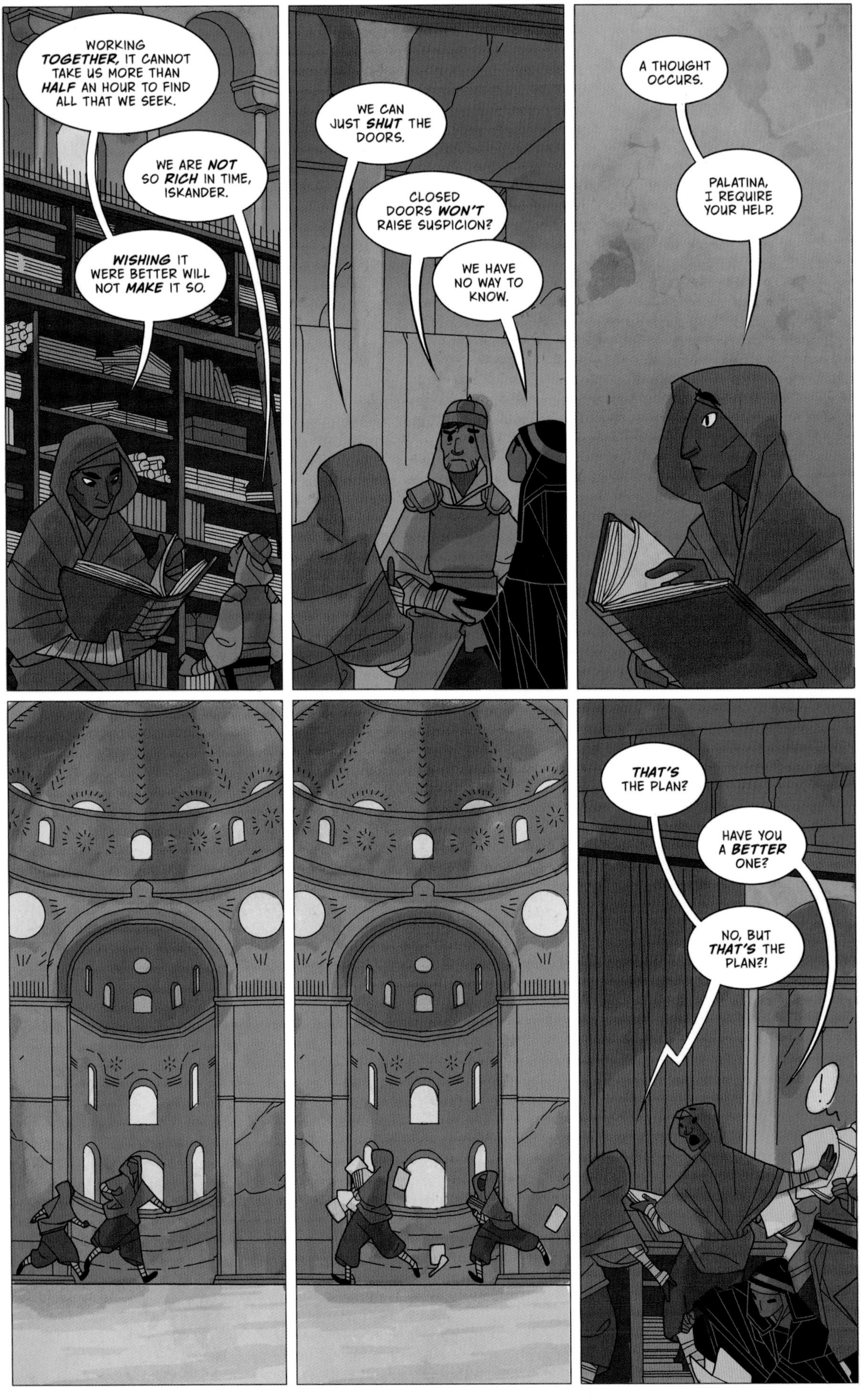
WORKING TOGETHER, IT CANNOT TAKE US MORE THAN HALF AN HOUR TO FIND ALL THAT WE SEEK.
WE ARE NOT SO RICH IN TIME, ISKANDER.
WISHING IT WERE BETTER WILL NOT MAKE IT SO.
WE CAN JUST SHUT THE DOORS.
CLOSED DOORS WON'T RAISE SUSPICION?
WE HAVE NO WAY TO KNOW.
A THOUGHT OCCURS.
PALATINA, I REQUIRE YOUR HELP.
THAT'S THE PLAN?
HAVE YOU A BETTER ONE?
NO, BUT THAT'S THE PLAN?!
!

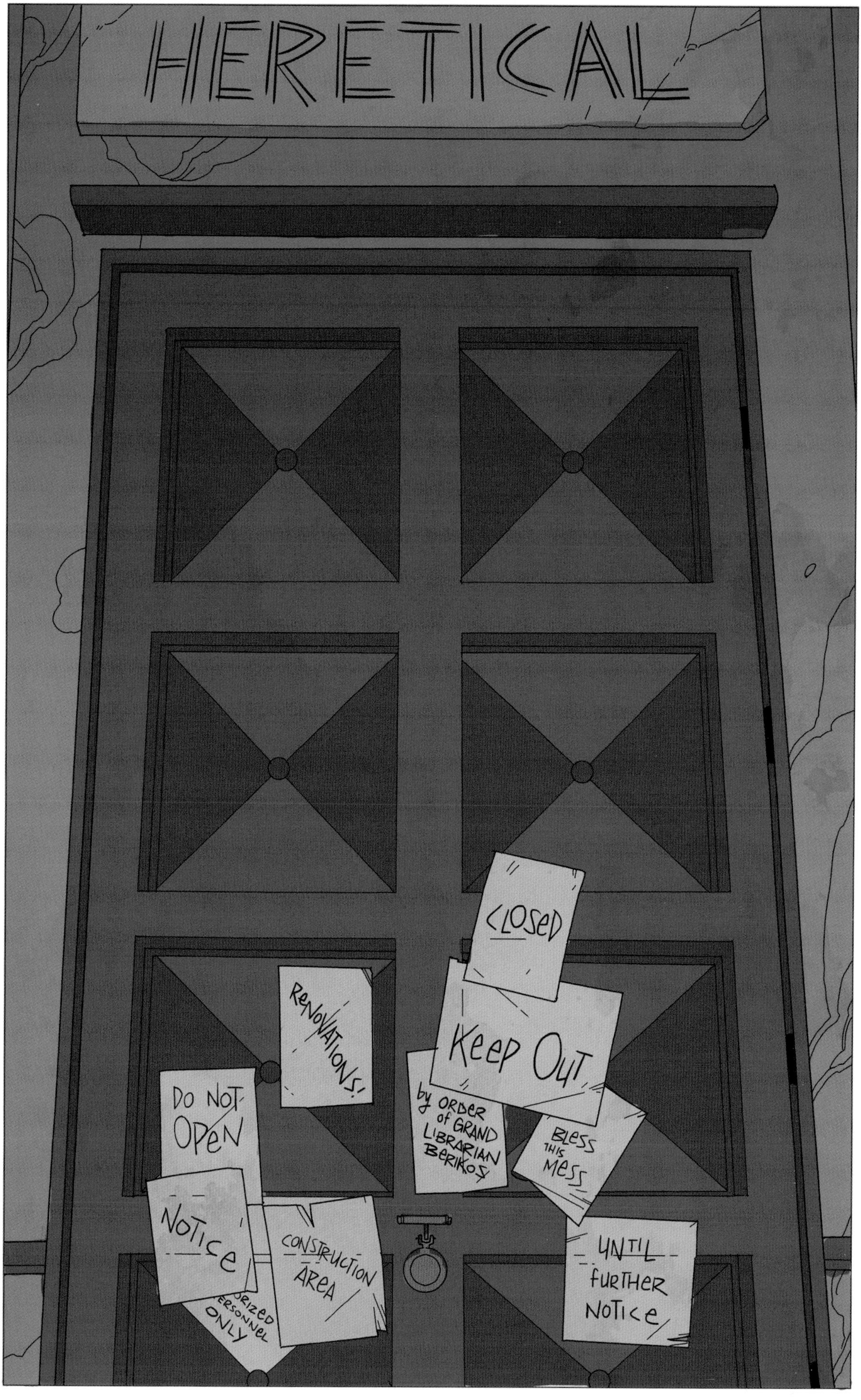
HERETICAL
CLOSED
Keep Out
by ORDER of GRAND LIBRARIAN BERIKOS
BLESS THIS MESS
RENOVATIONS!
DO NOT OPEN
NOTICE
CONSTRUCTION AREA
ORIZED ERSONNEL ONLY
UNTIL FURTHER NOTICE

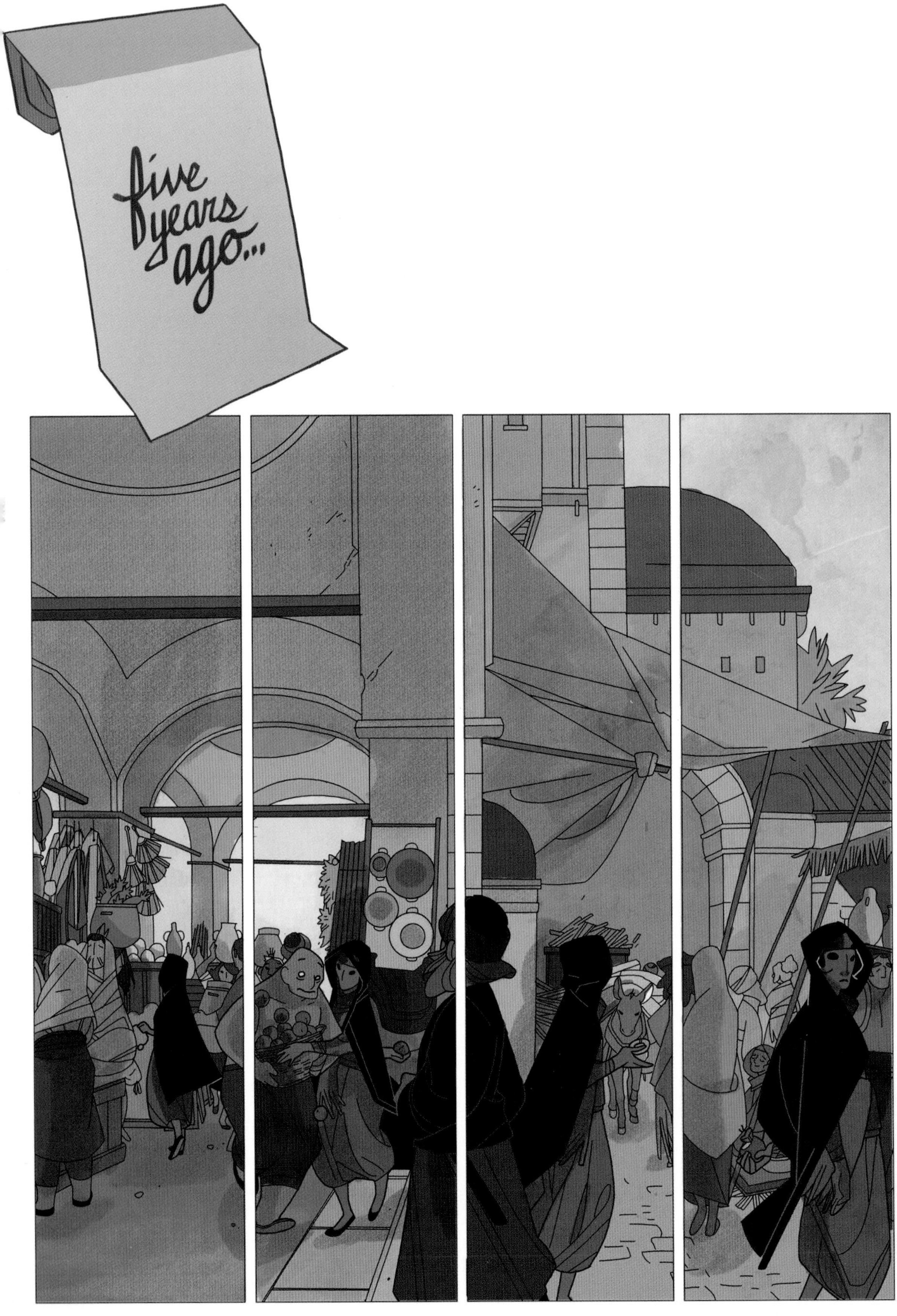
five years ago...

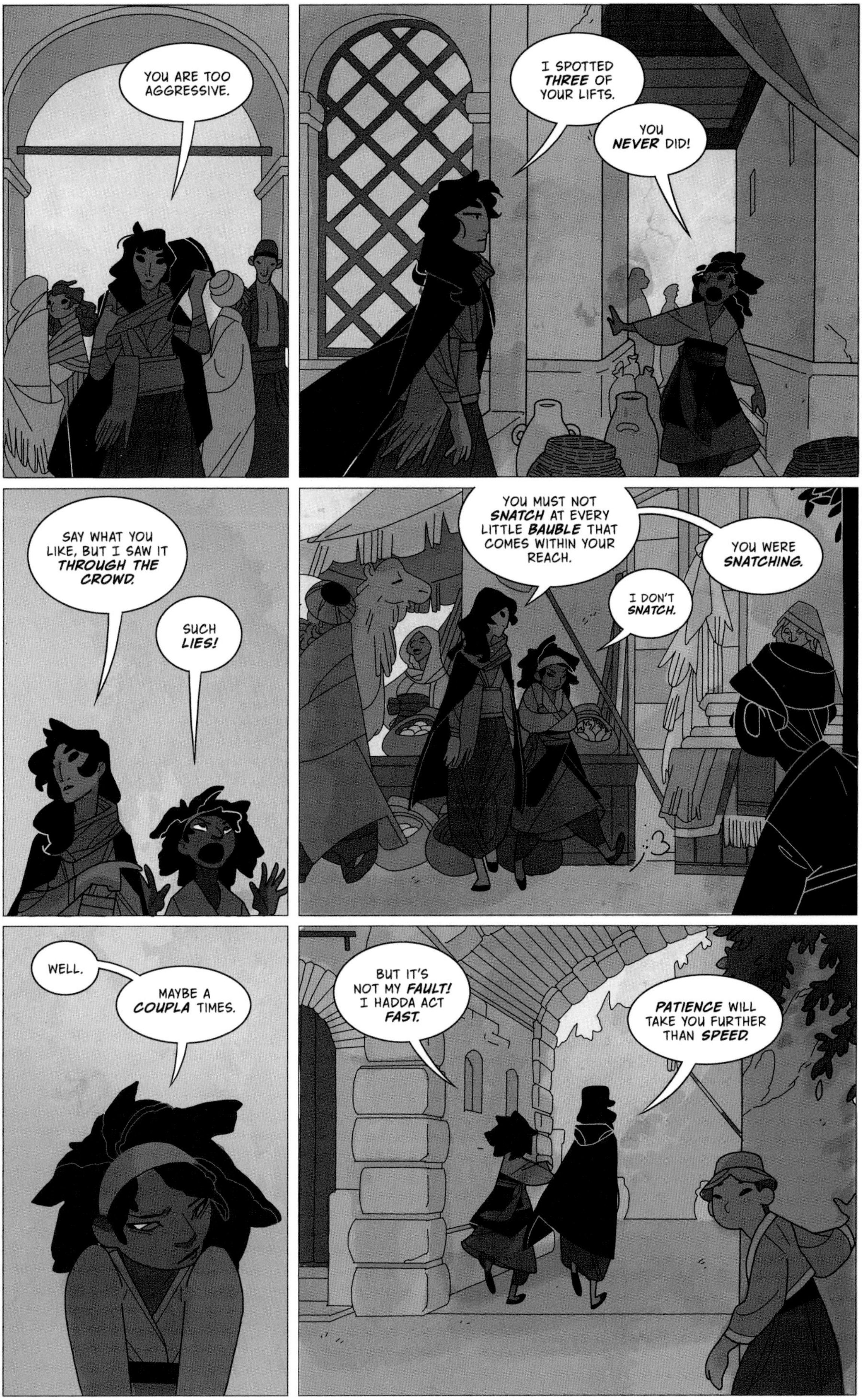
YOU ARE TOO AGGRESSIVE.
I SPOTTED THREE OF YOUR LIFTS.
YOU NEVER DID!
SAY WHAT YOU LIKE, BUT I SAW IT THROUGH THE CROWD.
SUCH LIES!
YOU MUST NOT SNATCH AT EVERY LITTLE BAUBLE THAT COMES WITHIN YOUR REACH.
YOU WERE SNATCHING.
I DON'T SNATCH.
WELL.
MAYBE A COUPLA TIMES.
BUT IT'S NOT MY FAULT! I HADDA ACT FAST.
PATIENCE WILL TAKE YOU FURTHER THAN SPEED.

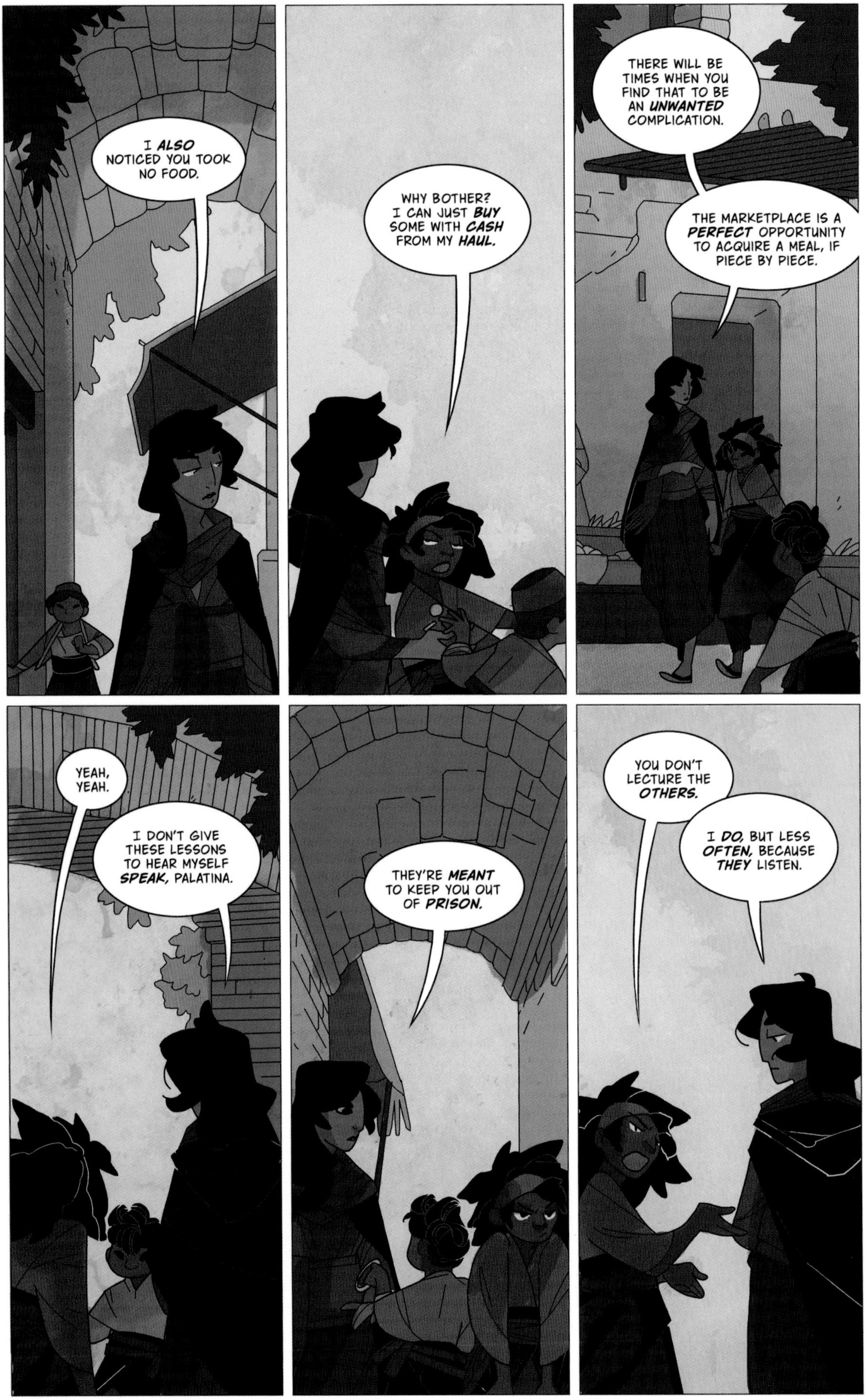
I ALSO NOTICED YOU TOOK NO FOOD.
WHY BOTHER? I CAN JUST BUY SOME WITH CASH FROM MY HAUL.
THERE WILL BE TIMES WHEN YOU FIND THAT TO BE AN UNWANTED COMPLICATION.
THE MARKETPLACE IS A PERFECT OPPORTUNITY TO ACQUIRE A MEAL, IF PIECE BY PIECE.
YEAH, YEAH.
I DON'T GIVE THESE LESSONS TO HEAR MYSELF SPEAK, PALATINA.
THEY'RE MEANT TO KEEP YOU OUT OF PRISON.
YOU DON'T LECTURE THE OTHERS.
I DO, BUT LESS OFTEN, BECAUSE THEY LISTEN.

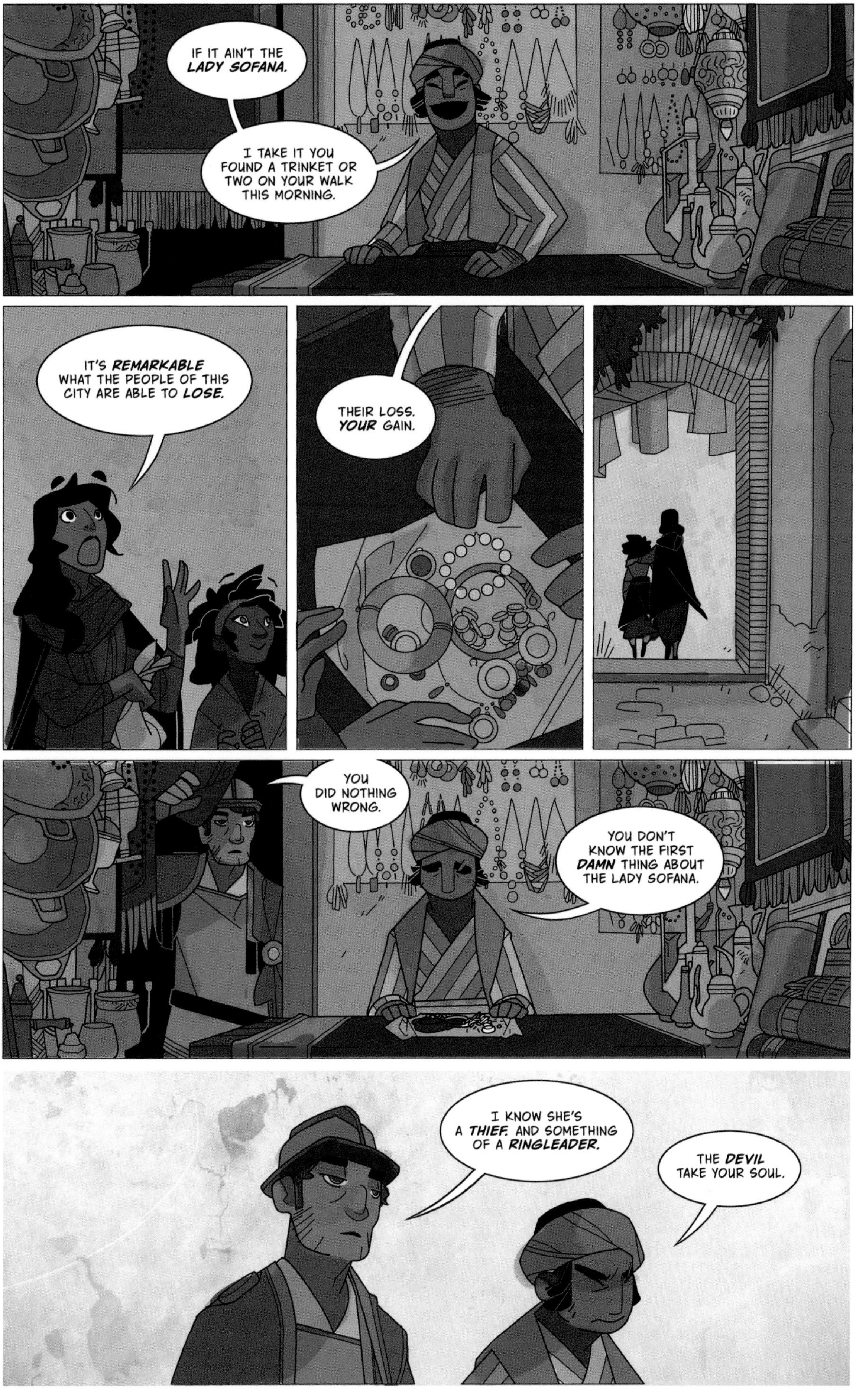

IF IT AIN'T THE *LADY SOFANA.*
I TAKE IT YOU FOUND A TRINKET OR TWO ON YOUR WALK THIS MORNING.
IT'S *REMARKABLE* WHAT THE PEOPLE OF THIS CITY ARE ABLE TO *LOSE.*
THEIR LOSS. *YOUR* GAIN.
YOU DID NOTHING WRONG.
YOU DON'T KNOW THE FIRST *DAMN* THING ABOUT THE LADY SOFANA.
I KNOW SHE'S A *THIEF.* AND SOMETHING OF A *RINGLEADER.*
THE *DEVIL* TAKE YOUR SOUL.

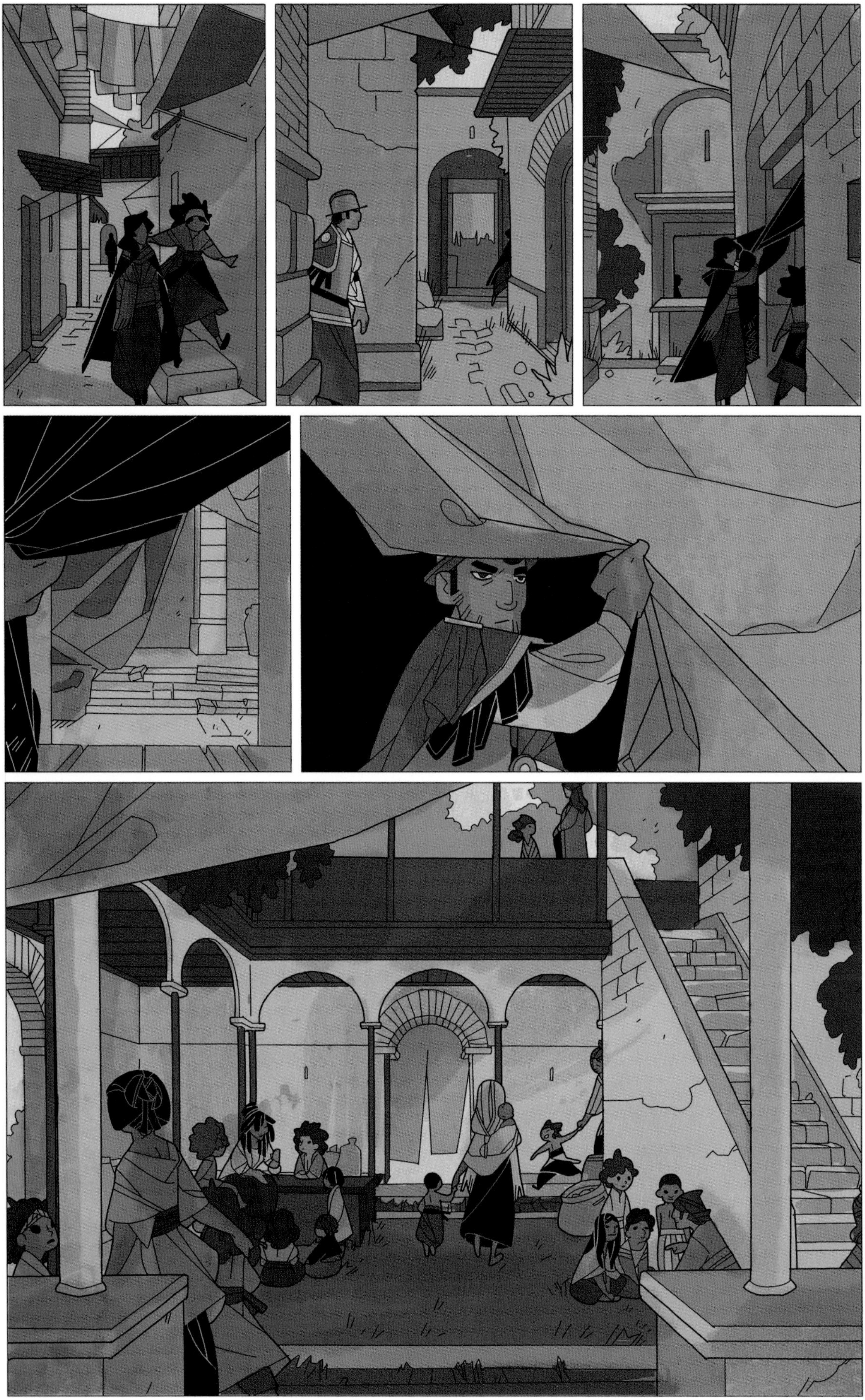

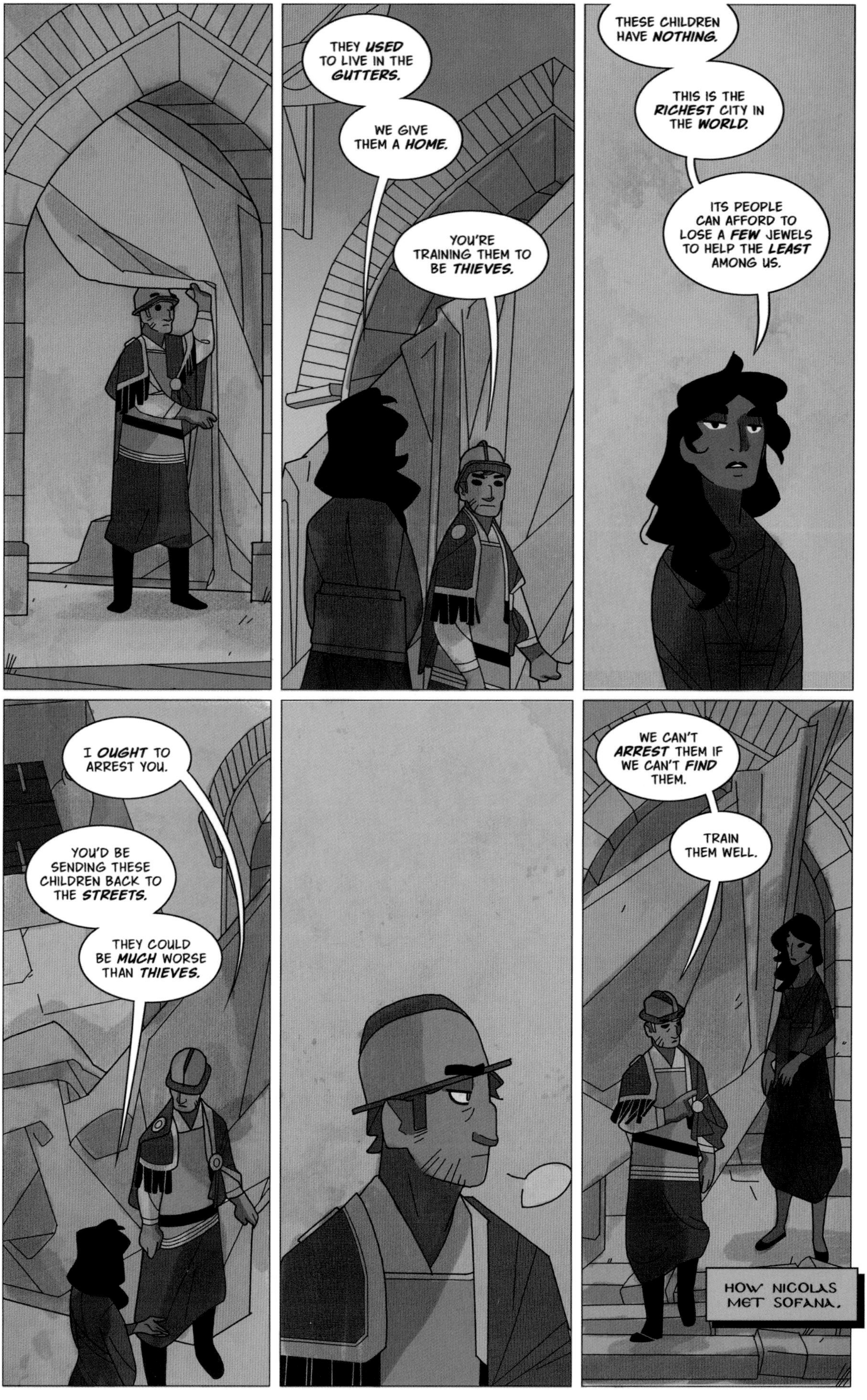
THEY USED TO LIVE IN THE GUTTERS.
WE GIVE THEM A HOME.
YOU'RE TRAINING THEM TO BE THIEVES.
THESE CHILDREN HAVE NOTHING.
THIS IS THE RICHEST CITY IN THE WORLD.
ITS PEOPLE CAN AFFORD TO LOSE A FEW JEWELS TO HELP THE LEAST AMONG US.
I OUGHT TO ARREST YOU.
YOU'D BE SENDING THESE CHILDREN BACK TO THE STREETS.
THEY COULD BE MUCH WORSE THAN THIEVES.
WE CAN'T ARREST THEM IF WE CAN'T FIND THEM.
TRAIN THEM WELL.
HOW NICOLAS MET SOFANA.

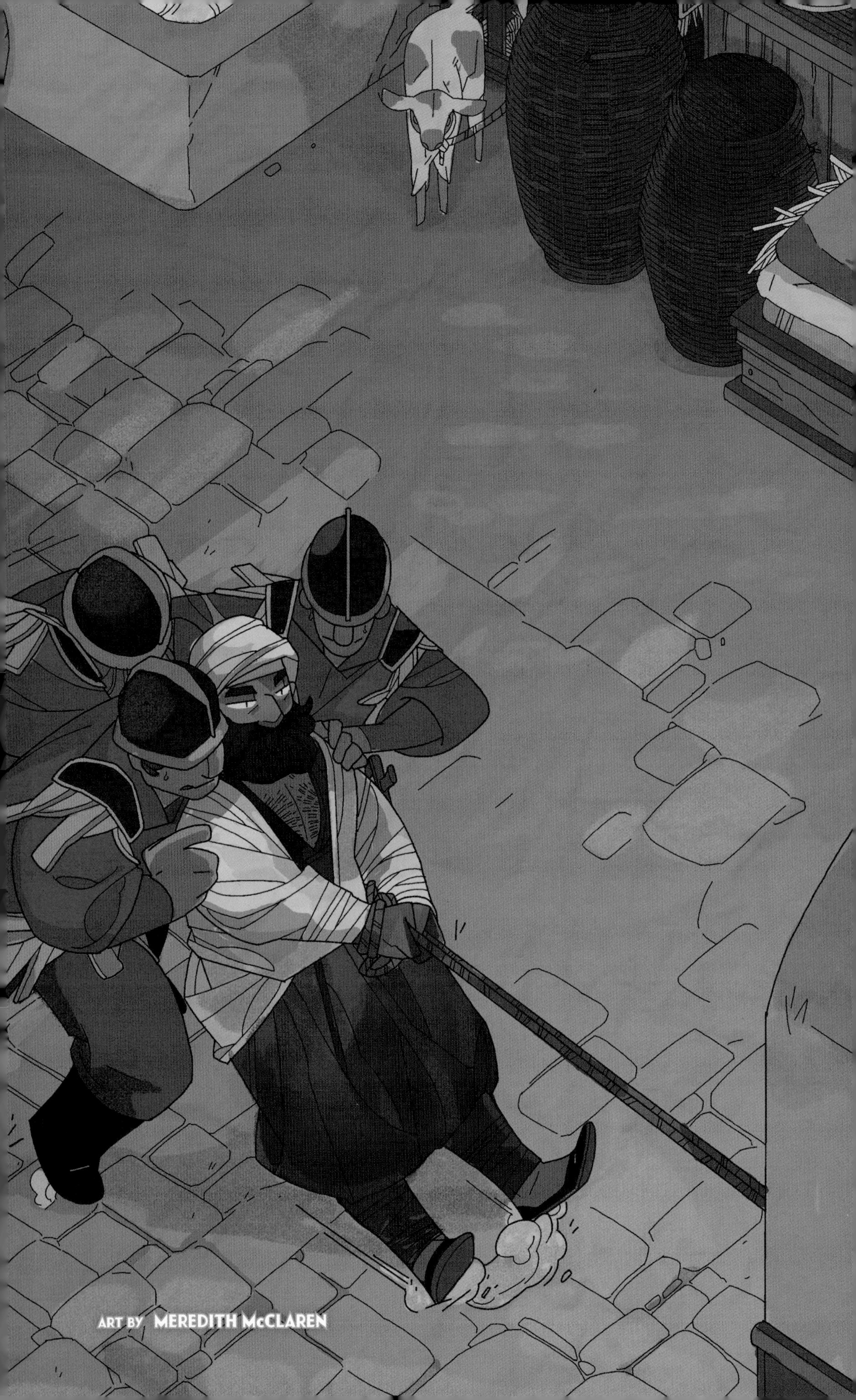
ART BY MEREDITH McCLAREN

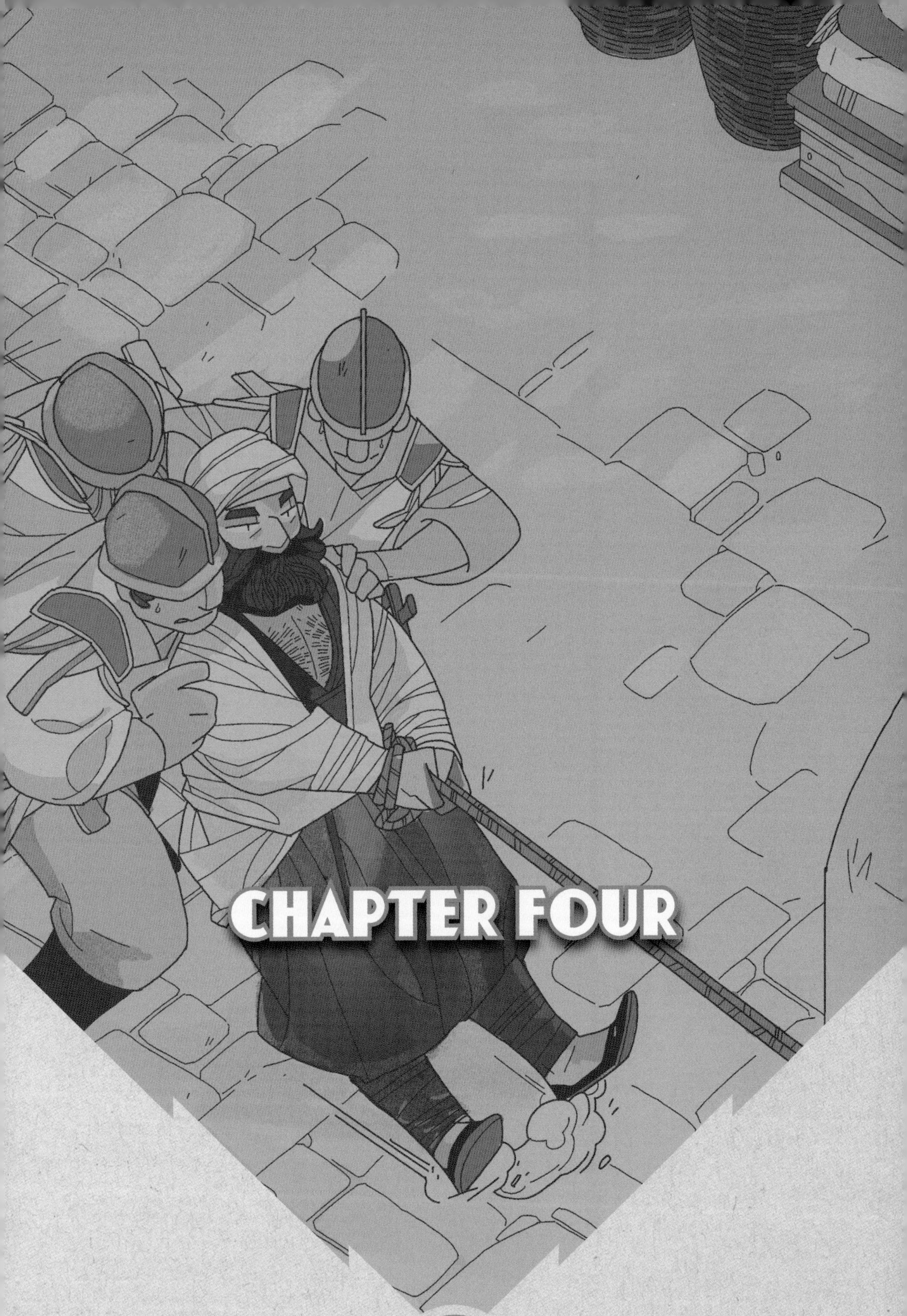

CHAPTER FOUR

4

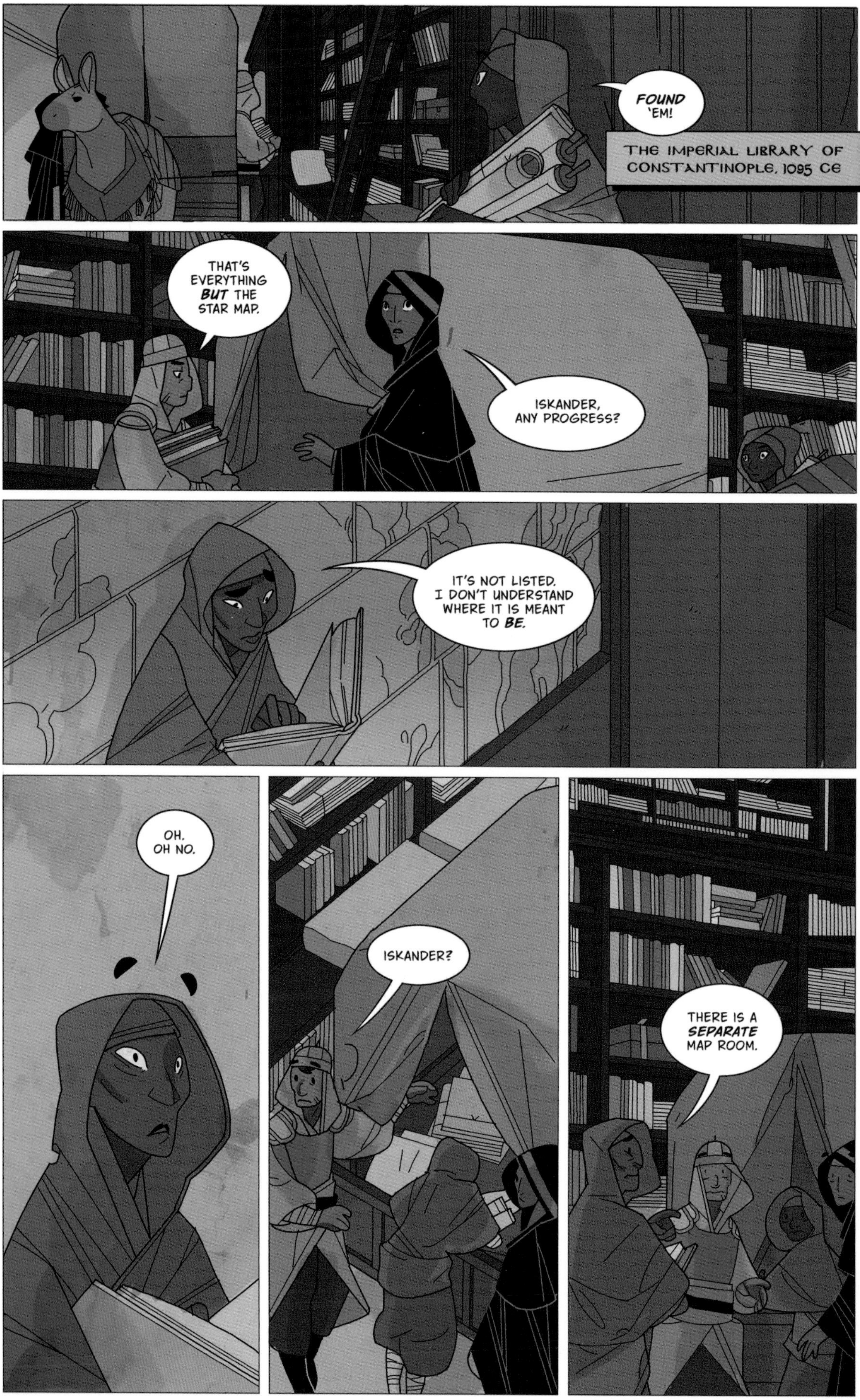
FOUND 'EM!
THE IMPERIAL LIBRARY OF CONSTANTINOPLE, 1095 CE
THAT'S EVERYTHING BUT THE STAR MAP.
ISKANDER, ANY PROGRESS?
IT'S NOT LISTED. I DON'T UNDERSTAND WHERE IT IS MEANT TO BE.
OH. OH NO.
ISKANDER?
THERE IS A SEPARATE MAP ROOM.

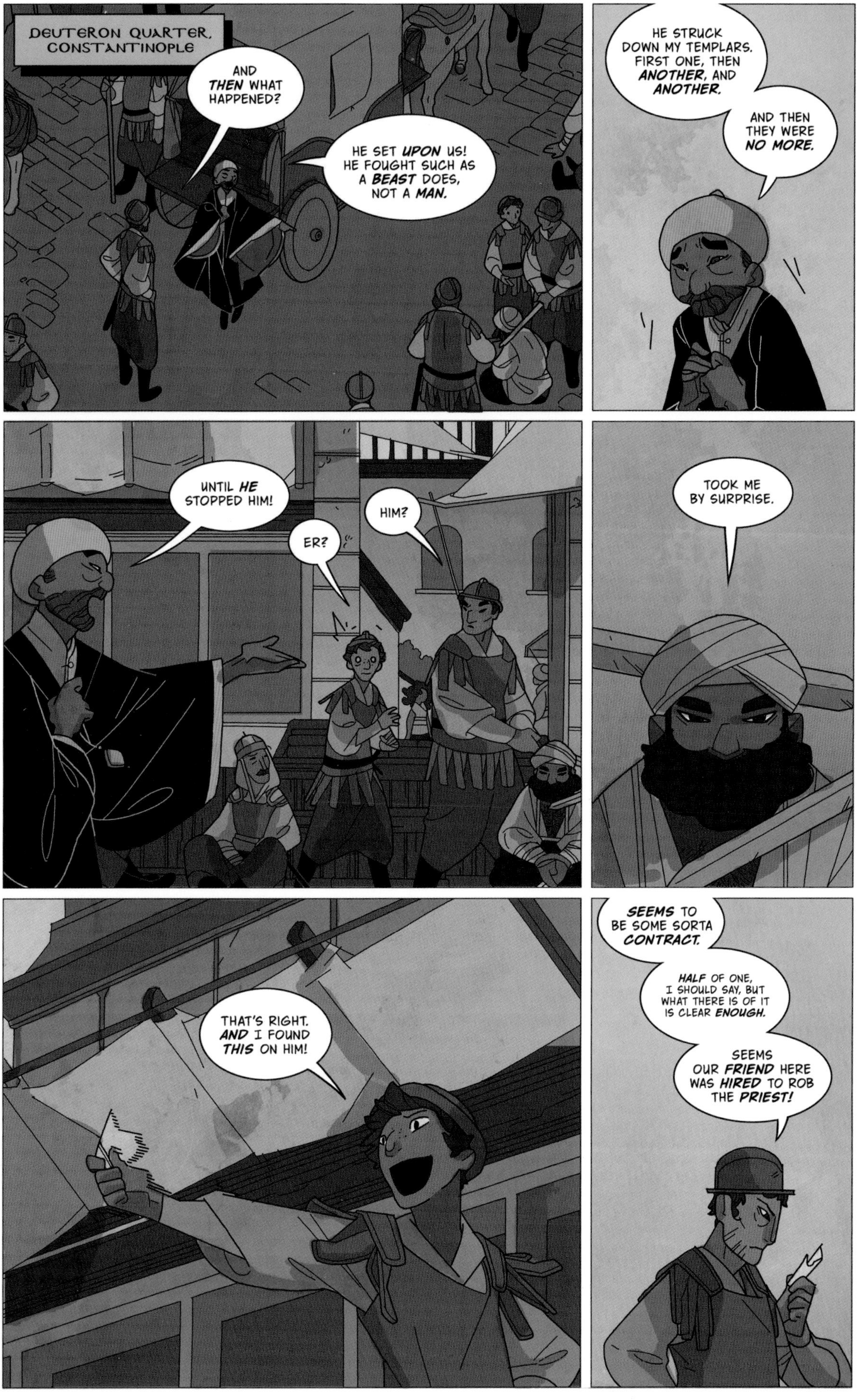
DEUTERON QUARTER, CONSTANTINOPLE
AND THEN WHAT HAPPENED?
HE SET UPON US! HE FOUGHT SUCH AS A BEAST DOES, NOT A MAN.
HE STRUCK DOWN MY TEMPLARS. FIRST ONE, THEN ANOTHER, AND ANOTHER.
AND THEN THEY WERE NO MORE.
UNTIL HE STOPPED HIM!
ER?
HIM?
TOOK ME BY SURPRISE.
THAT'S RIGHT. AND I FOUND THIS ON HIM!
SEEMS TO BE SOME SORTA CONTRACT.
HALF OF ONE, I SHOULD SAY, BUT WHAT THERE IS OF IT IS CLEAR ENOUGH.
SEEMS OUR FRIEND HERE WAS HIRED TO ROB THE PRIEST!

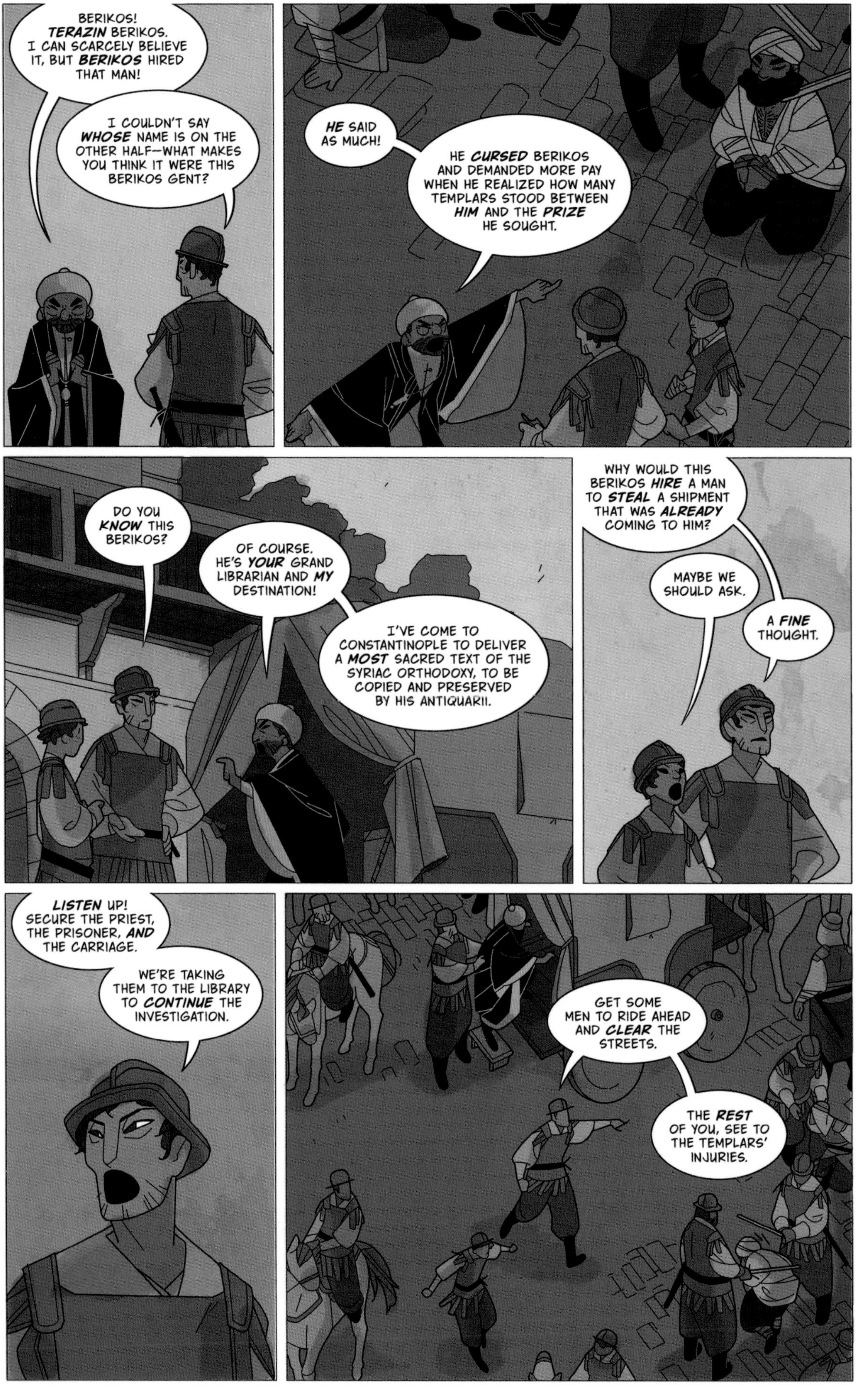
BERIKOS! TERAZIN BERIKOS. I CAN SCARCELY BELIEVE IT, BUT BERIKOS HIRED THAT MAN!
I COULDN'T SAY WHOSE NAME IS ON THE OTHER HALF—WHAT MAKES YOU THINK IT WERE THIS BERIKOS GENT?
HE SAID AS MUCH!
HE CURSED BERIKOS AND DEMANDED MORE PAY WHEN HE REALIZED HOW MANY TEMPLARS STOOD BETWEEN HIM AND THE PRIZE HE SOUGHT.
DO YOU KNOW THIS BERIKOS?
OF COURSE. HE'S YOUR GRAND LIBRARIAN AND MY DESTINATION!
I'VE COME TO CONSTANTINOPLE TO DELIVER A MOST SACRED TEXT OF THE SYRIAC ORTHODOXY, TO BE COPIED AND PRESERVED BY HIS ANTIQUARII.
WHY WOULD THIS BERIKOS HIRE A MAN TO STEAL A SHIPMENT THAT WAS ALREADY COMING TO HIM?
MAYBE WE SHOULD ASK.
A FINE THOUGHT.
LISTEN UP! SECURE THE PRIEST, THE PRISONER, AND THE CARRIAGE.
WE'RE TAKING THEM TO THE LIBRARY TO CONTINUE THE INVESTIGATION.
GET SOME MEN TO RIDE AHEAD AND CLEAR THE STREETS.
THE REST OF YOU, SEE TO THE TEMPLARS' INJURIES.

NEVER HAVE I SEEN THE FRONT DESK IN SUCH DISARRAY!

CODICIER LEONIUS SAYS OUR EXCESSIVE YAWNING THREATENS EVERY FACET OF ORDERLY SOCIETY— PERHAPS IT IS SO?

EH? WHAT IS THIS?

JACOBUS!

CLOSED

KEEP OUT

BY ORDER OF SOUND LIBRARIAN SERVICES

BLESS THIS MESS

REVITALIZE!

NO PEN

UNTIL FURTHER NOTICE

NOTICE

CONSTRUCTION AREA

DID YOU KNOW OF THESE RENOVATIONS?

HMM?

RENOVATIONS?

HERETICAL

I RECALL NO SCHEDULED RENOVATIONS.

DO YOU HEAR SOMETHING?

HRRMRR!

MMMR!

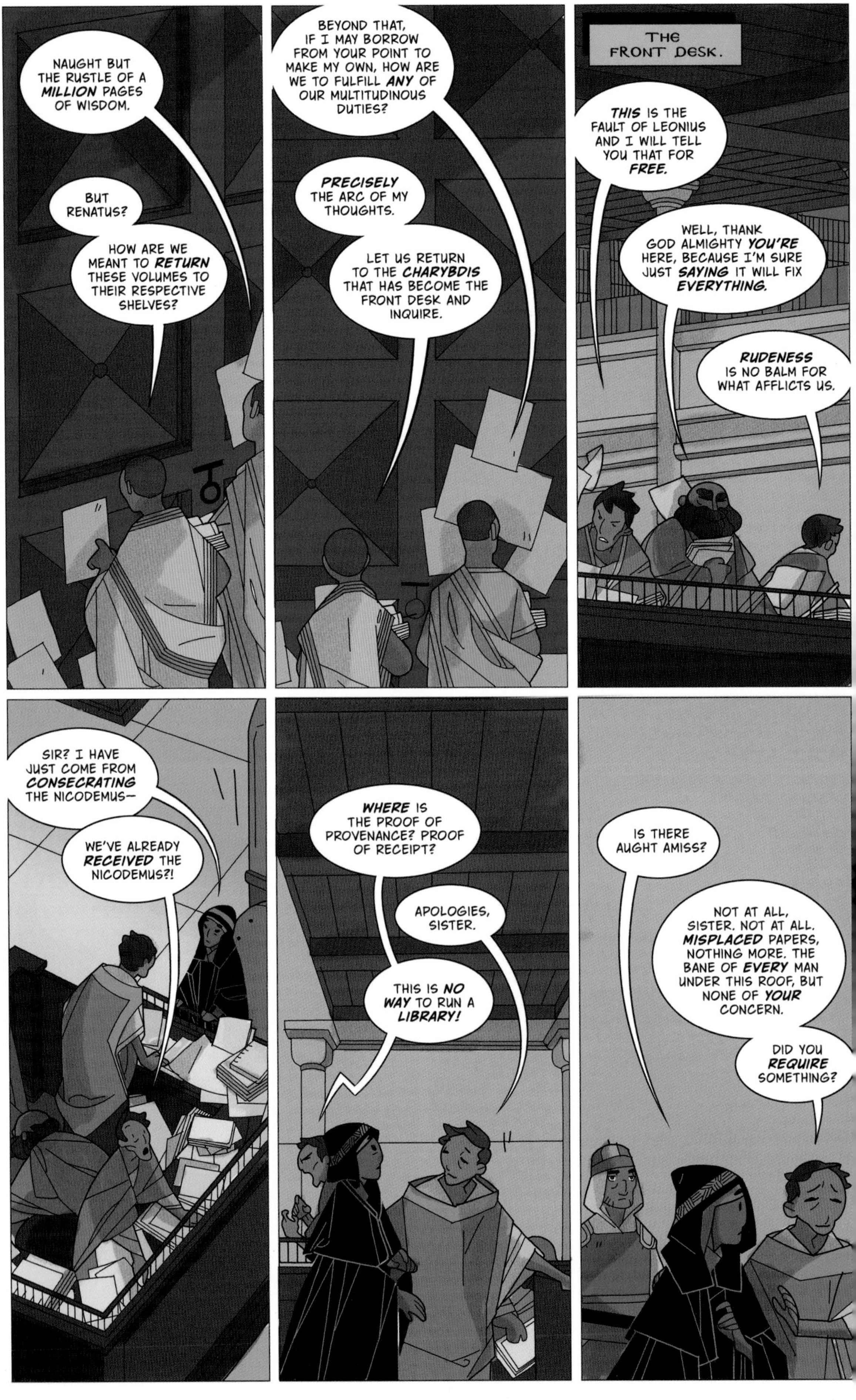
NAUGHT BUT THE RUSTLE OF A MILLION PAGES OF WISDOM.
BUT RENATUS?
HOW ARE WE MEANT TO RETURN THESE VOLUMES TO THEIR RESPECTIVE SHELVES?
BEYOND THAT, IF I MAY BORROW FROM YOUR POINT TO MAKE MY OWN, HOW ARE WE TO FULFILL ANY OF OUR MULTITUDINOUS DUTIES?
PRECISELY THE ARC OF MY THOUGHTS.
LET US RETURN TO THE CHARYBDIS THAT HAS BECOME THE FRONT DESK AND INQUIRE.
THE FRONT DESK.
THIS IS THE FAULT OF LEONIUS AND I WILL TELL YOU THAT FOR FREE.
WELL, THANK GOD ALMIGHTY YOU'RE HERE, BECAUSE I'M SURE JUST SAYING IT WILL FIX EVERYTHING.
RUDENESS IS NO BALM FOR WHAT AFFLICTS US.
SIR? I HAVE JUST COME FROM CONSECRATING THE NICODEMUS—
WE'VE ALREADY RECEIVED THE NICODEMUS?!
WHERE IS THE PROOF OF PROVENANCE? PROOF OF RECEIPT?
APOLOGIES, SISTER.
THIS IS NO WAY TO RUN A LIBRARY!
IS THERE AUGHT AMISS?
NOT AT ALL, SISTER. NOT AT ALL. MISPLACED PAPERS, NOTHING MORE. THE BANE OF EVERY MAN UNDER THIS ROOF, BUT NONE OF YOUR CONCERN.
DID YOU REQUIRE SOMETHING?

THE IMPERIAL LIBRARY OF CONSTANTINOPLE IS KNOWN THROUGHOUT THE WORLD FOR THE **BREADTH** OF ITS COLLECTIONS.

I MUST **CONFESS** A WEAKNESS FOR THE TOOLS AND PRACTICES OF **CARTOGRAPHY.**

AH, ALLOW ME A **GUESS**, SISTER, THAT IT MAY SAVE YOU THE EMBARRASSMENT OF BEGGING A FAVOR.

YOU MIGHT **BENEFIT** BY A TOUR OF OUR **RENOWNED** MAP ROOM, YES?

OH, I COULD SCARCELY—

NOT AT ALL! INDEED, YOU WOULD DO **ME** A FAVOR BY ACCEPTING. I SO **RARELY** HAVE AN OPPORTUNITY TO VISIT THE UPPER LEVEL.

YOU DO NOT **MIND?**

SISTER, THE **EMPEROR** CONSIDERS THE DELIVERY OF YOUR NICODEMUS TO BE A **PARTICULAR** FAVOR TO HIM AND TO THE EMPIRE.

THE CITY AND ITS WONDERS ARE OPEN TO YOU. IT IS MY DUTY **AND** HONOR TO ATTEND TO YOUR SAFETY AS LONG AS YOU WISH TO STAY.

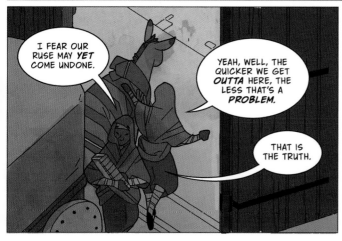

I FEAR OUR RUSE MAY **YET** COME UNDONE.

YEAH, WELL, THE QUICKER WE GET **OUTTA** HERE, THE LESS THAT'S A **PROBLEM.**

THAT IS THE TRUTH.

BUT CONFUSING OUR ENEMIES WILL BE OF GREATER BENEFIT TO NICOLAS AND SOFANA'S ESCAPE.

ISKANDER!

DAMMIT, **WAIT!**

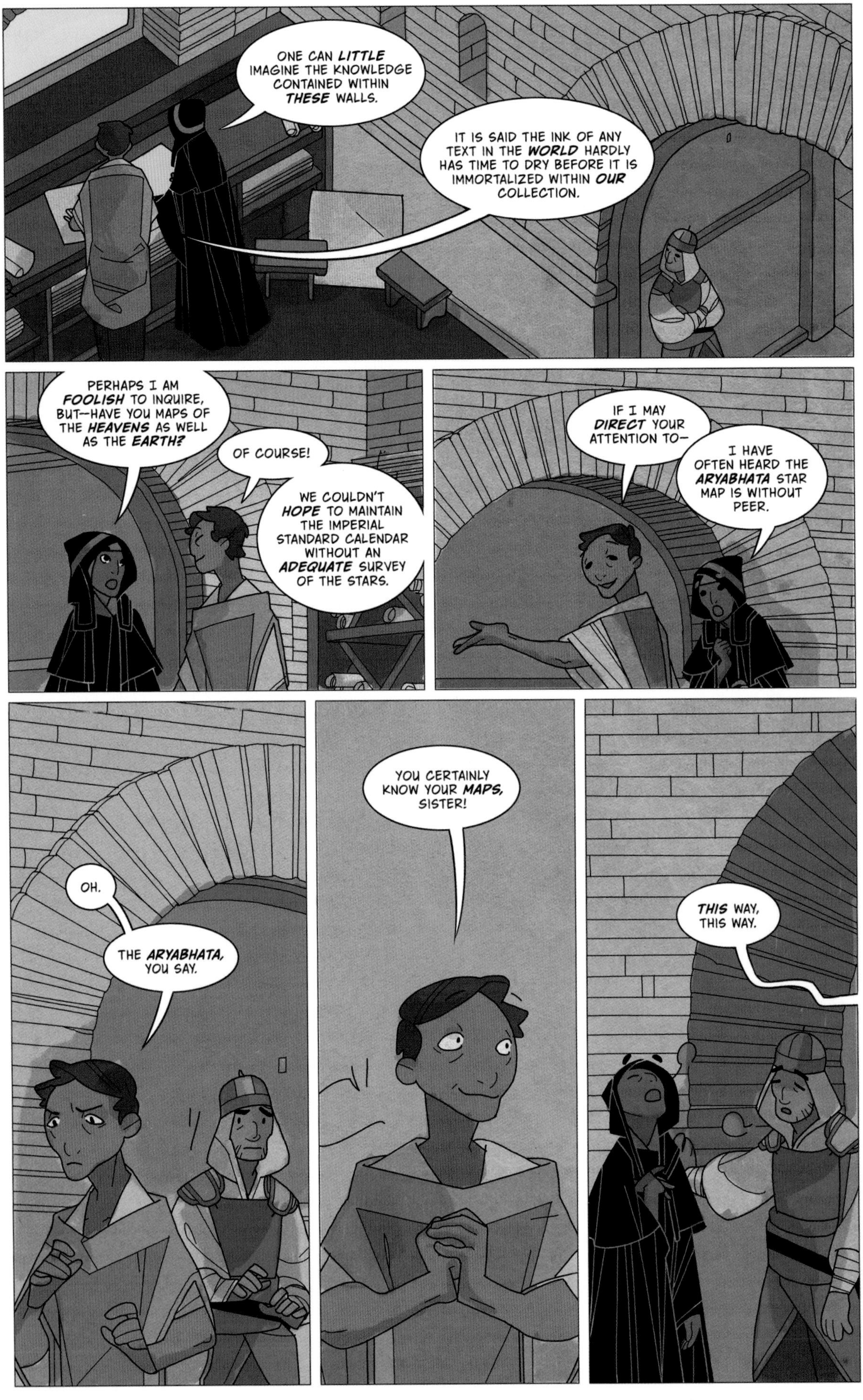
ONE CAN LITTLE IMAGINE THE KNOWLEDGE CONTAINED WITHIN THESE WALLS.
IT IS SAID THE INK OF ANY TEXT IN THE WORLD HARDLY HAS TIME TO DRY BEFORE IT IS IMMORTALIZED WITHIN OUR COLLECTION.
PERHAPS I AM FOOLISH TO INQUIRE, BUT--HAVE YOU MAPS OF THE HEAVENS AS WELL AS THE EARTH?
OF COURSE!
WE COULDN'T HOPE TO MAINTAIN THE IMPERIAL STANDARD CALENDAR WITHOUT AN ADEQUATE SURVEY OF THE STARS.
IF I MAY DIRECT YOUR ATTENTION TO—
I HAVE OFTEN HEARD THE ARYABHATA STAR MAP IS WITHOUT PEER.
OH.
THE ARYABHATA, YOU SAY.
YOU CERTAINLY KNOW YOUR MAPS, SISTER!
THIS WAY, THIS WAY.

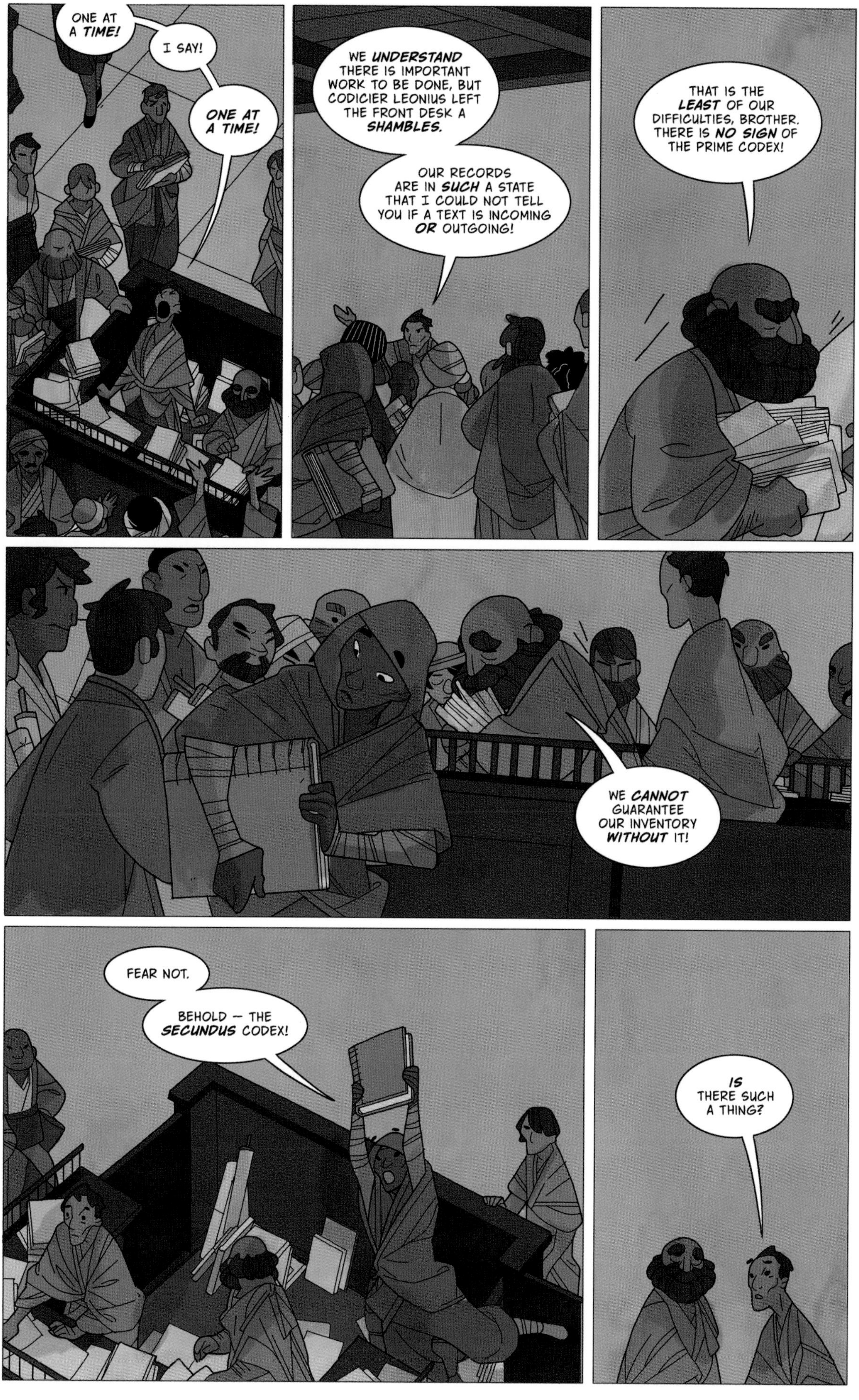
ONE AT A TIME!
I SAY!
ONE AT A TIME!
WE UNDERSTAND THERE IS IMPORTANT WORK TO BE DONE, BUT CODICIER LEONIUS LEFT THE FRONT DESK A SHAMBLES.
OUR RECORDS ARE IN SUCH A STATE THAT I COULD NOT TELL YOU IF A TEXT IS INCOMING OR OUTGOING!
THAT IS THE LEAST OF OUR DIFFICULTIES, BROTHER. THERE IS NO SIGN OF THE PRIME CODEX!
WE CANNOT GUARANTEE OUR INVENTORY WITHOUT IT!
FEAR NOT.
BEHOLD — THE SECUNDUS CODEX!
IS THERE SUCH A THING?

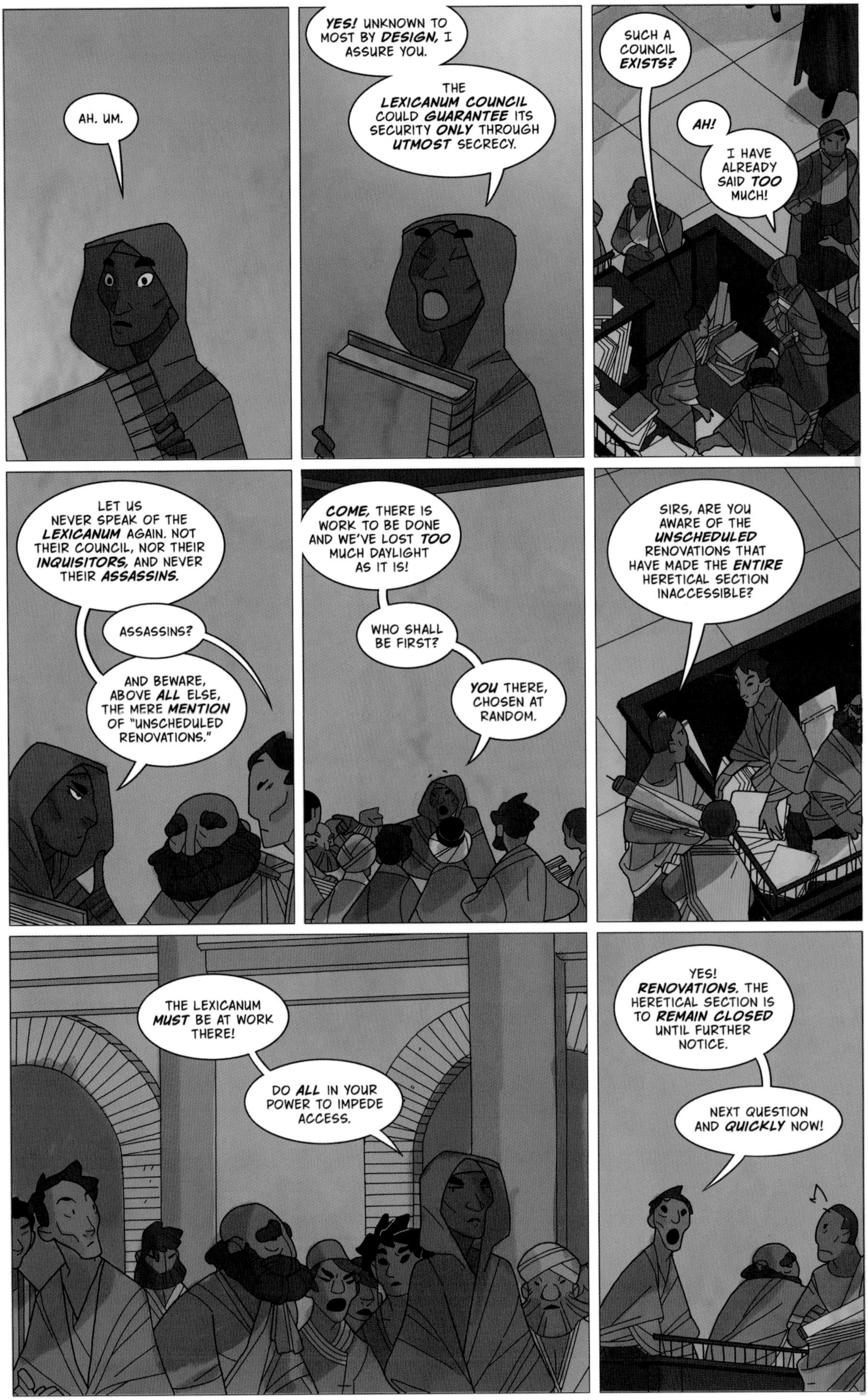
AH. UM.
YES! UNKNOWN TO MOST BY DESIGN, I ASSURE YOU.
THE LEXICANUM COUNCIL COULD GUARANTEE ITS SECURITY ONLY THROUGH UTMOST SECRECY.
SUCH A COUNCIL EXISTS?
AH!
I HAVE ALREADY SAID TOO MUCH!
LET US NEVER SPEAK OF THE LEXICANUM AGAIN. NOT THEIR COUNCIL, NOR THEIR INQUISITORS, AND NEVER THEIR ASSASSINS.
ASSASSINS?
AND BEWARE, ABOVE ALL ELSE, THE MERE MENTION OF "UNSCHEDULED RENOVATIONS."
COME, THERE IS WORK TO BE DONE AND WE'VE LOST TOO MUCH DAYLIGHT AS IT IS!
WHO SHALL BE FIRST?
YOU THERE, CHOSEN AT RANDOM.
SIRS, ARE YOU AWARE OF THE UNSCHEDULED RENOVATIONS THAT HAVE MADE THE ENTIRE HERETICAL SECTION INACCESSIBLE?
THE LEXICANUM MUST BE AT WORK THERE!
DO ALL IN YOUR POWER TO IMPEDE ACCESS.
YES! RENOVATIONS. THE HERETICAL SECTION IS TO REMAIN CLOSED UNTIL FURTHER NOTICE.
NEXT QUESTION AND QUICKLY NOW!

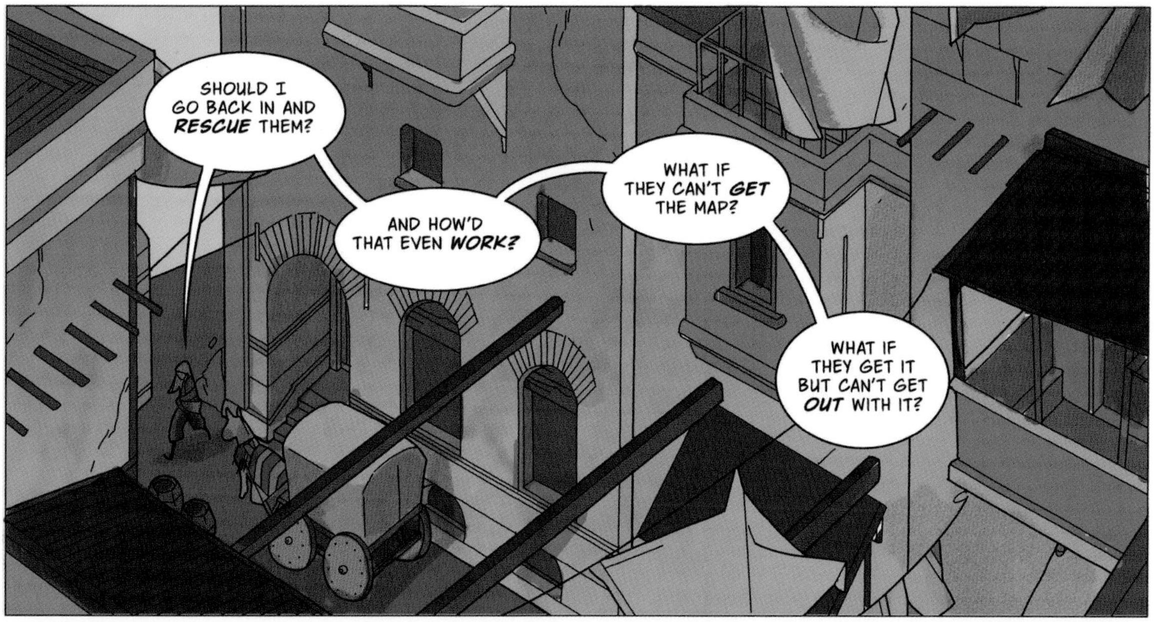
SHOULD I GO BACK IN AND RESCUE THEM?
AND HOW'D THAT EVEN WORK?
WHAT IF THEY CAN'T GET THE MAP?
WHAT IF THEY GET IT BUT CAN'T GET OUT WITH IT?

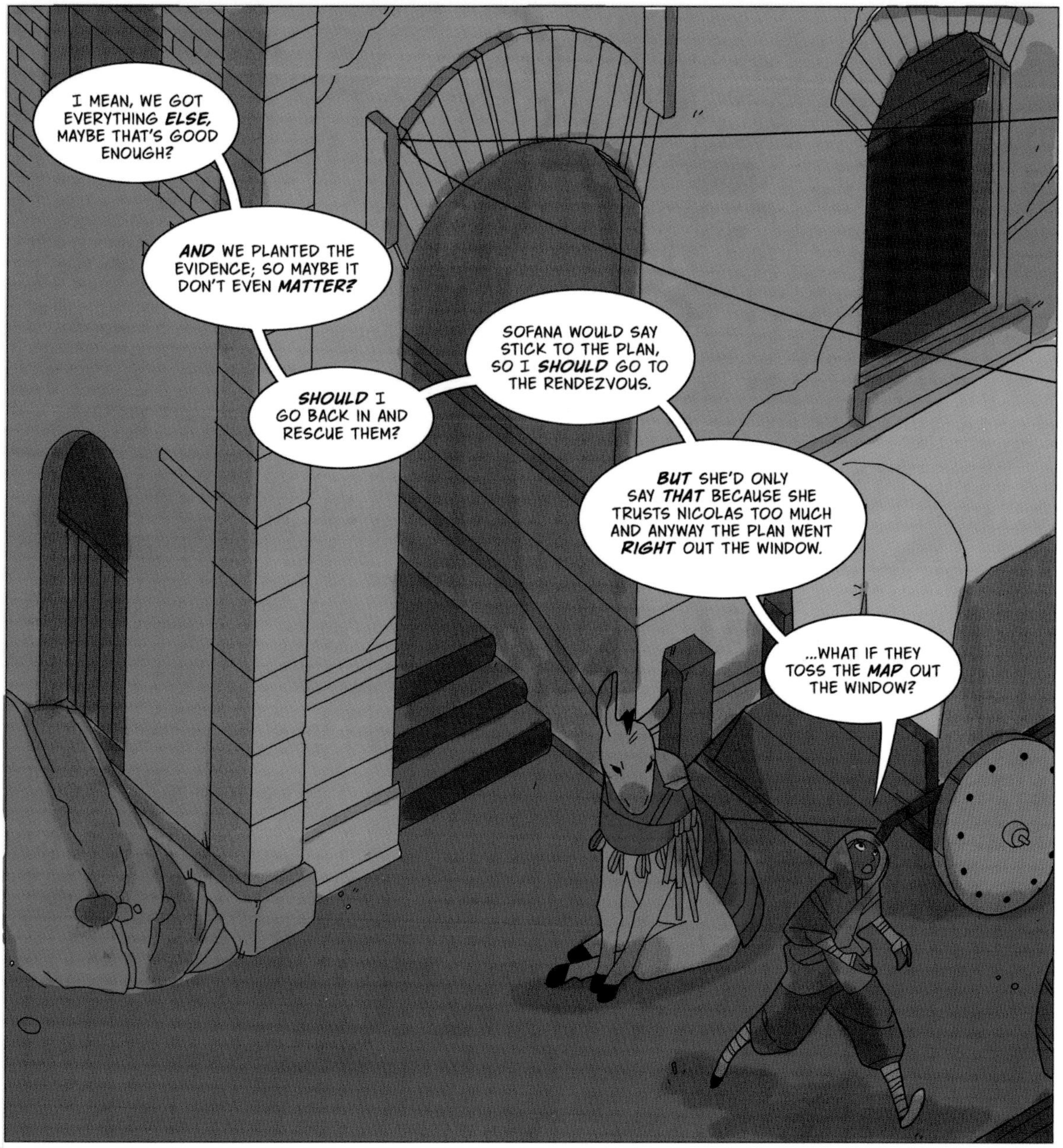
I MEAN, WE GOT EVERYTHING ELSE, MAYBE THAT'S GOOD ENOUGH?
AND WE PLANTED THE EVIDENCE; SO MAYBE IT DON'T EVEN MATTER?
SHOULD I GO BACK IN AND RESCUE THEM?
SOFANA WOULD SAY STICK TO THE PLAN, SO I SHOULD GO TO THE RENDEZVOUS.
BUT SHE'D ONLY SAY THAT BECAUSE SHE TRUSTS NICOLAS TOO MUCH AND ANYWAY THE PLAN WENT RIGHT OUT THE WINDOW.
...WHAT IF THEY TOSS THE MAP OUT THE WINDOW?

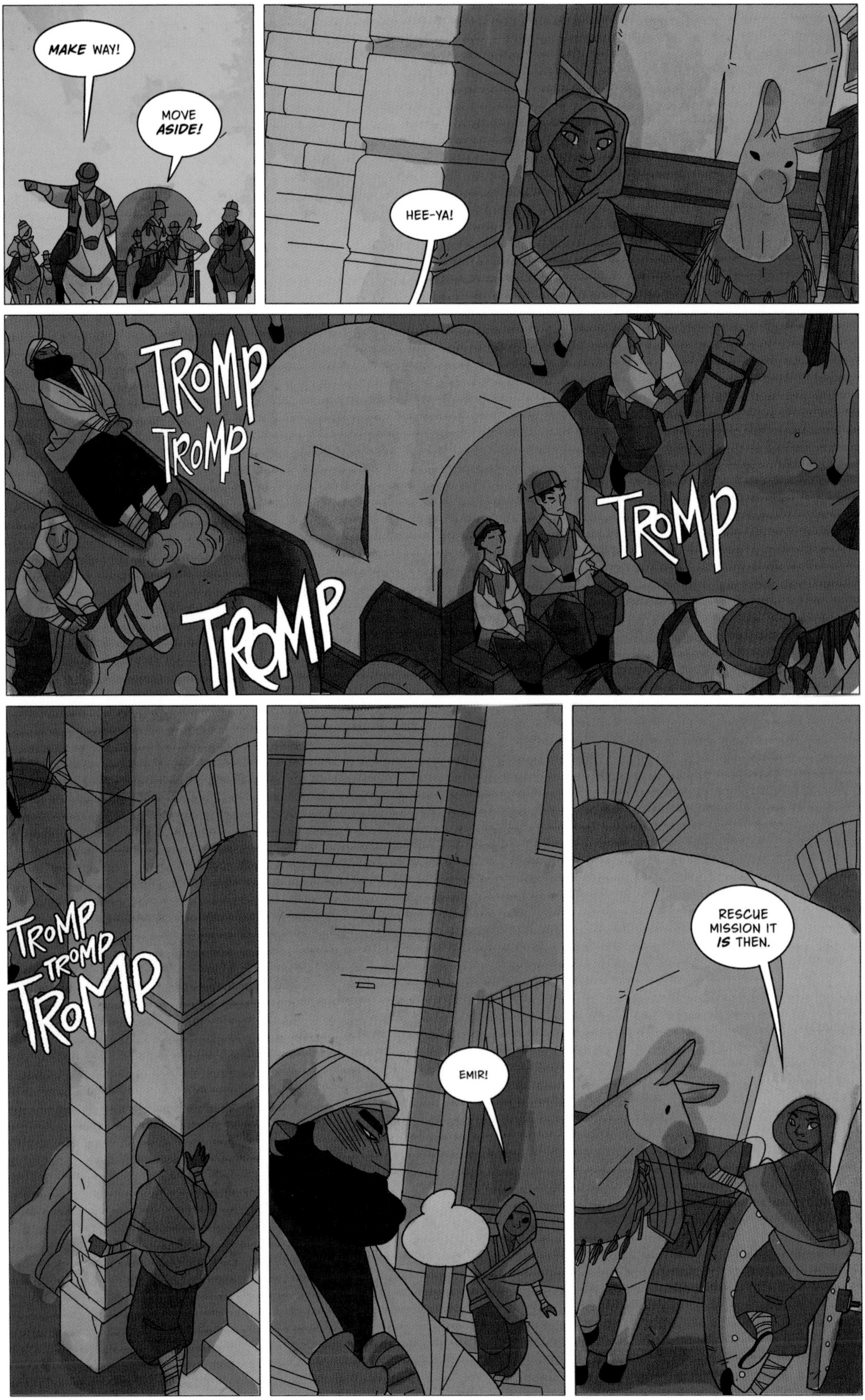
MAKE WAY!
MOVE ASIDE!
HEE-YA!
TROMP
TROMP
TROMP
TROMP
TROMP
TROMP
TROMP
EMIR!
RESCUE MISSION IT IS THEN.

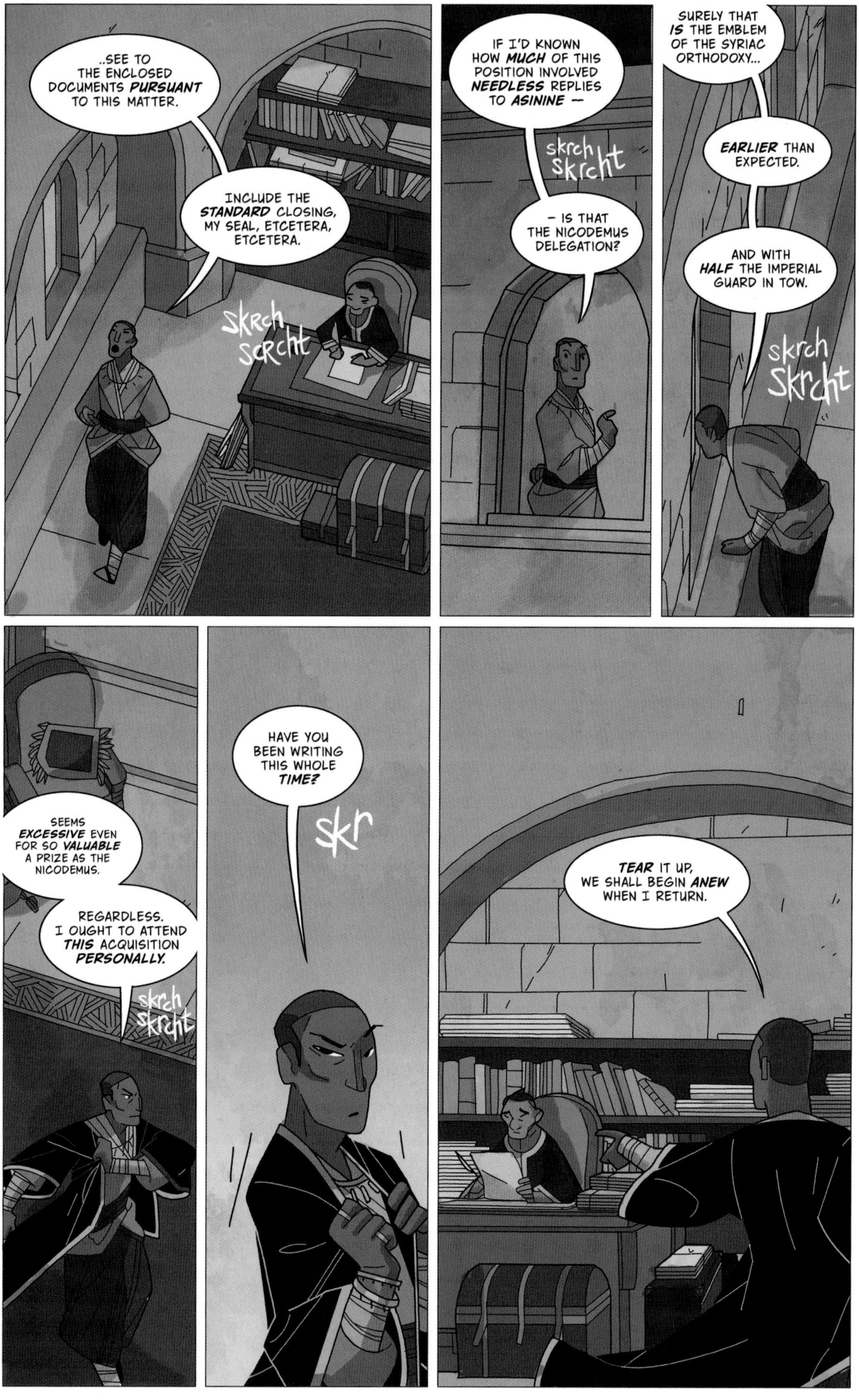
..SEE TO THE ENCLOSED DOCUMENTS PURSUANT TO THIS MATTER.
INCLUDE THE STANDARD CLOSING, MY SEAL, ETCETERA, ETCETERA.
skrch scrcht
IF I'D KNOWN HOW MUCH OF THIS POSITION INVOLVED NEEDLESS REPLIES TO ASININE --
skrch skrcht
- IS THAT THE NICODEMUS DELEGATION?
SURELY THAT IS THE EMBLEM OF THE SYRIAC ORTHODOXY...
EARLIER THAN EXPECTED.
AND WITH HALF THE IMPERIAL GUARD IN TOW.
skrch skrcht
SEEMS EXCESSIVE EVEN FOR SO VALUABLE A PRIZE AS THE NICODEMUS.
REGARDLESS. I OUGHT TO ATTEND THIS ACQUISITION PERSONALLY.
skrch skrcht
HAVE YOU BEEN WRITING THIS WHOLE TIME?
skr
TEAR IT UP, WE SHALL BEGIN ANEW WHEN I RETURN.

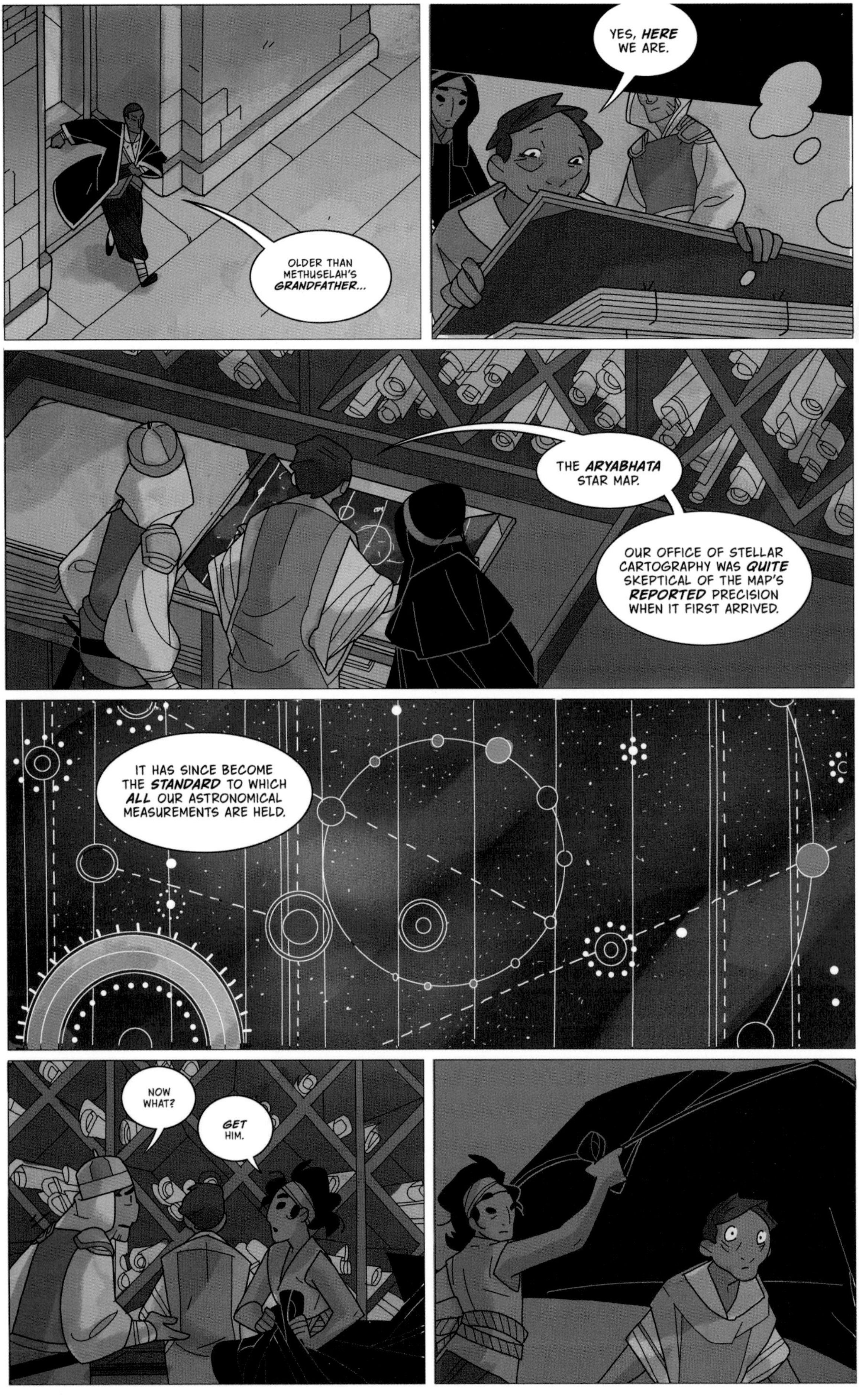
OLDER THAN METHUSELAH'S *GRANDFATHER...*
YES, *HERE* WE ARE.
THE *ARYABHATA* STAR MAP.
OUR OFFICE OF STELLAR CARTOGRAPHY WAS *QUITE* SKEPTICAL OF THE MAP'S *REPORTED* PRECISION WHEN IT FIRST ARRIVED.
IT HAS SINCE BECOME THE *STANDARD* TO WHICH *ALL* OUR ASTRONOMICAL MEASUREMENTS ARE HELD.
NOW WHAT?
GET HIM.

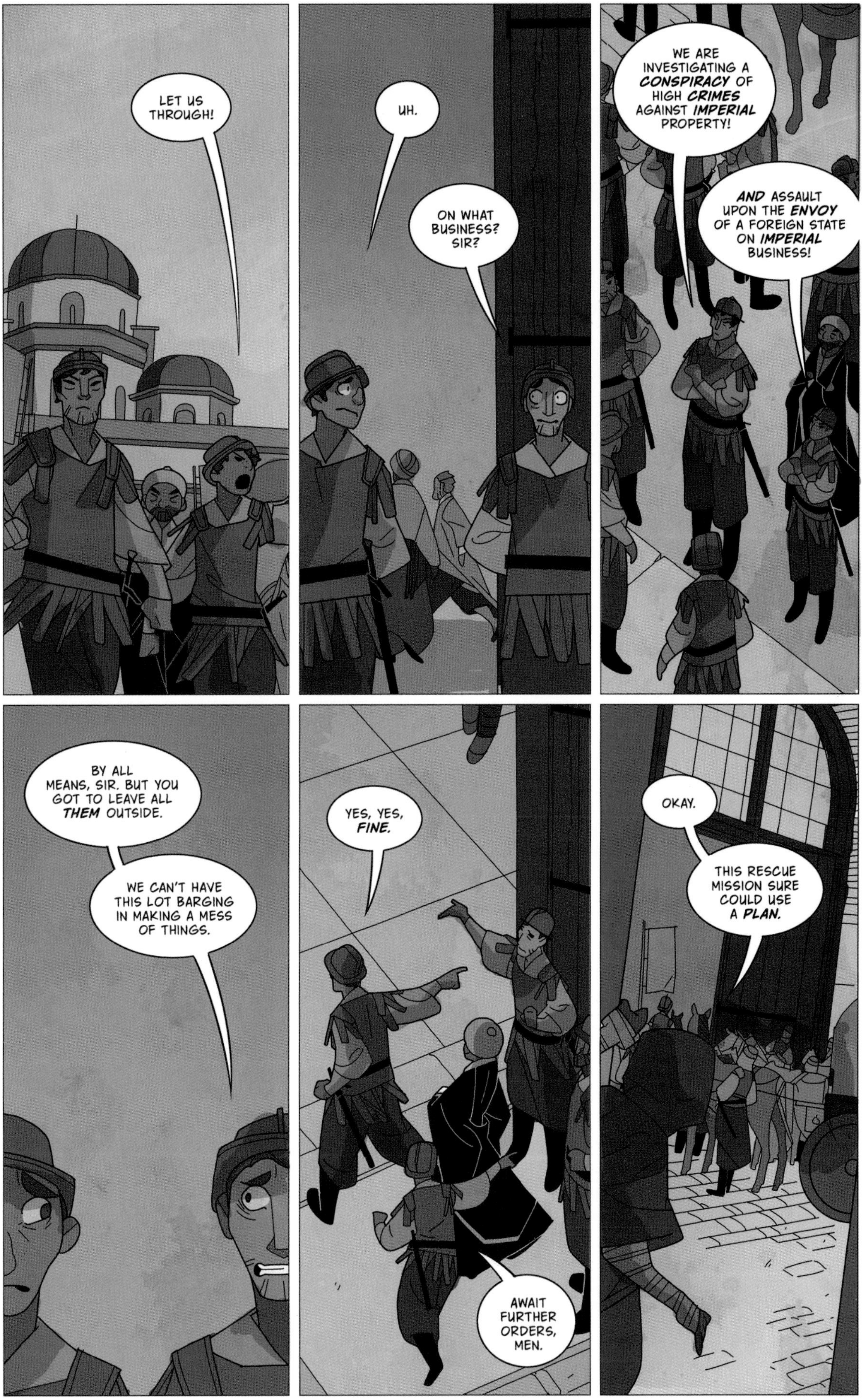
LET US THROUGH!
UH.
ON WHAT BUSINESS? SIR?
WE ARE INVESTIGATING A CONSPIRACY OF HIGH CRIMES AGAINST IMPERIAL PROPERTY!
AND ASSAULT UPON THE ENVOY OF A FOREIGN STATE ON IMPERIAL BUSINESS!
BY ALL MEANS, SIR. BUT YOU GOT TO LEAVE ALL THEM OUTSIDE.
WE CAN'T HAVE THIS LOT BARGING IN MAKING A MESS OF THINGS.
YES, YES, FINE.
AWAIT FURTHER ORDERS, MEN.
OKAY.
THIS RESCUE MISSION SURE COULD USE A PLAN.

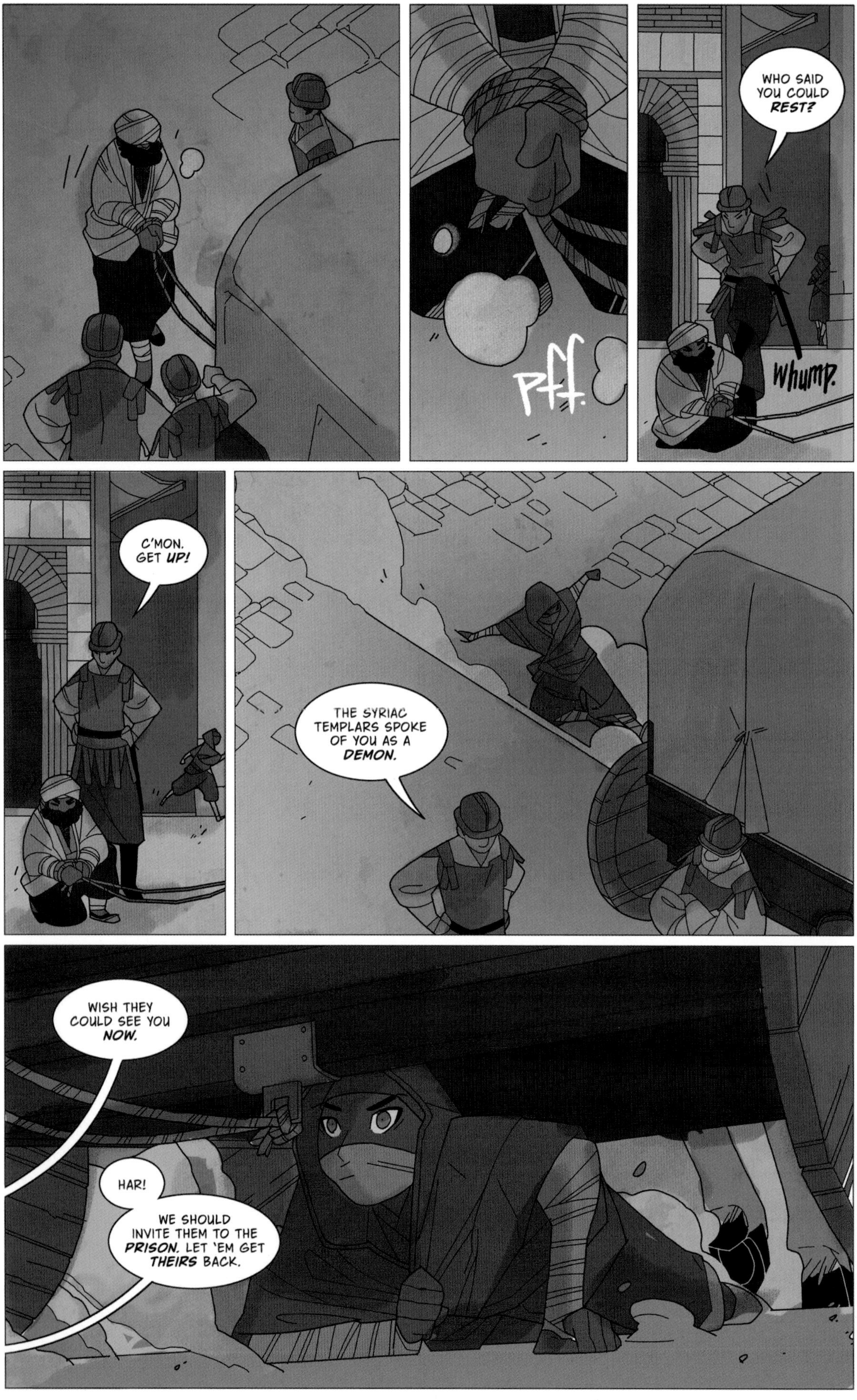
Pff.
WHO SAID YOU COULD REST?
Whump.
C'MON. GET UP!
THE SYRIAC TEMPLARS SPOKE OF YOU AS A DEMON.
WISH THEY COULD SEE YOU NOW.
HAR!
WE SHOULD INVITE THEM TO THE PRISON. LET 'EM GET THEIRS BACK.

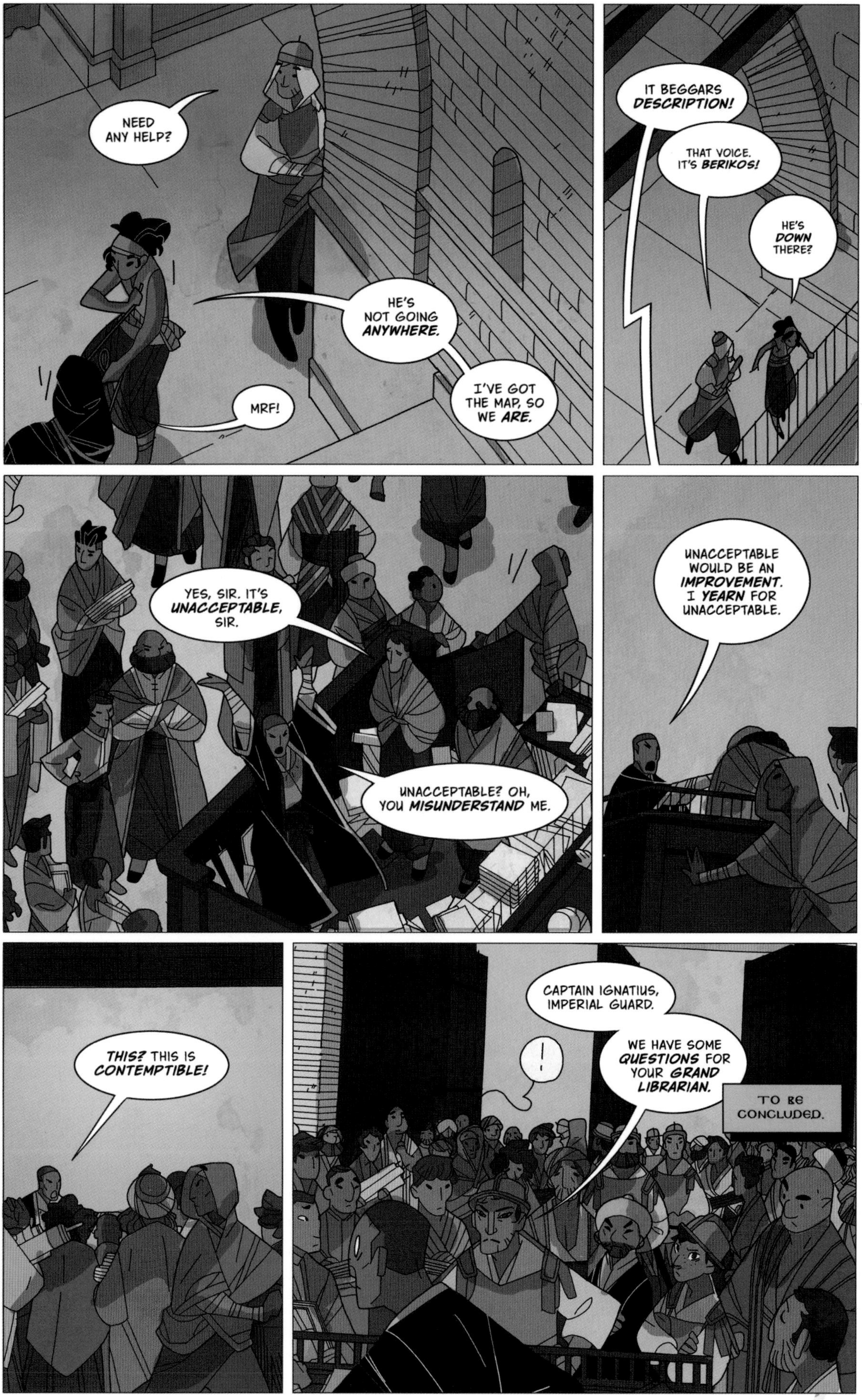
NEED ANY HELP?
HE'S NOT GOING ANYWHERE.
MRF!
I'VE GOT THE MAP, SO WE ARE.
IT BEGGARS DESCRIPTION!
THAT VOICE. IT'S BERIKOS!
HE'S DOWN THERE?
YES, SIR. IT'S UNACCEPTABLE, SIR.
UNACCEPTABLE? OH, YOU MISUNDERSTAND ME.
UNACCEPTABLE WOULD BE AN IMPROVEMENT. I YEARN FOR UNACCEPTABLE.
THIS? THIS IS CONTEMPTIBLE!
CAPTAIN IGNATIUS, IMPERIAL GUARD.
!
WE HAVE SOME QUESTIONS FOR YOUR GRAND LIBRARIAN.
TO BE CONCLUDED.

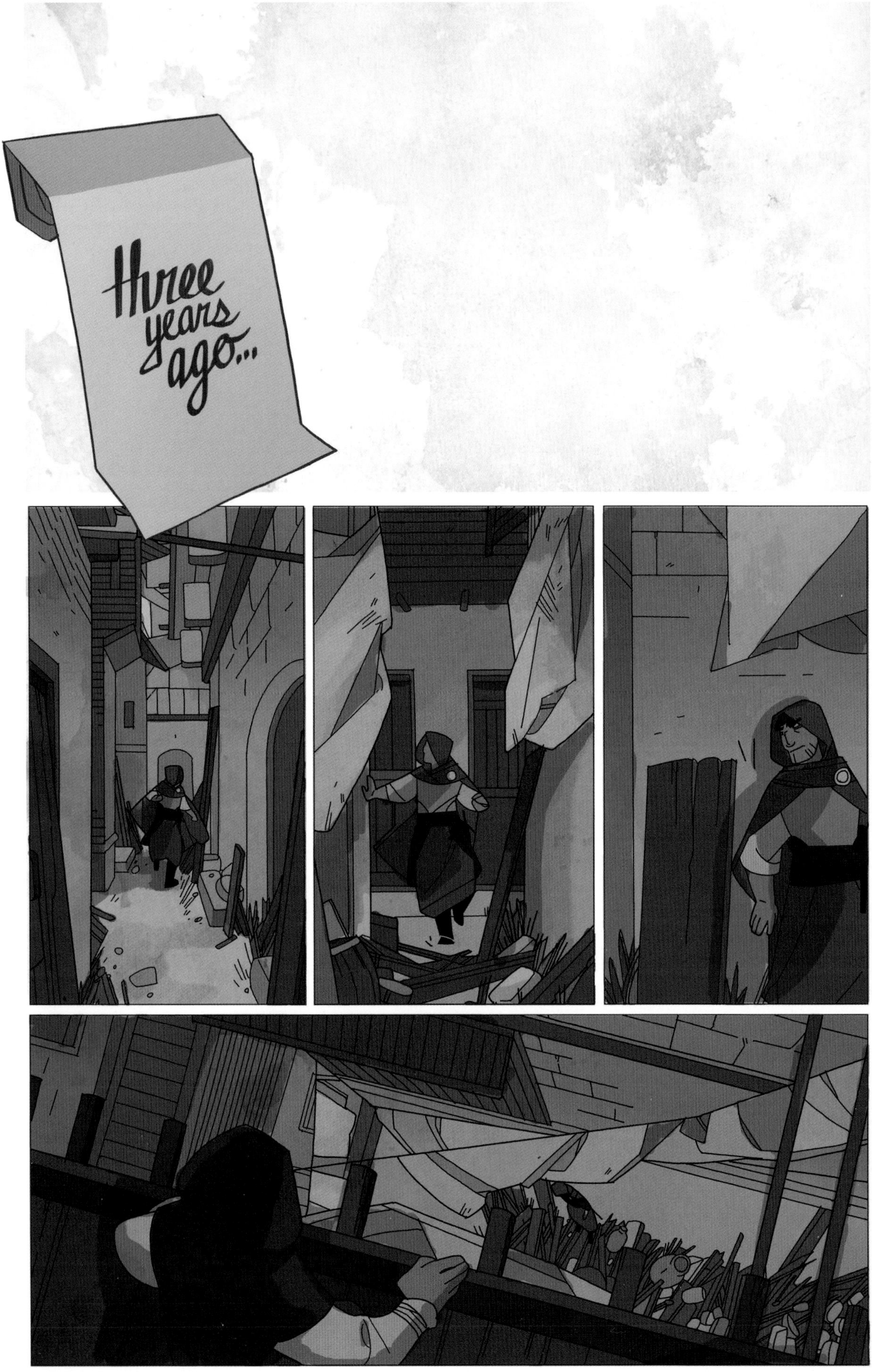
three years ago...

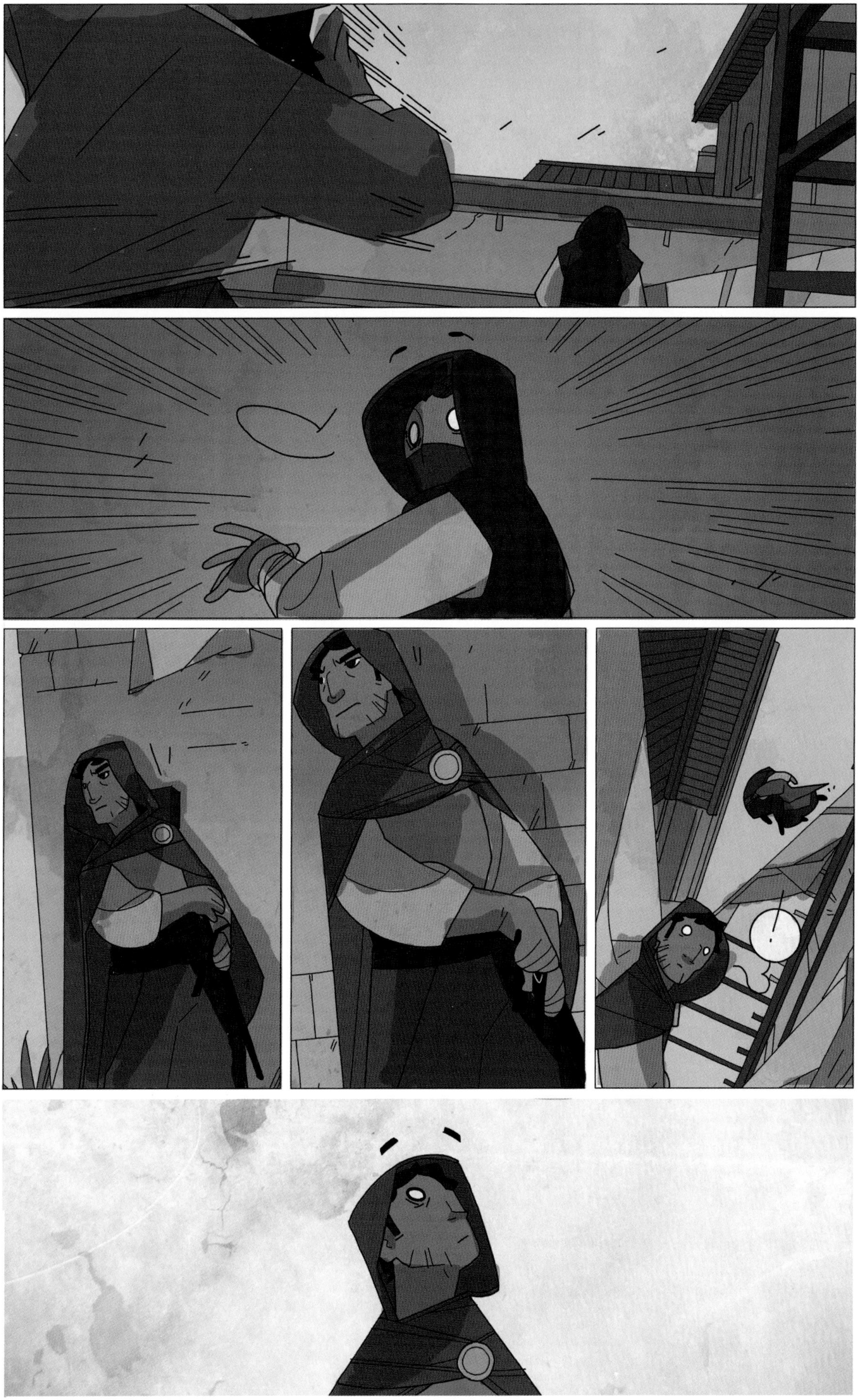

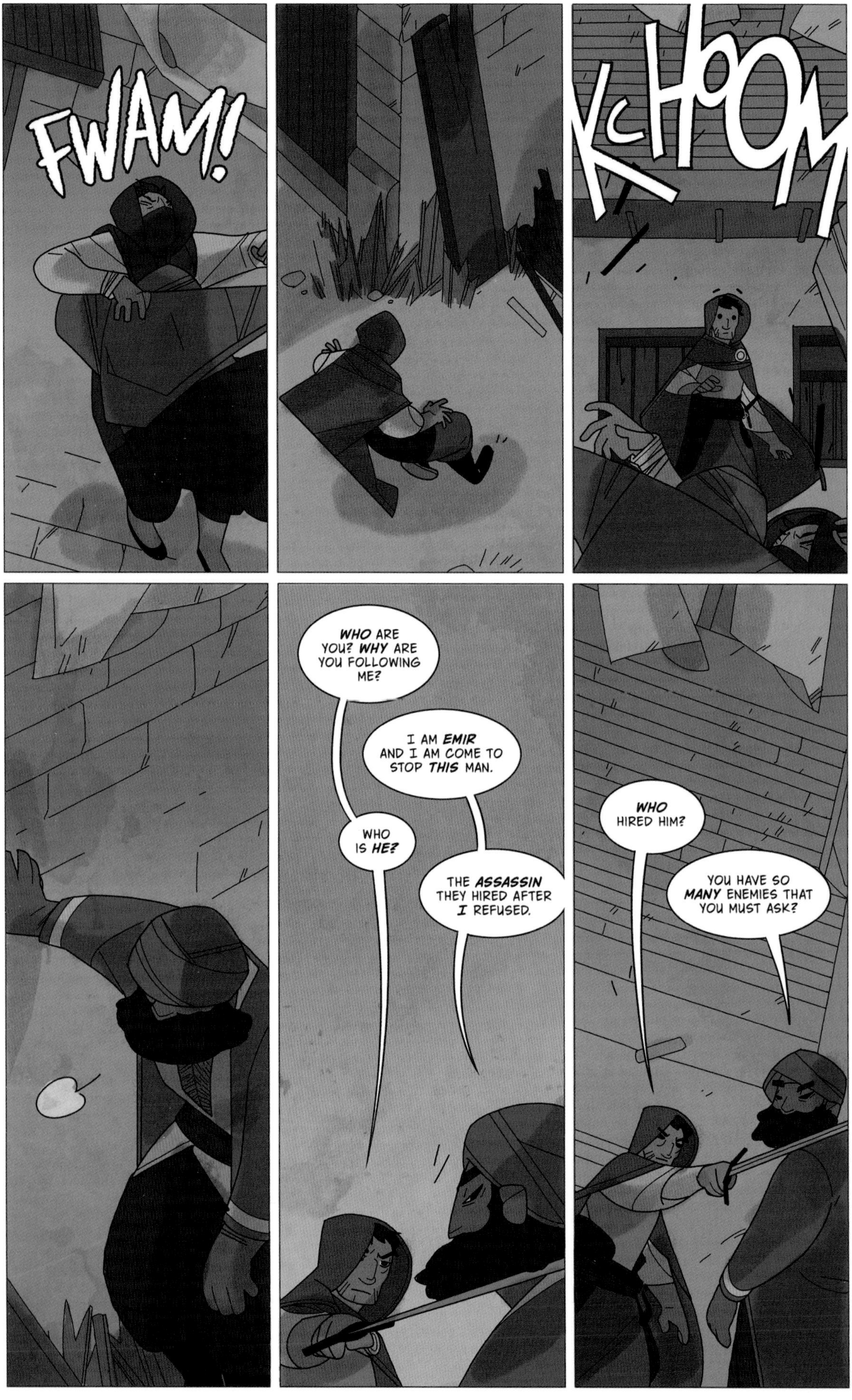
FWAM!
KCHOOM
WHO ARE YOU? WHY ARE YOU FOLLOWING ME?
I AM EMIR AND I AM COME TO STOP THIS MAN.
WHO IS HE?
THE ASSASSIN THEY HIRED AFTER I REFUSED.
WHO HIRED HIM?
YOU HAVE SO MANY ENEMIES THAT YOU MUST ASK?

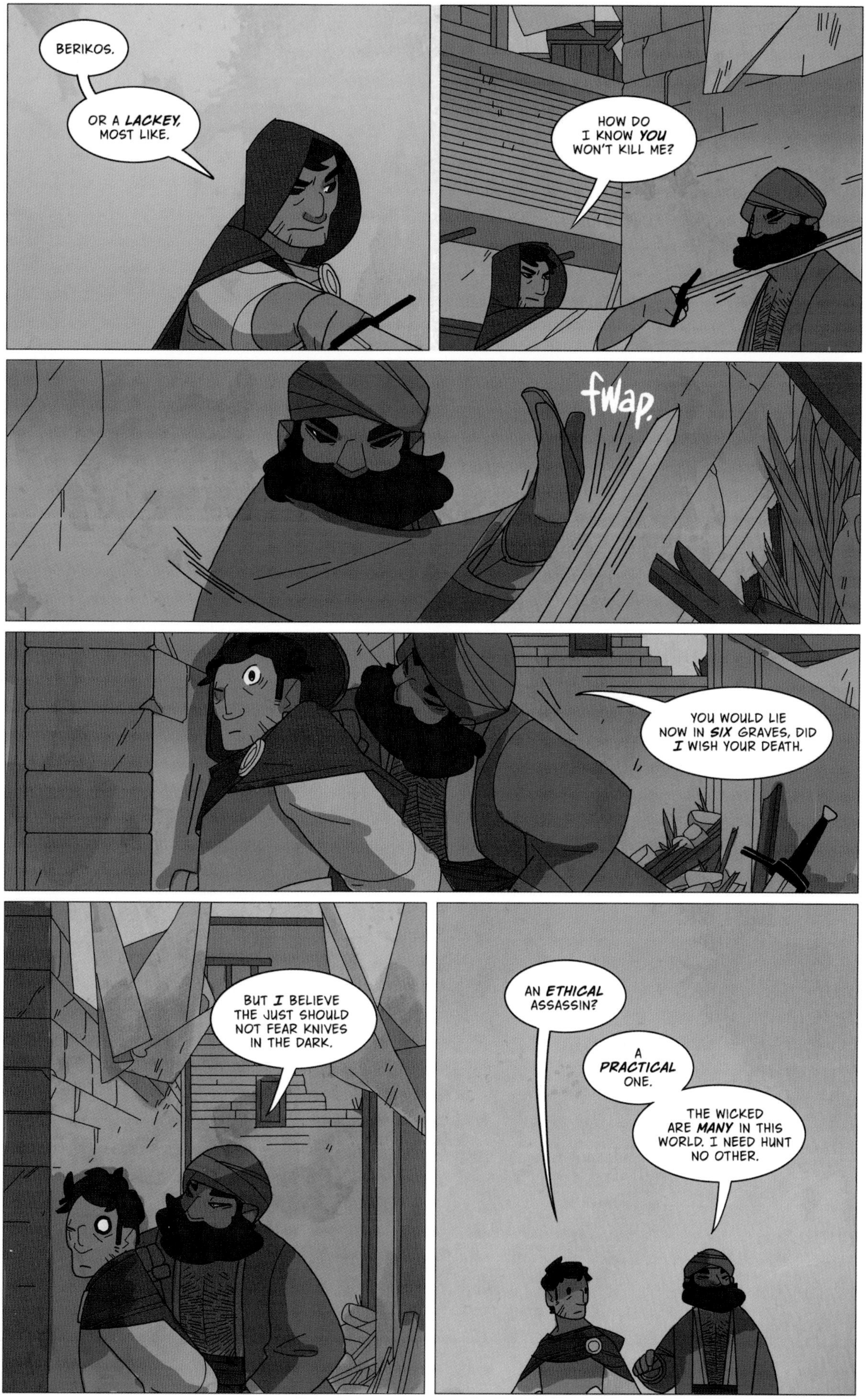
BERIKOS.
OR A LACKEY, MOST LIKE.
HOW DO I KNOW YOU WON'T KILL ME?
fwap.
YOU WOULD LIE NOW IN SIX GRAVES, DID I WISH YOUR DEATH.
BUT I BELIEVE THE JUST SHOULD NOT FEAR KNIVES IN THE DARK.
AN ETHICAL ASSASSIN?
A PRACTICAL ONE.
THE WICKED ARE MANY IN THIS WORLD. I NEED HUNT NO OTHER.

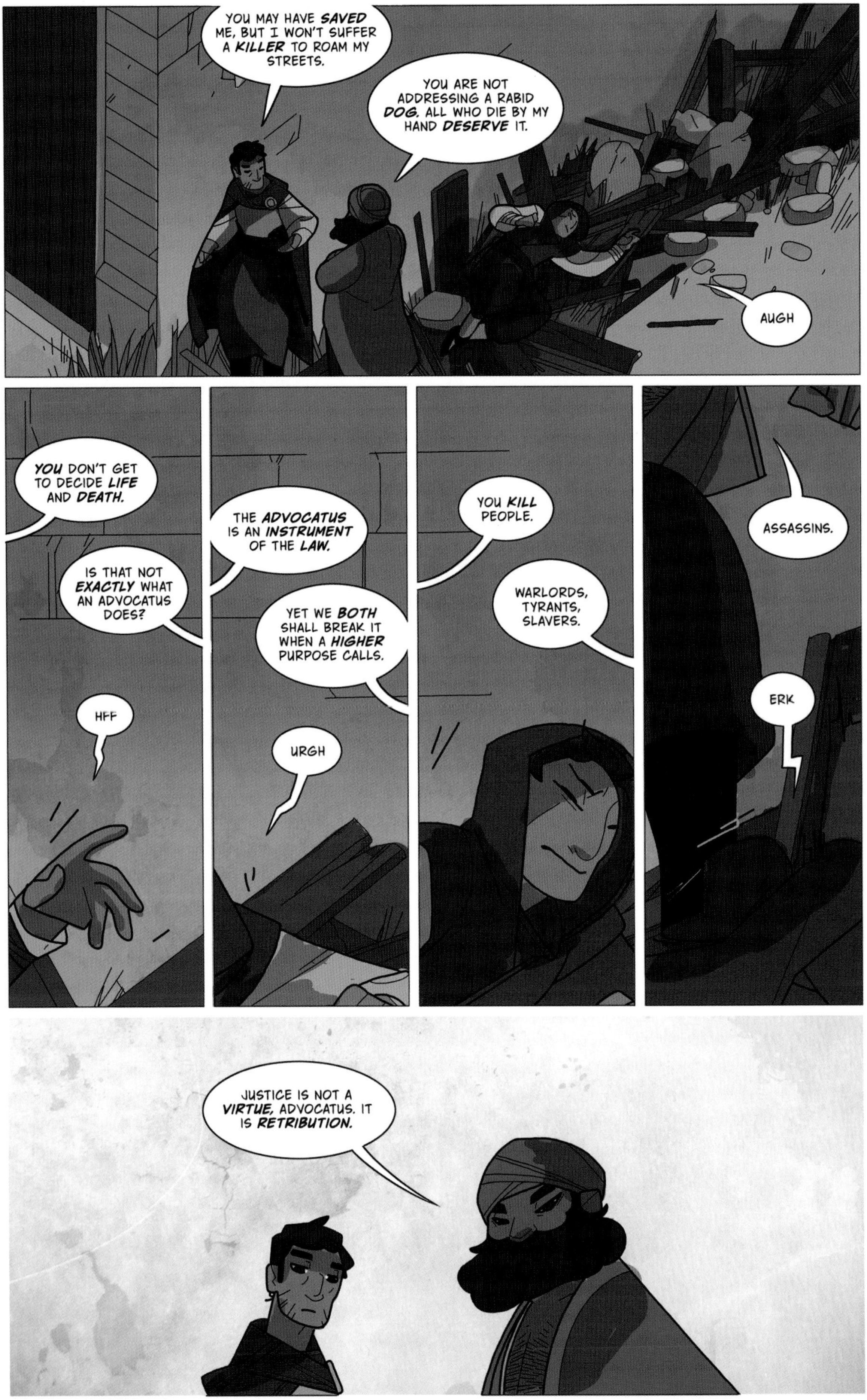
YOU MAY HAVE SAVED ME, BUT I WON'T SUFFER A KILLER TO ROAM MY STREETS.
YOU ARE NOT ADDRESSING A RABID DOG. ALL WHO DIE BY MY HAND DESERVE IT.
AUGH
YOU DON'T GET TO DECIDE LIFE AND DEATH.
IS THAT NOT EXACTLY WHAT AN ADVOCATUS DOES?
HFF
THE ADVOCATUS IS AN INSTRUMENT OF THE LAW.
YET WE BOTH SHALL BREAK IT WHEN A HIGHER PURPOSE CALLS.
URGH
YOU KILL PEOPLE.
WARLORDS, TYRANTS, SLAVERS.
ASSASSINS.
ERK
JUSTICE IS NOT A VIRTUE, ADVOCATUS. IT IS RETRIBUTION.

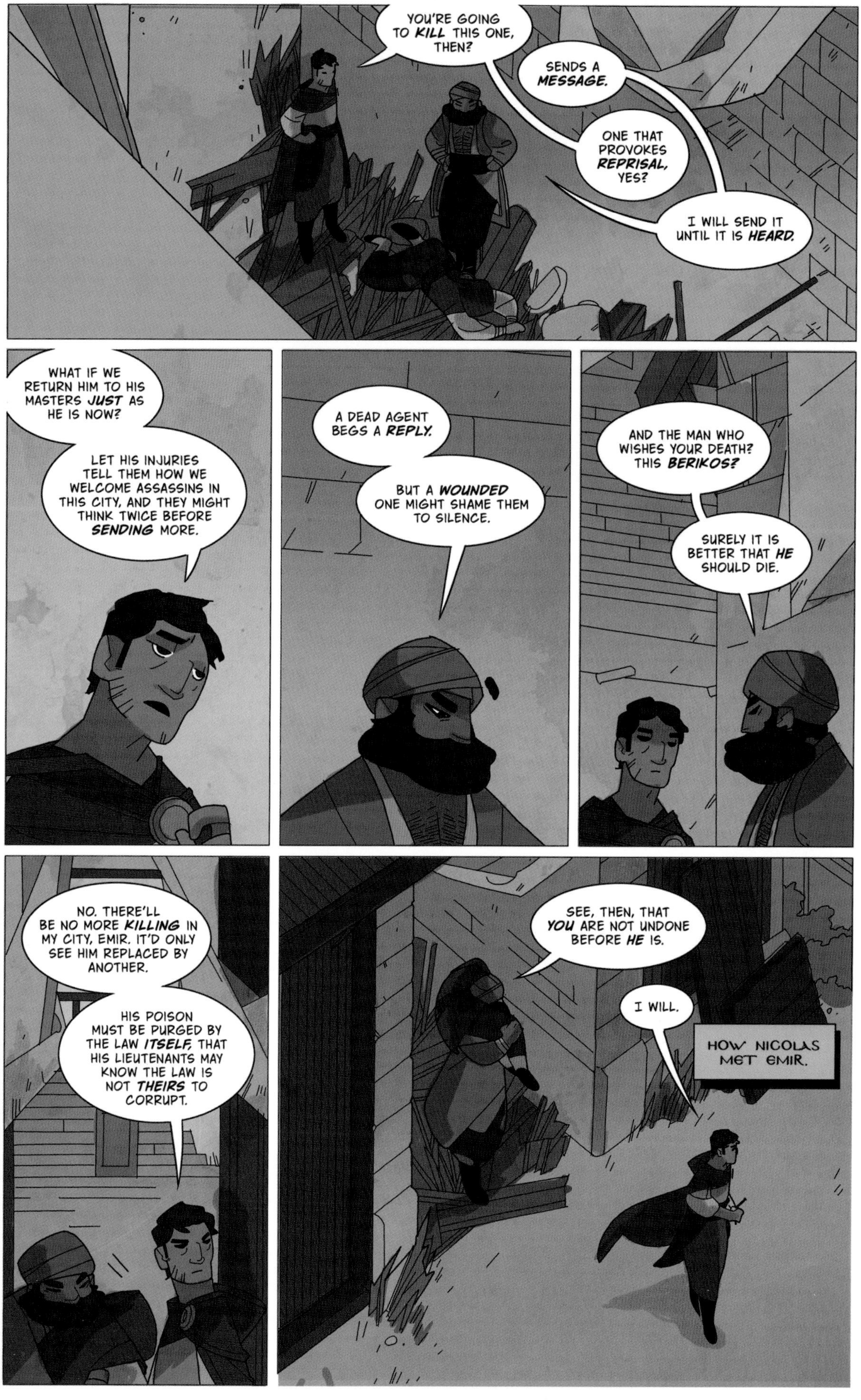

YOU'RE GOING TO KILL THIS ONE, THEN?
SENDS A MESSAGE.
ONE THAT PROVOKES REPRISAL, YES?
I WILL SEND IT UNTIL IT IS HEARD.
WHAT IF WE RETURN HIM TO HIS MASTERS JUST AS HE IS NOW?
LET HIS INJURIES TELL THEM HOW WE WELCOME ASSASSINS IN THIS CITY, AND THEY MIGHT THINK TWICE BEFORE SENDING MORE.
A DEAD AGENT BEGS A REPLY.
BUT A WOUNDED ONE MIGHT SHAME THEM TO SILENCE.
AND THE MAN WHO WISHES YOUR DEATH? THIS BERIKOS?
SURELY IT IS BETTER THAT HE SHOULD DIE.
NO. THERE'LL BE NO MORE KILLING IN MY CITY, EMIR. IT'D ONLY SEE HIM REPLACED BY ANOTHER.
HIS POISON MUST BE PURGED BY THE LAW ITSELF, THAT HIS LIEUTENANTS MAY KNOW THE LAW IS NOT THEIRS TO CORRUPT.
SEE, THEN, THAT YOU ARE NOT UNDONE BEFORE HE IS.
I WILL.
HOW NICOLAS MET EMIR.

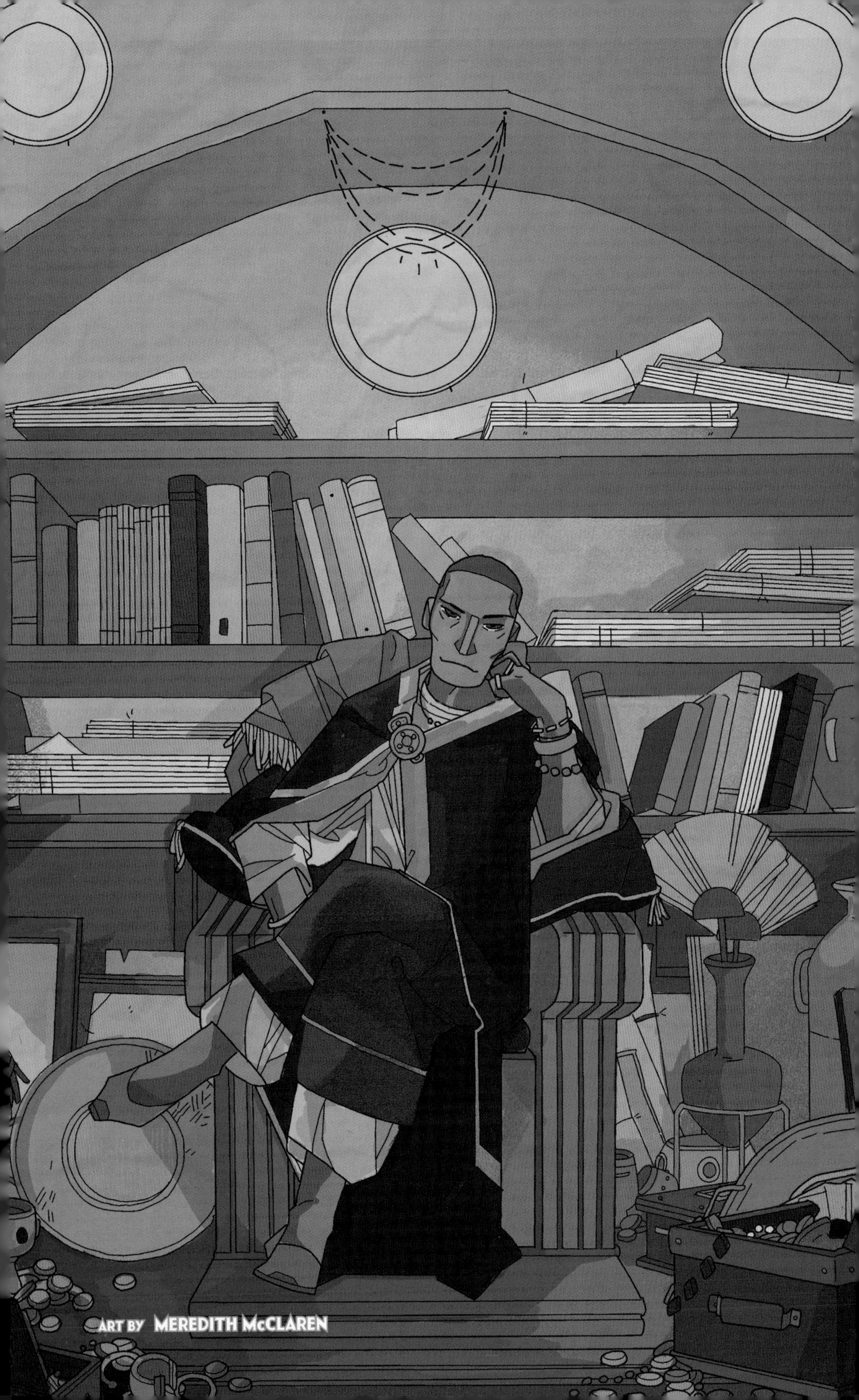
ART BY MEREDITH McCLAREN

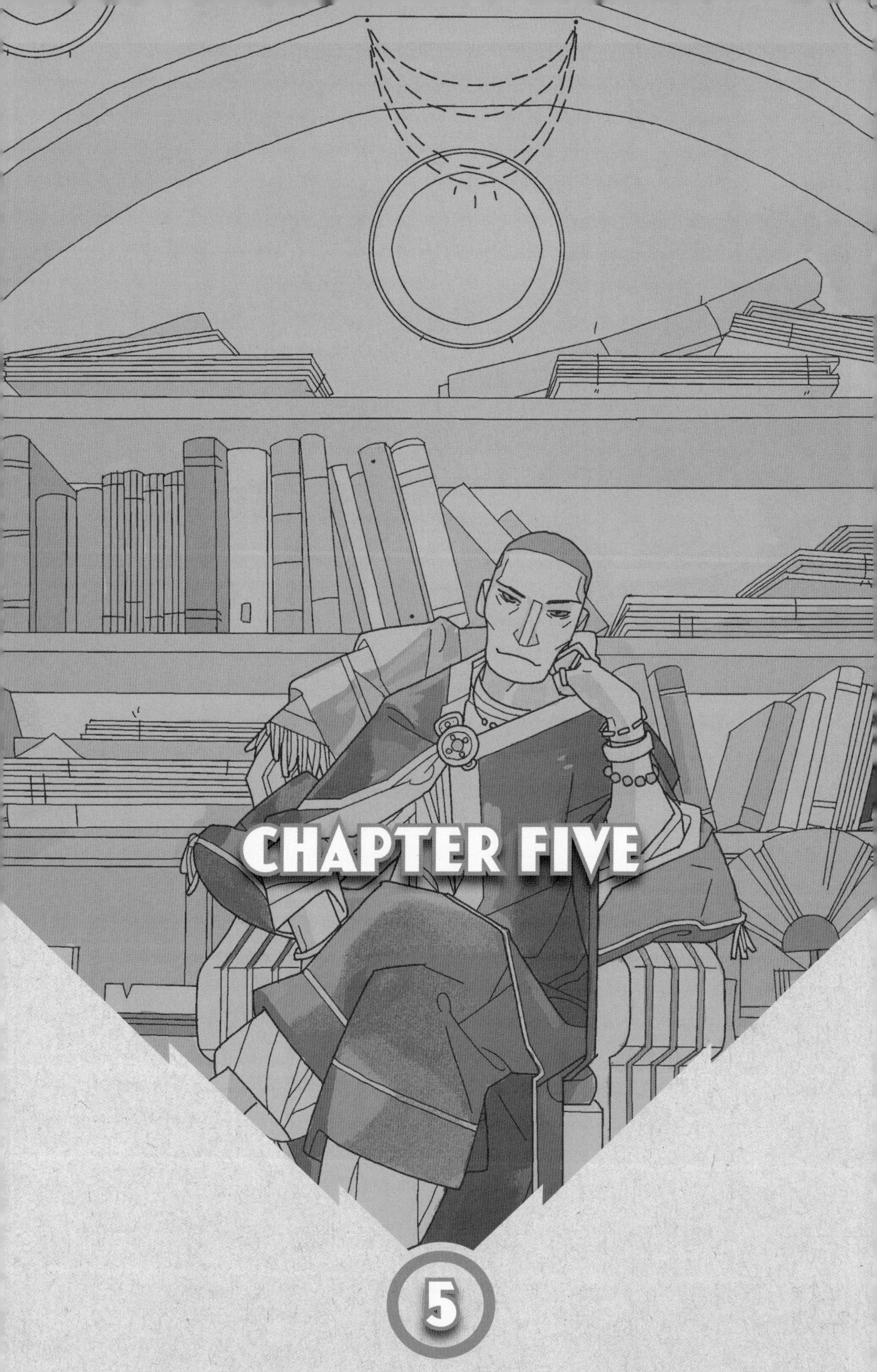

CHAPTER FIVE

5

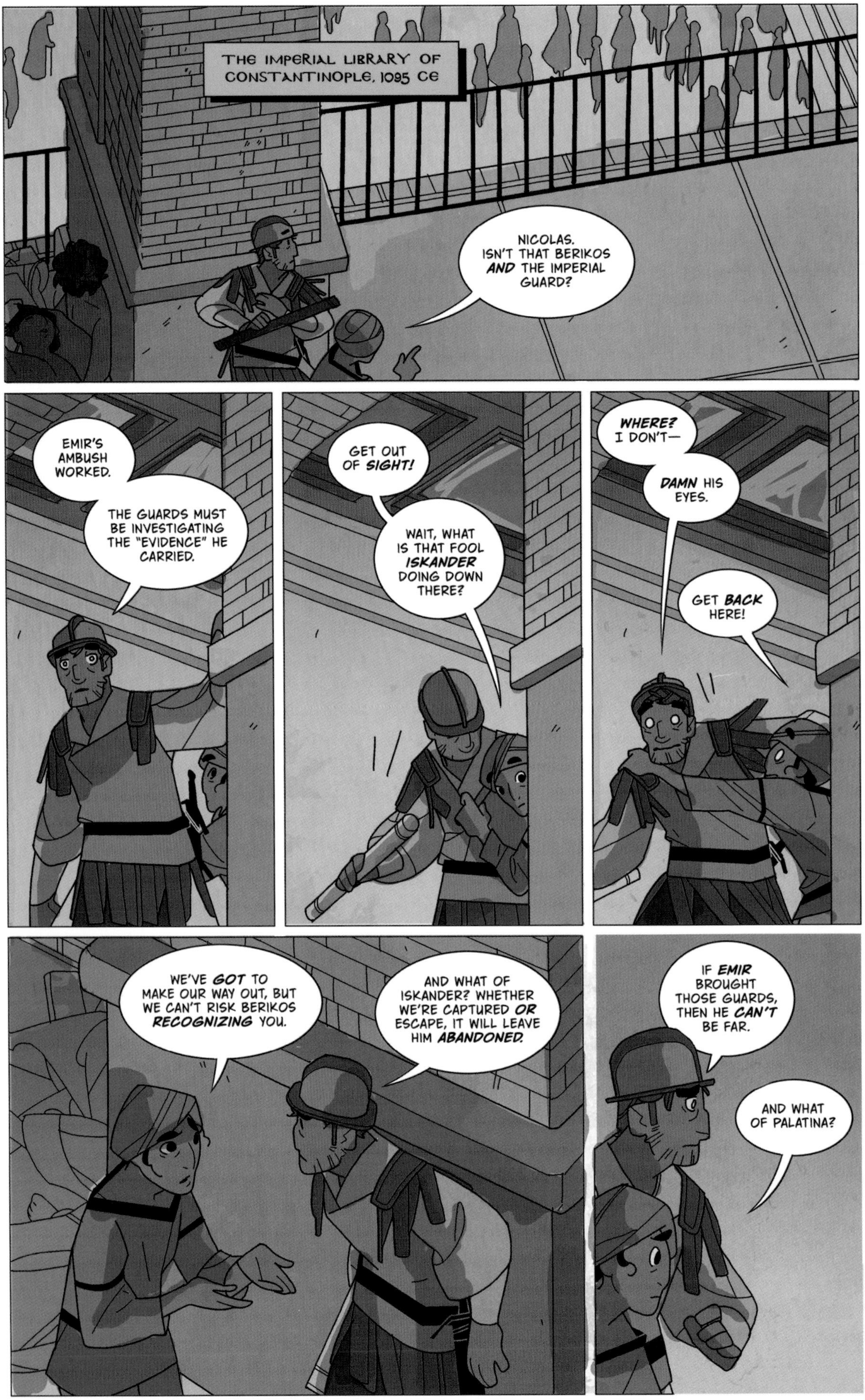
THE IMPERIAL LIBRARY OF CONSTANTINOPLE, 1095 CE
NICOLAS. ISN'T THAT BERIKOS AND THE IMPERIAL GUARD?
EMIR'S AMBUSH WORKED.
THE GUARDS MUST BE INVESTIGATING THE "EVIDENCE" HE CARRIED.
GET OUT OF SIGHT!
WAIT, WHAT IS THAT FOOL ISKANDER DOING DOWN THERE?
WHERE? I DON'T—
DAMN HIS EYES.
GET BACK HERE!
WE'VE GOT TO MAKE OUR WAY OUT, BUT WE CAN'T RISK BERIKOS RECOGNIZING YOU.
AND WHAT OF ISKANDER? WHETHER WE'RE CAPTURED OR ESCAPE, IT WILL LEAVE HIM ABANDONED.
IF EMIR BROUGHT THOSE GUARDS, THEN HE CAN'T BE FAR.
AND WHAT OF PALATINA?

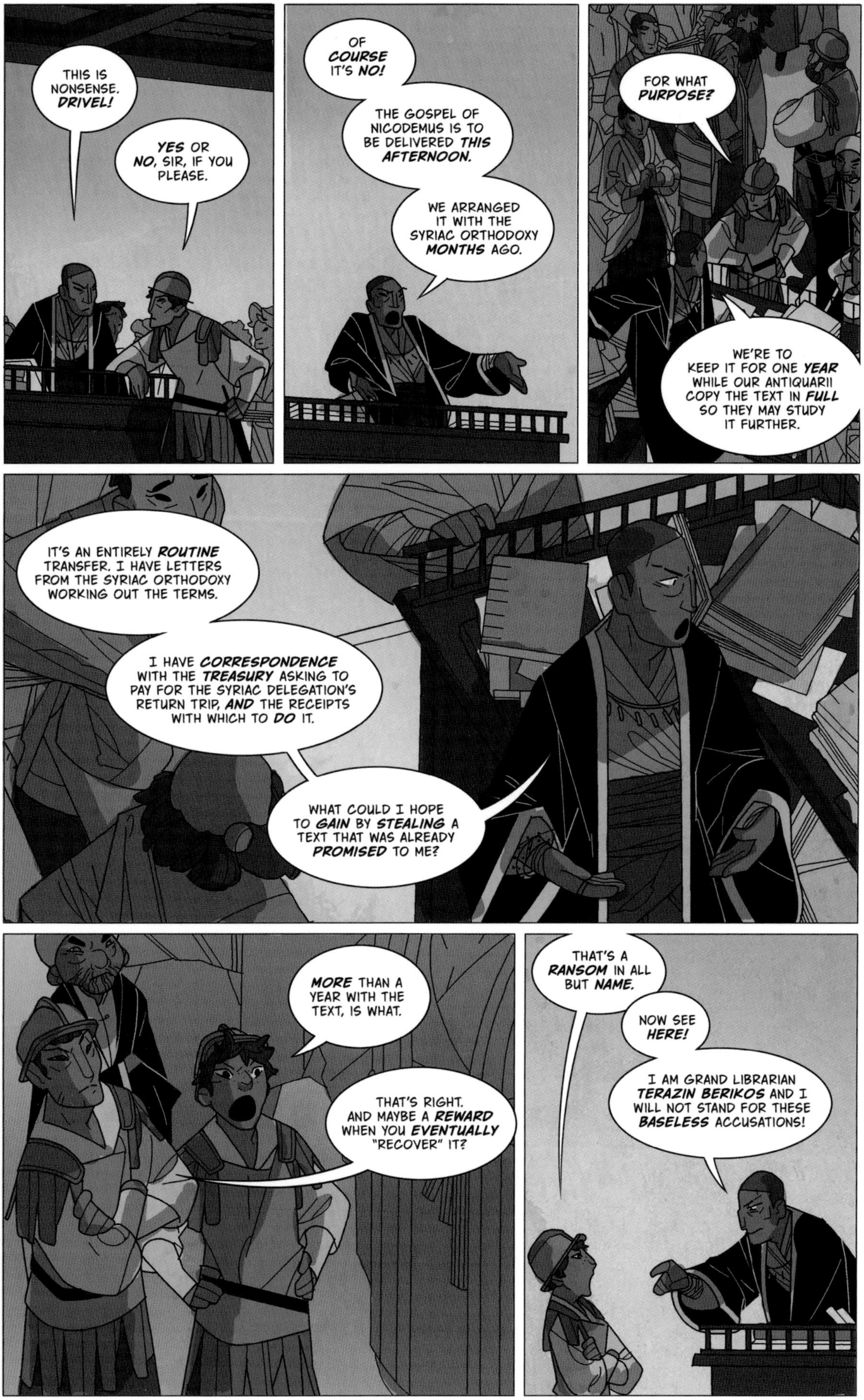
THIS IS NONSENSE. DRIVEL!
YES OR NO, SIR, IF YOU PLEASE.
OF COURSE IT'S NO!
THE GOSPEL OF NICODEMUS IS TO BE DELIVERED THIS AFTERNOON.
WE ARRANGED IT WITH THE SYRIAC ORTHODOXY MONTHS AGO.
FOR WHAT PURPOSE?
WE'RE TO KEEP IT FOR ONE YEAR WHILE OUR ANTIQUARII COPY THE TEXT IN FULL SO THEY MAY STUDY IT FURTHER.
IT'S AN ENTIRELY ROUTINE TRANSFER. I HAVE LETTERS FROM THE SYRIAC ORTHODOXY WORKING OUT THE TERMS.
I HAVE CORRESPONDENCE WITH THE TREASURY ASKING TO PAY FOR THE SYRIAC DELEGATION'S RETURN TRIP, AND THE RECEIPTS WITH WHICH TO DO IT.
WHAT COULD I HOPE TO GAIN BY STEALING A TEXT THAT WAS ALREADY PROMISED TO ME?
MORE THAN A YEAR WITH THE TEXT, IS WHAT.
THAT'S RIGHT. AND MAYBE A REWARD WHEN YOU EVENTUALLY "RECOVER" IT?
THAT'S A RANSOM IN ALL BUT NAME.
NOW SEE HERE!
I AM GRAND LIBRARIAN TERAZIN BERIKOS AND I WILL NOT STAND FOR THESE BASELESS ACCUSATIONS!

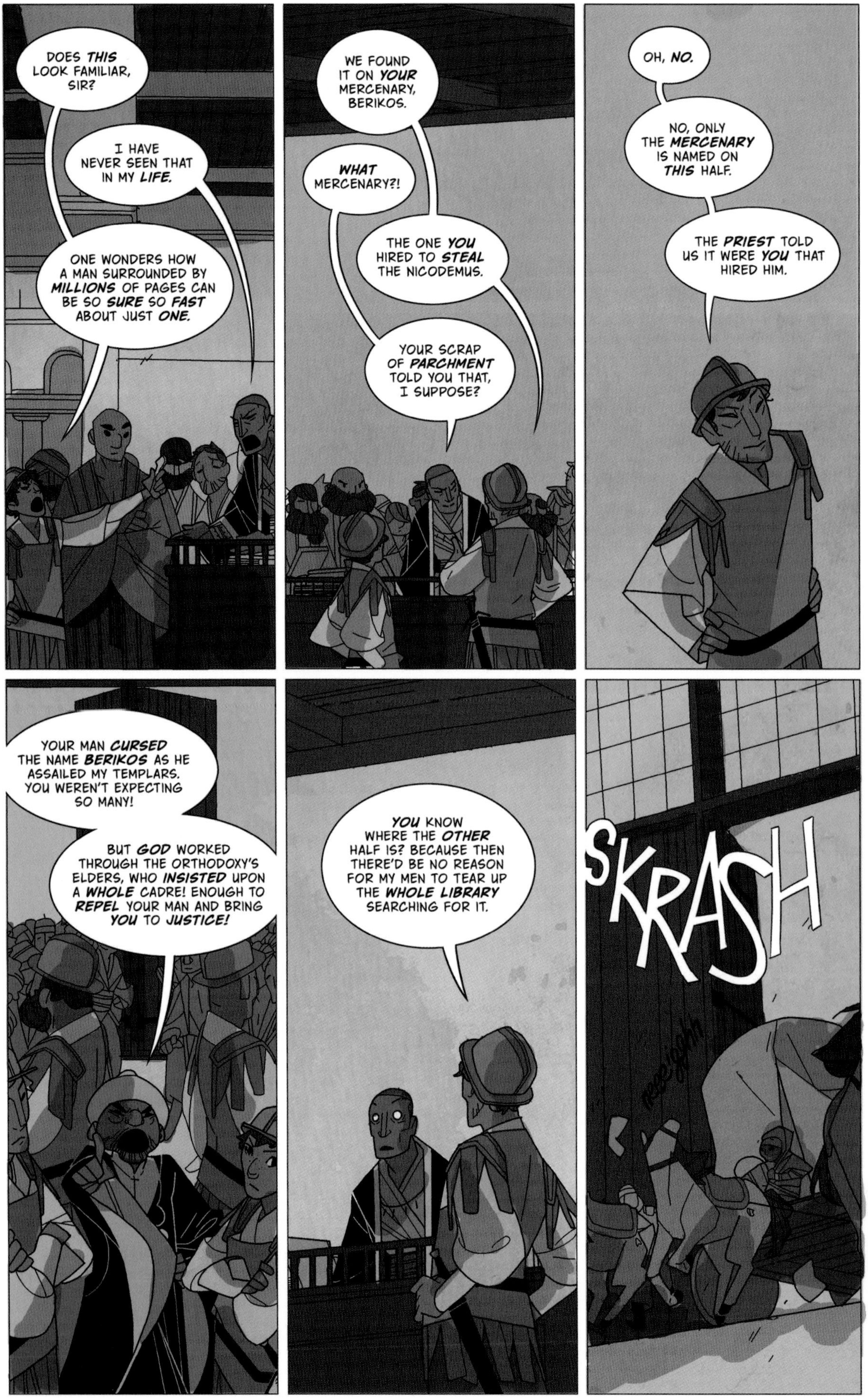
DOES *THIS* LOOK FAMILIAR, SIR?
I HAVE NEVER SEEN THAT IN MY *LIFE.*
ONE WONDERS HOW A MAN SURROUNDED BY *MILLIONS* OF PAGES CAN BE SO *SURE* SO *FAST* ABOUT JUST *ONE.*
WE FOUND IT ON *YOUR* MERCENARY, BERIKOS.
WHAT MERCENARY?!
THE ONE *YOU* HIRED TO *STEAL* THE NICODEMUS.
YOUR SCRAP OF *PARCHMENT* TOLD YOU THAT, I SUPPOSE?
OH, *NO.*
NO, ONLY THE *MERCENARY* IS NAMED ON *THIS* HALF.
THE *PRIEST* TOLD US IT WERE *YOU* THAT HIRED HIM.
YOUR MAN *CURSED* THE NAME *BERIKOS* AS HE ASSAILED MY TEMPLARS. YOU WEREN'T EXPECTING SO MANY!
BUT *GOD* WORKED THROUGH THE ORTHODOXY'S ELDERS, WHO *INSISTED* UPON A *WHOLE* CADRE! ENOUGH TO *REPEL* YOUR MAN AND BRING *YOU* TO *JUSTICE!*
YOU KNOW WHERE THE *OTHER* HALF IS? BECAUSE THEN THERE'D BE NO REASON FOR MY MEN TO TEAR UP THE *WHOLE LIBRARY* SEARCHING FOR IT.
SKRASH

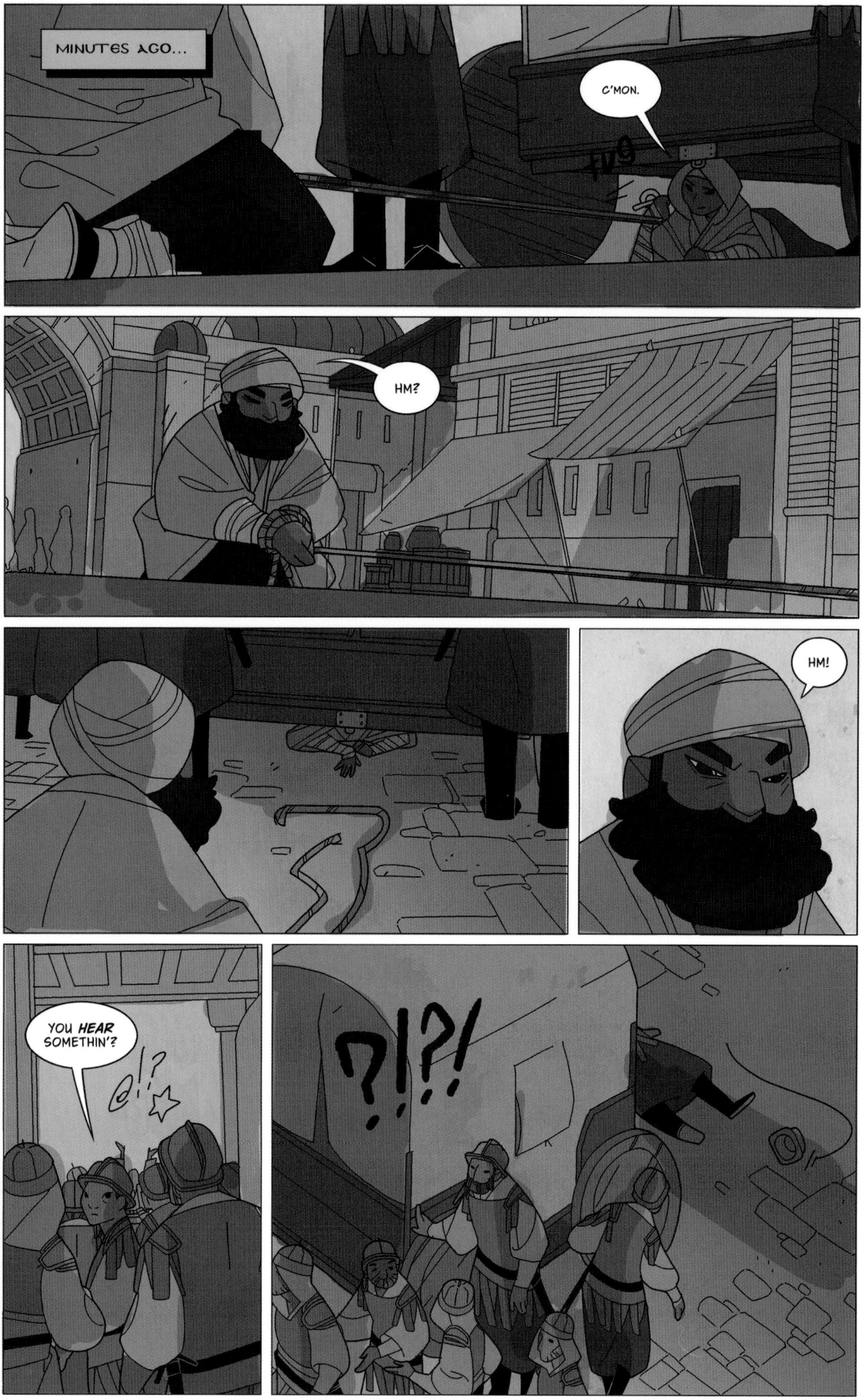
MINUTES AGO...
C'MON.
TUG
HM?
HM!
YOU HEAR SOMETHIN'?
?!?!

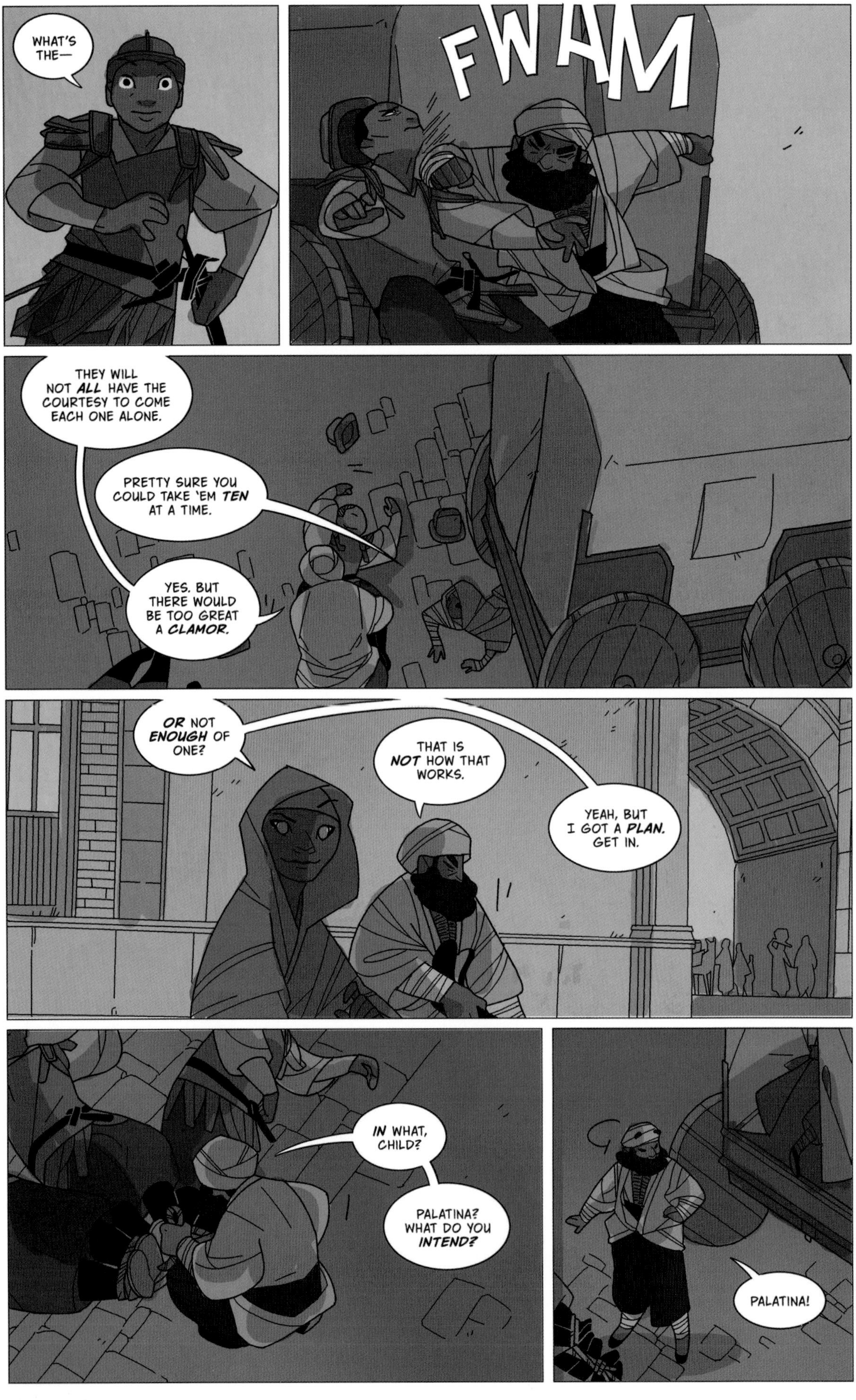
WHAT'S THE—
FWAM
THEY WILL NOT ALL HAVE THE COURTESY TO COME EACH ONE ALONE.
PRETTY SURE YOU COULD TAKE 'EM TEN AT A TIME.
YES. BUT THERE WOULD BE TOO GREAT A CLAMOR.
OR NOT ENOUGH OF ONE?
THAT IS NOT HOW THAT WORKS.
YEAH, BUT I GOT A PLAN. GET IN.
IN WHAT, CHILD?
PALATINA? WHAT DO YOU INTEND?
PALATINA!

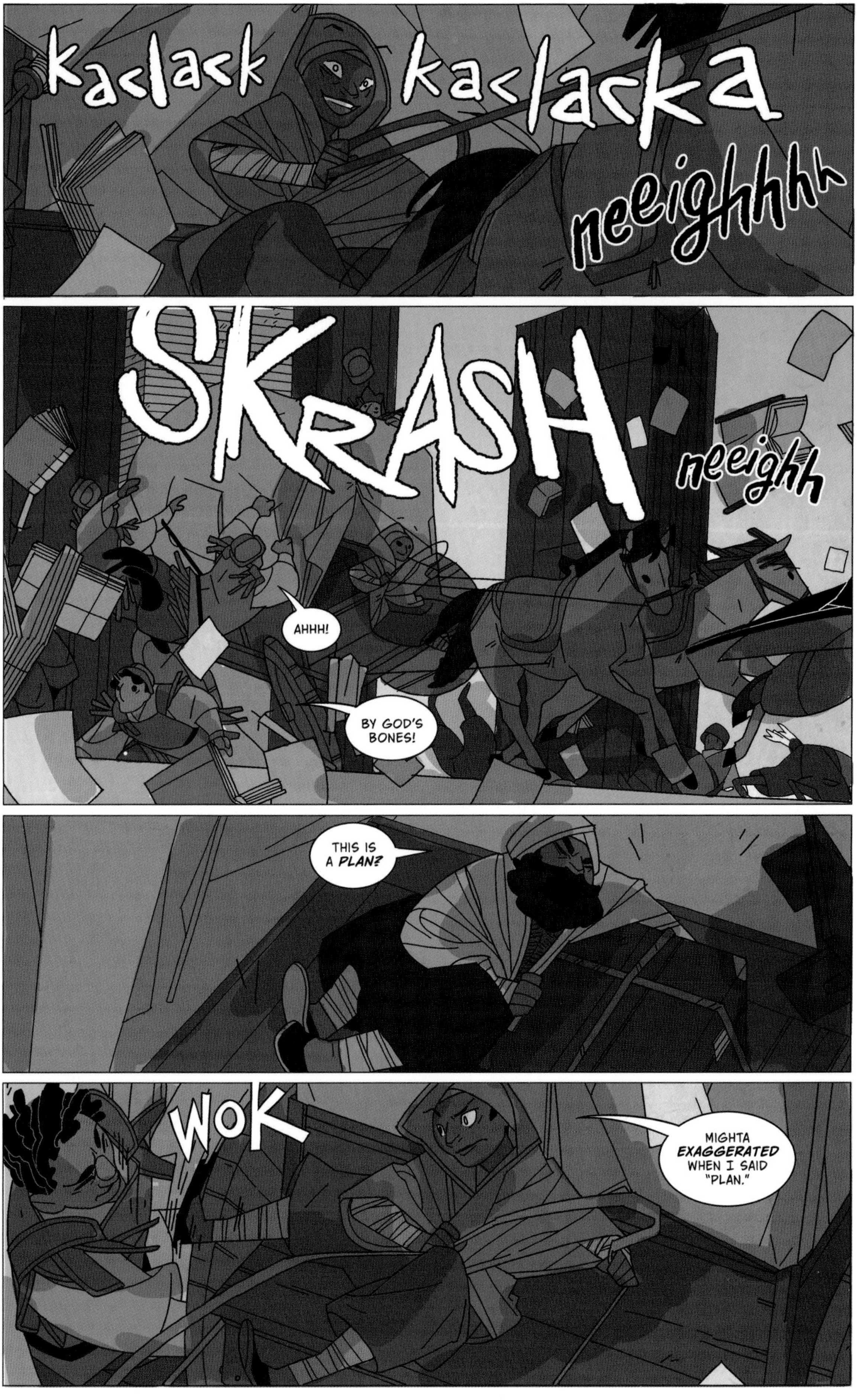
kaclack kaclacka
neeighhhh
SKRASH
neeighh
AHHH!
BY GOD'S BONES!
THIS IS A *PLAN?*
WOK
MIGHTA **EXAGGERATED** WHEN I SAID "PLAN."

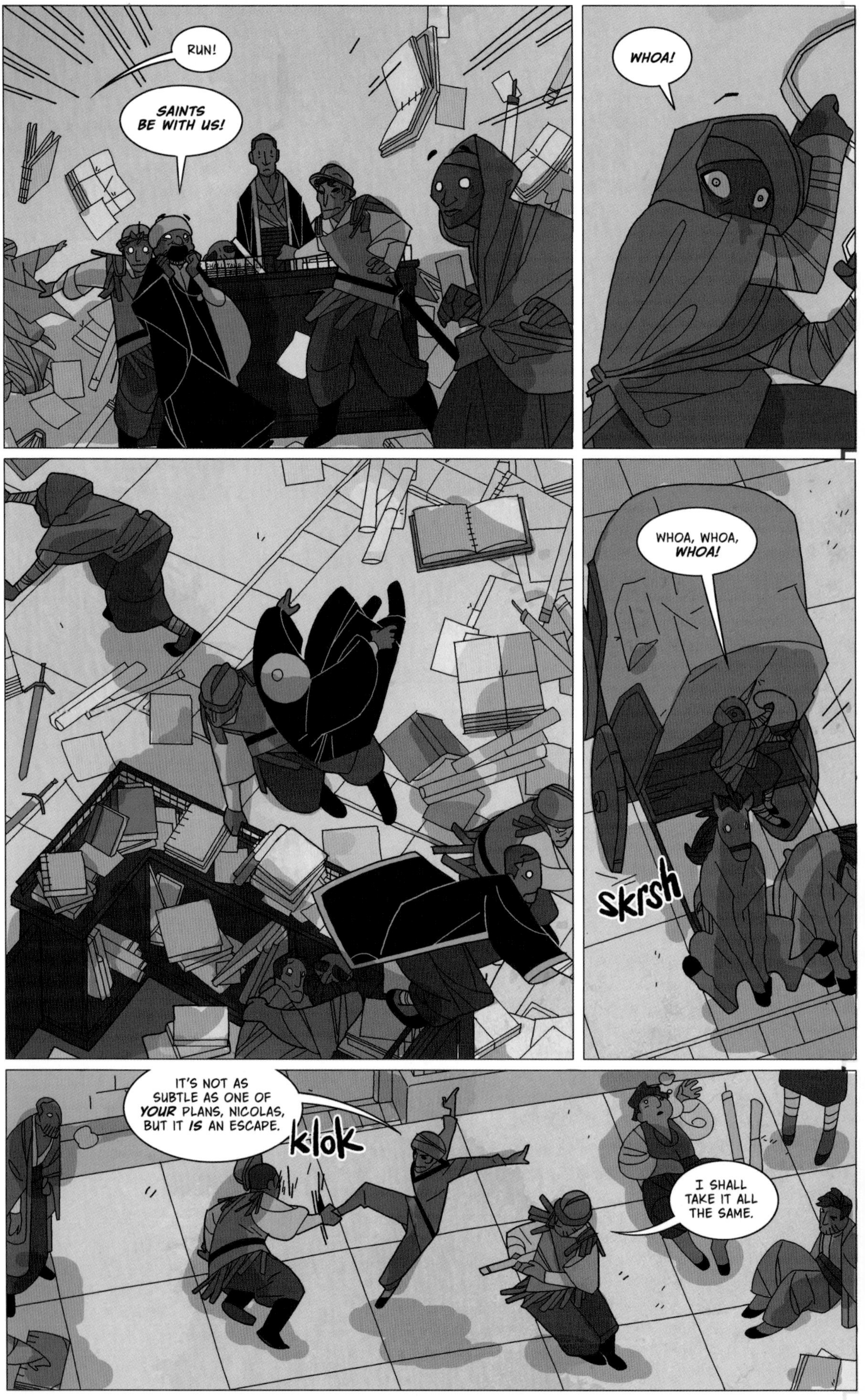
RUN!
SAINTS BE WITH US!
WHOA!
WHOA, WHOA, WHOA!
skrsh
IT'S NOT AS SUBTLE AS ONE OF YOUR PLANS, NICOLAS, BUT IT IS AN ESCAPE.
klok
I SHALL TAKE IT ALL THE SAME.

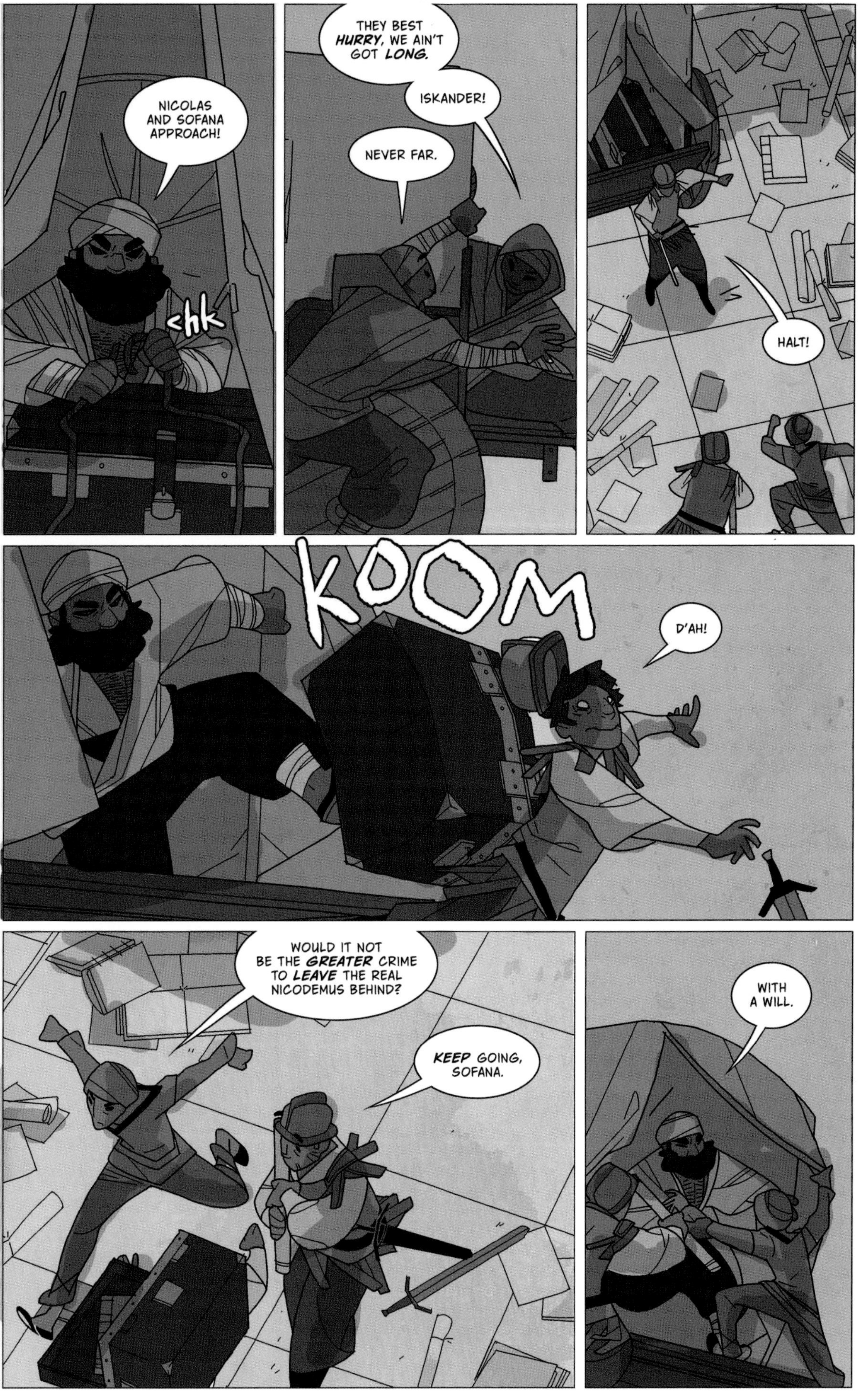
NICOLAS AND SOFANA APPROACH!
chk
THEY BEST *HURRY*, WE AIN'T GOT *LONG*.
ISKANDER!
NEVER FAR.
HALT!
KOOM
D'AH!
WOULD IT NOT BE THE *GREATER* CRIME TO *LEAVE* THE REAL NICODEMUS BEHIND?
KEEP GOING, SOFANA.
WITH A WILL.

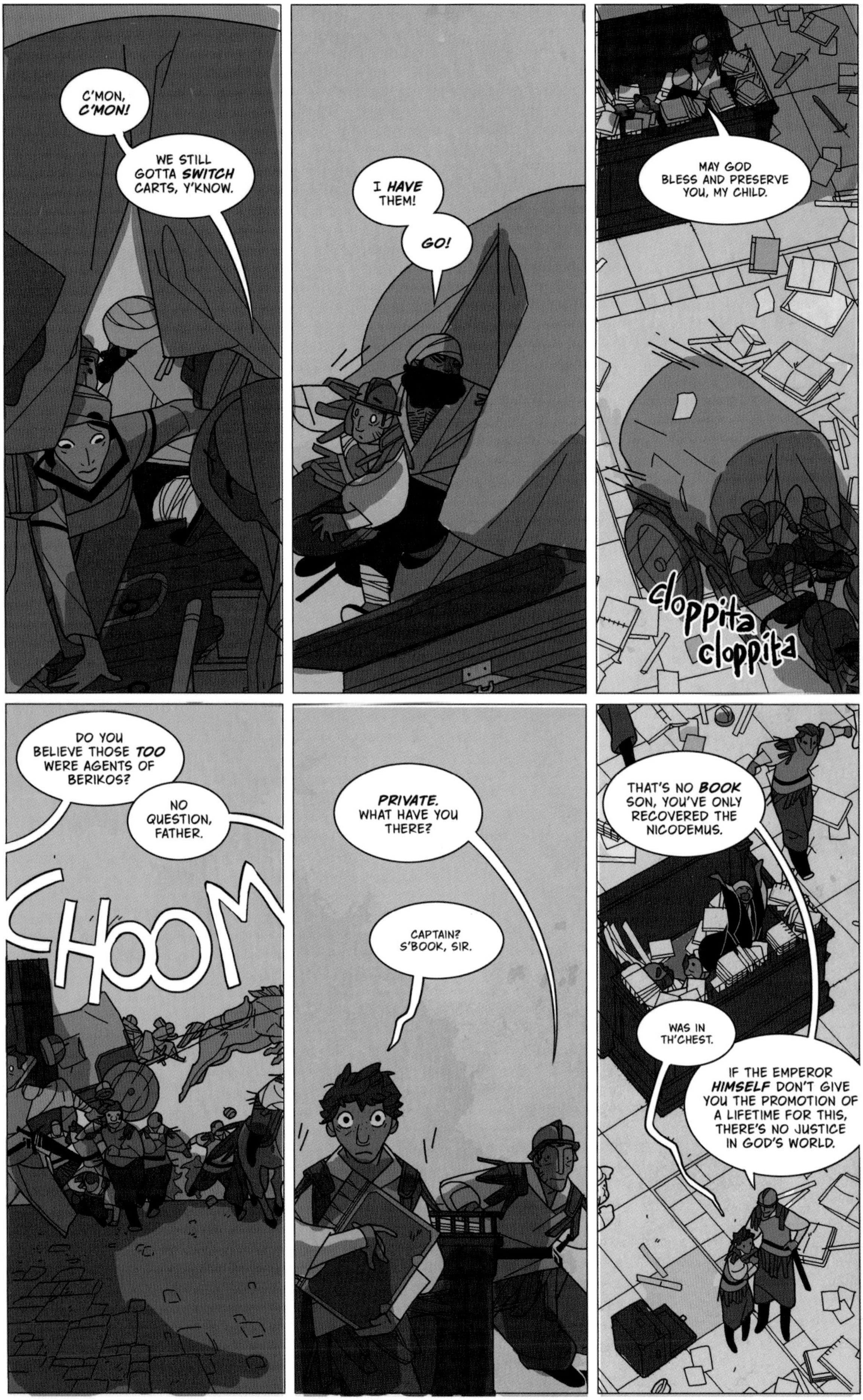
C'MON, *C'MON!*
WE STILL GOTTA **SWITCH** CARTS, Y'KNOW.
I *HAVE* THEM!
GO!
MAY GOD BLESS AND PRESERVE YOU, MY CHILD.
cloppita cloppita
DO YOU BELIEVE THOSE *TOO* WERE AGENTS OF BERIKOS?
NO QUESTION, FATHER.
CHOOM
PRIVATE. WHAT HAVE YOU THERE?
CAPTAIN? S'BOOK, SIR.
THAT'S NO **BOOK** SON, YOU'VE ONLY RECOVERED THE NICODEMUS.
WAS IN TH'CHEST.
IF THE EMPEROR **HIMSELF** DON'T GIVE YOU THE PROMOTION OF A LIFETIME FOR THIS, THERE'S NO JUSTICE IN GOD'S WORLD.

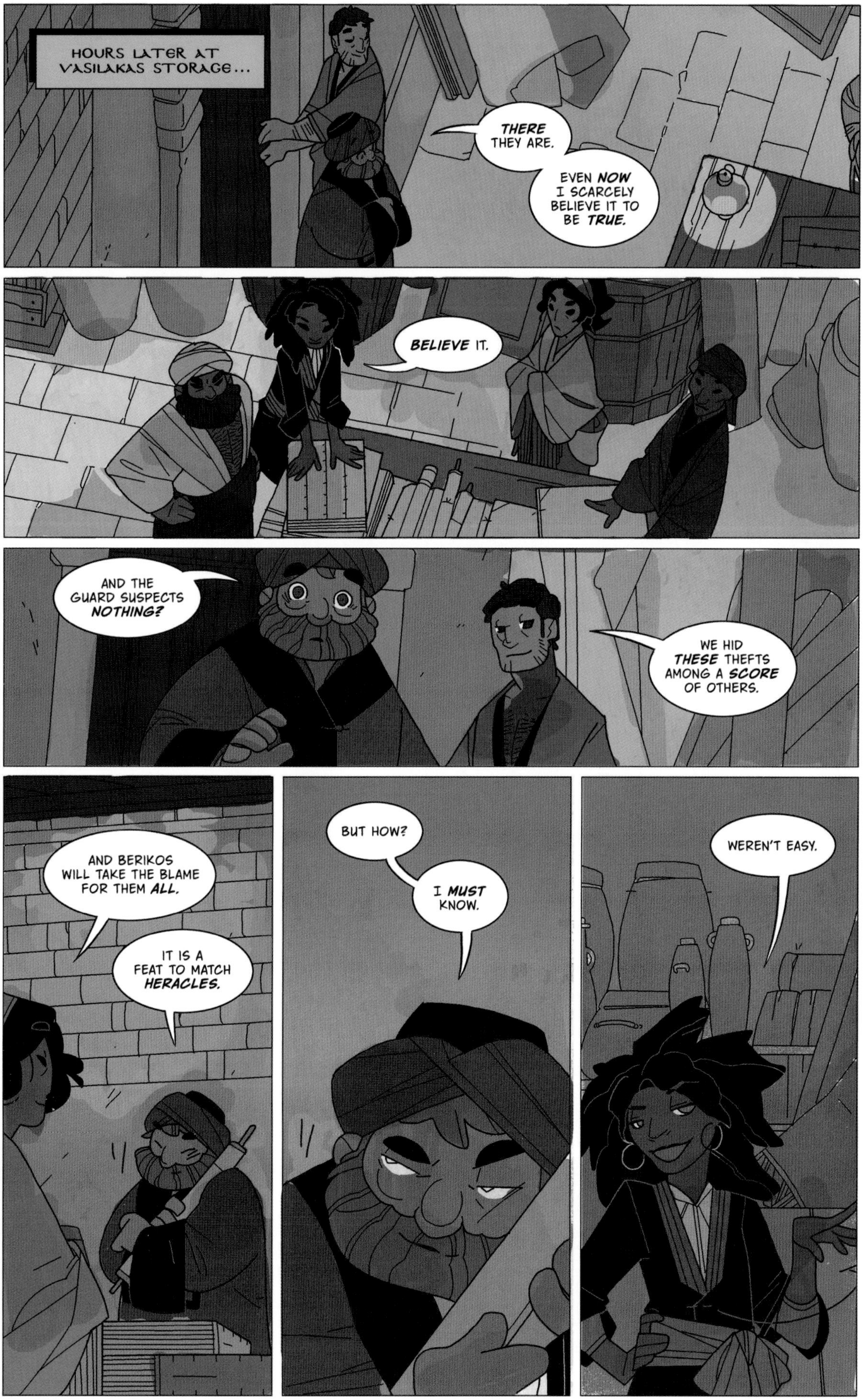
HOURS LATER AT VASILAKAS STORAGE...
THERE THEY ARE.
EVEN NOW I SCARCELY BELIEVE IT TO BE TRUE.
BELIEVE IT.
AND THE GUARD SUSPECTS NOTHING?
WE HID THESE THEFTS AMONG A SCORE OF OTHERS.
AND BERIKOS WILL TAKE THE BLAME FOR THEM ALL.
IT IS A FEAT TO MATCH HERACLES.
BUT HOW?
I MUST KNOW.
WEREN'T EASY.

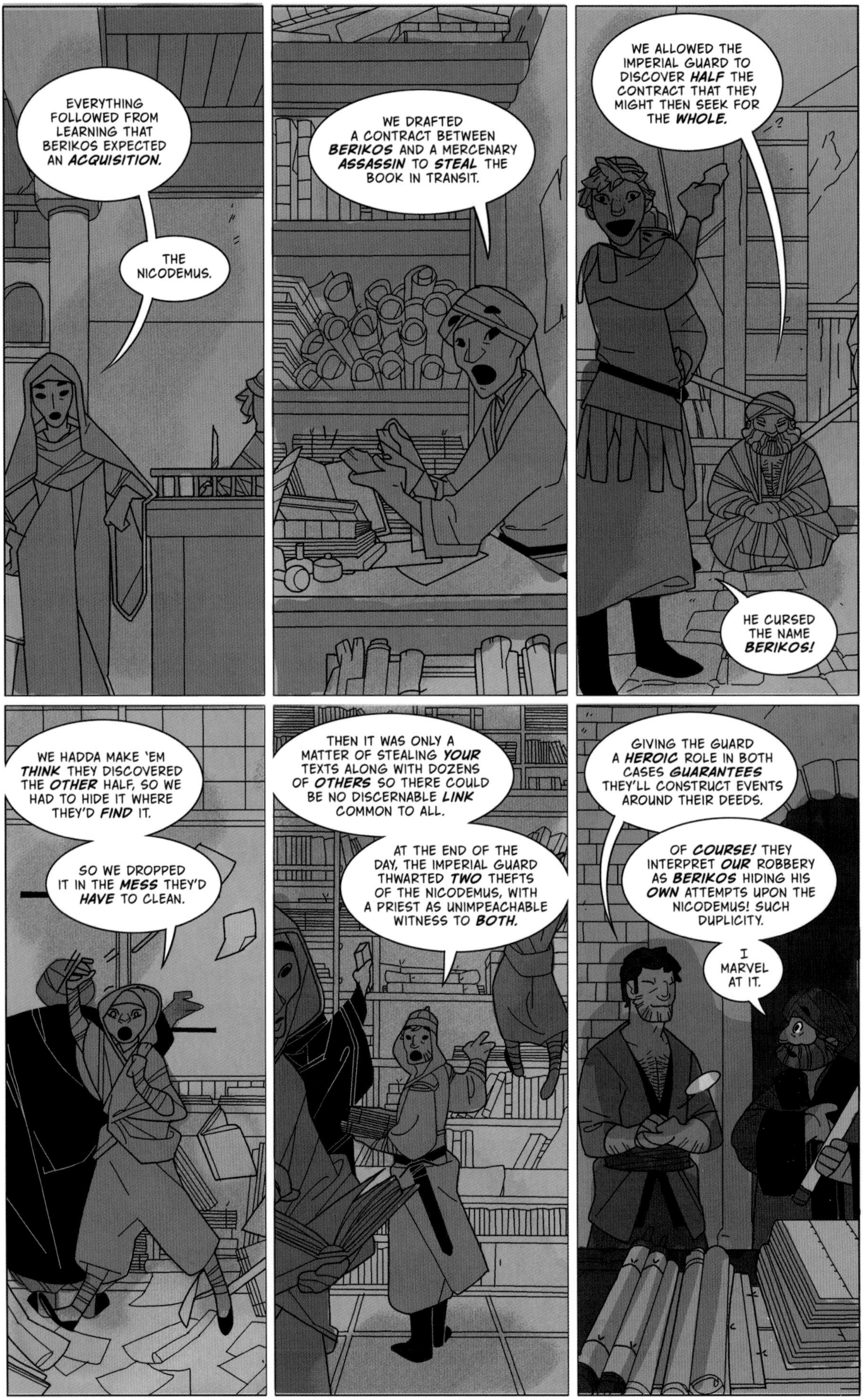
EVERYTHING FOLLOWED FROM LEARNING THAT BERIKOS EXPECTED AN *ACQUISITION.*
THE NICODEMUS.
WE DRAFTED A CONTRACT BETWEEN *BERIKOS* AND A MERCENARY *ASSASSIN* TO *STEAL* THE BOOK IN TRANSIT.
WE ALLOWED THE IMPERIAL GUARD TO DISCOVER *HALF* THE CONTRACT THAT THEY MIGHT THEN SEEK FOR THE *WHOLE.*
HE CURSED THE NAME *BERIKOS!*
WE HADDA MAKE 'EM *THINK* THEY DISCOVERED THE *OTHER* HALF, SO WE HAD TO HIDE IT WHERE THEY'D *FIND* IT.
SO WE DROPPED IT IN THE *MESS* THEY'D *HAVE* TO CLEAN.
THEN IT WAS ONLY A MATTER OF STEALING *YOUR* TEXTS ALONG WITH DOZENS OF *OTHERS* SO THERE COULD BE NO DISCERNABLE *LINK* COMMON TO ALL.
AT THE END OF THE DAY, THE IMPERIAL GUARD THWARTED *TWO* THEFTS OF THE NICODEMUS, WITH A PRIEST AS UNIMPEACHABLE WITNESS TO *BOTH.*
GIVING THE GUARD A *HEROIC* ROLE IN BOTH CASES *GUARANTEES* THEY'LL CONSTRUCT EVENTS AROUND THEIR DEEDS.
OF *COURSE!* THEY INTERPRET *OUR* ROBBERY AS *BERIKOS* HIDING HIS *OWN* ATTEMPTS UPON THE NICODEMUS! SUCH DUPLICITY.
I MARVEL AT IT.

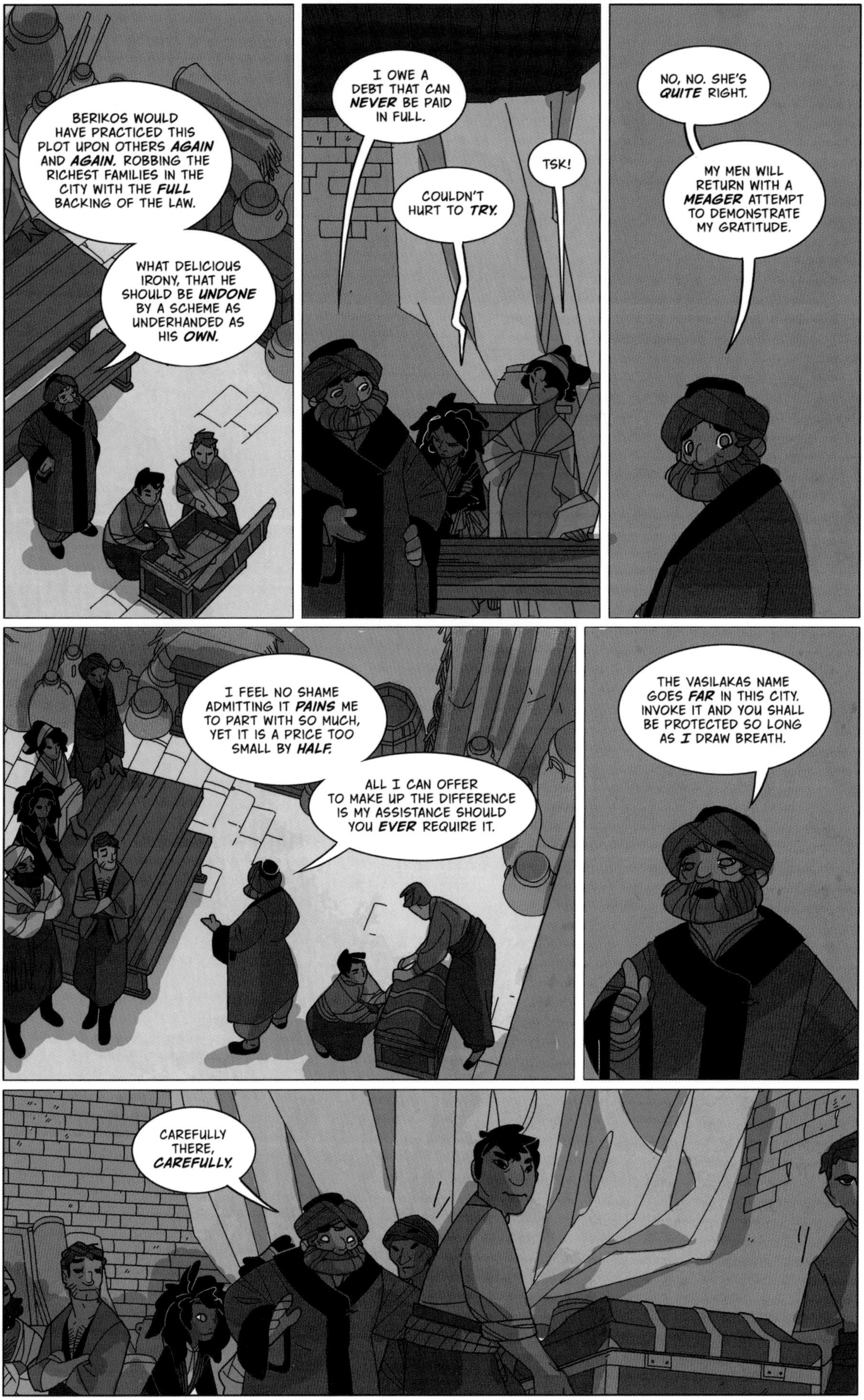
BERIKOS WOULD HAVE PRACTICED THIS PLOT UPON OTHERS AGAIN AND AGAIN. ROBBING THE RICHEST FAMILIES IN THE CITY WITH THE FULL BACKING OF THE LAW.
WHAT DELICIOUS IRONY, THAT HE SHOULD BE UNDONE BY A SCHEME AS UNDERHANDED AS HIS OWN.
I OWE A DEBT THAT CAN NEVER BE PAID IN FULL.
COULDN'T HURT TO TRY.
TSK!
NO, NO. SHE'S QUITE RIGHT.
MY MEN WILL RETURN WITH A MEAGER ATTEMPT TO DEMONSTRATE MY GRATITUDE.
I FEEL NO SHAME ADMITTING IT PAINS ME TO PART WITH SO MUCH, YET IT IS A PRICE TOO SMALL BY HALF.
ALL I CAN OFFER TO MAKE UP THE DIFFERENCE IS MY ASSISTANCE SHOULD YOU EVER REQUIRE IT.
THE VASILAKAS NAME GOES FAR IN THIS CITY. INVOKE IT AND YOU SHALL BE PROTECTED SO LONG AS I DRAW BREATH.
CAREFULLY THERE, CAREFULLY.

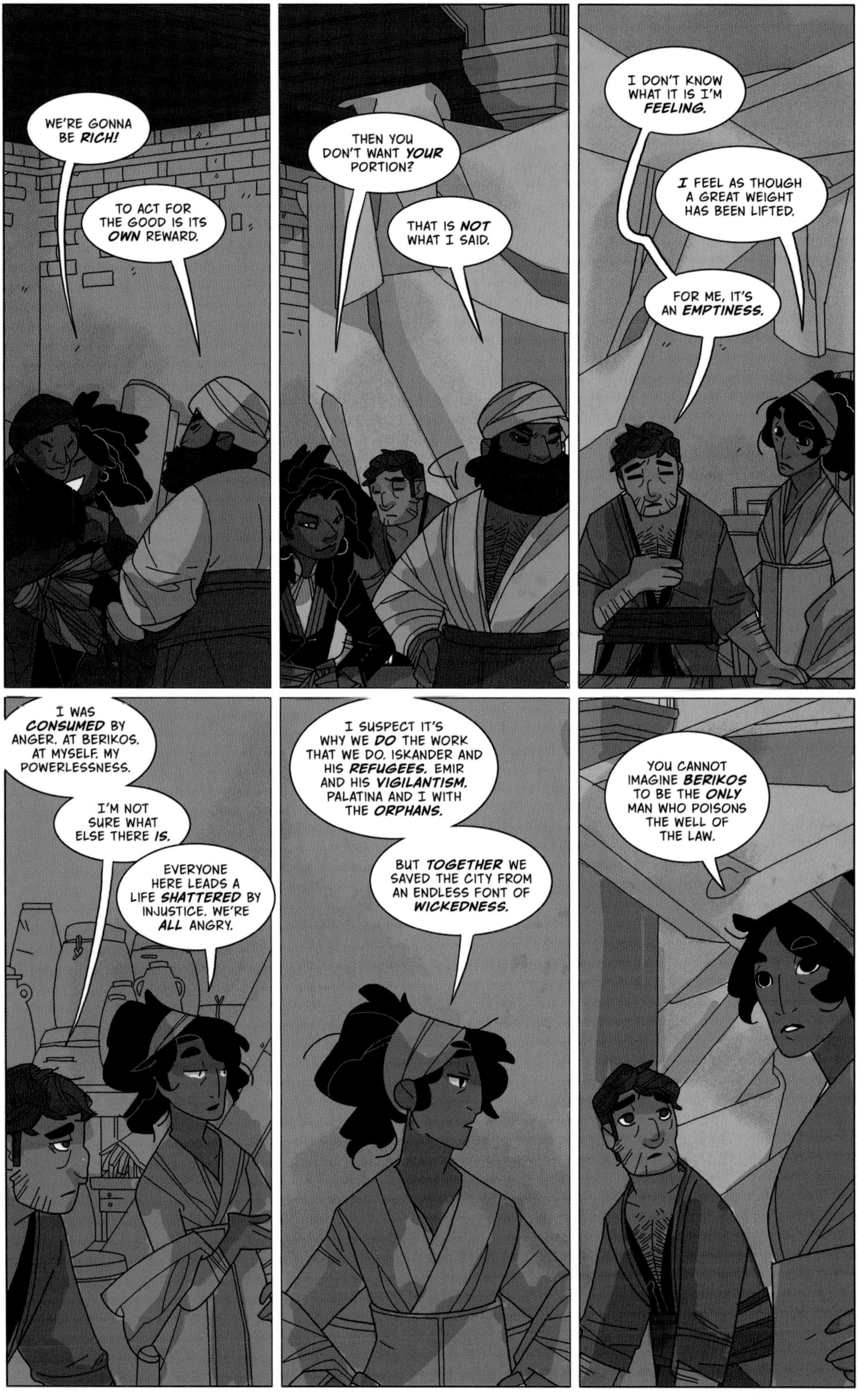
WE'RE GONNA BE ***RICH!***
TO ACT FOR THE GOOD IS ITS ***OWN*** REWARD.
THEN YOU DON'T WANT ***YOUR*** PORTION?
THAT IS ***NOT*** WHAT I SAID.
I DON'T KNOW WHAT IT IS I'M ***FEELING.***
I FEEL AS THOUGH A GREAT WEIGHT HAS BEEN LIFTED.
FOR ME, IT'S AN ***EMPTINESS.***
I WAS ***CONSUMED*** BY ANGER. AT BERIKOS. AT MYSELF. MY POWERLESSNESS.
I'M NOT SURE WHAT ELSE THERE ***IS.***
EVERYONE HERE LEADS A LIFE ***SHATTERED*** BY INJUSTICE. WE'RE ***ALL*** ANGRY.
I SUSPECT IT'S WHY WE ***DO*** THE WORK THAT WE DO. ISKANDER AND HIS ***REFUGEES.*** EMIR AND HIS ***VIGILANTISM.*** PALATINA AND I WITH THE ***ORPHANS.***
BUT ***TOGETHER*** WE SAVED THE CITY FROM AN ENDLESS FONT OF ***WICKEDNESS.***
YOU CANNOT IMAGINE ***BERIKOS*** TO BE THE ***ONLY*** MAN WHO POISONS THE WELL OF THE LAW.

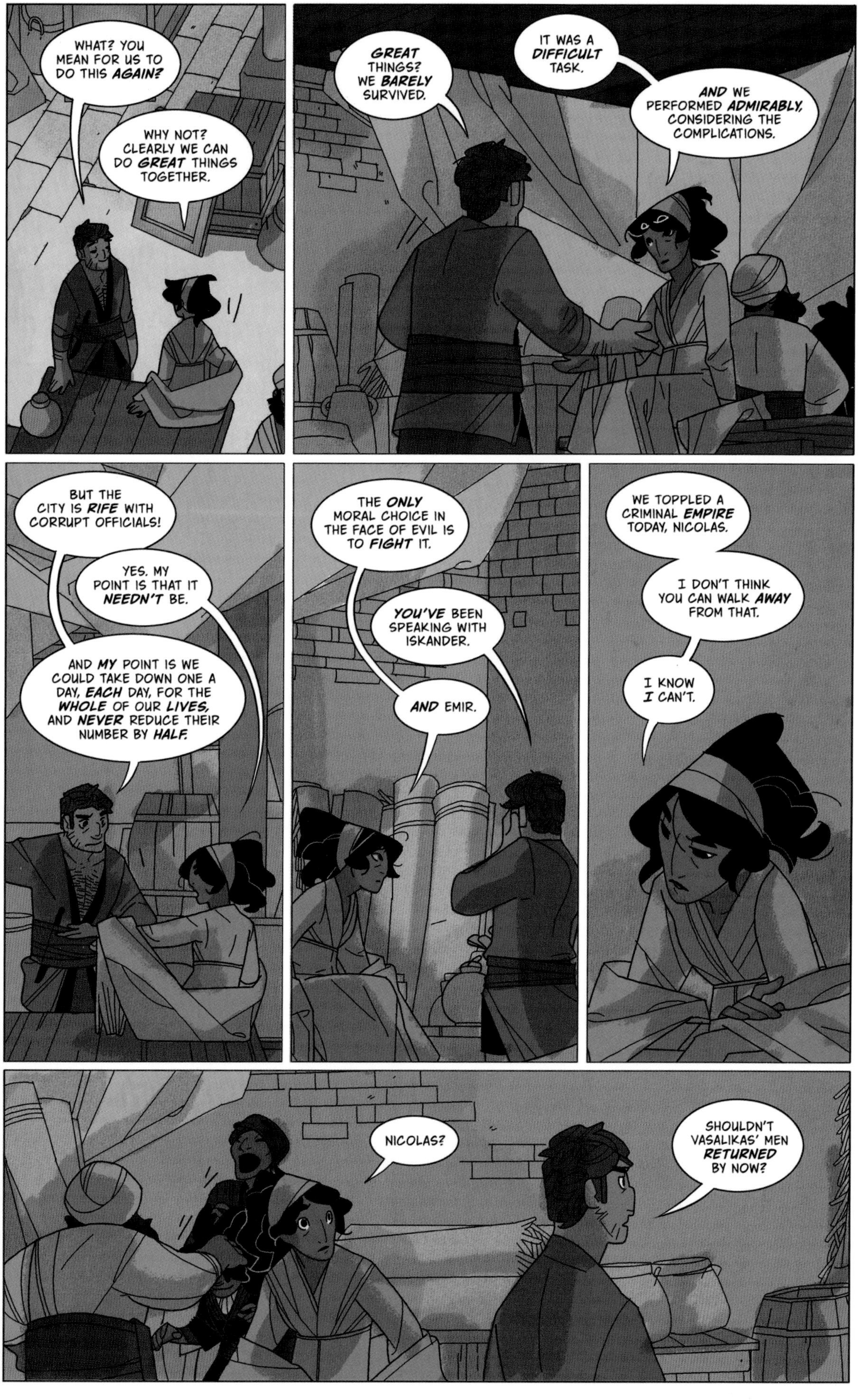
WHAT? YOU MEAN FOR US TO DO THIS AGAIN?
WHY NOT? CLEARLY WE CAN DO GREAT THINGS TOGETHER.
GREAT THINGS? WE BARELY SURVIVED.
IT WAS A DIFFICULT TASK.
AND WE PERFORMED ADMIRABLY, CONSIDERING THE COMPLICATIONS.
BUT THE CITY IS RIFE WITH CORRUPT OFFICIALS!
YES. MY POINT IS THAT IT NEEDN'T BE.
AND MY POINT IS WE COULD TAKE DOWN ONE A DAY, EACH DAY, FOR THE WHOLE OF OUR LIVES, AND NEVER REDUCE THEIR NUMBER BY HALF.
THE ONLY MORAL CHOICE IN THE FACE OF EVIL IS TO FIGHT IT.
YOU'VE BEEN SPEAKING WITH ISKANDER.
AND EMIR.
WE TOPPLED A CRIMINAL EMPIRE TODAY, NICOLAS.
I DON'T THINK YOU CAN WALK AWAY FROM THAT.
I KNOW I CAN'T.
NICOLAS?
SHOULDN'T VASALIKAS' MEN RETURNED BY NOW?

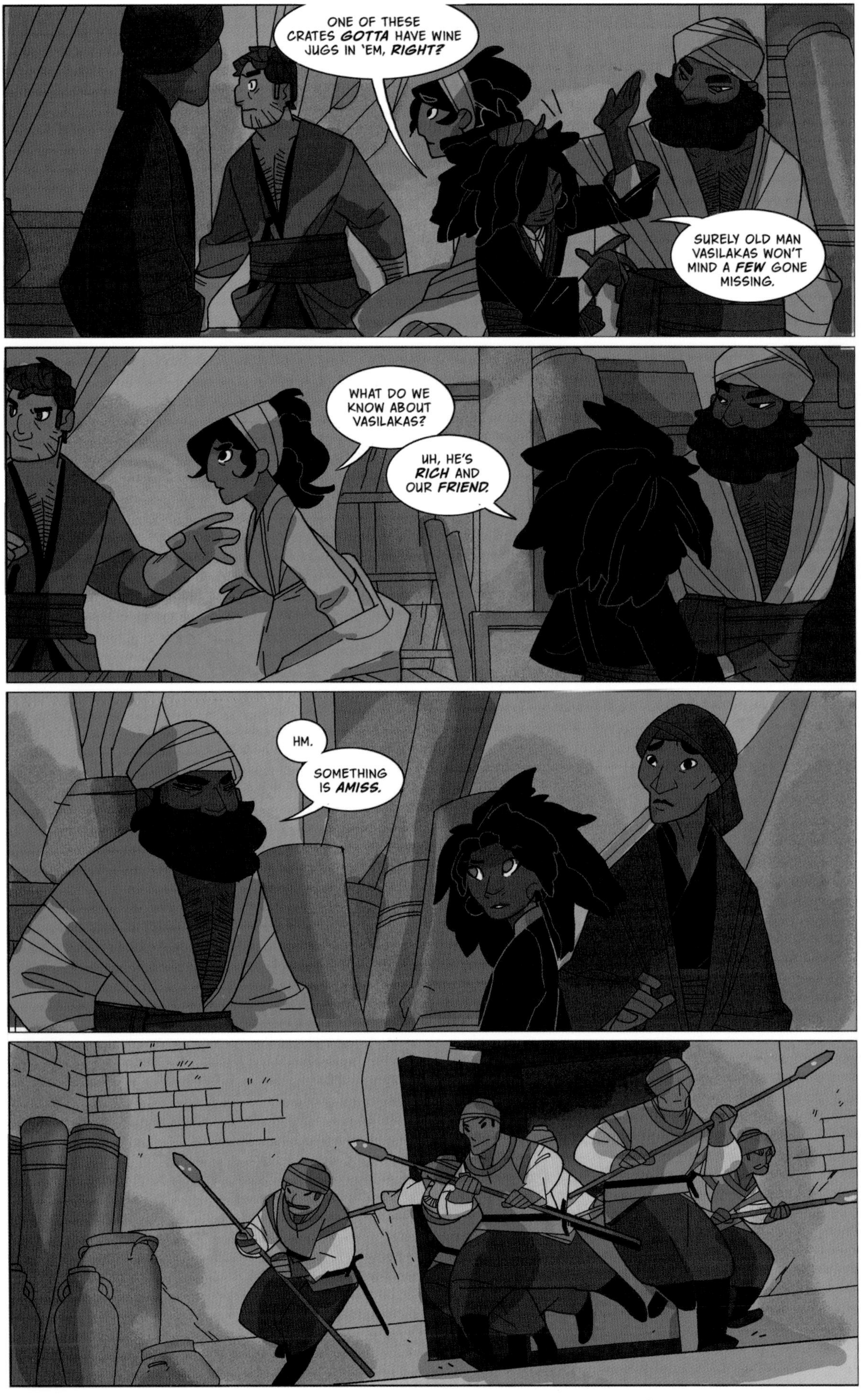
ONE OF THESE CRATES GOTTA HAVE WINE JUGS IN 'EM, RIGHT?
SURELY OLD MAN VASILAKAS WON'T MIND A FEW GONE MISSING.
WHAT DO WE KNOW ABOUT VASILAKAS?
UH, HE'S RICH AND OUR FRIEND.
HM.
SOMETHING IS AMISS.

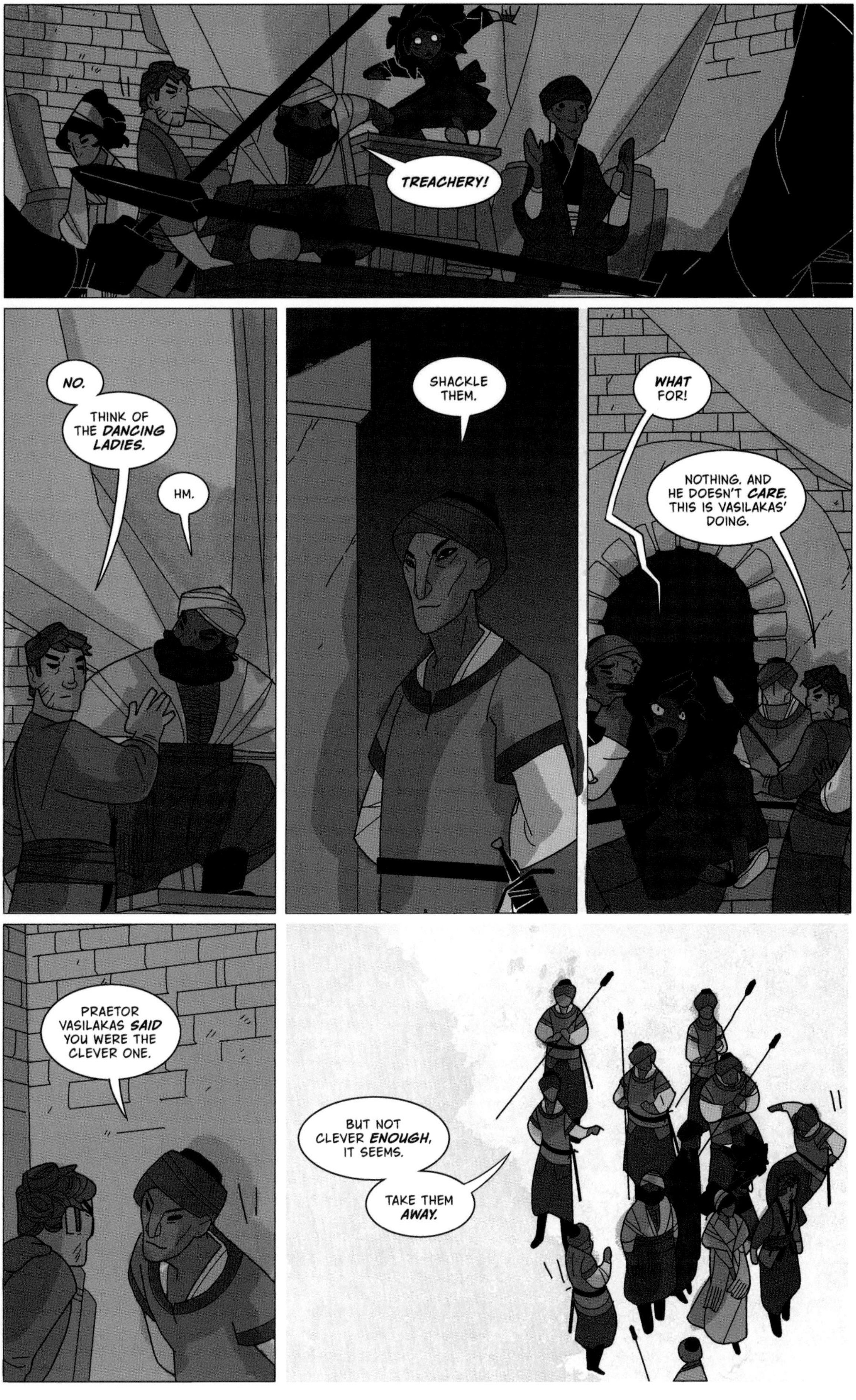
TREACHERY!
NO.
THINK OF THE DANCING LADIES.
HM.
SHACKLE THEM.
WHAT FOR!
NOTHING. AND HE DOESN'T CARE. THIS IS VASILAKAS' DOING.
PRAETOR VASILAKAS SAID YOU WERE THE CLEVER ONE.
BUT NOT CLEVER ENOUGH, IT SEEMS.
TAKE THEM AWAY.

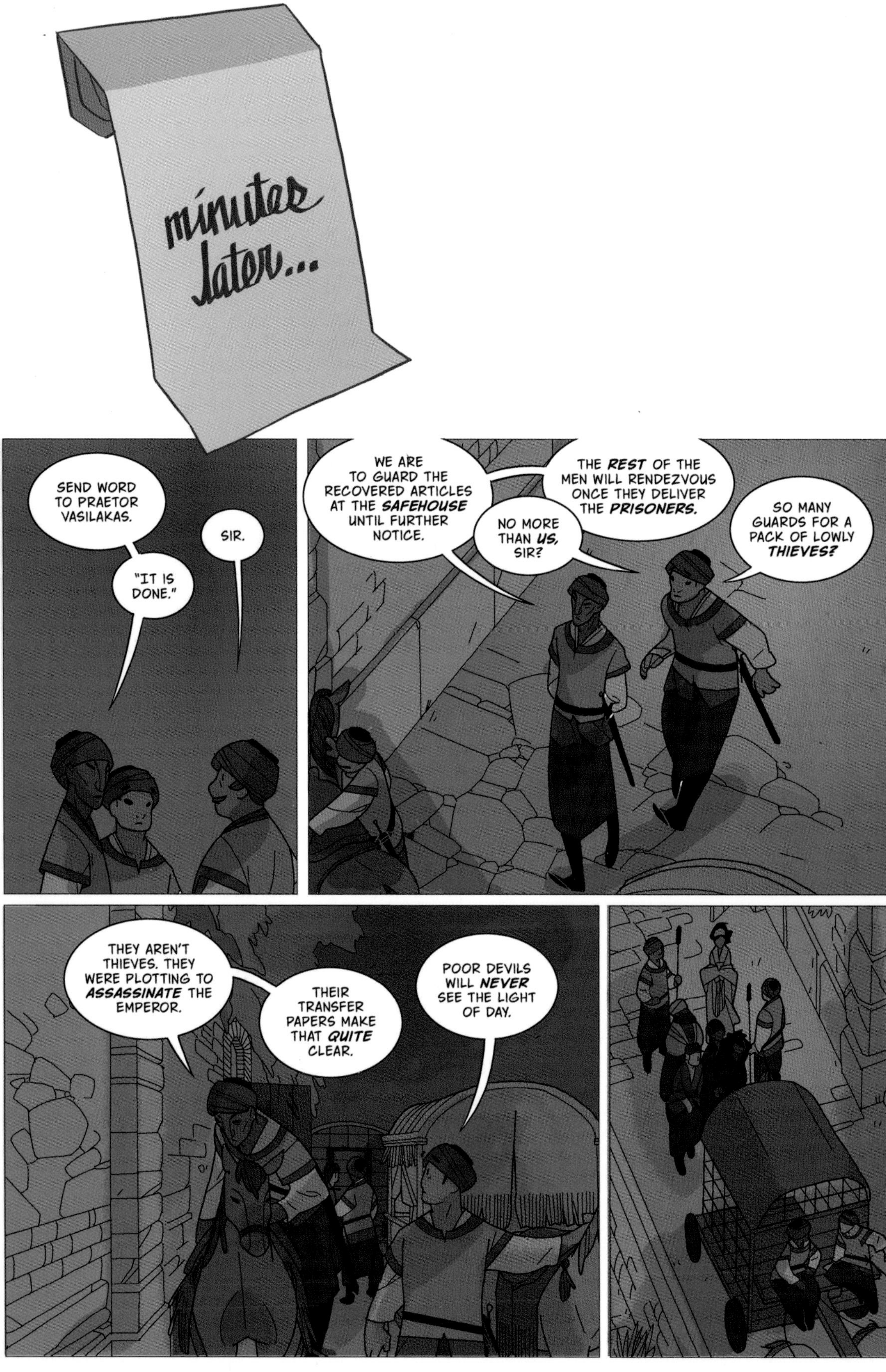
minutes later...
SEND WORD TO PRAETOR VASILAKAS.
"IT IS DONE."
SIR.
WE ARE TO GUARD THE RECOVERED ARTICLES AT THE SAFEHOUSE UNTIL FURTHER NOTICE.
THE REST OF THE MEN WILL RENDEZVOUS ONCE THEY DELIVER THE PRISONERS.
NO MORE THAN US, SIR?
SO MANY GUARDS FOR A PACK OF LOWLY THIEVES?
THEY AREN'T THIEVES. THEY WERE PLOTTING TO ASSASSINATE THE EMPEROR.
THEIR TRANSFER PAPERS MAKE THAT QUITE CLEAR.
POOR DEVILS WILL NEVER SEE THE LIGHT OF DAY.

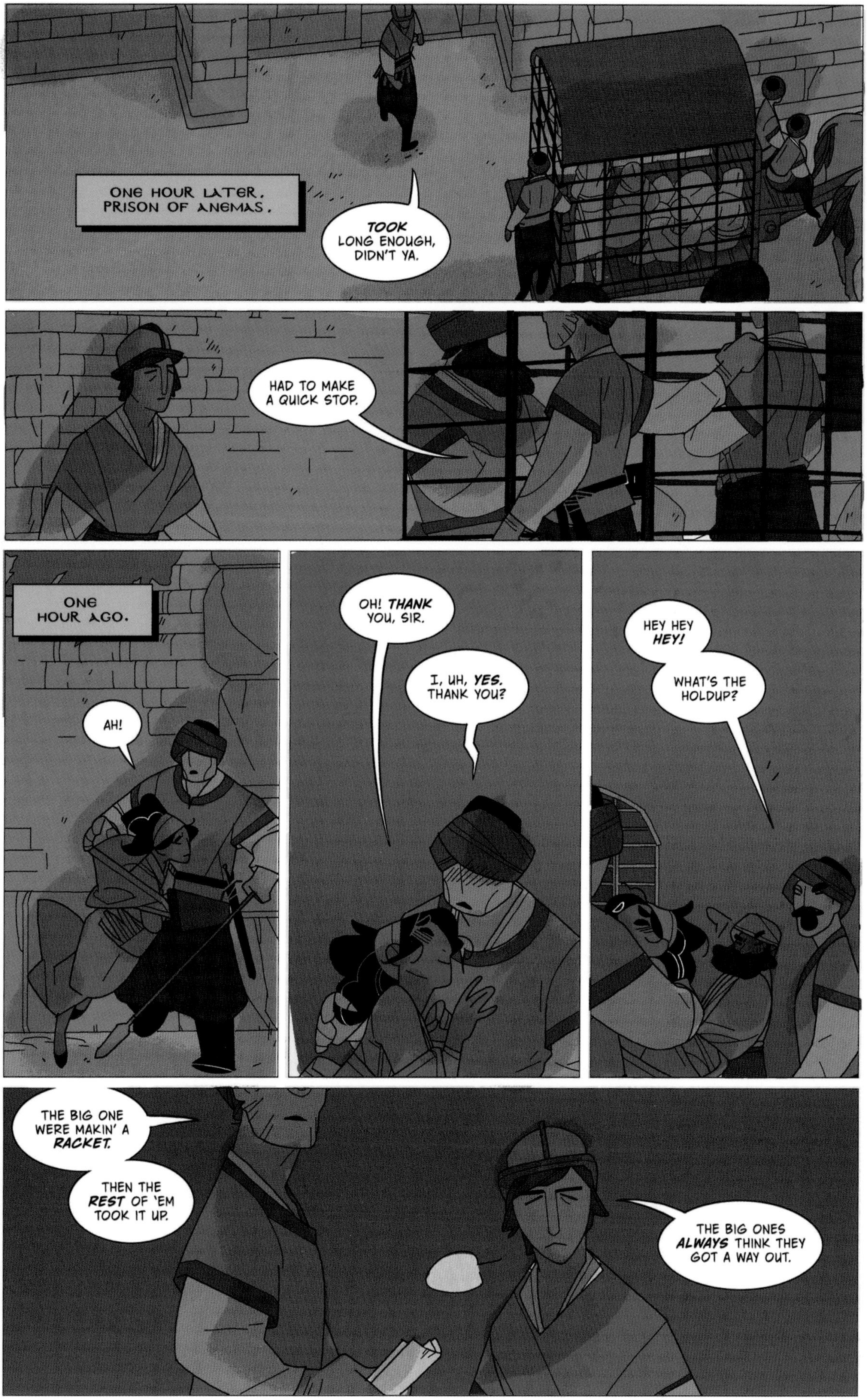
ONE HOUR LATER.
PRISON OF ANEMAS.
TOOK LONG ENOUGH, DIDN'T YA.
HAD TO MAKE A QUICK STOP.
ONE HOUR AGO.
AH!
OH! THANK YOU, SIR.
I, UH, YES. THANK YOU?
HEY HEY HEY!
WHAT'S THE HOLDUP?
THE BIG ONE WERE MAKIN' A RACKET.
THEN THE REST OF 'EM TOOK IT UP.
THE BIG ONES ALWAYS THINK THEY GOT A WAY OUT.

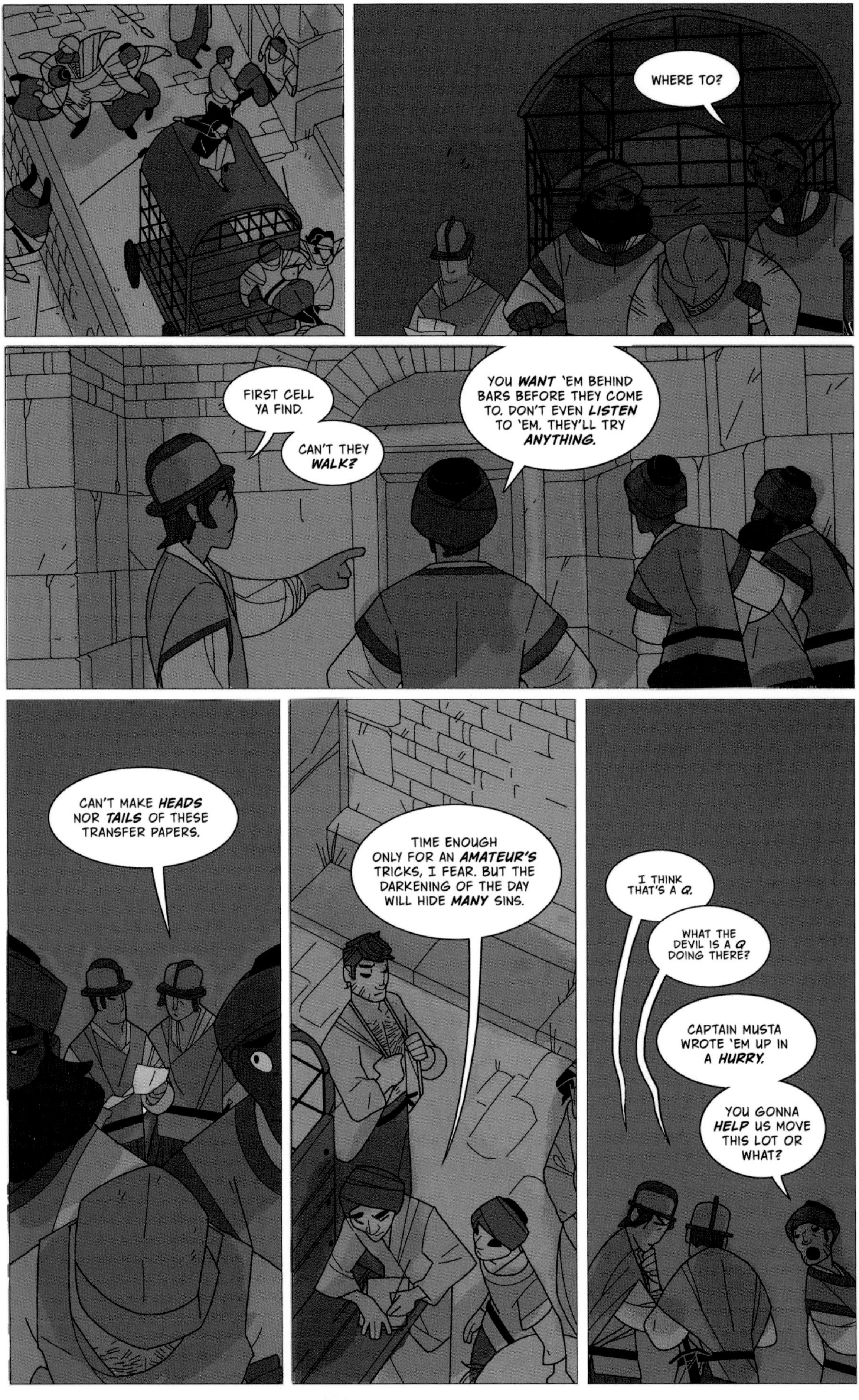
WHERE TO?
FIRST CELL YA FIND.
CAN'T THEY WALK?
YOU WANT 'EM BEHIND BARS BEFORE THEY COME TO. DON'T EVEN LISTEN TO 'EM. THEY'LL TRY ANYTHING.
CAN'T MAKE HEADS NOR TAILS OF THESE TRANSFER PAPERS.
TIME ENOUGH ONLY FOR AN AMATEUR'S TRICKS, I FEAR. BUT THE DARKENING OF THE DAY WILL HIDE MANY SINS.
I THINK THAT'S A Q.
WHAT THE DEVIL IS A Q DOING THERE?
CAPTAIN MUSTA WROTE 'EM UP IN A HURRY.
YOU GONNA HELP US MOVE THIS LOT OR WHAT?

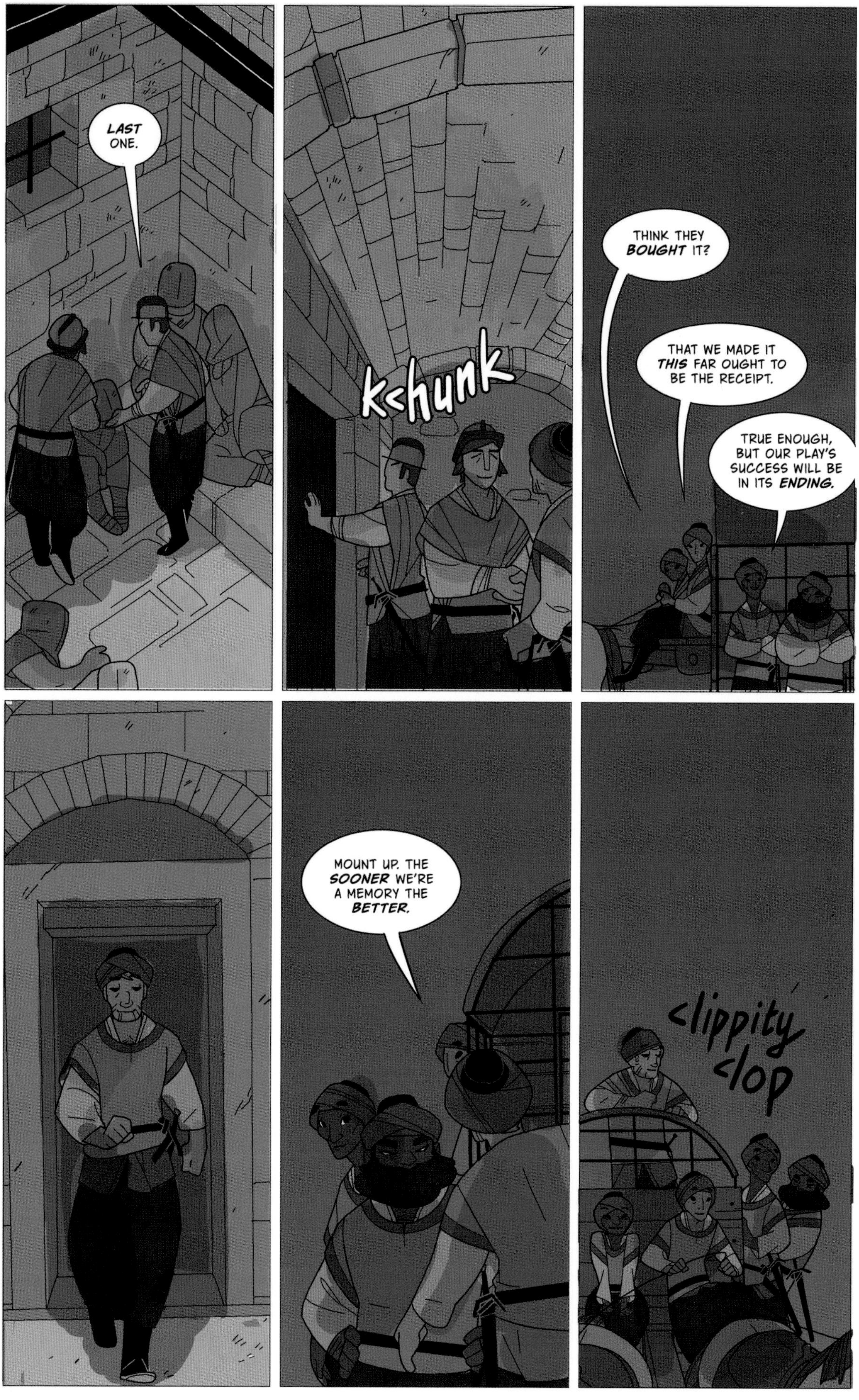
LAST ONE.
k<hunk
THINK THEY BOUGHT IT?
THAT WE MADE IT THIS FAR OUGHT TO BE THE RECEIPT.
TRUE ENOUGH, BUT OUR PLAY'S SUCCESS WILL BE IN ITS ENDING.
MOUNT UP. THE SOONER WE'RE A MEMORY THE BETTER.
clippity clop

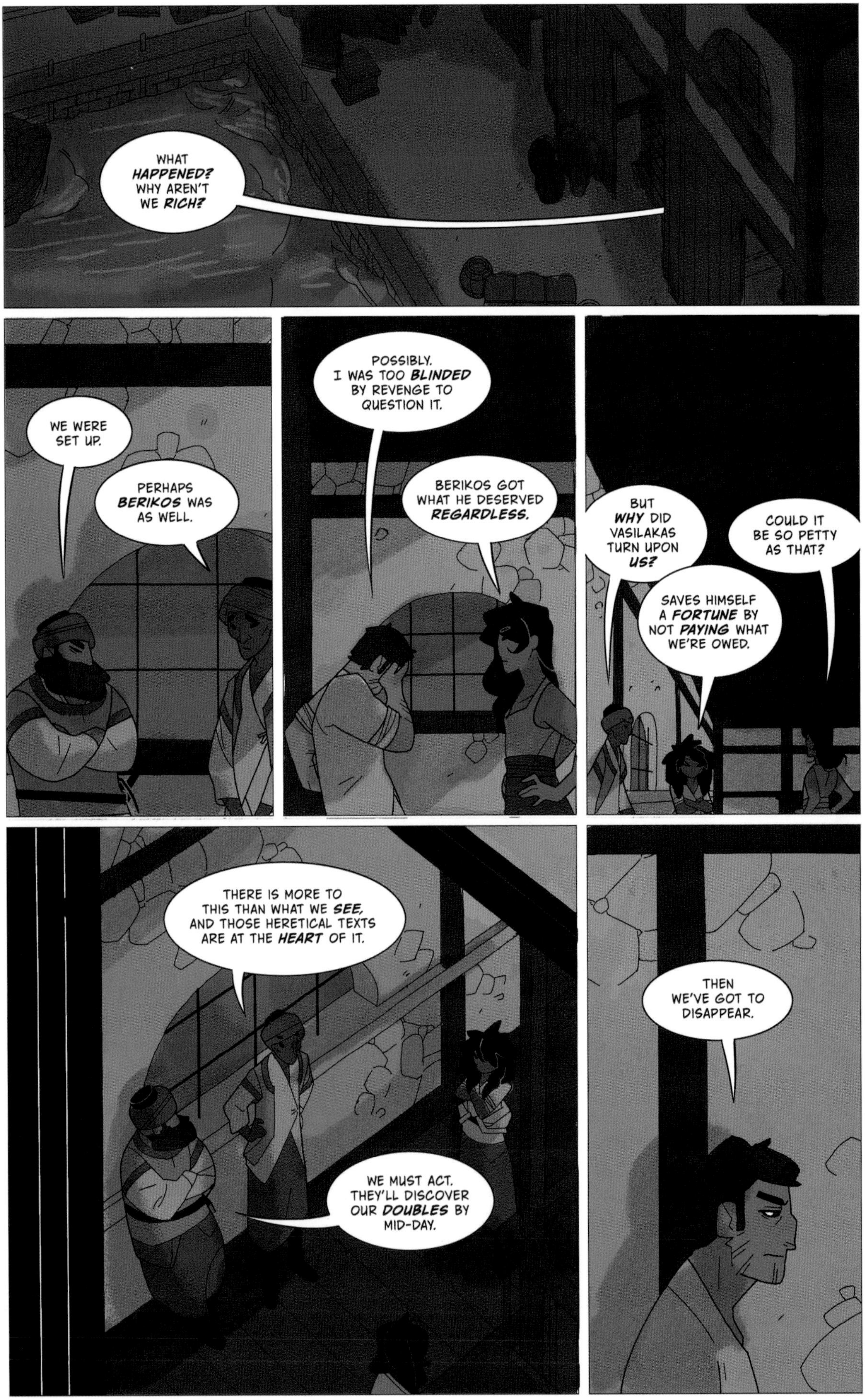
WHAT HAPPENED? WHY AREN'T WE RICH?
WE WERE SET UP.
PERHAPS BERIKOS WAS AS WELL.
POSSIBLY. I WAS TOO BLINDED BY REVENGE TO QUESTION IT.
BERIKOS GOT WHAT HE DESERVED REGARDLESS.
BUT WHY DID VASILAKAS TURN UPON US?
COULD IT BE SO PETTY AS THAT?
SAVES HIMSELF A FORTUNE BY NOT PAYING WHAT WE'RE OWED.
THERE IS MORE TO THIS THAN WHAT WE SEE, AND THOSE HERETICAL TEXTS ARE AT THE HEART OF IT.
WE MUST ACT. THEY'LL DISCOVER OUR DOUBLES BY MID-DAY.
THEN WE'VE GOT TO DISAPPEAR.

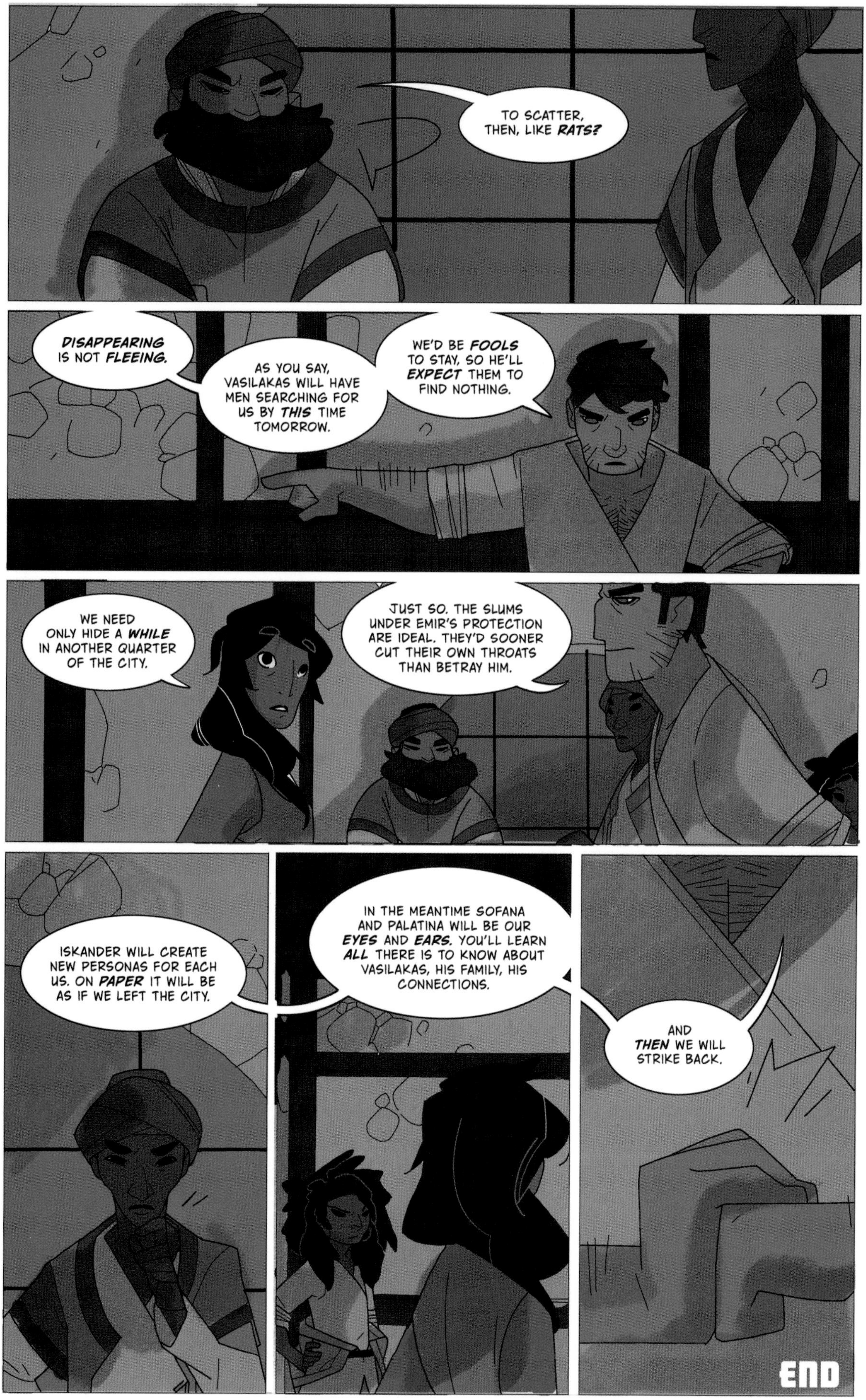
TO SCATTER, THEN, LIKE RATS?
DISAPPEARING IS NOT FLEEING.
AS YOU SAY, VASILAKAS WILL HAVE MEN SEARCHING FOR US BY THIS TIME TOMORROW.
WE'D BE FOOLS TO STAY, SO HE'LL EXPECT THEM TO FIND NOTHING.
WE NEED ONLY HIDE A WHILE IN ANOTHER QUARTER OF THE CITY.
JUST SO. THE SLUMS UNDER EMIR'S PROTECTION ARE IDEAL. THEY'D SOONER CUT THEIR OWN THROATS THAN BETRAY HIM.
ISKANDER WILL CREATE NEW PERSONAS FOR EACH US. ON PAPER IT WILL BE AS IF WE LEFT THE CITY.
IN THE MEANTIME SOFANA AND PALATINA WILL BE OUR EYES AND EARS. YOU'LL LEARN ALL THERE IS TO KNOW ABOUT VASILAKAS, HIS FAMILY, HIS CONNECTIONS.
AND THEN WE WILL STRIKE BACK.
END

HISTORY'S MYSTERIES

1 **OUR STORY TAKES PLACE IN 1095 CE,** the year before European armies amassed outside Constantinople to reclaim Anatolia for the Byzantine Empire. It's something of a departure from what we usually offer, so we wanted to hit you folks with some context.

Constantinople was founded upon the ancient Greek city of Byzantion in 330 CE and became the capital of the Eastern Roman Empire for the next twelve hundred years, the Latin Empire for a bit (didn't go great), then the Roman Empire again (even worse), and finally the Ottoman Empire from 1453 CE until its collapse in 1923.

Constantinople was the largest, richest, and most powerful city in the West for over a thousand years. It was so significant a political entity that it was never referred to by name within its realm of influence. It was always called The City. Situated upon the "Golden Horn" separating the Bosphorus Strait from the Marmara Sea, The City was always a crossroads. Christianity, Judaism, and Islam co-existed within its walls. Scholars, priests, and alchemists mingled in its streets. It's where the Silk Road ended or began depending on which direction you were heading.

I mean, good lord, I haven't even scratched the surface and that's already a boatload of history. And since this is the world of **Atomic Robo**, you better believe it's a history full of adventures and sci-fi conspiracies. Yes, even in the 11th century!

How do you have science fiction before science? Well, first up, I'd argue humans have always been scientific. You don't get calendars without astronomy, or agriculture without genetic modification, or architecture without engineering. Every civilization that ever left a ruin was built on observations and experiments. All we've really done since is to standardize the methods of inquiry so experiments are more easily reproduced and to make increasingly precise observations of those experiments possible. I mean, the ancient world is filled with people who figured out the shape and size of the Earth by measuring a few shadows. We have always been scientists.

So 11th century sci-fi ought to look like it does in the 21st just without all the projected holoscreens. You tell a story about people interacting with technology. Usually, not necessarily, a new technology, and almost always one or more novel applications of that technology.

What technology is this story about? Who's exploiting it? Why?

Keep reading!

2 THE WORKING TITLE OF THIS series was *The History of Everything* because it was originally conceived as glimpses of action science from 25,000 BCE through the 19th century. Turns out that was far too big a story to contain in a single volume. After a lot of denying that obvious fact, I scrapped the scope of that story to instead concentrate on one part of it.

Y'know, like I should've done from the start.

But still, I thought you guys might like to see the original notes for what *History of Everything* would have been. Just the broad strokes. There's enough material in the full notes that we could still use these plots one day. Probably by expanding every issue described below into its own volume.

HISTORY OF EVERYTHING

Each era presents a battle between order and chaos with a variety of technologies/knowledge. Loose brotherhood of agents dedicated to studying the world to understand it (order) or to transcend it (chaos).

#0 The Far Seer (bonus pages in each issue) – 25000 BCE introduces us to culture (language, songs, traditions as generational memory): the first attempt to build data and transmit it to the future. "As above, so below."

#1 Gilgamesh and Puabi – 2500 BCE. Order vs. Chaos as Understanding vs. Transcendence. A tome of astronomical records going back a thousand years to accurately project the new calendar, stolen to plot the course of Tiamat.

#2 Akhenaten and Nefertiti – 1330s BCE. Aten vs. Kadath / Sacred Forms. Immortality. Attempts to counteract sympathetic geometries to unravel civilization so that it may be remade anew.

#3 Jabir ibn Hayyan – 770 CE. Secret Forms. Alchemy. As above; so below. Chemistry shows the transformational nature of information and demonstrates that nothing is absolutely real, therefore everything is possible.

#4 Shen Kuo and Wife – 1040 CE. Computation as key to understanding or transcendence/ Yijing computer to computer astronomical data to precisely project auspicious dates further forward into time; baddies want to input false data to test hypothetical futures to find the one where transcendence can occur.

#5 John Dee – 1550 CE. Cryptohedron, transcendence via unity instead of

"WHO KNEW SUMMARIZING ~27,000 YEARS OF ACTION SCIENCE WOULD BE SUCH AN ENORMOUS UNDERTAKING?"

destruction. John Dee investigating sacred geometries. Great library. Monad. Reality as an act of numbering (cut this one if only doing five issues).

#6 Ada Lovelace – 1840s CE. Singularity cult with alchemical echoes. Ada mechanizes information. Whereas previous records externalized memory, this new method allows the externalization of thought/process. A world machine or machine world.

I got as far as tackling the first outlines but couldn't get more than halfway through before scrapping it. This happened, let's say, several times.

Who knew summarizing ~ 27,000 years of action science would be such an enormous undertaking? One much larger than the page count we were giving ourselves. Each of the chapters above would only run 16 pages with another 4 "bonus" pages of the issue #0 story.

And in those 16 pages we'd have to introduce you to a completely new set of protagonists, their new antagonists, their new culture and setting, their new time, their new supporting cast, and new technologies while everyone involved in each chapter is in the midst of the newest action science crisis.

It's just, I mean, that's a lot to do in sixteen pages only to reset it all over again for the next sixteen. Especially when each of these could easily be its own volume. Sure, we hop around history in each issue of ***Atomic Robo***'s first four volumes, but all of them happen within a single century. One that you almost certainly lived in. There's enough familiarity built into it that we can skip a lot of worldbuilding because we know the audience has seen enough TV or movies to have a basic idea of a given modern-ish era. We can't assume our audience is that familiar with, say, ancient Sumer.

So we scrapped ***History of Everything.*** It was simply unworkable as a single volume. But I wasn't ready to give up on the idea of a pre-industrial action science story! I went back to my notes and looked at the different eras we'd considered that didn't make the list above to see if we could find one adventure on one time and one place that would at least touch on the ideas I wanted to dive into.

That gave us Constantinople in 1095 CE.

It's the heart of the Byzantine Empire. The Turks have taken holy lands previously held by Byzantium. What would become known as the First Crusaders are amassing outside Constantinople's walls to get them back. Meanwhile, inside its walls, Constantinople is one of the largest, richest, and most diverse cities in history and home to one of the great libraries of the ancient world.

I mean, we could launch a whole franchise on what Constantinople gives us. But for now let's just see if we can this crew through their first big adventure.

3 SO THE STORY TELLS US THAT the ringleader of our Crew, Nicolas Farads, used to be an Advocatus. What the heck is that?

Well, it's made up. Sort of.

The story was plotted out with the idea that Nicolas used to be an officer of the law. Nicolas thought the law was impersonal. It's just words in a book somewhere. And there's no way for any law to fully encapsulate the nuance and subtlety of human life—much less a million human lives—bumping into one another. Nicolas did not believe it was his job to blindly enforce the law, but to make sure the law as written was tempered with mercy. Yes, stealing bread is a crime. But is it justice to punish a man for stealing bread to feed his starving family? An argument can be made that justice would be to help this man find work so he can pay to feed his family.

The idea was that in his old life as an arbiter of justice, Nicolas came across people committing crimes, not because they were cackling villains or even bad people, but because they were trapped in a cycle of systemic injustices. Their crimes were attempts to redress that injustice. And instead of punishing them, he helped them to achieve justice—by turning a blind eye, by nudging the bureaucracy. Nicolas' police work was meant to demonstrate that law without mercy is tyranny.

Our story would open with Nicolas a destroyed man. Now he would be a victim of injustice, deemed a criminal by a corruption of the very system he had worked for, and stripped of everything. Nicolas drowns his sorrows until one day he's given a lifeline, this one chance to extract some measure of justice against the man who used the office of the Advocatus as little more than a protection racket and destroyed Nicolas for discovering it. Nicolas calls upon those he helped as an Advocatus and they are more than eager to help him achieve justice in return.

The chasm between law and justice comes up a few times in this series. Criminals on one side, the law and its agents on the other, and mercy bridging the two.

Just one problem. Twelfth century Constantinople did not have anything like a policing body as we would understand it. Indeed nowhere in the world would have one until the 19th century.

That's not to say these were lawless times. Just that the law worked differently for the vast majority of history. The most common solution, and indeed what was practiced in Constantinople, was to have a portion of the military garrisoned in a given city to go on patrols. The idea was that crimes should be difficult to pursue if criminals know a gang of the most heavily armed men in the city were wandering around looking for trouble. These patrols were typically given wide latitude to "investigate" crimes, which was absolutely a recipe for corruption and random violence. An order enforced through fear. Whereas in modern policing there are forensics so criminals are occasionally caught.

But this wasn't the only way to keep the law. At various times in various places there were traditions of, in essence, elite detectives. Magistrates, marshals, medley, judges, advocate. People training and trusted to wander the land as an instrument of justice. This, of course, was also a recipe for corruption or, possibly worse, pure chaos. The punishment for stealing bread might be a small fine in one country, death in another, and a massive "fine" (bribe) in yet another.

So we kind of invented the Advocatus. It's a real position, but it didn't exist in Constantinople. It comes from medieval Europe, but was inspired by ancient Roman law. And since medieval Constantinople considered itself the true inheritor of the Roman Empire, it seemed only fair to bring the Advocatus back to them in our story. We never dive too deep into what exactly our version of the Advocatus is supposed to be. The details are essentially irrelevant to the action, so we never bog things down with a bunch of legalese backstory. But my thinking was that it should look something like a private investigator and a beat cop. Our Advocatus should be part of the community he patrols. He should know the people in it so he can bring the most just version of the law to them. And if there's a problem too big for one Advocatus alone, he can call upon his comrades with the full backing of The City and even the Imperial Guard if need be.

We catch glimpses of Nicolas as an Advocatus through occasional bits of dialog and some flashbacks. He's clearly respected, often feared; he thinks nothing of wandering the city alone; he carries a sword like he intends

"THAT'S NOT TO SAY THESE WERE LAWLESS TIMES. JUST THAT THE LAW WORKED DIFFERENTLY FOR THE VAST MAJORITY OF HISTORY."

to use it; he speaks bluntly and defers to no one. But it's never haughty or imperious, it's a no-nonsense professionalism.

There is no unique quality of our fictional Advocatus that immunizes it against corrupt practices and, indeed, this is what brings Nicolas to the lowly state we find him in the first page of the first issues.

I suppose all this is to say it's okay to invent things that will help make your story work. One thing I've learned while writing historical adventure stories is that you can drive yourself mad chasing accuracy. And, really, for what? Most people don't know or care what you're being accurate about and the people who do will gleefully point out trivial inaccuracies.

These are stories, not documentaries. You don't need accuracy, you need only plausibility.

The Advocatus did not exist in Constantinople but they make sense in **The Nicodemus Job**. It's plausible that the largest and richest metropolis in Western history would have a body of law enforcement officers. It's plausible that among them there would be detectives. It's plausible that, lacking forensic technologies, these detectives would be given a wide latitude to decide how the law is enforced and that they would be embedded in specific communities to better understand them.

It's not accurate. But who cares?

 YOU EVER READ OR WATCH THE NEWS and run into someone trying to push an agenda that only makes sense if you never investigated the ideas of history you got back in elementary school?

I always wonder, do they have these agendas because their view of history is wildly simplified? Or do they espouse these simplified ideas of history to justify their agendas to the rest of us? Maybe it doesn't matter. Either way they end up peppering our cultural consciousness with false notions about how the past worked, how the present is, and what the future ought to become.

You should study history is what I'm saying.

The dead outnumber the living by, oh, what is it, 7-to-1? Or is it 17-to-1? Either way we'll never win the skeleton war should it ever come to pass. History simply contains a vast wealth of human experience and wisdom–more than we'll ever get from our lives. It's just sitting there waiting to be used. Instead it seems like we spend a lot of energy reinventing solutions that didn't work the first time to problems we recreated after forgetting why we fixed them in the first place.

It doesn't even take us long to screw this up. It's why we're living through **Gilded Age 2: This Time With Nazis**.

The stories we tell about history define what we're able to believe not only about the present but the future.

The stories we tell about history define what we're able to believe not only about the present but the future. If we never probe the origins of power structures that shaped the modern world, then we aren't equipped to challenge them today or to replace them tomorrow.

Or if you have a specific vision about the populations of, say, medieval Europe or America's Old West, then you probably have a specific vision about what they look like today and what they should look like tomorrow.

Those who don't study history are doomed to repeat it, yes, but it's also true they're doomed to spread someone else's version of it. *What we believe to be true about our past sets limits on what we believe to be possible about our future.*

If you interrogate the source of these ideas, you might find they're entirely fictional, usually rooted in simplistic 20th century media. Or from a spurious survey of "world history" that goes from Ancient Greece to the Roman Empire to the Dark Ages to the Renaissance to the American Revolution and World War 2 that most of us got in middle school.

That rather rushed survey creates the illusion of the inevitability of Western triumph so the injustices and power dynamics of the modern world appear to be the natural and inevitable result of all human activity–simultaneously projecting the injustices and power dynamics of the future. But it's a vision of the past, and the present, and the future, that only makes sense if you ignore the rest of the planet. History is never so simple. Genius is not limited to any one group. Ideas and technologies never stay put. The Industrial Revolution may have happened in Britain but they built it out of thousand year old Middle Eastern and Chinese technologies. Nothing was invented in a vacuum.

People who want to convince you that the world is simple or that facts don't matter are just frustrated that their agendas don't work in a complex world because facts illuminate the absurdity of their ideas. One wonders how yawning the void in their hearts must be that they would rather destroy

"THE STORIES WE TELL ABOUT HISTORY DEFINE WHAT WE'RE ABLE TO BELIEVE NOT ONLY ABOUT THE PRESENT BUT THE FUTURE."

"FOR THE RECORD, MY AGENDA IS TO GET PEOPLE TO ACTIVELY ENGAGE WITH HISTORY."

everything to preserve their little ideas than to be excited to be wrong and learn what else might be true.

But I digress.

The only defense against this sort of manipulation by bad actors is to investigate history yourself. And to remember that every version of history, including this one, is trying to shape how you think about yourself, your fellow humans, and the world you create to inhabit together. Always ask yourself—who benefits from this version of history? What are they leaving out? Why?

For the record, my agenda is to get people to actively engage with history. To think of it as more than a list of dates and kings. To realize the world has always been full of genius, humor, and tragedy. That our ancestors were not unknowable aliens with bad teeth and weird clothes and nothing to teach us.

We're all we've got in this universe. It's worth our time to learn about one another.

5   HOPE YOU ENJOYED OUR CRIMINAL ROMP through Constantinople at the close of the 11th century. I don't think this is the last we've seen of Nicolas, Sofana, Palatina, Iskander, and Emir. You just can't keep a good crew down!

So for the last few years I've been drawn to wuxia stories. Wuxia is a genre of Chinese literature that arguably dates back to their earliest written histories, but the modern wuxia story has its roots in fiction from the Ming Dynasty. What I like most about them is their structure.

See, in the West, we have Three Act Structure. Or Five Acts. They're the same, just one has three labels and the other has five. You've got your (1) Introduction, your (2) Conflict, and your (3) Resolution. It's a solid arc and it's served us well. But I find myself writing stories that delay the Resolution in favor of adding more complications that extend the conflict. This way readers can't be sure what'll happen next and they should be worried about the heroes until the very last minute. Well, if I've done it right, anyway.

Turns out this is similar to the Four Act Structure that wuxia stories generally follow. It's similar to the Three Acts we're familiar with but it shifts the focus. It starts with, (1) Introduction of characters and setting, then there's a (2) Development that reveals secrets about one or more characters and/or their setting, then there's a (3) Twist on those developments that reveals unexpected relationships or truths about the characters and/or their setting, then the story (4) Concludes now that we know the real truth(s) illuminated by the story of these characters. What I like about this is that it lets me put the narrative pedal to the metal, so to speak, and drive an adventure right off a cliff.

But the big difference between these two models isn't the number of acts or how they're divided up. It's this: one is about Conflict and the other is about Learning. A story with either structure will almost certainly have both–what's the dramatic point of a conflict if the character or audience learns nothing new from it; what's the dramatic point of revealing a new truth if it doesn't produce a new conflict or complicate an existing one?

Neither is better than the other and the line between them is fuzzy anyway. Hell, I'm pretty sure we do both at the same time–they both have Introductions, the Development and Twist are part of the Conflict, and the Resolution is just Concluding the story. But thinking *specifically* about what the characters or the audience *learn* based on the decisions characters make seems like a valuable way to approach something like a heist story. Well, I hope so anyway, because that's what I tried to do here.

Broadly speaking I liked to break down **Atomic Robo** volumes into five parts:

Issue One – Introduction of Conspiracy
Issue Two – Discover the Conspiracy
Issue Three – Confront the Conspiracy
Issue Four – Defeated by the Conspiracy
Issue Five – Defeat the Conspiracy

I'm not sure which sort of structure we use to navigate that path. Probably a mix of both since there's value in each.

We're usually taught that Conflict is the engine of a story because that's where the dramatic stuff comes from. But every scene in a story should tell the reader *something* about one or more characters, or their setting, or both! Whether that's re-emphasizing a known fact, or seeing a known fact in a new light, or revealing a new fact that changes or enhances our understanding of an old fact. Doesn't that sound dramatic too?

THE CREATORS

BRIAN CLEVINGER lives in Richmond, Virginia and writes comics like *The Avengers and the Infinity Gauntlet*, *Atomic Robo*, and *The Phantom* in between feeding his cats 800 times a day.

MEREDITH McCLAREN is an assortment of random thoughts consisting mostly of a desire for sleep and a need to eat. She's worked on such comics as *Jem and the Holograms*, *Heart in a Box*, and *Hinges*.